THE PRINCES

Praise for *The Princes*

'In this fast-paced account Malgonkar traverses an India that was, a fascinating world of princely states—from their aura of power, tiger hunts, champagne and pearls to their integration into the modern republic. Legitimacy and illegitimacy, fidelity and infidelity, bravery and cowardice go hand in hand—whether of the ruler or the ruled—in this unputdownable novel.'

—Rana Safvi, author

'Neither an elegy for nor an indictment of the eponymous princes … Malgonkar draws from his own life to create a memorable portrait of the past in this cleverly paced and finely wrought masterpiece.'

—Devapriya Roy, author

'Manohar Malgonkar writes with detachment and wit … The character of the father is vividly and boldly drawn; that of the son subtly and attractively matures; the social and political history is blended into the novel with considerable skill. And the measured, stately prose of old England proves itself to be still a wonderfully serviceable instrument.'

—*The Times Literary Supplement*, London

'Abiding interest … *The Princes* is a wonderfully decent and informative story.'

—*The Sunday Times*

'A brilliant picture of a vanishing, if not vanished, scene, the world of the small princely states of India … Manohar Malgonkar writes wittily and dispassionately.'

—*British Book News*

'A brilliantly realised novel about India as seen through Indian eyes.'

—*The Western Mail*

THE PRINCES

A NOVEL

With an Introduction by Anita Nair

MANOHAR MALGONKAR

HarperCollins *Publishers* India

This edition published in 2022 by HarperCollins *Publishers*
4th Floor, Tower A, Building No 10, DLF Cyber City,
DLF Phase II, Gurugram, Haryana – 122002
www.harpercollins.co.in

2 4 6 8 10 9 7 5 3 1

PISBN: 978-93-5629-085-3
EISBN: 97-89-3562-9086-0

This is a work of fiction and all characters and incidents described in this book are the product of the author's imagination. Any resemblance to actual persons, living or dead, is entirely coincidental.

Typeset in 10.5/14 Adobe Caslon Pro at
Manipal Technologies Limited, Manipal

Printed and bound at
Thomson Press (India) Ltd

For Mai and Baba
Looking back over many monsoons

Also by Manohar Malgonkar

A Bend in the Ganges
The Devil's Wind: Nana Saheb's Story
The Sea Hawk: Life and Battles of Kanhoji Angrey

Contents

Introduction

W. H. Auden in his *Lectures on Shakespeare* writes that in ancient tragedies, the universe refuses reconciliation, while in modern tragedy, the failure is the result of an individual's choice.*

So how then must one read *The Princes*? As an ancient tragedy where time will do what it must and mortals can do nothing to change the course of the universe? Or as a modern tragedy where people choose who they wish to be and thus have to live with its resultant consequences?

That the trajectory of *The Princes* is tragic is indisputable. But it is neither an ancient nor a modern tragedy. Instead, here is a remarkable story that defies the boundaries of classification and is as much an account of a time that saw India shrug the yoke of colonial powers and come into its own as it is the story of the lives caught in that ensuing chaos and the choices made thereon.

There are many things to delight in Manohar Malgonkar's *The Princes*:

The setting is the Kingdom of Begwad caught in the cusp of the period as it turned from a princely state to a part of the Indian union. So even as we are whirled from royal banquets and tiger hunts to Etonesque boarding schools and military camps, we also learn of a life far removed from the enchanted life of the princes'

---

* Auden, W.H. *Lectures on Shakespeare* (Princeton University Press, 2002).

and their palaces. A time where the nationalist movement drawn from all rungs of the social strata would turn norms and mores on its head as it sought to root out all that was considered a symbol of white privilege.

It is amidst such turbulence that we meet the characters who are all drawn from what is representative of this changing India. Prince Abhayraj and his larger-than-life father, the unnamed Maharaja; princesses, concubines, illegitimate siblings, Englishmen both gentlemen and scoundrels, Anglo-Indian girlfriends, huntsmen, Dewans and Political Agents, tribesmen and even a slighted Dalit boy who goes on to become a facet of emerging India.

But what makes *The Princes* an exemplary book is its writing. This is a writer who is at his peak and the story he tells is one where the demand of the external world on the characters and the state of their interior lives come together with such arresting command that one can only marvel at the writer's ability. There is something that happens with the happy marriage of research and experience and nowhere is this more evident than in *The Princes*. With such a wealth of detail and conflict, almost every scene leaps off the pages with a three-dimensional effect.

The Princes is not just the story of how the princely states were swallowed whole by the new republic called India. It is also a bildungsroman of a prince named Abhayraj. A prince born to the certainty that one day he shall be king. Abhayraj's evolution from boy to man is fascinating. When we meet him first, he is someone who has come to terms with his change in circumstances. A once-maharaja. A sovereign who chose to abdicate. It is easy to dismiss Abhayraj and his story as yet another narrative of a dispossessed monarch. After all, he says right at the beginning of the novel, 'we were the princes; no one mourned our passing.'

But then comes the first glimpse of Abhayraj, not quite eighteen and a head full of undigested knowledge. He is with his father, the Maharaja. The ruler is sitting crossed-legged and barefoot on a white mattress in the room with the tiger rug.

'Fifty-eight tiger skins had been sewn together to make that rug which covered the room from wall to wall. All of them had been killed by my father.' The simplicity of the sentence is deceptive. It talks of entitlement that would brook no interference. It talks of a life far removed from the reality that was India. It also indicates an acceptance of privilege in a matter-of-fact manner.

The young prince and the Maharaja are discussing the new constitution which the latter proposed to introduce in their state. The prince does not understand the need for one as it seems to be written with the monarch's interests. Abhayraj is certain the nationalists won't accept it. And that once the British leave India, the 'collective wish of the people' will prevail. The king is astounded that his heir can consider such heresy. And with that scene the stage is set for the rest of the book. As the princely states struggled to keep alive what and who they were, an India that was beyond their comprehension begins to shape.

Here is a monarch who refuses to accept that the death knell of the princely states has been rung. And here is also a monarch-in-making who can hear the bells tolling vehemently: the end is near, the end is near.

Here is a father who cannot condone his son for accepting the loss of his heritage without rage or recrimination. And here is a son who cannot accept his father's easy dismissal of all that he holds sacred by reducing it to sordid personal levels.

Again and again, the king and Crown Prince—the father and son—are to decry each other's belief systems. Resistance thus becomes the leitmotif of *The Princes*.

The resistance of Abhayraj to the demands of his heritage. The Maharani's resistance to her circumstances with the only weapon available to her; the agency of her body. The resistance mounted by the king's tribesmen, the Bhils. The resistance to monarchy by Kanakchand and his Praja Mandal. And eventually, in probably what is one of the best scenes ever seen in Indian Writing in English, the Maharaja's resistance to having to accept that he and his kingdom no longer have a place or standing in the new India.

The success of a novel for me isn't drawn from whether it is good or bad. I would rather opt for the choice between whether it draws me into the narrative with an effortless ease or if its tedium makes plodding through it a penance, a punishment even. For when a novel is fascinating, it is born of the fact that several dimensions come together to create a whole that makes the book unputdownable. Such is Manohar Malgonkar's *The Princes*.

It is a period novel where pomp and circumstances, duck shoots and treasure chambers and retainers who are the epitome of loyalty abound. But it would be reducing the novel to classify it as one. For *The Princes* is as contemporary as anything written today. The emergence of a new order which in Malgonkar's words is hallmarked by the 'vengeance of sheep' could very well be about the India in the here and now. The Maharaja and Abhayraj's anguish at seeing the steady erosion of what constitutes fairness and fair play is one that echoed within me about the times we live in.

Perhaps that is the true hallmark of a fine piece of writing. That it is relevant no matter what era the book is set in. Time changes; the nature of the human condition doesn't.

Bengaluru **Anita Nair**
July 2022

Author's Note

The characters in this novel are intended to personify the thoughts and ideas of a somewhat tightly-knit social group: the one-time ruling princes of India. Since over six hundred Princely States were integrated into the Indian Union within a matter of months, it is possible that certain incidents described herein may seem familiar enough for some readers to associate them with persons of their acquaintance. It is, therefore all the more necessary to explain that with the exception of such well-known names and events as have figured in the public press, all incidents and characters in this book are entirely fictitious and that no reference is intended to any actual person, whether living or dead.

—M.D.M.

Prologue

1 November 1858

Victoria, by the grace of God, of the United Kingdom of Great Britain and Ireland, and of the colonies and dependencies thereof in Europe, Asia, Africa, America and Australia, Queen, Defender of the Faith …

Whereas, for diverse weighty reasons, we have resolved by and with the advise and consent of the Lords Spiritual and Temporal and Commons, in Parliament assembled, to take upon ourselves, the Government of the territories of India …

We hereby announce to the native princes of India that all treaties and engagements made with them … are by us accepted, and will be scrupulously maintained …

We desire no extension of our present territorial possessions … We shall respect the right, dignity, and honour of the native princes as our own …

And may the God of all power grant to us, and to those in authority under us, strength to carry out these our wishes …

—Extract from the Queen's Proclamation read out at Allahabad.

1

'So Long as the Sun and the Moon go Round'

The map was red and yellow. The red was for British India; the yellow for the India of the princes: the Rajas and the Maharajas, the Ranis and the Maharanis, the Nawabs, the Rawals, the Jams.

For more than a hundred years, the red and the yellow had remained exactly as they were. Then the British left, and in no time at all, the red had overrun the yellow and coloured the entire map a uniform orange. The princely states were no more.

We were the princes; no one mourned our passing. We were a jest of history, a tribe that had lived long beyond its day because it had been carefully preserved in the strong chemicals of British protection. And when that protection was withdrawn and all of us were exposed to the harsh glare of the sun like frogs under an overturned slab, it was inevitable that we should perish.

I realize that it could not have been otherwise and yet I cannot rid myself of a purely selfish sense of loss; and above all, I cannot help wondering at the suddenness of it all: one day we were ruling princes, the next we were frogs shrivelling under burning sun. I often catch myself longing for the days under the slab; the days of silk turbans and egret plumes and brocade robes and velvet slippers and the glittering life that went with them.

They say that even the Government themselves were surprised at the speed and ease with which they were able to do away with the princely states. As for us, we had always been brought up to believe that nothing could assail us, that we were meant to go on as we were for all time, so long as the sun and the moon themselves went round, as our treaties stipulated, our rights guaranteed by the pledged word of the British crown. As late as the summer of 1938, I remember my father himself pronouncing in a trembling voice:

'There will always be a Begwad, and there will always be a Bedar ruling it—so long as the sun and the moon go round!'

I remember it so well because that was the only time my father and I had exchanged words of anger, the only time he had ordered me to leave his presence.

It was early in the evening and he had just returned from his audience chamber. He was drinking Scotch and soda, sitting cross-legged and barefoot on the white mattress and leaning against the bolster in the room with the tiger rug. He wore his purple velvet cap which never looked out of place or theatrical on him. Fifty-eight tiger skins had been sewn together to make that rug which covered the room from wall to wall. All of them had been killed by my father.

The A.D.C. on duty, Captain Haibat Ram, came in and switched on the lights, and my father jumped to his feet and folded his hands in a reverent namaskar to the chandelier overhead, and myself and the A.D.C. in our turn did a mujra to my father by bowing low and touching our foreheads with our right hands three times. The room was still dim though, for the chandelier had many of the bulbs missing and the wall lights had not been put on. My father sat down and sipped his whisky and pulled at his hookah pipe. He dismissed the A.D.C. with a curt nod because he wished to continue the discussion we had been having before. We were talking about the new constitution which my father proposed to introduce in our state.

I was in my last year at college then, not quite eighteen years old, and my head was full of undigested knowledge. I should have known better, but I had gone on contradicting my father, almost taking a malicious delight in the way he was reacting.

'But all you have done, Dada, is to increase the number of your Councillors from three to six,' I said.

'Ah, but one of them is elected,' Father pointed out.

'Hardly elected. It says each of the other five members are to put up a name, and from these names you will select one.'

'There you are! Chosen from amongst names put up by others; not nominated.' At times he could be so infuriatingly impervious to logic.

'Besides, the Council has no power to discuss your privy purse except to increase it, and in any case, you can always overrule anything it may decide if you don't approve of it.'

'But naturally. That is the power of the veto; a ruler's privilege.'

Somehow, as I sat face to face with my father in that room with no chairs—only the tiger rug and, along one wall, the white mattress and the bolster covered in pale blue brocade—I could not help feeling that we were both acting in a play.

The clock on the palace tower chimed the half-hour. It was seven-thirty, and as though at a signal, almost as though to heighten the illusion that we were acting in a play and surrounded by stage props, two servants carried in brass bowls containing burning incense. They marched silently around the room, taking no notice of us, leaving a smothering, heavily scented trail of smoke in their wake. I waited for them to go, listening to the quiet gurgle of my father's hookah and looking at the swords and shields and the odd-looking guns and pistols of olden days that hung on the walls.

'This is so like a play,' I remarked.

'What is?'

'All this, us.'

My father smiled. 'All life is a play,' he said. 'All the world's a stage, and all the men and women merely players.' Have you done *As You Like it*?'

I did not answer his question. Instead I asked: 'Why was this necessary at all?'

'You mean the new constitution?'

'Yes.'

My father threw back his head and laughed. He had such a natural, gurgling laugh, just like a child's, and with the shadows thrown by the light that hung directly overhead, his tanned, sharply chiselled face looked ruggedly handsome; like a black and white portrait done in bold strokes.

'The federation of India,' he explained. 'The Political Department insists … well, desires, really, that the princes must introduce a substantial measure of responsible government.'

'And does the Political Department consider this adequate?'

'Oh, perfectly,' my father said, beaming. 'They are quite pleased with it.'

I could detect the note of derision in his voice. Of late my father had begun to take liberties with the Political Department. Indeed with him it had become a sort of game to see just how far he could push them without inviting any serious consequences.

'What about the people?' I asked. 'The nationalists are not going to accept it.'

'The nationalists!' my father said with a sneer. 'Gooandas led by traders and lawyers!' For the nationalists, my father had nothing but contempt. The British were our traditional enemies, for they had taken our kingdom by treachery. But that was long ago, and he had become resigned to their domination. The adversaries of the moment were the nationalists, out to grab whatever the British had spared by resorting to treachery far greater than the British were capable of—by subverting the loyalty of the people towards their rulers.

'I don't think we need bother about hurting the feelings of the agitators. As far as I'm concerned, they just don't exist.' The sneer was even more pronounced.

'But they can't be swept aside by merely ignoring their existence,' I told him. 'They have won quite overwhelming majorities in the British provinces—are actually running the governments.'

'Sometimes you talk almost like an agitator yourself,' Father chided. 'As though you condone their heresy … approve it. Almost like that boy I horsewhipped—the one with the mean little face. What was his name? Oh, yes, Kanakchand. Kanakchand the dhor, the untouchable. Remember how he squealed? Do you still see anything of him?'

The boy he had horsewhipped. For seven years, that incident had stood between us like a steel spike. This was the first time my father had spoken about him. It seems strangely appropriate that Kanakchand's name should have come to his mind just then: the boy he had flogged publicly.

'We don't speak to each other,' I said. 'He is doing well at college, though; bound to pass with honours. Then he will take up law.'

'All thanks to you—you and your mother. Otherwise he would still be curing leather. And the way he shows his gratitude is by not speaking to you! It is important to choose carefully those you wish to elevate. Breeding always tells.'

I had not known till then that my father knew that it was my mother who had been paying for Kanakchand's education. 'He certainly deserved to be helped,' I said, stung by his air of all-knowing assurance. 'He was quite the most hardworking boy at school. He'll be a lawyer soon.'

'Oh, I am sure he will. And then he will go and join the nationalists; all misguided lawyers go and join the nationalists—the opposite camp.' He shook his head in disapproval.

'Even the British have had to accept them,' I pointed out.

'All to the good! Let them fight one another. We don't want either of them here. The fear of the nationalists has made the British swing more and more to our side—they have suddenly become the friends of the princes.'

'It all seems so distorted,' I protested. 'In the colleges, the British tell us how proud they are of the unfettered democracy in their own country. Yet here in India, they see nothing wrong in making common cause with the princes to deny basic rights to the people ...'

Something in the way my father was staring at me made me stop. 'It is surprising how quickly the horns grow on the foreheads of lambs,' he remarked. He was shaking his head gently from side to side.

I did not know what he could be talking about. He had a habit of resorting to obscure quotations. 'With what face can they—the British—side with the princes against their own people?' I asked.

'That is hardly the point. What is important is that today the British need our support. The topiwallas are getting scared of the white-capwallas. We must take the fullest advantage. This is the time to try and win back our privileges, one by one.'

'How can any rights and privileges, guaranteed by treaties, withstand the collective wish of the people?' I asked, quoting from my textbook on political science. But my father was not listening to me any more. A dreamy, faraway look had come into his face.

'Why, the day might come when we shall get back what was ours,' he said in a voice that had dropped to a dry whisper. 'The Kali river shall be our boundary, the Kali and the Nashi. Let the nationalists bleed the British. The more they weaken, the stronger do we emerge.'

'But how long can this go on? When India gets independence, the British will have to leave. What happens to the princes then?'

The dreamy look on my father's face vanished. He was back in the present. 'The British will never leave this country—never!' he pronounced. There was a glint of anger in his eyes and the lines around his mouth had grown tight.

He no longer looks handsome, I thought. Indeed, whenever my father was angry, his features took on a strange resemblance to the portrait of my namesake, the first Abhayraj, known in history books as 'Abhayraj the terrible'—once he had festooned the walls of the old fort with the heads of his victims.

But my father's voice was still calm and even as he went on. 'No, Abbay, the British will never leave this country. We shall see that they don't. It is up to us, the ruling princes of India, to see that they remain here, for our own sakes—remain here for ever.'

'Does it mean that you would be prepared to support the British against the nationalists?'

'Every time,' my father said with emphasis. 'Every time. Mind you, I am no friend of the British, as you know; I hate them far worse than Gandhi can do. He was only thrown out of a railway carriage. My grandfather was certified mad by them—certified mad and deported just because he refused to kowtow to the Resident. My great grandfather was declared a rebel for almost the same reason. And they took our raj by the vilest treachery. But I would prefer the British to the Gandhi-ites any day, so that the integrity of our state is preserved for all times. It is more important than anything else—more important than our own lives, yours and mine. And if it can be achieved only through British bayonets, let us keep British bayonets here by all means. Keep them for all time, so that Begwad remains ours, the descendants of the Bedars, the fearless chieftains—ours for all time.'

'How can we separate the destiny of Begwad from the rest of India?' I taunted him, feeling a rising anger, a recklessness provoked as much by my father's composed, disdainful voice as by his refusal to face facts. 'India is far more important than the heritage of her biggest prince, the Nizam or the Wadiar. Our state is as nothing, insignificant ... '

I stopped in mid-sentence, aware that I had overstepped the mark. Across the snow-white mattress, my father's face stared at me, contorted with pain and shock and anger as I had never seen it before.

'Is there nothing sacred to you?' he asked in a voice trembling with anger, and almost in spite of myself, I experienced a surge of achievement, knowing I had pierced his armour. I had made him come down from his pedestal; he was no longer regal, no longer a prince but an angry man ranting at his son.

'That you, who will one day rule this state, should think of it as nothing, as something to be thrown on the streets for a feast of crows—I can hardly believe it! Sometimes—sometimes I even doubt whether you are a true son of mine, born of my loins; a true Bedar.'

That remark made me lose all self-control. 'You are not yourself, Dada. Do you realize you are alluding to Her Highness my mother—sullying her name. If it had been anyone else, I would ... I would ... '

'Yes, what would you have done?' he jeered.

'I would have slapped his face. I would have made him touch my feet, for saying what you have just said—you who are not fit to walk in her shadow.'

'I think you have said quite enough,' my father said. 'Get out of my sight—at once!'

l jumped to my feet and ran out without doing mujra to him as custom demanded.

'Wait!' my father ordered. 'Wait!' And almost in spite of myself, I stopped in the doorway and turned to face him.

'Bear this in mind,' he said, and once again his voice was low and without a quiver and his face had regained its normal composure except that it was very pale. 'Bear this in mind. No matter what anyone tells you, there will always be a Begwad and there will always be a Bedar as its ruler, so long as the sun and the moon go round. Now you may go.'

His words rang in my ears long after I had left his presence.

I knew I had gone too far, but I was not sorry. I owed it to myself not to permit the sullying of my mother's honour; to him there was nothing more sacred than his heritage. We had hit at each other by assailing something we held sacred above all and we had both drawn blood. And yet I was conscious that the mark of corrosion left by our exchange of angry words would remain for a long, long time.

My father lived in a world of his own—the world of princely India, remote from the twentieth century, encrusted with taboos and clinging with pathetic desperation to a time when our fortunes were at their highest and our kingdom had reached its greatest extent. It was a wholly composite world, made up by adding bits and pieces from many an indeterminate past and forming the rosy, intoxicating picture of wealth and achievement he carried within himself.

It was also a world built on make-believe and half-truths and legends, as for instance the myth about the British having taken the kingdom of the Bedars by treachery.

'All the officers of the East India Company were low-born men—sudras,' my father would pronounce. 'The better class Englishmen did not come to India in those days. And Perkins was the lowest born of the lot. No one else would have stooped to such downright treachery.'

But there had been no treachery involved. General Perkins had beaten our forces squarely and fairly in the battle of Patalpat. We were numerically superior, but we were hopelessly outgeneraled. The troops of the company were better trained and disciplined and they routed the Bedar's army by first driving a wedge between his main force and his artillery, and then swooping down upon the men caught up helplessly in the Bulwara valley and cutting them down systematically. That was what my father had always termed treachery.

'They had won over our French gunners, the mercenaries, long before the battle,' he would explain. 'So that we were left to fight with nothing but muskets and spears. And then they fell on us with everything they had.'

No, it was not treachery; it was sheer superiority of tactics. Perkins was one of the most brilliant officers in the Company's service. But you could never have argued the point with my father.

Again, there was his exasperating tendency to reduce the national political agitation to sordid personal levels. Nothing would have convinced him that Gandhi's movement for self-rule was not wholly motivated by his bitterness against the British because he had once been thrown out of a railway carriage reserved for the whites, or that a well-brought-up man like Motilal Nehru was supporting him only because he had been blackballed in the club at Allahabad. I am sure he had never cared to find out whether Motilal Nehru really had been blackballed, or whether the man who had insulted Gandhiji in South Africa was an Englishman.

The painful scene between my father and myself had brought into the open a resentment which had been growing within me for a long time. Hitherto, I had never shown, any open resistance to his ideas. He, on the other hand, must have always assumed that I had absorbed without question all that he had taught me to believe. Lately, I have wondered what psychological quirk in my character made me take a perverse delight in having digs at him about the growth of nationalism in the country and the hopelessly insecure position of the princes, for although I would not have admitted it readily at the time, I myself went a long way inwards sharing his views and values as far as our state was concerned. Indeed it seems to me that with the passing of the years, l have come to identify myself more and more with those values, with the result that today I feel myself a spokesman for whatever the princely order once stood for.

'Maharaja Abhayraj proved to be just as much of a reactionary as his father,' the Settlements Minister wrote in his memoirs. He was referring to me, of course, and instead of feeling resentful, I was elated by the rebuke, proud of being thought like my father.

Towards the end I was to become just as proud of our heritage as my father had been, the only difference being that I was prepared to take everything just as it was. I loved the forests and the hills and the river with a sense of belonging, just like our own palaces and shooting lodges, and I loved the tribesmen of the Bulwara valley with the same clannish, almost touchy fierceness as my father's—the half-savage yet intensely civilized Bhils, loyal, quick-tempered, fierce and proud subjects to whom the Bedar was both king and god, and who have suffered so much during recent years because of the virtues and vices inherent in the characters of primitive men. At least I like to think that I learnt to accept everything just as it was, and if my early ancestry were nothing but professional bandits, the dreaded wielders of the double axe, who happened to rise to high command in the service of the Peshwas, it was all the more reason to be proud of them. To me it was something of a sacrilege to falsify the past; to whitewash it was to render it sterile.

My father thought quite differently. He had brought down an historian from Allahabad University to write the family history, and between them they had made out the Bedars to be a race of heroes, brave, noble, virtuous, intensely patriotic, and in the process had divested them of their fire and turbulence, and even of normal human frailties.

For instance, they had put out a neat little legend showing how the first Abhayraj began to be called the 'Bedar' because of his courage in battle in the war with the Rohillas.

'It was then that they began to call him "Abhayraj the Bedar—the fearless",' my father used to explain, and as though to invest his statement with the hallmark of truth, he added: 'The Peshwa's army was at Shukratal then.'

Abhayraj may have been a quite fearless man, but both my father and his historian, Dr. Niyogi, were aware that we were the Bedars long before the Rohilla wars, and that we were called the Bedars because we belonged to the Bedar community, casteless professional highwaymen from the hills of Sutgatta. Our weapon was not the sword or the lance of the fighting man, but the double axe of the bandit, and we still have it emblazoned on our crest and on our flag. Throughout history we had lived by plunder and indulged in pagan worship including human sacrifices. It was only when the hard-pressed, leaderless Maratha noblemen engaged our earliest known ancestor, the first Hiroji, for harassing the Mughal columns then operating in the land, that we became soldiers—mercenaries, as my father would have termed them. From then on we were plunderers with the sanction of a monarch, looting the rich Mughal bullock trains and building up the family treasure at Patalpat, and at the same time, receiving payment for our services too.

It was almost inevitable that we should grow rich. The hoard of gold in the Jamdar-khana, the secret vault at Patalpat, soon grew to such proportions that its protection became the primary concern of the Bedars. They devised a special set of rules for its safety and invoked the curse of the family goddess upon those who would covet it. Even the head of the family himself was forbidden to enter the vault unless he was blindfolded. I myself had to wait until I was twenty-six years old before I was taken to see our Jamdar-khana.

But we became powerful too, and at the time of the first Abhayraj, we had risen to the command of a column and were among the half-dozen leading generals who were permitted to carry their own flag and drums into battle. But in spite of the wealth and power and prestige, we still continued to be known as the Bedars; the Marathas never accepted us as one of themselves.

To me, personally, there is no humiliation attached to being born in a family originating from a clan of highwaymen, but my values were not those of my father. To him it was unbearable that we should not be among the high-born, and should therefore not be permitted to wear the sacred thread or to offer prayers in the temples except through the brahmin priests.

And above all, not considered sufficiently high-born by both the Rajputs and the Marathas to marry into their families.

The religious slights that he had been subjected to in his early days goaded my father to spend a good deal of money and energy in trying to establish that our family did have the right to wear the janwa, the sacred thread of the high-caste Hindu, and to offer prayers in the temples as the equals of caste Hindus. In the end, he did succeed in obtaining a ruling from a panel of high priests in Gokarn conceding these rights, but it was common knowledge that he had paid a whole lakh of rupees for the repairs of the Durga-ghat at Gokarn as the price of the concession and that he had also made several undisclosed personal gifts to the priests themselves.

For my part, I gave up wearing the sacred thread within a few days of my thread ceremony, and this fact may well represent my whole attitude towards religion, and particularly towards the concessions that my father had striven so hard to obtain.

Religion, which was such a tangible, living matter of faith with my father, tended to become another point of difference between us, and the more strenuously he strove to convert me to his beliefs, the more unreceptive did I seem to become to all religious teaching.

My mother was religious too, but her religion was a simple, almost personal affair. Her pooja was done in solitude; her temple was a small alcove next to her bedroom; her goddesses the seven satis in the family, the Maharanis before her who had immolated themselves on their husbands' funeral pyres. The satis, by giving their lives, had found a place in the family shrine. I have seen my mother shed tears while she was at her prayers, so that I was filled with shame for being there, in her prayer room, as though I had stumbled on sacred ground and defiled something by my intrusion.

My father's religion, on the other hand, was blatant, noisy, almost an orgiastic affair, with clash of cymbals and the chanting of devotional songs and the burning of incense and the distribution of silver coins. In a way, I felt slightly ashamed in the presence of my father's religion too, but it was a wholly different kind of shame.

I have read somewhere that the growing resentment I had begun to feel towards my father during the years of my youth may be ascribed to a natural oedipus complex, which, of course, is quite absurd. In spite of all that has happened, I like to think that the one thing of which my father was really convinced was my extreme devotion to him. I am sure that, if necessary, I would have willingly sacrificed my life for him. But this again, someone told me only the other day, could have been the outcome of an exaggerated sense of duty and that it could not be called either love or affection; that, strangely enough, it may even have been the outward manifestation of a subconscious hatred.

The fact remains that during my years at college I drew more and more away from him, feeling I could no longer be natural in his presence, conscious that instead of getting to know each other better we were becoming strangers; two men who had little in common thrown together by an accident. Between us there was always a curtain of increasing formality. He was the Maharaja with almost absolute power over five hundred thousand people; I was his heir. Imperceptibly the curtain thickened, and suddenly we were no longer merely a father and son, but a Maharaja and his successor. The days when I rushed into his arms on the rare occasions he chose to be playful during my evening visits to him, to be pressed against his chest, to be enveloped into the maleness of tobacco smoke and whisky, the powerful arms lifting me higher and higher, terrified yet squealing with delight, belonged to my childhood. Now he was someone I had to do mujra to whenever the light came on in the evenings, for he was the source of all light, someone with whom I could begin to speak only after I had bent down and touched my forehead with my right hand three times in token of putting the dust of his feet on my head. In his presence, I could not altogether push away the awful thought that he was someone who would have to die before I could come into my own. There was no question of my being able to fulfil my own destiny like other men; I had to wait on the sidelines for another man's death.

That unhappy scene in the room with the fifty-eight dead tigers and the old swords and shields nailed to the walls was like the ending of a phase. For many years from that day, our relationship became even more coldly formal than before. Whatever had held us close had broken away, only the shell of our proprieties now kept us together, like two men living under a flag of truce.

And, of course, the years have given the lie to my father's impassioned pronouncement: 'There will always be a Begwad, and there will always be a Bedar ruling it. So long as the sun and the moon go round!'

Begwad is still there, a name on the map, an untidy cluster of houses and streets and two palaces which have been converted into a college and a research laboratory respectively, and the statues of my ancestors at street corners encrusted by the droppings of birds. A town where they have the district's headquarters and a cement factory belching smoke against the hoary old fort. Nothing can obliterate the place itself unless they drop a nuclear bomb on it or something. Begwad is as much there as it ever was, and if anything it has grown in size. But the Bedars are certainly not ruling it. Within ten years of my encounter with my father, the state of Begwad was merged with the vast totality of India.

My father just missed being the last ruling Maharaja of Begwad. I was the last, and it fell to me to sign that doleful document known as the instrument of merger, surrendering all powers as the ruler.

2

Of Lambs and Lions

As I have said, perhaps the most dominant urge of my childhood was to prove my devotion to my father; he strode my horizons like a knight in shining armour, his smile or frown capable of covering the full range of my emotions. And yet, even in those days, there were occasions when I hated him with an overpowering bitterness, hated him enough to have wanted to kill him with my own hands. But the occasions that gave cause for such blind anger on my part had nothing to do with my affection for my mother, which just proves how misguided the psychologists can be. It seems perfectly absurd now, but the first time I wanted to kill my father, it was all over a pet ram which I had acquired within a day or two of my tenth or eleventh birthday.

He was a small, month-old lamb at the time, only a bundle of soft, brown fleece with a jet black nose. I was returning from my riding lessons and had just taken a short cut from the paddock on my way to my mother's apartment for breakfast when I saw one of the servants carrying it on his shoulder.

'Oh, what a pretty lamb!' I said. 'Let me see.' I jumped off the pony and the syce who was running with me caught up the reins.

The man put the lamb down for me to see and I petted it and put my arms around it.

'Do you think I can lift it?' I asked.

I could. It was so light that I could lift it clean off the ground. It was not a bit frightened, though, and as soon as I put it down, it began to rub its head against my knees.

'What will it eat? Bring something for it to eat, a banana or something,' I ordered, and the servant ran off to the kitchen wing while I played with the lamb. But we found that it was not interested in a banana. It went on rubbing its forehead against my knees and making queer little lamb noises. And I thought of the sugar cubes in my pocket. I always carried some sugar cubes during my riding school days. The lamb curled its lips and began to nibble at the cube somewhat messily.

'What is its name?' I asked.

'It has no name, Bal-raje,' the servant told me. All the palace servants called me Bal-raje in those days.

'We'll give it a name. Let's give it an English name.' There was a moment of caution. Accustomed to horses and dogs from childhood, I knew that names had to go with sex. 'Is it going to become a papa or a mama?' I asked.

'Papa. Bal-raje.'

'Oh. good! We will call him Cannonball, because of the way he butts his head. Can I keep him for a pet?'

'The khansama is waiting for it.'

'Does it belong to him?'

'He is waiting to have it slaughtered for tomorrow's pallav; Bal-raje's birthday lunch.'

'Oh, you can't kill the poor thing! He's so tiny.'

'They have to have tender meat for the pallav.'

'But he is such a sweet little fellow. Look at the way he keeps butting. Go and bring some more sugar cubes.'

'But what shall I tell the khansama, Bal-raje?'

'Tell him he can't kill poor little Cannonball! I want to keep him as a pet.'

The Dewanji who looked after the household marketing and the cooks between them must have found another lamb for the day's feast. Cannonball was spared. He was given a shed to himself in the stables and one of the dog boys, Kishen, was to look after him.

The boy kept him clean and brushed his fleece every day until it shone like gold. I used to go and play with him every morning on my way back from riding, and sometimes in the afternoons too. Within a few months he grew to an enormous size, but he was full of mischief as ever. Our play used to begin by his running up to me whenever he heard my voice and demanding carrots and sugar cubes and nuzzling my pockets for them. After finishing whatever titbit I had brought for him, he would begin his butting. I would keep pushing him back with both hands and he would come charging back, his head down, asking for more. Between Kishen and myself we soon trained Cannonball to be a confirmed butting ram so that he would charge at anyone who came near him. Once he broke the wooden bars of his shed and got loose and attacked one of the chaprasis who was carrying a load of account books. Cannonball sneaked from behind, felled him and sent his books flying all over the courtyard.

The Dewanji pretended that he was going to report it to my father, but in the end all that happened was that he had a new steel-barred gate installed on the shed. Whenever Cannonball heard my voice he would cock his head and begin to bleat and give funny little sideways jumps and come scampering to the gate. But as soon as he had finished eating, he would be ready for battle, chasing Kishen and myself in turns and butting viciously at the little wooden tables we used to carry to fend off his attacks.

By the time Dassara came, Cannonball was nearly a year old. He had become so big that neither the dog boy nor I could have lifted him off the ground. A few days before the festival, when I went to see my father in the evening, I happened to speak to him about Cannonball. Father was in a particularly expansive mood that evening. He was surrounded by half a dozen courtiers and they were discussing the programme for the Dassara sports.

'How many entries have we got for the ram fights?' my father asked.

One of the men looked at his notebook and said: 'Eleven. Your Highness.'

'Only eleven? Last year we had eighteen.' My father had an extraordinary memory for such detail.

That was when I told him about my pet ram. 'I have the best butting ram in the world.'

My father patted my shoulder indulgently. 'Oh, here we are,' he said. 'Abhay has got a ram. Why don't we enter him for the bouts. Would you like to enter him? Is he any good as a fighter?'

'Cannonball is the best fighter in the world,' I said. 'He even breaks bars. He has broken all the plaster on the walls of his shed.'

A ram fight must be one of the cruellest sports in the world. They always do their best to match the rams evenly, but the more evenly matched they are, the more heartless the contest.

Before each bout, the opposing rams are taken round and exhibited to the spectators so that bets can be placed. The rams are then taken by their handlers into the roped-off arena and made to stand facing each other at a distance of twenty feet. Then the whistle blows and they are released.

They charge, aiming with their bodies, and their foreheads crash with a thud. As though repelled by the impact they draw back a few paces and then charge again, still in a perfect straight line, seeming to observe some inflexible rule of their own. They repeat this again and again and stop only when one of them falls down thrashing its legs.

I do not know what courage means unless it is the will to go on attacking even when you know you are beaten, giving up only when you are dead. If so tigers or lions cannot be called the bravest animals in the world, for there is nothing to match the blind courage of fighting rams. For them, each bout is a fight to the finish. When the rams are well-matched, often both die side by side, their skulls broken in one last mighty collision.

The betting was not heavy on Cannonball, although my father had put a hundred rupees on him to win. His opponent was a grey and black Jaisalmir ram with twisted, goat-like horns, called Sandogama. I crossed my fingers and kept trying to convince myself that Cannonball would win.

They crashed into each other with a soft thud, and then they went back and came in again, and this time it was like the whack of a washerman beating a wet sheet on a stone slab. All the palace staff roared their cheers for Cannonball to win:

'Come on, Cannonball! Kill that scrawny goat!'

There was an even greater roar from the opponents:

'Oh, Sandogama. Kill that little pet lamb! Kill him!'

Even after the first half-dozen crashes, I realized that Cannonball was not in the same class as Sandogama, who was a seasoned fighter. But he was so brave. His legs were already trembling under him, but he went on, straight and true, charge after charge.

I could not stand it any more. 'Oh stop the fight! Stop it at once!' l yelled.

The two handlers looked uncertainly at me, and then they both ran in and grabbed the rams by their hind legs and pulled them away.

'What are you doing? Bewakoofs! Ulloos!' my father's voice thundered. 'Let the fight go on.'

The fight went on. I watched, my lips trembling, my fingers tearing at the velvet padding of my chair, my eyes pricking with tears. In the next chair was my father, calmly smoking a cigarette and pulling at his moustache. Cannonball's head was no longer like gold and the blood had begun to run out of his ears. But he went on, my brave Cannonball, thud upon thud, each louder than the last, until that inevitable last mighty explosion of two heavy-boned heads, and he lay on the grass, his legs jerking and the blood spurting from his jet black mouth and ears in thick gouts. His burnished brown coat was caked with mud and blood.

'Sandogama wins,' the bland voice of the Master of Ceremonies announced as soon as the clapping had stopped.

I wanted to rush into the enclosure and hug my Cannonball, to say something to him just before he died, to hold his head in my arms and comfort him and tell him how brave he was. Of course I did not do any of these things, but I could not prevent the tears flowing down my cheeks. Someone came and dragged his body away. The entries for the next bout were already being paraded, their handlers singing their praises. I saw it all through a blur of fractured light.

As in all Maratha states, the Dassara was our most important festival. It was on Dassara day which comes at the end of the rains and when the harvest has been brought in, that our ancestors used to set out on their campaigns. Most of the states still kept up a pretence that Dassara was somehow a warlike occasion; that we were celebrating it because we were setting out for the wars.

That same evening, my father and I went out in procession to the old palace in the city, riding on our state elephants. We wore jewels with our eighteenth century costumes and carried swords. The courtiers too were in costume and even the elephants were painted and caparisoned with silver bells round their necks. The procession went from the new palace to the old. In the courtyard before the old palace was the ceremony of distributing 'gold' to the populace; only, instead of gold coins, we gave away the leaves of the apta tree. After that we offered prayers in the family prayer room in the old palace, laying our swords at the feet of Ambica and seeking her blessings in the campaigns we were setting out upon.

Even as I knelt beside my father, my hands folded in prayer, I could not help feeling that it was all a great pretence, that there was no campaign of any sort for us to go on. The two bowls of incense were throwing full columns of scented smoke and the tall, many-flamed oil lamps were making weird shadows on the angry face of Ambica. She had eight hands and she was painted in red lacquer and dressed in a green sari. Seven of her hands bore weapons of combat—the mace, the wheel, the sword, the dagger, the trident, the bow and the arrow—and the eighth carried a still-bleeding human head, terrifyingly life-like, as though it had just been severed from the trunk.

I glanced sideways at my father. His eyes were tightly shut and his face looked dead white, like a bloodless mask, so that the caste mark of red sandalwood on his forehead stood out like a streak of blood. Even as I was looking at him, I saw him open his eyes wide. For a moment I thought he was going to admonish me for not concentrating on the pooja. Then I realized that he was not looking at me, or at the goddess, or at anything at all; that he was in a trance, staring at something no one else could see.

I went on looking at him as though spellbound, at my father who sat next to me and yet was somewhere far away, his palms held out rigidly to receive the blessings of Ambica. The head priest with his luminous, shaven head went on mumbling prayers in a soothing, singsong voice, pouring spoonfuls of water over the flowers heaped at the feet of the goddess, lighting more and more joss-sticks and camphor cakes and offering her meat and wine and music and perfume, all in make-belief symbols, and beseeching her protection in the coming campaign:

> 'Oh, Ambica, goddess of all gods!
> Bless thy son as ever in the past,
> Thy son who brings to thy feet the sword of his ancestors,
> Seeks now your blessings for victory …
> For power … for glory … for good and evil …
> Undertaking to be true to the salt of his ancestors,
> For ever and for ever.'

The priest picked up some flowers from the goddess's feet and put them in my father's hands, and even as I looked, the flowers rolled off and fell on the floor. After that the priest picked up the sword, anointed it with sandalwood paste and red ochre and placed it firmly into my father's hands, closing his fingers round the hilt.

I saw my father give a start, as though he had been woken from a deep sleep. He clutched the sword and bent down and touched his forehead with it. Then he rose to go.

'Come,' he beckoned to me.

We went down some stairs, narrow and winding like a secret passage, and we ended up in a small dark room above the banqueting hall where my father usually waited before making his formal entry into the durbar.

There was only one chair in the room, an elaborate chair of carved sandalwood and ivory, black with age and shining with natural oils, the seat and the back upholstered in purple velvet. It was more like a throne than a chair.

'Haibat! ' my father called.

Captain Haibatram, who must have been standing outside, said 'Huzur!' and came into the room.

'I want some whisky, and after that I don't want to be disturbed.'

'Huzur!'

The whisky came, already in a glass, looking fierce and red exactly the way my father liked it, with the glass nearly a quarter full of whisky and then topped with ice and soda. My father took the glass from Haibatram, who left the room and shut the door behind him.

'Sit down,' my father said to me, pointing to the chair.

'I will sit on the floor.'

'No, no; sit on the chair.' His voice sounded tired, as though he had undergone some great physical exertion.

I sat down in the absurdly high, high-backed chair, my feet dangling under me, and my father stood directly in front, holding the glass of whisky in his hand but not drinking.

He stood tall and powerful and handsome in his robe of rose and pea-green brocade and the purple silverwork slippers and the purple three-cornered pagri of the Bedars. Even the costume of long ago and the vulgar chains of pearls and diamonds did not make him look as though he were dressed up for a part in a play. He was one of the lucky ones, like Jaipur and Bikanir, who carried the trappings of their order with a natural ease; the pigeon-blood ruby cluster on his pagri, the collar of rows of outsize pearls, the dark-blue K.C.I.E. sash with the flamboyant star that come with it, the enormous chain of twisted gold around his left ankle.

'I have been praying,' my father told me. 'Praying for you.'

I did not know what to reply to such a private admission. I waited for him to go on.

'I prayed to Ambica that you should be the one to be given the strength to reconquer all our possessions; to re-establish the raj of the Bedars between the Kali and the Nashi rivers. And beyond ... why, up to Delhi itself.'

Even at the time, I knew enough to realize that Father was only speaking of a dream; that neither I nor any of my descendants were going to be able to restore the glory of the Bedars as my father had conjured it in his mind.

'What is this in my hand?' he asked.

'Whisky, sir.'

'That is right, whisky. It is a man's drink. A man's,' he repeated in a soft voice. 'Men who weep cannot call themselves men. They should wear bangles and hide their faces.'

'I am sorry, Dada,' I said.

'We, the Bedars, are fearless. "Bedar" means without fear. You know that, don't you? We are like lions, we do not weep for dead lambs.'

'What about dead lions?' I asked. 'Do we weep then?'

My father looked coldly at me with his hard, black eyes, as though he was looking deep into my mind, hypnotizing me with his stare. Then he went on: 'No, not even for dead lions—at least not when there are others present. In fact we never break down in public. There are, in everyone's life, moments when it is so much easier to weep; but it is always more manly not to. Sorrow, grief, is a private thing, like … like making love.'

'Yes, Dada.'

'We all have to take a whipping now and then, and the sooner we learn to take it without flinching, without showing that we are hurt, the better. It is like … like a well-bred dog. If you kick a pie dog, it sets up a howl. Will a well-bred dog do that?'

'No. Dada.'

'It is most important not to squeal, to show hurt. Be a man, my son. There is a great English poem you must read some time. Ask Mr. Moreton to show it to you. "Make me a Man, O Lord." It is a great thing to be a man … a true man. Tears are the refuge of the weak. Will you promise me that you will never break down; at least when you are not by yourself?'

'Yes, Father.'

'Promise me by all that is sacred to you; our ancestors, the goddess Ambica, your mother.'

'I promise.'

'Now drink this,' Father said, and held the glass before me.

'Drink it all down, and then we will go down to the banquet. The court must be waiting.'

The drink burnt its way down my throat and caused me to gasp, but it was important not to cough or splutter or show signs of distress.

'Remember what I told you. Remember what you promised,' he whispered a few moments later as we stood near the head of the curving staircase of the durbar hall before going down to the Dassara feast, and he gave my hand a slight squeeze. His fingers were like ice.

The heralds in their green and gold cloaks were already calling out the titles of the Maharaja—English, Sanskrit, Persian and Hindi—and announcing his approach.

'Valorous as the sun, the chosen of the gods, the source of light,' they were proclaiming in their rhythmic chant as my father went down the steps, slowly so as to give them time to run through the list. 'Wazir-e-farzand, Intezam-e-daulat, sar-e-sar-band, prithwi-naresh, sena-dhurandhar who holds undisputed sway over all the dominions between the Kali and the Nashi rivers, His Highness, Maharaja of the clan of the Bedars, Hiroji the fourth, Knight commander of the Star of India.'

We walked through the glittering ranks of the courtiers in their flamboyant turbans and pagris doing mujra, their heads bowing before us in a continuous wave, and once again my father was his usual self, gracious and charming, radiating good fellowship, smiling, playing the part of a prince at his own court and yet it was wrong to say that he was playing a part because it was all so real to him.

On the long, damask-covered dining-table, on a salver the size of a cartwheel, was the main dish of the evening: a great mound of saffron rice with all the spices the palace cooks had been able to conjure and with a whole roast sheep on top. Even as I glanced at it, my mind reeled with the thought that Father had had my Cannonball cooked for the Dassara banquet, and only then did I appreciate the full meaning of his whispered warning at the top of the stairs.

'We are going to have an Arab speciality,' Father was telling his guests. 'And I want the Yuwaraj to be the chief guest of the evening. His is the rising generation; the generation that will redeem the past. We shall observe the formalities of Arab hospitality, where the chief guest is personally served by the host. I shall myself serve the Yuwaraj.'

He picked up a sharp, gleaming carving knife, carefully carved out the eyes from the head of the sheep and placed them in a plate.

'That is how the Arabs honour their guests,' he announced as he handed the plate to me. 'The others may begin now; please carry on.'

I held the plate in my hands and managed to put one of the eyes in my mouth. It stuck in my throat and for a moment I thought I was going to choke. The glittering chandeliers, the enormous piles of food, the courtiers in their many-coloured robes, the white marble staircase, all began to go round and round in a pattern of broken light and shade as I tried desperately to swallow.

'Here, drink this,' my father was saying, and once again there was the fiery flash of almost neat whisky coursing down my gullet, and the eye, as large as a marble and just as hard, went slowly down. I shook my head and glared at the image of hate that was my father, and everything came into focus once again, falling into place under the thousand lights of the chandeliers.

'Make me a Man, O Lord,' I said to myself. 'Make me a Man.' Was this what it involved, the process of becoming a man? I threw away my fork and it fell with a clatter amidst the dishes piled on the main table. I grabbed the other eye firmly with my fingers and thrust it into my mouth, deliberately and defiantly, and once again my father held out the glass of whisky before me.

'No, thank you, Your Highness,' I said. 'I can manage. I don't need the whisky.' I chewed on the rubbery mouthful, slowly and purposefully, and swallowed it down.

'Shabash!' my father whispered, placing a hand on my shoulder. 'Well done!'

I kept my promise. I did not break down, and I felt a surge of triumph. I had met the challenge thrown at me by a hated adversary. The victory was mine. But that was one time I could have cheerfully killed my father; I, who loved him and revered him all my life.

3

'Fikra-fight!'

Driving into Begwad from either direction, you can see the Hirabagh palace from at least five miles away, separated from the pink and grey town by a belt of forest. Its domes and spires rise out of the surrounding green like great fingers of rock, providing a counterpoint for the jagged walls of the old fort towering on the hill behind. From that distance, you cannot see the river at all, just the craggy black structure in the fold of the hills, like a castle or a fortress, its unrelieved darkness accentuating the illusion. As you get closer, the sweep of the Kamra river comes into view and the cluster of outbuildings begin to separate themselves so that now the palace looks like an uninspired public building, like a prison or a post office of extravagant proportions, and you find yourself wondering how anyone could actually have lived in a structure like that.

And yet, for fifty years and more, my family lived in it, and we all loved it as people love their homes, and when I was at school or college, and even later during the war, I used to long to get back to it.

The Hirabagh palace is an unattractive basalt structure, a uniform grey in colour like the hides of elephants. It was built by my grandfather at the beginning of the century in a well meaning effort to bring together all that was good in the architectural styles of both the east and the west, and which turned out to be a nightmarish grafting of a maze of turrets and domes on an ornate and quite hideous Victorian edifice of arches and corridors that was complete in itself.

Its boundary walls circumscribed my childhood world, its four-faced chiming clock ruled my waking hours, its nooks and corners were my hiding places as a boy, its dim, echoing corridors harboured the formless ghosts of my childhood, its lawns, its woods, its tanks, were the signposts of my surroundings, and the arch of the drum-gate was my window on the outside world.

It was I who laid out the rose garden behind the drum-gate lawn, but I did not have time for much more. It was my father who planted all the fruit trees in the north orchard; the loquats, the Malta oranges, the mangoes and the cashews. My grand father confined himself to the decorative trees. He planted the gul-mohurs, the casuarinas, the silver oaks and the eucalyptus trees all leaning to one side as though bending in a storm and which were cut down last year for the factory expansion. A hundred peacocks used to inhabit the park in my childhood, making raucous love calls. I wonder what has happened to them.

I cannot say, as do many people I know, that my childhood was the happiest time of my life. Perhaps I am one of those who cannot think of any prolonged period of their lives as having been a happy one, to whom happiness is a fleeting thing, a state of mind lasting only a few minutes or an hour or so, and only occasionally for a whole day, but never longer. I remember my childhood as a blur of perpetual bewilderment, of an almost constant awareness of inadequacy, of a desperate striving to make adjustments. Perhaps it is not given to any child brought up by a hoard of ayahs and supervised by a grim Anglo-Indian nanny to look back upon a happy childhood. The ayahs were fat and clammy, the nanny angular and icy, and I was glad when, by the time I was about eight years old, they were replaced by male attendants and tutors. From then on, I seemed to be always doing some kind of lesson or other: riding lessons, cricket lessons, boxing lessons, music lessons, even lessons in wielding a sword. My father had laid down a rigid time-table for my up bringing.

I saw very little of my parents. Usually I saw my mother at breakfast. By the time I got to her apartment, she had finished her prayers and ceased to be 'untouchable', for between her early morning bath and her pooja, contact with anyone who had not had a bath and was not dressed in sanctified silk garments would have been defiling. In the mornings, Mother always looked peaked and tired, as though she had not slept well, or as if the pooja had in some manner drained away her vitality.

In the evenings I saw my mother again, just before going to bed, and then she looked radiant and beautiful, dressed in gorgeous silk saris with gold borders, wearing her pearls and surrounded by an aura of perfume, delicate and distinctive. She always had some special sweet or an ice-cream waiting for me. For a while we would talk, just like grown ups, and then Mrs. Hinks would come to take me away.

Before going to my mother's apartment in the evenings, I saw my father, too. I was given a bath and dressed in pyjamas, a dressing-gown and a velvet cap and taken by Mrs. Hinks to the door of the billiard room with many a whispered warning about how to behave. We waited for the stroke while Mrs. Hinks tip-toed to the door and peered through the glass peep-hole. When the stroke had been played and the balls were clicking, I was pushed into the room which always smelt faintly of hookah tobacco. And there was my father, bending over the table or sitting on one of the high-backed benches and the marker calling out the score in a jargon of his own and marking up the board. My father would look at me, almost in surprise, as though he had not expected me, and then rush forward and lift me in his arms. Occasionally, however, his mind seemed far away, and his greeting perfunctory. At such times I felt an intruder.

I hardly ever saw my parents together, for they lived in compartments sealed off from one another, never intruding. Lessons occupied most of my days and, oddly enough, gave rise to some of the happiest moments of my childhood; for they were the moments of achievement, of getting over fear and breaking new frontiers, discernible landmarks in the process of acquiring proficiency, like making a clean dive into the pool without breaking water and coming out to hear the instructor clapping his hands and shouting 'Shabashe! Shabashe!'

'Shabashe! Shabashe!' The words had an exhilarating ring, perhaps all the more so because they were so grudgingly uttered. The tall, thin figure of Gonsalves, white-clad in cricketing cottons or pitch black and shining in swimming trunks, breaking into a smile—a flash of white in black which could be seen from a hundred yards away—and applauding a cover drive or the way I had mastered the crawl and yelling 'Shabashe! Shabashe!' or scowling and throwing his hands up in despair at my clumsiness, meant far more to me than the praise or censure of my tutors.

And there was riding, my favourite sport, pastime and diversion, carried out under the coaching of Hamidulla, passionate exponent of the forward seat. I can still recall his trim figure, dressed in soft riding boots, breeches, a tattered tweed jacket with patches on the elbows and a polo helmet. He would be carrying a leather crop which he never used, leaning languidly against the paddock rail, shouting words of encouragement at the horse or myself and giving the curt orders: 'Fikra-fight! Fikra-fight!'

I would twist my wrist and shift the reins and prod lightly with the opposite heel for the horse to change his feet and go into the figure of eight. But I never seemed to be light enough, gentle enough for the riding master. 'Now, now, stop pulling, stop jerking, don't kick! You are not riding a railway engine, Balraje. Lightly, lightly … panje-undher, eddie-bahar … nai, nai, nai!'

And only occasionally, 'Shabashe! Shabashe!'

The sights and sounds come back to me in sharp jabs, clearing away the mist of the intervening years: the noise of the hooves pounding on the sawdust-covered ring in an easy rhythm, matching the panting of the shining, sweating horse; the acrid smells of the riding school on a winter's morning, and of refuse being burnt in a nearby incinerator; the grass drenched with dew; the sunlight slanting through the trees in dusty shafts and falling on the white-painted paddock rails; the terrifying jumps built of bamboo and straw. And dominating all, the wiry, bandy-legged figure of Hamidulla, the true aristocrat of the ring, praising me and cursing me in hunting field oaths and the quaint ring of the orders in an unlearnt foreign language. 'Fikra-fight! Fikra-fight!' which had nothing to do with fighting but which was Hamidulla's way of saying 'Figure of eight'.

Until I was eleven years old, I had no friends I can think of, only 'companions' chosen by my father. One of them, Charudutt, was my father's son by a concubine. He was a year older than I was, and he was a loud-mouthed bully. He was fairer than me, and bigger made, and his hair curled in thick waves. All the boys at school were terrified of him.

As boys, Charudutt and I were always scrapping, using fists and elbows and feet. Once when, for the second time in a week, my father saw fresh bruises on my face and body, he told me he was arranging to have me taught boxing. Within two months, I found I could hold my own against Charudutt, and then one day I lashed out at his face with such fury that his mouth began to bleed. That was the last time I used my fists against Charudutt, but my boxing lessons continued until my last year at school, when my father ruled that I was not to box any more.

It was only when I was much older that I began to understand why Charudutt used to hate me as much as he seemed to: if only his mother had been legally married to my father, he would have been the Yuwaraj. But although he was my father's first-born son, he could never aspire to his gadi merely because his mother happened to be a concubine.

Charudutt's mother, whom we all knew as Bibi-bai, was the first of my father's concubines, and she remained his favourite for many years, encouraging him to do the sort of unorthodox and often foolish things that men do to please the women they are infatuated with. At one time it was rumoured that she had cast some kind of spell over him by making him eat a love potion administered in the paan she used to make for him. But of course the rumour may have had its roots in the fact that, at one time, my father never ate paans made by anyone else.

Charudutt joined the police when he grew up. Within the next two or three years he should become the Inspector-General of the state, and I have no doubt that he will make an excellent police chief. The way things have turned out, perhaps he no longer regrets not having been born a prince.

My other companion at the time was Ranjit, a boy from the Hazarnis family, the premier noblemen of Begwad. I don't remember much about him except that he was a meek little boy who seemed to know a surprising number of bad words, and also that he never passed any examination but had to be promoted because of his family's claims upon our state. He died of drink and dissipation before he was thirty. It was almost hereditary for the men of his family to die of drink.

Every morning the two-horsed carriage would be sent to collect my two companions, and by the time I had finished breakfast they would be waiting for me in the verandah. At nine we would all drive to the school in the city, in the same creaking, two-horsed carriage. In the afternoon, after school was over, they would both come back to the palace with me and we all had tea together.

After that we would play games, mainly hockey or football, until Pandit Sharma came to teach me Hindi and Sanskrit and the scriptures. At six o'clock came Mr. Fredrick Moreton, my English tutor, and I spent the rest of the evening in his company.

In addition to English and history and geography, Mr. Moreton was supposed to teach me English customs and manners; how to use the correct knives and forks, and wear western style clothes 'like a gentleman', what to do with a hat, and how to tie a neck-tie. He always said that anyone who wore a ready-knotted tie had not been properly brought up. Most evenings we went for a ride in one of the palace cars, and often we used to sit and listen to western music on the wireless. He even attempted to teach me to play the piano, but without success.

I liked Mr. Moreton. I now feel he may have been the greatest single influence of my early days. He was perhaps the only man in the palace who treated me as an equal, not as a child, but as an adult and, for much of the time, not as a prince either, but an ordinary man. He was always interested in what I had to say, and above all he never betrayed my confidences. Even though he represented authority, I found myself regarding him more and more as a guide and mentor, even as a companion. To this day, we still write to each other occasionally.

It was about this time that I made friends with a cobbler's son. His name was Kanakchand. He went to the school my companions and I attended, the Ashokraj High School, which had been established by my grandfather at the time of Queen Victoria's diamond jubilee. He was in the same class as myself, but being an untouchable, he was made to sit at the back, away from the others, and on the floor. I am sure I would never have noticed him or found out his name if one day Charudutt had not picked a quarrel with him.

It was during the fifteen minute break at eleven o'clock. About six of us were playing mango-seed football in the school verandah which suggests that it must have been soon after the summer holidays, otherwise there would have been no mango-seeds lying about. The children who usually sat on the floor at the back of the class were watching our play from a respectful distance. Once, when the mango-seed had gone into the courtyard, one of the boys had retrieved it and kicked it back into the game. As though that act had established some sort of claim, two of them came and joined the game on opposite sides. It was just when Charudutt had dribbled the seed past our team and was about to shoot a quite unopposed goal that a boy sneaked up from behind and hooked his leg with his foot.

Charudutt went sprawling on the stone-flagged floor. When he not up, his face was white.

'Thu!' he spat. 'What are the stinking cow-eaters doing in our midst? Bhag-jao! Go away!'

'The stinkers, the untouchables. Bhag-jao!' we yelled.

The two boys who had joined our game fled, but one of them, the boy who had tripped Charudutt, had left his satchel behind, leaning against a pillar. Charudutt ran and grabbed hold of it.

'Let's throw the stinker's books in the pond,' he shouted.

'That will teach the untouchables to come and muck up our game,' agreed Ranjit, my other companion.

'Let's teach the cow-eaters a lesson,' we all yelled.

The owner of the satchel came up with a hang-dog look and said: 'Please give me my books.'

'Go away, shoe-maker, don't you dare touch us—cow-skinner!' Charudutt cried.

'Forgive me this time. I will never interfere with your game again,' the boy said very humbly. 'Please tell him to give me my books, Bal-raje,' he appealed to me.

This must have angered Charudutt all the more. As though to demonstrate that I had no authority over him, he ran to the fountain and hurled the satchel into it. For a moment he stood there, defiant, crowing with exultation, and then the boy rushed and began to pommel him, screaming, 'My books! Oh, my books!'

Charudutt kicked out and knocked him down and then he fell on him, pinning his shoulders down. 'Come on, fellows,' he called. 'Let's throw him in the pond to fish his books out … how dare he lay hands on me … stinking cow-skinner!'

Three or four of our crowd ran up to Charudutt and between them they lifted the boy bodily and pushed him into the pond. 'That will teach you to come and fight with princes and noblemen,' Charudutt yelled at him. 'Chamar, cow-skinner, shoe-maker!'

'Bastard!' the boy yelled back from the fountain. 'You are no prince. You are a whore's son.'

For a moment, we all stood speechless. Charudutt was breathing heavily and his face was flushed as though on fire. I don't know how it would have ended if the bell had not rung just then. All of us fled into the classrooms, almost glad to escape.

After school, as our carriage passed the fountain, the boy was still sitting on the wall. He had retrieved his satchel from the bottom and had spread out all the books on the stones to dry. By now his clothes had dried on him, but he was still shivering. As we passed the fountain, Charudutt stared straight in front, pretending he had not seen the boy, but there was an angry scowl on his face.

The dark, skinny boy shivering silently beside his limp books was Kanakchand, although I did not then know his name. Nor could I have known that thereafter our destinies were to be inextricably interwoven.

We drove to the palace and kicked a football about until tea. As soon as my companions had gone away, Pandit Sharma came in for the Sanskrit lessons. I asked him the meaning of the word 'bastard'.

'Chhi-chhi! You must never utter such a word,' Sharmaji told me, and patted his own cheeks as though to register shock. 'His Highness will be very angry if he finds out that the Yuwaraj has been using such words.'

'I did not use it,' I said. 'But what does it mean?'

The pandit pushed back his gold-edged pagri and pushed it forward again. 'No, no. This sort of thing cannot go on. We shall now take up the study of the sandhi rules.'

'I will ask Moreton sahib,' I said.

'Chhi-chhi! Moreton sahib will never approve. You will only shock him. You must not ask anyone.'

'But if I don't ask how can I find out?'

'It is not necessary to find out the meanings of all the words one hears,' Pandit Sharma pronounced. He played with his pagri again, pushing it back and then forward again, and we plunged into the sandhi rules.

Mr. Moreton came in soon after five, and Sharmaji left in what I thought was something of a hurry. As soon as he was out of earshot, I asked Mr. Moreton what a bastard was.

Mr. Moreton gave me a sharp look. In his brown, pill-box cap and western style suit complete with a club tie, he looked like a dummy I had seen in the tailor's shop my father patronized in Bombay. Mr. Moreton always wore a cap, indoors or outdoors, because he had heard my father say that it was bad form to keep one's head uncovered in company. Mr. Moreton was most particular about not doing anything that might hurt Indian sentiment. He had given up eating beef, and invariably wore Indian dress for my father's durbars.

'Where on earth did you hear such a word, Abbey?' he asked.

Mr. Moreton must have been the first person who called me 'Abbey'.

'A boy at school used it. He is a cobbler's son.'

'That may explain it, perhaps. It is not a word that people … well, people like ourselves, use. Not a nice word.'

'So Panditji said.'

'Oh, have you been asking Mr. Sharma? You must have quite shocked him.'

'He said the same thing … that I would shock you if I asked you. What does it mean?'

'You first tell me why the cobbler's son used it. What made him say it?' Mr. Moreton could be so exasperating at times.

'Charudutt had thrown all his books into the fountain. They began to fight, so … so they threw him into the fountain too.'

'They? You too?'

'No, sir.'

'Did you call the boy any names yourselves?'

'We called him cow-eater and stinker.'

He took out his tobacco pouch and began to fill his pipe. 'Well, you see, there are fathers and mothers, and they have children,' he began, his eyes concentrating on the pipe. 'Everyone has a father and mother, and the father and mother always, well, nearly always, happen to be married to each other. Only sometimes it happens that a child's father and mother are not married. There may, of course, be some very good reason for … for such a state of affairs. It can … it can happen to any of us, for reasons none of us can do anything much about. Such children are referred to as bastards. But mind you, it is a bad word, and you must not use it at any time. And you should not have thrown the poor boy's books into the fountain. And you say you threw him in too! Perhaps he hasn't got any other clothes. Perhaps his father can't afford to buy him another lot of books.'

He trailed off and began to light his pipe with great deliberation, taking his time, his slender hands cupping the pipe lovingly, his long, tapering fingers tapping the bowl.

I could understand his embarrassment. He was a sensitive man, and he knew about Charudutt and about the numerous uparaja sons in our family—children born to the rulers out of wedlock. We went on with the lesson; we were reading 'The Charge of the Light Brigade' because my father wanted me to recite it before Colonel Broom, the Political Agent, during his forthcoming visit. It was when the clock in the central tower chimed six and the car came to take us for our evening drive that I fired my main question at Mr. Moreton:

'Charudutt is a bastard, isn't he? The boy also called him a whore's son.'

He gave me another of his sharp looks down his long, bony nose, almost as though he had been expecting the question and had the answer ready. He puffed at his pipe for a few seconds before he spoke. 'Well, in certain societies, there are … what may be called degrees of marriage. Charudutt is a half-brother of yours, and that is how you should regard him.'

'I don't like him,' I said.

'He is a fine boy, and you will grow to like him. And remember, Abbey, whether you like him or not, a prince is, first and foremost, a gentleman, and no gentleman uses such words in polite conversation. Now forget the whole thing,' and Mr. Moreton began to empty his pipe in the ash tray.

And with that we went for a drive. The car took us through the bazzar and out of the city, over the bridge and past the old fort on the hill destroyed by the British during the 1857 revolt. Beyond that were the brown and yellow fields of bajra and jwar, and the scrub jungle where my uncle Ashokraj had died of a riding accident, and then finally the endless folds of the Sattawan range.

But I did not forget the whole thing, as Mr. Moreton had advised. Were all the uparaja sons in our family, those who were still given pensions and treated as ranking noblemen, bastards? There had been so many of them, and some of them had been legendary figures in the history of the family. Could a bastard become a hero?

The next morning, we had what used to be called 'rapid reading' at school. When the teacher found that Kanakchand did not have his books with him, he promptly sent him out of the class.

At the end of the day, as our carriage was passing the fountain, we saw the boy, looking miserable and downcast, still squatting on the wall. He had a vacant look on his face, but he was not crying or shivering. None of us spoke to him.

Again the next morning, I saw the boy sitting on the fountain wall, almost as though he had gone on sitting there since the previous evening. But he did not come into the class. That day, Charudutt was shamming a stomach ache because he wanted to stay at home and listen to Talyarkhan's commentary on the Bombay cricket match. In fact, he had told me the previous evening that he would not be coming to school. He always used to take his mother in with such tricks.

During the break, I went and spoke to the boy. 'Why don't you come to the classes?' I asked.

He gave me a sullen look but did not say anything.

'You were not hurt or anything when they threw you into the water, were you?'

At that, for some reason which I could not understand, Kanakchand burst into sobs.

'If you don't attend classes, why come to school at all?'

'But I cannot stay at home either, Bal-raje,' he said between sobs. 'My father will give me a beating if he finds out my books are gone—what is it to you whether I come to the classes or not?'

'Can't you buy new books?'

He wiped his eyes with his sleeve and scowled belligerently.

'New books! They cost eight rupees. Even second-hand ones will cost three rupees. Where are we to get three rupees? We haven't even got three annas.'

'You meet me here tomorrow, during the break,' I told him without thinking. 'I'll get you the money.'

I had no money either; until then I had never handled money. Most of the things I could call my own had been given to me. Anything that I needed for my daily needs was always supplied by the Dewanji, who did all the purchasing for the palace. I just had to send for him and tell him whatever it was I wanted, and within a few hours, it was delivered at my rooms.

In the end I made no effort to raise the money, but when Kanakchand met me the next morning, I gave him my own books instead. I was pleased with myself when I saw him come into the class and take his usual place near the back wall.

That afternoon Pandit Sharma took me in the scriptures, and there was no need for any of the textbooks. But as soon as Mr. Moreton came in, he discovered that I did not have my books.

'Are you ready with the "Charge of the Light Brigade"?' he asked.

Only then did I realize that I had given away my *Highroads Treasury* with my school books.

'Can't we do it tomorrow?' I asked.

'But why not today? We had decided to do it today.' The one thing Mr. Moreton was particular about was our time table.

'Come on, where is the *Highroads*?'

The *Highroads Treasury* was one of the few books I really loved. It was a thick green book with glossy, gold-edged pages, and it had the loveliest pictures in it. It was Mr. Moreton who had given me the *Highroads* for my previous birthday.

'I haven't got the *Highroads*, sir,' I said.

'What have you done with it?'

'I lost all my books.'

'Lost them?'

'Yes, sir.'

'How did you happen to lose them?'

'I shall get them back tomorrow.'

'Let's get this straight, Abbey. Just what has happened to your books?'

'I gave them away.'

'Gave them away! Who to?'

'To the boy they had thrown into the fountain. The teacher had put him out of the class because he had no books. He is the cobbler's son.'

'Oh really! But why?'

'His father would have given him a hiding if he found he had lost his books.'

'I mean, wouldn't it have been much simpler to have given him the money to buy the books—instead of giving him your own books?'

'It needed three rupees, even for second-hand ones. I did not know where I could have got the money, but the Dewanji will get me another set of books. So I gave him my own books.'

'But don't you know you cannot buy books like the *Highroads Treasury* here? It has nothing to do with your school books.'

'I'm sorry I gave away the books,' I said.

'You're not really sorry, Abbey; are you now?'

'No, sir.'

'It is one of the most satisfying things in life to be able to give someone what he really needs; only it takes a long, long time for most of us to find it out.'

'But I am sorry about the *Highroads Treasury*.'

Mr. Moreton's face broke into pleasant creases, and there was a glint in his eyes. For a few seconds he did not say anything, and as he began to fill his pipe, a part of the smile was still on his face.

'I will ask the boy to give me back the *Treasury*,' I said. 'Explain that I had given it to him by mistake.'

'No, no; don't do that,' Mr. Moreton said. 'Oh, no; you mustn't. I am sure we'll get hold of the poem somewhere else. It is a different thing if the boy himself returns it.'

'I am sure he will.'

'Also, I shall speak to your father about giving you an allowance for pocket money. It is time you started getting used to handling money.'

'Then I will save up and buy the *Highroads Treasury*,' I promised.

'Oh, don't let it worry you any more,' he said with another grin. 'I am really pleased you thought of giving your own books to the boy.'

I did not even have to ask the Dewanji to get me the books. Mr. Moreton must have sorted it out. The next morning a set of new text books was on my table. And as soon as I went to school, Kanakchand came up to me with a shy grin and handed me the *Highroads Treasury*.

'One of your own books was in the lot you gave me, Bal-raje,' he said. 'It was a present. Here, I have brought it back.'

He was sound as a silver rupee when he began. What made him turn so sour and twisted in later life?

4

Of Queens and Concubines

From that day, my friendship with Kanakchand may be said to have begun. A few days later, he happened to help me out with the sums we had been given for homework, and after that we began to help each other in our studies regularly. He was an exceptionally hard-working and diligent boy, and good in all subjects except English. I, on the other hand, was far in advance of the class in English, but I found maths a bore.

One day he brought me some enormous bean-seeds as a present, each as big as the palm of my hand and smooth and shining like glass—the rich, dark-brown glass of wine-bottles when the wine is still inside.

'What do you use them for?' I asked.

'Oh, you don't *use* them for anything really,' he said, a little embarrassed. 'It is just that they are … well, they are the biggest bean-seeds you can find, and they look so pretty when dried and polished with coconut oil. I polished them for a whole week. Don't you like them?'

'Oh, yes, I like them very much, I really do,' I assured him, vaguely distressed at my first contact with the playthings of the poor—bean-seeds found in the forest, just something to look at and polish and run through your fingers. I gave him two of my best marbles, and after that I began to give him little things regularly: coloured pencils, little mirrors, and things like that, and once I gave him a brand new English-made hockey stick which Charudutt had had his eye on.

I did not realize it then, but Kanakchand was my first direct contact with the quivering poverty of India, and one day when he showed me what he had brought with him for his mid-day meal—a single black roti smeared with a mess of oil and chillis and a whole raw onion—for no reason at all I felt close to tears.

It seemed that even the onion was something of a treat, and that bajra or millet bread and chilli powder mixed with groundnut oil formed his main meal of the day. I watched with fascination as he ate, hungrily and with relish, and I felt a little ashamed of the extra-large chocolate which I had just bitten into and which seemed to taste slightly bitter in my mouth. He wolfed the very last crumb, biting alternately on the charred bajra roti and the onion. And when he finished the very last mouthful, he licked his fingers clean before going to the tap to wash his hands.

There was another chocolate in my pocket; one even larger than the one I had eaten. I had found the two chocolates on my table, beside my schoolbooks, as I came running down the stairs after breakfast. I didn't know who could have put them there, but as I picked up my books, I put the chocolates in my pocket, meaning to eat them during the break.

'Here, eat this,' I said, and held out my chocolate to Kanakchand. I can still remember what it looked like. It was very large, the size of a match-box, and it was nobbly with the nuts in it. It was wrapped in green foil.

'What is it?' Kanakchand asked.

'Chocolate. Eat it.'

'Sukr, Bal-raje,' he said politely. 'Thanks.' He took the chocolate and stuffed it into his mouth.

Of course, he could never have eaten a chocolate before, and even as I was saying 'No, no, what are you doing! You don't eat the wrapping,' he had realized that something was wrong. He quickly spat it out and looked at me reproachfully.

'You have to remove the wrapping before you eat it,' I said.

'Oh. I didn't know. I thought Bal-raje was playing some kind of joke on me—making me eat green paper. I am very sorry. I have never seen anything like it in my life.'

'Oh, never mind,' I told him. 'I'll bring you some another time.'

I was very ill that evening, suffering from painful cramps in my stomach, wanting to be sick and not being able to. Sometime during the night, I must have become unconscious. I remember very little about what happened for many days afterwards, and I did not find out about the two doctors who had been sent for from Bombay until some days after they had gone away.

During my illness, my mother came to live downstairs, in the room next to mine, only going up to her own wing in the mornings for her pooja and then rushing back to my bedside. From the blurred, only half-alive and half-dead world of my sickbed, I saw her as a vision, a goddess holding promise of life, coaxing me to sip my orange juice and the bouillon she had prepared herself, her hands always cool to the touch and soft as velvet and smelling delicately of lavender. I came to depend on her being there, whenever I awoke, reading a book or knitting, or sometimes just sitting with her eyes closed. She looked anxious and pale in the beginning, but as I began to feel better, she became radiant and serene and happy, a goddess in pastel saris, sweet and gentle and incredibly beautiful. She was always there, a part of my surroundings, like the dim light of the sickroom and the low voices in the background, the smell of disinfectants, the flowers, the hum of the fan going at slow speed; and whenever I had anything to say, her face was close to mine, the hands with their clean lavender scent holding a bowl of fruit juice or jelly.

For many days I lay between sleeping and waking, a drugged, exhausted sleep and drowsy wakefulness mingling together and leaving behind a confusion of dreams and reality, only the flimsiest of textures separating moments of agony and bliss, of cold terror and sheer ecstasy. How much was reality, how much from the realms of dreams and nightmares—who can say? The only thing I could be certain about was that whenever I came awake, my mother would be there, waiting.

Everyone knows what cruel and shocking hallucinations a fevered brain can conjure, and in my half-awake moments, I seemed to be haunted by a face; a broad, unrefined face with a thin moustache and smelling of cigar smoke and cheap liquor. I began to loathe that face with a hatred I did not know I was capable of, for it was associated with the most shocking and shameful nightmare of my illness.

In my dream I seemed to come awake and it must have been night because there was a dim light burning by my bed. I was sweating and in the grip of an unknown fear, wanting to scream but unable to make a sound, my tongue dry and powerless within my throat, my eyes unable to pierce through the white, choking mist that surrounded my bed. I flung away the sheet in panic, wanting to run away from whatever was smothering me, and stumbled out of the room, not seeing where I was going, holding on to the walls for support. I remember walking out of the room and into the blackness of the verandah, and everything seemed so real that I remember feeling the marble floor cold against my bare feet. I dropped uncertainly against a door and opened my eyes in relief, for there was a light burning, and saw a sight which hit me like a bullet.

Through a gap in the curtains, I could see my mother lying in a high, four-poster bed, white and naked and abandoned and locked in the embrace of a man with an enormous curving back covered with thick hair. And my nostrils, rendered hyper sensitive by the fever, caught the scent of tobacco smoke and rum ...

For a moment I stood, staring wide-eyed, between paralysis and hypnosis, and then I must have swooned ... swooned back into sleep, as it were, for when I came to, I realized it had all been a dream, and I was once again in my own bed, bathed in a cold sweat. It was a long time before I could focus my eyes to peer through the cobweb shroud around me; and there was my mother, as ever, bending over me and holding out a spoon of chilled orange juice. In a sudden surge of gratefulness and relief, I put my arms around her and lay trembling with my head pillowed against her breast. And even as I cuddled against her, I could smell, instead of the warm smell of a woman's body mixed with the scent of lavender, the nauseating fumes of stale cigar smoke and liquor, as though my nightmare had left some kind of contamination so that its smell transmitted itself to everything I touched.

It was as a result of my illness that Abdulla Jan had been brought to Begwad, and when, a few days later, I was allowed to sit up in bed my father brought him in and introduced him.

'This is Abdulla Jan, the new Palace Officer,' my father said. 'I have had old Kabraji sacked.'

Then I realized how irrational dreams could be, for this was the man I had seen in my dreams; with his broad, heavy-jowled face, thick, wavy hair, pencil moustache, and the backs of his hands covered with thick hair, just as I had seen.

He had in fact already been working in the palace for nearly two weeks. I must have seen his face in one of my fitful waking moments, and not knowing who he could be, a total stranger in my surroundings had built up my nightmares around him. And yet I took an instant dislike to him, knowing that I was being unfair, that I was allowing myself to be influenced by my sickbed hallucinations.

'He was the Security Officer in the Government House in Nagpur,' my father said. 'He will look after you.'

And there was Abdulla Jan, bowing to me and touching his forehead with his thick, spatulate fingers. I turned my head away.

'I have had all the servants in this wing sacked—the whole lot. Dhaniram and everyone,' my father was saying.

Dhaniram had been my personal servant ever since I could remember, and I had been very fond of him. I was sorry to hear that my father had had him dismissed.

I learnt that Abdulla Jan had been brought over specially from the police service in British India as a sort of personal bodyguard for me. He was to sleep in the room next to mine and not allow anyone to come into my rooms without his permission.

It must have been nearly a week later. As I lay propped up in bed, still unable to get up without help, Abdulla Jan came in and told me that a boy from the school had been hanging about outside the drum-gate and asking everyone who came in how I was.

'What's his name?' I asked.

'I don't know, Bal-raje. But he seems to come every day. I have told them to send him away.'

'No, no, don't send him away,' I told him. 'He must be my friend Kanakchand.'

It was Kanakchand. When I began to go to school again some weeks later, I gave up playing with my other companions altogether and spent all my spare time at school with Kanakchand. In March, when I was having my annual party for the children of the palace staff, I invited Kanakchand to it.

Charudutt was wholly against it. But by now I paid very little heed to what Charudutt had to say.

'He is an untouchable, and if Dada-maharaj were to find out, he is bound to get very angry,' Charudutt warned. We were on our way back from school in the carriage, and Charudutt had just found out that I had asked Kanakchand to the party.

'Dada-maharaj is in Simla,' I said. 'Seeing the Viceroy. He is not coming back for a week at least. The party is the day after tomorrow.'

'But he will find out when he returns.'

'How can he find out? Of course, Dada-maharaj cannot find out.'

'Oh, can't he? I will myself tell Bibi-bai, and she will tell Maharaj.'

'Go to hell,' I said. The phrase had stuck in my mind because Mr. Moreton had told me it was not to be used in polite conversation. 'Go to hell. I will invite just whoever I choose. You don't have to come if you don't want to.'

'I will die before I eat in the same room as a cow-eater.'

'Englishmen too eat cows,' I pointed out. 'And you always sit at the table when we have tea with Mr. Moreton.'

'Englishmen are not Chamars—untouchables! '

'Go to hell,' I said. 'Oh, go to hell.'

'Wait till my mother tells Dada-maharaj,' Charudutt threatened again.

Then I said something cruel to him. 'There is no danger of that. His Highness never visits your mother these days.'

And I did not regret saying it.

It was quite true. My father had given up seeing Bibi-bai. It was almost as though the spell she had cast over him had suddenly broken, as though the doctored paans she was said to make for him had suddenly lost their potency.

A year or two later, when I learnt what it was that had made my father change so abruptly, it had made me ashamed of my own attitude towards him. It seems that the doctors had told my father that my illness had been due to some kind of food poisoning, and when he had found out about the two chocolates which had been so temptingly put beside my school books, he had jumped to the conclusion that someone had tried to poison me.

No one had been able to discover how the chocolates had come to be where they were. It was believed that one of the palace servants had been bribed to put them there. That was why my father had dismissed all the servants in my wing and brought in Abdulla Jan, who was experienced in security duties, as the Palace Officer.

The coincidence between my illness and my father's sudden abandonment of Bibi-bai was so marked, that everyone seemed to take it for granted that my father was convinced that Bibi-bai had tried to murder me in an effort to secure the succession for her own son: it was not unknown for a prince to adopt a son born of a concubine if there was no direct heir to the gadi. Personally I never paid much heed to that kind of talk. At the same time, it was quite true that hardly any Indian state was free of such rumours, for poisonings were almost the recognized weapons of succession disputes, a sort of occupational hazard for growing princes.

The fact remains that within a month of my illness, my father had Bibi-bai's residence shifted from the old palace to a tumble down house near the elephant gate.

But Bibi-bai's place did not remain vacant for long. Soon after my father's return from Simla, he installed a Muslim dancing girl in it. Her name was Amina, and being Muslim, she came to be called Amina-begam. It was said that my father had seen her in one of the courtesan's houses in Simla and that he had paid twenty thousand rupees to her mother for agreeing to her coming to Begwad.

Until I returned from war service, I used to squirm with shame at the thought of my father's private life. I now realize that, obsessed with the narrowness and naive values of youth, I judged him harshly, as indeed most of his world seems to have judged him. It was the war that helped me to grow up and to broaden my vision, the war and also the sudden explosion of the urges of my own body; and then I acquired what I like to think is a civilized tolerance for human frailties, learnt to tear my mind away from the petty and often false loyalties of childhood and youth.

In those days I used to side with the world in condemning my father's infatuation, first with Bibi-bai and then with Amina and later still with Sherawathi, the South Indian girl, while taking for granted all the sterling attributes of his character: his contagious high spirits, his unquestioning pride in the achievements of his ancestors, his abounding, often misplaced kindness, his courage, his devotion to his values, his passionate veneration of his inheritance.

There was, of course, the difference of years between us: I was youth, progressive, righteous; he was age, reactionary, taboo-ridden. If I had allowed for the natural resistance of the rising generation to everything that the previous one stood for, and had perceived that he was, in many respects, drawn to a different scale from the rest of us, some kind of superman born several decades too late to be understood and appreciated by ordinary men and women, that he was a giant caught in the snare of contemporary values but trying to be true to the values of a lost world, I would not have been so completely separated from him in the days of my youth. As it was, whatever good qualities he had, in my estimation they were hopelessly overshadowed by his blatant and consistent infidelity to my mother.

At the time I could not understand how any man in his senses could have preferred another woman to my mother who, I think, was one of the most beautiful women of her times. She was fair and slim, with a well-set, small-boned figure and finely chiseled features. She had a mass of raven-black hair which had a touch of metallic blue in the waves, and which she wore severely swept back and caught in a bun on the nape of her neck. Her eyes were large and black, an iridescent black like the backs of beetles, and they shone with a brilliance that was almost spiritual. She wore make up with the utmost restraint and the most delicate and refreshing perfumes and she walked with the natural grace of a Bharat-natyam dancer.

Bibi-bai, on the other hand, was earthy and raw-boned, and to me she always looked unwashed with her hair straying all over her face. She had a vulgar, mannish laugh, her lips were always heavily painted and her teeth dark with the stain of betel leaf. And she sang bawdy, camp-fire songs and told bawdy, camp-fire jokes.

Compared to Bibi-bai, Amina, who came after her, was almost refined, even though she never learned to read or write. Almost surprisingly, as the years passed, I grew to like Amina-begam, and l felt genuinely sorry for her when my father brought Sherawathi, the temple dancer, from Tanjore.

Amina-begam was only six years older than I was, a naive, bubbling, gay, and wholly natural person who treated me just as though I were a younger brother. Now that I come to think of it, she must have been one of those rare human beings who are entirely happy with their lot in life. I occasionally went and had tea in the bungalow near the polo ground which my father had had built for her. She had brought her young niece, Zarina, to keep her company, and one of Amina-begam's favourite jokes was to tell me that she was bringing her up as a concubine for me.

'I am keeping her as a companion for myself now,' she used to tell me. 'But I am bringing her up to be a companion for you when she grows up.'

Zarina was a shy wisp of a girl when they first came to Begwad, always dressed in prim children's clothes and wearing her hair in pigtails. I, on the other hand, was a grown up boy, big for his age, as everyone said. I used to share my sweets with her and laugh at Amina-begam's joke. But as time passed and she kept repeating the same joke every time I saw her, it ceased to amuse me, because Zarina was growing up into an extraordinarily pretty girl.

I was friendly with Amina-begam; but, I hardly ever spoke to Sherawathi. I always felt awkward in her presence. She was the one woman I have seen who gave the impression of being absolutely naked even when fully clothed; sensuous and slim, supple, dark and shining like a black cobra swaying.

They were a study in contrasts, Amina-begam and Sherawathi; as though my father had gone to special trouble to find two perfect specimens of Indian womanhood, one from the extreme north, the other from the extreme south; the one fluffy, light-haired, light-eyed, fair, giggling, the other svelt, dark, raven-haired, sombre; the one straight out of a Mughal painting, the other a sex symbol in polished ebony.

These were the three women, Bibi-bai, Amina and Sherawathi, who were my father's concubines. None of them had my mother's look of breeding and refinement, or her grace, charm and dignity. And my father's open preference for them was a continued torment to me. Now of course I can understand how even the loveliest of women can make themselves hateful to men; that love, as much as mere sex, is not necessarily concerned with looks, and still less is it concerned with refinement; that a woman's very chasteness, her touch-me-not air of purity, can curdle a man's desires.

If the world I myself grew up in seems so remote today, it is almost impossible for me to reconstruct the world my father grew up in. In his youth, princely India was more embedded in the past, more reactionary, than at any time before or since. It was a dim, sealed-off world, a sort of island removed from the earth, and it had more in common with the India of Shivaji or even the India of Ashoka than the India of my own day. Many of the traits in my father's character, which defeated analysis or explanation, must have had their origin in these early influences of his life.

Begwad, lost in the hills and forests of Padmakoshal, had always been something like the Tibet of twenty years ago, totally walled off. It was only in the last years of the nineteenth century, after the railway and telegraph lines had penetrated into Padmakoshal, that the outside world began to break into its segregation. But the tenets of Victorian morality, the discipline of western social values, indeed the advent of the industrial age, were stoutly resisted in the states as British impositions, the tightening bonds of slavery. It was only in my father's childhood, when the telephone and motor cars came, that Begwad became fully exposed to the influx of twentieth century manners and morals and was caught up in the race for economic development.

It seems that it was on my father's sixteenth birthday that he was presented with his first concubine, Bibi-bai, a girl chosen from among a number of aspirants. This was a custom coming down from the earliest Bedars, and it was a common enough one in many of the Rajputana and Padmakoshal states. My father was to have occasion to tell me that he was sorry he had not honoured it when I was myself sixteen.

It all went back to the days when perhaps the safest way of protecting the young men of the chieftain families from venereal diseases was to ensure that they were provided with healthy concubines from a relatively early age. In those days of incessant warfare, the soldiers who used to be separated from their wives for years at a time were in the habit of taking their mistresses to the wars. The wives had to be protected and cared for; the concubines were, in a sense, expendable, and no one felt much compunction at making them undergo the risks and rigours of warfare. Only rarely was a mistress elevated to become a wife. But after that, she too was left behind with the other wives, in the relative safety of the ancestral villages. When the British first came into contact with our troops in the days of the second Hiroji, it was quite usual for every Indian military commander of any consequence to have anything up to a dozen wives staying at home and an equal number of concubines accompanying him to the wars.

But all these wives were not necessarily Maharanis, and there was always only one Senior Maharani, the Badi-Maharani. She was the one entitled to fly her own flag and to wear a gold chain on her ankle. It was her son, if she had one, who would become the next Maharaja. And above all it would be she who would have the privilege of performing sati in case her husband died before her. There were seven satis in our family.

Sati, the practice of widows immolating themselves on their husbands' funeral pyres, had been abolished by the British, but in the segregated world of the princes, the other customs died hard. In many states, the wealth and prestige of the ruler were judged as much by the size of his harem as by the gun salutes accorded to him by the British. I think even my father must be regarded as something of an exception, for right up to the end, when all the princely states were liquidated, there was nothing unusual in a prince having three or four wives at the same time, to say nothing of several concubines.

Bibi-bai was a couple of years older than my father. She was said to have been trained in the art of making herself agreeable to men by one of the greatest courtesans of her time who lived in Delhi's Chandni-Chowk. They also spoke about some mysterious ayurwedic powders she possessed for retaining a man's infatuation. For my part, I have always believed that there was some truth in this, for Bibi-bai, uneducated and coarse as she was, certainly managed to hold my father's interest for more than twelve years.

At the time of his marriage to my mother, my father was nineteen years old, and Charudutt had been already born.

The princes usually married off their sons and daughters at an early age, and nineteen was almost too old in those days. But my father's marriage had been delayed for nearly two years because of my grandfather's anxiety to find a bride for him from a ruling family, and by the reluctance of the major Rajput and Maratha princes to allow their daughters to marry beneath their caste. As a matter of fact, our family seems to have run into these difficulties of finding suitable matches for its sons and daughters in every generation, and it is on record that nearly a hundred and eighty years ago, the first Sekhoji went to war with the ruler of Joida because the latter had refused his daughter's hand in marriage.

My mother's marriage to my father was in the nature of a compromise, a compromise directly springing out of tragedy. My mother did not belong to a princely family, and my grandfather had never regarded her as a suitable bride for his elder son. She was the daughter of the Chandidars of Kurandi, and initially she had been engaged to my uncle, my father's younger brother Ashokraj.

The Chandidars had not been eager for an alliance with our family. They prided themselves on belonging to one of the 'thirty-seven families' of the Deccan, tracing their descent to the days of Shivaji as the hereditary headmen of Kurandi. At one time they were so rich that the doors of their mansion had been made of solid silver. This, incidentally, gave the family its name: 'Chandidar' means silver door.

But in the early years of the century, the Chandidars were no longer rich, nor were they the hereditary landlords of the district of Kurandi. Over the years, their wealth and position had vanished. The silver doors had been carried away by Mughal invaders or had been melted down to pay off creditors; the estates had been dissipated by a succession of profligates; and the Chandidars lived insignificantly, clutching at the prestige of the family name. My grandfather, on the other hand, was a powerful and wealthy prince. He offered to pay a dowry of eight lakhs of rupees, and the hard-pressed Chandidars relented. After that my grandfather turned his energies to the major task confronting him: that of finding a suitably high-born bride for my father. My mother's engagement to my uncle Ashokraj was announced with the usual fanfare, and both families agreed to hold back the time of the wedding until after the wedding of the elder son, my father, had taken place.

It was just when my grandfather had succeeded in securing the consent of the dowager Maharani of Ninnore to give her eldest daughter in marriage to my father, that tragedy struck.

My uncle Ashokraj died. He and my father had gone off riding after pig in the scarred jungle on the other side of the old fort, and there he had fallen off his horse while jumping across a dried up nullah and had broken his neck.

The older courtiers tell me that my grandfather did not shed a single tear, nor did he attend his son's cremation, although Ashokraj is said to have been his favourite. It was my father, himself dry-eyed and stiff as ever, who lit the funeral pyre and performed the necessary rites. The only thing that my grandfather did do was to invoke the curse of the family goddess on the scrub jungle beyond the old fort, and to forbid my father from going on horseback into it.

It is odd how a family tragedy leaves a mark on future generations, for both the restriction and the curse were carried down to my own days. I always regarded the foothills beyond the Kamra bridge, where the peepuls and banyans were growing out of the wall of the old fort, as a haunted land, and my riding master took good care never to let me go there.

My uncle's death had made the Maharani of Ninnore go back on her word. At best a delicately balanced affair, my father's proposed marriage to a princess was suddenly broken off. The Indian princes, perhaps more superstitious than any other class of people anywhere else in the world, would never have dared to challenge so unmistakable a warning of the gods.

The Chandidars for their part had been hit far more badly. In the face of the tragedy, they could not hope to find another eligible bridegroom for their daughter. She was now an ill-starred woman, the girl with the white foot, a daughter of Mars. It was an act of almost inescapable compromise when both families decided that my father should marry the girl who had been affianced to my uncle.

My grandfather tried desperately hard to make the match appear less of a compromise. He doubled the agreed dowry and, in addition, bestowed three thousand acres of paddy and wheat land on the Chandidars, once again bringing back to them a semblance of their past wealth. He spent money lavishly on the festivities. For the entertainment of the guests, he got a brass band from a British regiment, a fireworks expert all the way from Peking, and the best dancing girls from Kerala and Goa. But he must have known it was no use. None of the princes came to the wedding, although they all sent suitably imposing missions bearing expensive gifts for my father and mother. The Indian princes were not going to tempt the fates by attending the wedding of a girl with the white foot.

That was how my mother's life as a Maharani began.

The shock of his brother's death, the humiliations that the Bedars were made to undergo at the hands of the other princes, the cancellation of his own marriage to the daughter of another ruling prince, and above all, the fact that not a single prince came to his wedding, seem to have had a profound effect on my father's mind. At the same time, he must have realized the fact that as far as the family was concerned, his marriage to my mother was an elevation in the hierarchy of castes. My mother belonged to the thirty-seven families and any children born to her would be higher-born than himself. And as though fulfilling some obligation, as though undergoing a penance to make the succession secure, he produced an heir, myself, and then promptly turned back to Bibi-bai, making it clear that he too regarded my mother as the woman with the white foot, destined to carry bad luck wherever she went.

For several years afterwards, Bibi-bai continued to be the only woman in his life. Her apartment was in the old palace in the city which now houses the research laboratory. It was a vast, shapeless conglomeration of masonry that had gone on growing and changing shape as though it had a life of its own; a hotchpotch of basalt and laterite and mud and straw bricks, where the medieval and the modern stood cheek by jowl: an ornate stone pillar with a chariot-race frieze and tubular chairs, carved woodwork and black glass, Bokhara carpets and linoleum, naked electric lights hanging from fine lacework ceilings; a jumble of dark, dank rooms connected by twisting corridors and narrow stairs, bursting at the seams with the junk of two centuries.

My father would go down to the old palace every evening; Bibibai never came to the new palace. Nor could she be invited to any of the official functions. She may have been his mistress, but she was not his wife, and in my father's mind the two compartments were absolutely separate. The Maharani had her own Daimler, flew her own flag and lived in a wing of the palace. She was almost like a status symbol, the woman who was entitled to wear a gold chain around her left ankle.

My mother lived alone with her dignity, next to the shrine of the satis, in a part of the palace which my father rarely, if ever, visited. She lived in the strictest purdah, surrounded by a horde of women servants and a few ladies-in-waiting. Even the windows of her apartment were screened by heavy bamboo curtains. When ever she went for a drive, or for her daily visit to the temple in the city, she went in the sky-blue Daimler with the windows made of smoked glass, unseen by anyone, with her tiny purple and yellow flag fluttering from the bonnet. She could not be seen except as a hazy outline behind the windows. She was someone already removed from the world, not to be seen or heard, someone condemned to the shadows while still in the land of the living. A sati even though her husband was still alive.

5

The Education of a Commoner

The days of my boyhood were also the days of Mr. Gandhi's nation-wide agitation for self-rule, and nothing that the Political Department or my father between them could do succeeded in keeping the movement from seeping into our state.

My father had banned all the nationalist papers such as the *Chronicle of Bombay* and the *Hindustan Times* of Delhi, and had promulgated ordinances in the state to keep in step with the Viceroy's ordinances legalizing preventive detention, and indeed had kept well ahead of the British parts of India in the race for repressive legislation. He bustled about energetically, trying to make 'examples' of people associated with the agitation. He dismissed a clerk in his octroi department because he had seen the man's son wearing the white khaddar cap. And once he was so enraged by a group of people shouting 'Inquilab-zindabad', which meant 'long live the revolution', after his car had passed, that he had all of them rounded up and sent to prison for three weeks.

For a time, my father's repressive measures were virulently attacked by the leftish papers, and one day the *Awaz* came out with a leading article entitled 'Depravity in Begwad'. Despite the fact that the *Awaz* was totally banned from the state, copies containing the article seemed to find their way into all sorts of places. I discovered one in my satchel at school, and I still remember the hot flush of shame and anger that came over me when I saw it and the cartoon accompanying it. The cartoon showed my father with a dog collar round his neck. On the table before him was a bottle of whisky. One of his-arms was around a bosomy, seminaked woman. The other hand hugged the chain attached to the dog collar. The caption said:

'LONG LIVE SLAVERY!'

I did not read the article. I stuffed the paper back into my satchel and when I reached the palace, I tore it into little bits and flushed the bits down the lavatory. I doubt if my father ever saw the article, for none of his courtiers would have dared to show it to him or to admit that they had come across it. He went on tightening his 'security measures' as he called them, matching his wits against the enemy. He passed orders that any boy found wearing the white cap was to be instantly removed from school. He stopped the sale of the photographs of Tilak and Gandhi in the state. He also reintroduced horsewhipping as a punishment for these and similar crimes, and the next time someone shouted a nationalist slogan in his hearing, he had the offender flogged in the market square.

And right enough, the political movement seemed to disappear from our state. At least people did not go about shouting slogans any longer, or wearing the white cap in defiance of the ordinances, and Father took that as evidence of a complete victory. He was convinced that it was his stringent measures for security, his 'exemplary' punishments, that had eradicated Mr. Gandhi's movement from his state.

'To teach the people to destroy their own gods is the alphabet of heresy,' my father pronounced. 'It must not be allowed to raise its head here.'

It sounded so convincing when my father said it.

'Let the Viceroy make me responsible for the security of the whole of India,' he used to say, tugging at his moustache proudly. 'I will put the damned nationalists right in no time. No use being weak-kneed about the thing. I rule with the baton and the horsewhip. That's the way to keep order in this country. The ordinances by themselves are no good.'

But the reason why the national agitation never really took root in the outlying parts of the state was quite different. It was the people's backwardness, their inability to respond to the pressures of the twentieth century. Steeped in illiteracy and almost medieval ignorance, the population of the princely states had not acquired the political consciousness of their brethren in the rest of the country. And even today, after fifteen years of independence, many of our villagers have still not realized that their country is free.

The British never had any direct contact with the people of the states, and their departure meant little to them. But the removal of the Maharajas was quite another thing. It brought about drastic changes in their daily life. Freedom from foreign domination was less tangible than the fact of being transferred from the rule of a Maharaja to the rule of the petty official, from the rule of flamboyance to one of niggling austerity and total prohibition, from one of direct, easy access to the source of all authority, their ruler, to the faceless hierarchy of clerks.

'He would come to us on horseback, like a king should,' they say of my father. 'Riding through our fields, talking our own language.'

'And whenever he was amongst us, he would always share our food—whatever we were eating. Because a king should know what his people eat, how they live.'

It is true that my father did range the countryside on horseback, inspecting crops, talking to his people and sometimes sharing their meals. He ate their coarse jwar roties and fierce chutneys with evident relish, licking his fingers to wipe off the surplus oil. He had always been fastidious about his food, finding fault with the meals cooked by the palace cooks who were reputed to be among the best in Padmakoshal, and yet I am convinced that there was nothing artificial in his performance, that in some way he did enjoy the meals he shared with the peasants.

And even though I say it myself, most of them would gladly give up their right to vote for a return to the severities of the old order, for they still long for what they refer to as the good old days, the days of the Maharajas: the rough and ready justice, on the spot and promptly delivered, the large number of holidays, the pomp and pageantry, the frequent ceremonials, freedom to drink and dance and not have to pay any income tax. They cannot divorce the creeping joylessness of life, the crippling rise in the cost of living, the infliction of prohibition, from the change in the administration. Many of them still look back upon the days of princely rule with a sentimental longing, transforming the states into some golden land flowing with milk and honey.

'In the days of Hiroji Maharaj,' they will tell you in recalling the days of my father's rule, 'we used to get wheat at sixteen seers to the rupee.'

'He was a real food-giver, the ann-data, was our Dada Maharaj.'

'Yes, and jwar was twenty seers to the rupee. A man could live on five rupees a month and still have money for tobacco … '

'Tobacco! It has become like gold and silver … and they sell you wood husk.'

'And whenever anyone wanted to see the Maharaj, all he had to do was to go to the evening audience … or in an emergency, hold up the car when he was driving past. Now you cannot even see a Tahsildar for three days … and then you have to pay a rupee to his chaprasi.'

'At my daughter's wedding, I had the state military band given free … just as at the wedding of the prince himself.'

'The band as well as the utensils were always given free—the taats and the waties for the wedding feast. You could feed a hundred … '

'Nowadays it costs at least a hundred rupees to hire the cooking and serving utensils.'

'But who can think of feeding a hundred people these days!'

If you let them go on being sucked in by their nostalgia, they would soon begin to shed tears, and they would almost convince you that life was a glorious thing in those days, when they had all lived in the shadow of some Maharaja. In a sense, it is the tragedy of the people who are ruled by instinct more than reason, sentiment more than logic. No one will be able to convince them that the old order had little to do with the cheapness of food and clothing, that, if anything, the cheapness itself was the major evil of those times. If the cultivator had to sell his wheat at sixteen seers to the rupee, there was little enough he could buy with the proceeds. It is just that they take an altogether distorted view of progress, associating a quite imagined prosperity with the rule of my father.

And yet there is no doubt that there was some kind of bond between my father and his rural subjects, as I venture to say there is between myself and most of them to this day, something deep and incorruptible, stretching right back to the roots of our history, a bond which makes it difficult for me to analyse their shortcomings with detachment.

It was the blind sentiment of men such as these that kept the nationalist agitation from making much headway in the outlying areas of our state. But in the capital itself, it was beginning to be a live force, steadily gathering momentum despite my father's vigilant security measures.

The year Charudutt left for Kitchener College at Delhi, the anti-salt tax campaign was in full swing. It was Kanakchand who told me about it; he always seemed to be fully in touch with the political happenings in the country.

I did not know how salt was made, nor that there was a tax on it.

'It is made out of sea water,' Kanakchand explained.

He no longer addressed me as Bal-raje, and although I did not mind it for my own sake, I was glad that Charudutt was not around to carry tales.

'And when you make salt, they … the government, make you pay money for making it,' he said.

'Why?' I asked.

'Sea water belongs to the British. All over the world. When you take the water, they make you pay for it.'

'Then why not pay it?'

'The poor people cannot afford to pay it.'

'How much does salt cost?'

'About a pice per seer.'

'So little! And what is the tax on it?'

'Oh, I don't know,' Kanakchand admitted. 'But it is bad. There should be no tax, and Mahatma Gandhi has defied the government and prepared salt. They have put him in jail.'

It all seemed so utterly pointless. The tax on salt could not be more than a pice in the rupee, an insignificant, almost infinitesimal sum. I could not understand why anyone should refuse to pay it. Also, I was quite taken aback to hear Kanakchand refer to Mr. Gandhi as the Mahatma, the great man. My father always spoke of him as 'that man Gandhi'.

'Oh, how I wish I were old enough to join the agitation!' Kanakchand said, quite carried away by his fervour. 'To break the law and defy the British police … shout slogans at the white-faced monkeys—obscene slogans. Write things about their king on the walls at night … "White man go back!" … "Topiwalla Bhag-jao". And parade before them wearing the white cap … '

'You must never talk of wearing the white cap,' I said.

'But everybody is wearing it.'

'You know you will be sent out of school.'

'But I am not going to be in this school for ever. If I don't get a scholarship to the High School, I will have to start earning my living. Then I can wear my white cap openly.'

'What sort of work will you be doing?' I asked.

'Why, cure hides, make chapplies and bullock harness.'

'But won't you be ashamed to be seen in the white cap?'

'Ashamed! Toba! Never! I shall wear it proudly.'

'The most honourable cap in the world is the purple cap of the Begwad rulers,' I said.

'It may be so in Begwad, but no one knows anything about it outside. Also, your cap is the ruler's cap; the white cap is the people's cap.'

'It is only the Marwari business man's cap,' I said. 'Only potbellied baniyas wear it.'

'It is Mahatma Gandhi's cap.'

'Why do you call Gandhi a Mahatma?'

'Because he is a Mahatma, the greatest man in the world.'

'Greater than the Maharaja?'

'Greater than the King Emperor himself. And he wears the white cap.'

'Have you ever worn one?'

'I always wear one. Look!' He pulled a folded white cap out from his pocket and put it on. 'I always keep this in my pocket. In school, I wear a brown cap. But in our own bustee, you dare not be seen in any other cap but the Gandhi cap.'

'What would they do if you didn't have it on?'

'The boys would pelt me with stones, tear my clothes, and throw cow-dung at me.'

'Well, don't you get caught with it at school,' I warned him.

Just as I could never have told anyone in the palace that I had seen a cartoon that showed my father as a dog, I could never have divulged what I knew about the national agitation or Mr. Gandhi's salt march, or said anything about the people in the bustees booing the boys who did not wear the white cap. But it seems I gave myself away without realizing it.

'What is depravity?' I asked Mr. Moreton that evening.

'Depravity means corruption. It is as though … well, if a dog eats rubbish, it is said to have a depraved appetite. Same with men. If they do something that is morally beneath them, they are said to be depraved.'

He had taken out his pouch and was filling his pipe. 'Is there a salt tax in England?' I asked.

Mr. Moreton finished filling his pipe and was looking for a match. After tapping his pockets, he called out for a box of matches, and the Palace Officer, Abdulla Jan, who was reclining in an armchair in the verandah smoking a cigar, came in and offered him his own box.

'What were you saying? Oh yes, the salt tax. Have we a salt tax in England? I'm sure I don't know. Somehow we don't seem to bother ourselves much about this kind of thing.'

'Is it because there are no poor people in England?'

'Oh, I wouldn't say that. There certainly are a lot of poor people.'

'Then is it because the people are free?'

'Well, that may be the reason,' Mr. Moreton said. 'But why do you ask, Abbey?'

'Mahatma Gandhi is going to go on making salt, and he is not going to pay any tax.' I had used the word 'mahatma' almost unconsciously, and I remember Mr. Moreton raising his eyebrows slightly. But I went on as though I had used it deliberately. I liked to shock Mr. Moreton now and then. 'Do you think it is right to refuse to pay a tax?'

'Of course it isn't! Well, unless it is an unjustified tax. Or again, if it happens to be a matter of principle. But you mustn't concern yourself with such things. Whoever told you about Mr. Gandhi's salt march?'

I paid no attention at the time, but Abdulla Jan was still hovering in the room. Ordinarily I would have told him that he had no business to be lurking about when I was doing my lessons. But I was always careful how I spoke to any of the servants or staff in Mr. Moreton's presence.

Later, I learnt to shut my mouth whenever Abdulla Jan was around. But on that day I was indiscreet. I had no secrets from Mr. Moreton, or only a few. I told him everything.

'My best friend told me. He knows all about the salt march. He keeps a white cap in his pocket at all times and puts it on the moment he goes back from school.'

'What an extraordinary character,' Mr. Moreton laughed.

'He'll certainly go far … oh, dear me! Pipe gone out again. Could I have a match, Abdulla Jan?'

Although it called itself the Ashokraj High School, our school had only five classes. When originally established, it was intended to have seven classes and prepare its students for the matriculation examination. The name High School had been given in anticipation of such a development. But in the beginning they did not have enough pupils for the higher classes. Meanwhile my grandfather had died, and my father, whose ideas about the spread of education had been somewhat unorthodox, had refused to sanction money for expanding the school. He earnestly believed that education was at the back of most of the political troubles that the British were encountering in India.

'No use trying to educate every Tom, Dick and Harry,' he used to say. 'It is like gunpowder: precious, but equally dangerous. It must always be in the right hands. If you cheapen learning, you are just asking for trouble. Look at British India.'

And so the Ashokraj High School had remained a high school in name only. My father's own contribution to the cause of higher education in his state was to grant five annual scholarships. Five boys from our school were selected and were paid twenty-five rupees every month for three years to enable them to continue their studies in the High School at Jubblepore. These scholarships were given for proficiency in English, decided on the merits of an essay written by the candidates. That year's subject was 'Lord Kitchener'.

It was doubtful if, left to himself, Kanakchand would have been able to win a scholarship because he had always been weak in English. He himself was not at all confident of winning, and spoke of his future with despair if he had to give up studying and make a living as a cobbler.

One day he asked me whether I would help him with his essay. I was considerably in advance of the class in English and at once offered to co-operate. I should perhaps make it clear that at the time I never felt there was anything wrong in what I was doing.

Sometimes I wonder how different our lives would have been, both his and mine, if Kanakchand had never asked me to write his essay or if I had declined to do so. But then I have come to accept that these things are ordained, that what we are given in life are cards dealt out by other hands. You could not deal out the cards yourself.

I was convinced that no one was more deserving of getting a scholarship than Kanakchand, who had always been at the head of the class, and that it was wrong to penalize him for not being sufficiently proficient in a foreign language. He had certainly worked harder than anyone else and was desperately anxious to continue his studies. Without a scholarship, he could not have done so.

This is my justification for what I did. But of course, at the time, I had not bothered to reason things with myself. I had acted on an impulse and offered to write his essay. I worked on it in my bedroom for three days, and when it was finished, I showed it to Mr. Moreton, who praised it and made certain suggestions to improve it. Mr. Moreton had no idea I had written the essay for another boy. I incorporated all his suggestions in the essay and gave it to Kanakchand, who copied it in his own handwriting and submitted it as his own effort for the competition.

As we had both expected, his name was first in the list of successful candidates.

I now know that it was Abdulla Jan who informed my father that it was I who had written Kanakchand's essay. But I did not know it on the day that the awards of the scholarships were made. I was happy and yet a little sad because it was my last day of going to the Ashokraj High School, for I too had finished my five standards and was due to go to the Princes' College at Agra. The joy was perhaps due to the vicarious thrill that something I had written had been regarded as the best essay submitted in many years.

It was a hot, breezy day in March. The school building looked gay and festive. The drive and the building itself had been festooned with purple and yellow bunting, and two special archways had been built of matting and mango-leaves. One of them said 'Welcome to our Beloved Maharaja and Maharani' and the other said 'Annual Prize Distribution 1931'.

The drive had been watered to keep the dust down, and volunteers were flitting about, distributing sprays of flowers and sprinkling khas-water on the guests. By the time I arrived, most of the others were already in their places, waiting for my father.

I was sitting in the front row, clutching the arm-rests of my chair, and Charudutt, who was down from Kitchener College, was on my left. There was the preliminary booming of drums and the band broke into the state anthem. All of us jumped to our feet and stood to attention. The moment the anthem was finished, my father came in, smiling and bowing to acknowledge the mujras. He looked resplendent in his brocade achkan and his purple turban. He was accompanied by two A.D.C.s in their full-dress uniforms. Although he had driven up in a car, he was carrying his riding crop in his left hand.

My mother could not be seen, but I had seen her car parked near the porch and I knew she was there, in the special purdah balcony, screened off from public gaze by bamboo curtains lined with blue muslin. And then my eyes were drawn to the odd group under the ladies' balcony, the five prize winners and their parents. Prominent among them was Kanakchand, wearing freshly laundered clothes. He was flanked by a man and woman who I knew must be his father and mother. The father was a bent old man with a frayed red turban and a wispy grey moustache. The mother was surprisingly young-looking and was wearing a neat yellow sari and a thick chain of mogra flowers in her hair. Both of them had the slightly dazed look that only the poorest and the humblest can achieve when they are deliriously happy.

The head master made his speech of welcome. My father sat in a big red chair they had brought over specially from the palace, twirling his crop idly and staring straight ahead. At the end of his speech, the head master announced the names of the successful candidates and invited my father to distribute the prizes.

'Kanakchand Dhor!' the head master called out, and I saw Kanakchand going up the steps of the platform and doing a mujra to my father. I glanced at his parents. His mother was wiping her eyes with the end of her sari and his father was looking as if he were in a trance, unable to take his eyes away from his son.

My father rose to make his speech. 'Your Highness, ladies and gentlemen, and the staff and students of the Ashokraj High School,' he began. I thought his voice sounded dry and edgy.

'In my sense of values, perhaps old fashioned, the basic human virtues have a far higher place than mere learning or wealth or position. Truth, honesty, faith in God, and above all, loyalty, add up to far more than the gaining of worldly rewards.'

For no reason at all, he seemed to stop for a few seconds and look at me directly. I had a feeling that something awful was going to happen.

My father went on: 'And whenever I find dishonesty, lying, cheating, disloyalty, I have made it an act of faith to eradicate it with all the authority at my command. Cheating and disloyalty are bad enough anywhere else, but in the sacred atmosphere of the school, where the very lives of the coming generation are being moulded, it is a most despicable crime.'

His voice was even, easy, smooth, only slightly higher pitched than usual.

'Now, to my personal knowledge, this boy who stands before you as the first among the prize-winners, did not himself write the essay submitted for the competition. It was written by someone else and then it was corrected by another and re-written before it was submitted to the examiners. Therefore, this boy who stands before you is nothing but a cheat. And as to his loyalty, his loyalty to the ruler of this state, the man from whom he seeks to receive help for further studies, to the house whose salt his family have eaten for generations—look what he carries in his pocket!'

My father reached out and put his hand into Kanakchand's pocket, and there was a gasp in the audience as he pulled out the white cap and held it before them. They reacted as they were conditioned to react, taking their cue from my father, just as though he had whipped out a snake.

'Ladies and gentlemen, you are no doubt aware that the use of this cap is banned in my state.' And he pushed it away with the end of his crop as though he were prodding at something unclean. Then he raised the riding crop high and brought it down on Kanakchand's back. I saw Kanakchand fall down, more in fear than in pain, trying to ward off the next lash of the whip.

There were two more. Swish-slap, swish-slap, the crop descending through the air and ending in a sharp crack. The reports seemed to hang in the air, repeating themselves as in some whispering gallery and when they died out, there was a pin-drop silence except for the thin moaning of the boy cowering beside the table.

I kept wishing that Kanakchand would stop moaning, that he would stand up erect and defiant and soundless, denying to my father the satisfaction of a complete victory. But he cowered and whined. No one could have told him about lions and lambs and how important it was to take one's punishment without squealing.

My father put away his crop and wiped his hands delicately on a handkerchief. He looked at the boy as though in disgust, and ordered his A.D.C.s to have him taken away.

'Let us now proceed with the rest of the programme,' he announced. For the rest of the hour, he was just as charming, just as gracious as ever, as though whatever had happened was merely some horrible nightmare, something that you could not associate with anyone so handsome and gay and godlike, making jokes with the boys and chucking them under their chins.

I had not once looked at Kanakchand's father and mother to see how they had taken it. I could not take my eyes away from the riding crop that lay on the table, coiled like a snake beside the brass flower vase filled with dahlias.

I lay awake for a long time that night, listening to the owls and the tree-frogs and the night-time shufflings of pigeons. Somewhere a window was banging in the breeze and the clock chimed every fifteen minutes. And then with a start I realized that someone was standing near my bed. It was my mother. I never knew how she had found out that I had something to do with Kanakchand's flogging.

I thrust my face into the pillows and burst into sobs. My mother's nearness seemed to remove all shame from the act of shedding tears. I was grateful for her presence, her soothing words, her hands soft and fragrant, pressing my forehead. She was wearing a chain of white mogra flowers in her hair. Kanakchand's mother too had worn the same kind of flowers.

'I promise I will do something,' Mother kept telling me.

'Nothing can be done, Maji, nothing,' I told her. 'He will always think that it was I who told Dada.'

'Never mind about it now. Go to sleep.'

'And it was so important for him to go to the High School. They are so poor … they only have chilli powder with their roti. I have ruined his life … '

'Don't blame yourself too much, Abhay. It was not the essay alone. It was the cap more than the essay.'

'Father is a demon, Satan himself … '

My mother pressed my hand. 'You must never say such things.'

'I *will* say them. I wish something would happen to him. I wish he would die.'

'Your father is not like other men. Sometimes we do not understand him.'

'I don't want to understand him, ever.'

'Go to sleep now. I promise everything will turn out all right.'

'It cannot turn out all right, Maji.'

'I will pray for you, you and your friend. Then everything will be all right.'

Prayer seemed to be such an inadequate remedy for what had happened, and I was about to say something about it when out of nowhere came the nightmare that had been haunting me for more than a year, creeping up and filling my mind. And over the scent of mogra flowers in her hair and the lavender on her hands, came the hateful, hated man-scent of cigars and rum. I turned my face away, my flesh shrinking from her contact, and buried it into the pillows once more.

About a week later, my mother told me that it had all been sorted out. She had arranged it through Abdulla Jan. She had sent word to

Roopchand, Kanakchand's father, that she would not only bear all the expenses of his son's high school education, but would pay for his going to college as well. From that day my mother paid the money demanded by Roopchand every month for the next nine years, until Kanakchand passed out of the law college.

It was hardly likely that Kanakchand did not know where the money for his education was coming from, but not by a word or gesture did he ever show his gratitude to my mother or myself.

I must say I cannot altogether bring myself to blame him, for you could not wipe out a public disgrace by gifts of money; and yet I cannot help feeling that if he had not broken down under the punishment, he might have found it more easy to forgive. It is our humiliations that we carry through life, not our acts of defiance.

6

The Education of a Prince

Two months later, I went to the Princes' College at Agra.

Pandit Sharma gave me advice but no presents. 'It is important to perform one's tasks,' he told me quite unselfconsciously, 'without giving thought to the rewards.' He was quoting from the Geeta, somewhat inadequately. I could not appreciate the line of thought.

'Don't be afraid of the raggin', Mr. Moreton said. 'All schoolboys have to go through that; only builds up character.' He gave me a copy of *Tom Brown's School Days* with gold-edged pages and bound in red leather.

'Remember you are a Bedar—the fearless clan. You don't have to take any nonsense from the other fellows,' my father reminded me. 'It is important to remember that at one time the Bedars were just as big as the twenty-one gunners, if not bigger.' He gave me a shotgun, my first twelve bore, complete with leather case and gold fittings. It was a lovely hammerless double made by Holland and Holland with shining blue twenty-eight inch barrels and a design of hounds and pheasants etched into the metal parts of the stock. On a tiny gold disk fitted into the crook of the butt was my monogram.

My mother looked sad, but she smiled as she said good-bye. 'Learn not to be cruel,' she warned me. 'Try and develop tolerance and understanding. And come back soon.' She gave me a pocket watch, a half hunter by Patck Philippe, with the hours and minutes done in gold and radium. I still possess the watch, and although it has numerous scratches and one or two dents, it still keeps perfect time.

Of the three presents, I liked my Holland best. I fondled it as though it were a live thing, rubbing my cheek against the smooth, black-walnut stock shining with the natural glow of the wood, studying the intricate engraving of dogs and birds, shouldering it and swinging it. It handled beautifully, like a part of myself, almost weightless in my hands.

But we were not permitted to take our firearms to the Princes' College. I had to leave the gun behind, locked up in my cupboard with the two-two Remington and the old twenty-bore shotgun. The shooting season did not open till October anyway and in October I was going to be back home for the Dassara holidays. The watch and *Tom Brown* went to school with me.

Mr. Moreton was wrong. There was no raggin' in the Chelmsford Princes' College, which was no more than a sort of finishing school for the sons of the princes, and where all of us lived in our own, spacious, four-roomed, semi-detached bungalows, and all of us lived in roughly equal comfort, with our personal servants and horses and cars.

The college was somewhat like our High School at Begwad in that although it called itself a 'college' it was really only a high school which prepared its princely students for the matriculation examination of the Agra university, and it didn't even do that very well since our percentage of students passing the examination was almost the lowest in the province. It was called a 'College' for the sake of dignity.

But examinations hardly mattered. What our head master, Mr.Walter Ludlow, was really proud of was the fact that we had produced three eight-handicap polo players and one all-India tennis champion and that we never had less than three of our ex-students in the provincial cricket team. I myself played for the provincial team for a season, three years later.

For the first few days I was lonely and homesick, and, oddly enough, I seemed to miss my father most. Although he represented all the authority, the sternness, the discipline I had encountered in my life, he was also someone I had always striven to live up to. And I missed my mother too, for she had been the source of all the kindness and love and laughter and lightness that had come to my share. I vowed that I would never allow myself to be separated from the watch she had given me, and I also made a resolve not to grow up to be cruel and to develop tolerance. Did she really think that there was a cruel streak in me? Was she, I wondered, telling me not to grow up to be like my father?

But above all, I missed the palace, the ugly black extravaganza which looked more like a prehistoric place of worship than a dwelling house: the peacocks in the park, the leaning trees, the riding school, the pungent smoke belching from the incinerators, the barn-like rooms, the echoing corridors, the smells of floor-way and furniture polish, the pre-dawn music of the sehnai players in the drum-gate, the elephants oscillating in their stalls in the hati-khana, the inexorable quarter-hour chiming of the clock in the tower, the insolent grunts of the pigeons making love under the turret walls—they were all a part of me now, and I felt a sense of separation as though I had been wrenched away from things to which I had become joined.

But gradually the shadowy longings, the feeling of separation and loss, melted away as I began to grow into my new surroundings and an awareness of freedom began to take their place. Pandit Sharma, Mr. Moreton, Gonzalves, Abdulla Jan, or my father and mother, were no longer around. Now I was on my own, with a brand new Morris Oxford and a chauffeur, three personal servants and a cook, three riding ponies, and I had half a burnt-brick bungalow to myself situated right at the back of the school grounds. From my bedroom window, I could see both the Jumna and the Taj.

And just as Mr. Moreton had been wrong about the ragging, so was my father about the danger of higher-gunned rulers' sons looking down on me, for that was something that the Head, Mr. Ludlow, was extremely punctilious about: at Chelmsford College all the students were equal. We were given identical half bungalows and allowed only one car each, and the Head saw to it that the cars were among the lower priced ones, Chevrolets, Fords, Morrises and Citroens. We were all allowed the same number of horses and servants, and we were addressed by our surnames, so that if there were two brothers, they became Major and Minor.

He was a remarkable man, the Head, determined to mould our characters according to his lights even if he did not succeed in getting many of us to pass our exams. He went about in his flapping gown and mortar-board, erect and with his hands folded behind him, a man of steel in the untidy garb of a professional school master. We learnt to accept him as a substitute for our parents, for their discipline and their affection. But as time passed, we also learnt to respect him and revere him for his own sake, so that by the time he had finished with us, his values had become our values. Kipling's 'If' was our daily prayer, the college motto 'Never Give In' our guiding principle.

We were gentlemen first and princes afterwards, we were taught. 'A gentleman carries his manners with him at all times,' the Head would remind us. 'And remember he carries nothing else—except perhaps a walking stick.' And he would smile wryly at his own joke.

He had simplified life for all of us, reducing both religion and ethics to a few simple maxims; so long as we obeyed the rules, we had nothing to fear.

'We have all come here with dealt-out hands,' the Head would say. 'And some of us may be holding better cards than the others. I don't care as much about whether you play your cards well or badly as about whether you play them honourably. That is what you are going to be taught here.'

And the one thing he was intolerant of was snobbery. If any of his students had any differences, they were made to settle them with their fists, in the boxing ring, and afterwards made to shake hands and forget all about the differences.

We tried to, we really tried, and as often as not, we did forget. The Head was a great influence in our lives, and the problems of youth could be solved by rule of thumb.

And yet this school of princelings was ridden with snobbery, not the snobbery of precedence or wealth, but the snobbery of proficiency in sports. Whether your father was a nineteen gunner or held the G.C.S.I. mattered far less than whether you played cricket for the school eleven.

I got on well at school, just managing to hold my own in studies, but getting into the first eleven at cricket during my very first year. During my last year, I captained both the cricket and hockey elevens.

It was a heady feeling to be wearing the school colours, to be regarded with envy by those outside the circle, and above all to be trusted by the Head to 'play the game and play for the team'.

I made friends. Inevitably, they were the boys from my own circle of cricket, hockey, tennis and boxing, for we sportsmen rather tended to stick together, a caste of our own, tightly knit and jealous. It was perhaps unfortunate that to us the clever ones, those who made the 'A' grades in the exams or who were interested in playing the sitar or the piano or in electric motors or in flying toy aeroplanes, were almost like outsiders.

Jumbo Kanil, the present Maharaja of Rajgoli, was with me. He was called Kanil Minor then. His elder brother, who won the posthumous V.C. in the Aracan, was called Kanil Major. Perhaps my closest friend was the Maharaja of Ninnore, Snappy Baindur, who broke my nose in the welterweight championship during my final year at school. He joined the Air Force during the war, and some years later was nearly, in the official phrase, derecognized as Maharaja, but was lucky to be let off with a warning. The Nawab of Waranda was our star pace bowler, although no one who sees the Nawabsahib today, with all those rolls of fat and his glazed, drink-sodden eyes, would think of him as a thin and wiry youth with the grace of a panther and a spark of genius in his fingers, or imagine that he could ever have run the four-forty in sixty seconds. Ranjit Singh, the Raja of Joida, was there too during my time, the one who scored the first century against the M.C.C. touring side and then died in a polo accident. Sandy, the Maharaja of Usoda and String, the Raja of Pusheli were in the hockey eleven with me, and the Thakur of Konshet was my doubles partner at tennis.

And admittedly, while all these Maharajas and Nawabs are today only titled nonentities, living on pensions and in constant dread of the Home Ministry's axe, they were true princes once, the very salt of the earth. I am proud that they were my friends, that many of them are still my friends.

Those were days of steady sunshine, exhilarating in spurts, at times even intoxicating, but never dismal; we lived from one cricket fixture to the next and never thought beyond. But in themselves, these happy days cannot be of interest to those who did not form a part of that closed circle of growing princes committed to the guardianship of the Head. I have no doubt in my mind that they were the ideal surroundings for a young man's upbringing even though I now realize that they represented a way of life that was already dying. We had a clean, carefree, time, sheltered from the outside world. Like birds in antiseptic cages playing their own games. Perhaps if I had been more diligent in my studies, I would have got much more out of them than I did, and possibly even have prevented myself from making such a hash of my life. All I can say is that I took the cards as they were dealt out and played my hand as best I could, without trying to peep at the other man's cards. And I have no regrets. Whatever faults there were in me were not those of the institution, and least of all were they the result of any shortcomings in the Head. If I had my days all over again, the period of my life I would unhesitatingly choose to live exactly as I had, would be the years at the Chelmsford College at Agra.

But if my schooldays now seemed bathed in sunshine, my holidays from school were certainly shadowed with moments of anguish and bitterness, as though they were a foretaste of what was to come.

For suddenly the holidays were upon us. The old ties began to reassert themselves. I wanted to be back with my father and mother, and I wanted to see Kanakchand. I wanted to go fishing for mahseer with Gonzalves and to improve my backhand at tennis. I wanted to go on long rides with Hamidulla and to try out the new jumps and convince Hamidulla that I was good enough to carry a spear at the next pig-sticking meet that my father would get up.

And above all, I was longing to blood my Holland, desperately hoping to get a clean right-and-left with the first two shots, for that, as everyone knows, is the only way to blood a good shot-gun. I am almost ashamed to admit it, but when I went home for the Dassara holidays, I was more anxious to try out my shotgun than I was to see my father and mother.

My father was away on one of his horseback tours of the state, but was coming back to Begwad for Dassara which was still ten days away. Even before going to see my mother, I ran to my cupboard and took out the Holland. I took it out of its case and assembled it and broke it and looked through the barrels. I nearly dropped the gun.

'God damn!' I said. 'Oh, damn and blast!'

They were no longer like tubes of mirror glass, my perfect, unblooded barrels. Someone had been using my gun, and had cleaned the barrels carelessly afterwards, leaving the unmistakable mist of gunpowder. My eyes pricked with a hot rage. And then, when I snapped the barrels back, I roared like an animal in rage, for there was a long scratch on the lovely black-walnut stock.

'What—has been using my Holland?' I shouted at the room boy who was emptying my suitcases.

He gave me a speechless, frightened look and began to gesture with his hands. I flung the gun on the sofa and clutched his shoulders and shook him. 'Have you been struck dumb, you bewakoof!' I screamed, forgetting myself, for I had never before shouted words of abuse at my personal servants. 'Why don't you speak? Who has been … '

'I have no idea, malik. I never touched the gun … I swear … '

'You had the keys. Who else could have opened the cupboard?'

'Malik, the keys were taken away from me.'

'Who took them? Who's been opening my cupboard?'

'The Palace Officer has taken all the keys in his own charge, huzur, for the last three weeks … I don't know anything … anything about … '

'Abdulla Jan? Has he been using my gun? Did he take it out?'

'I don't know, malik, I only … '

I pushed him away, and he staggered against the sofa. 'Go and call him at once … get him here, the swine!' I yelled.

The servant ran out and I paced the room in my rage. It seemed a long time before I heard the clit-clat of the Palace Officer's shoes. He came in, suave as ever, cocky, smiling a tight-lipped smile and smoking a cigar.

I pointed to the gun. 'What do you know about that?' I asked.

'Your gun! What about it?'

'You have been using it.'

'I did take it out once, just for an hour or so. I have had it cleaned … '

'Who gave you permission to use it?'

'Permission?' he asked. 'Permission?'

I had a crawling sensation at the back of my neck, a tightness around the eyes. 'Yes, permission, you bit of dirt,' I said.

'You cannot call me names!' he said, looking belligerently at me. There was an angry flush on his face. 'I won't stand for it. It is only a gun. I shall at once report this to His Highness … '

'You are nothing but a lowdown cur—a thief! And I will myself tell everything to His Highness the moment he returns. I won't be waiting for you, you filthy cigar-smoking bit of dirt! Drop that thing out of your mouth … drop it at once, or I will bash your face … daring to smoke in my presence!' And I went close to him, my fists curled, determined to hit him, measuring my distance for a swing at his jaw.

He stood his ground, his face a grim mask of hatred, almost daring me to hit him, the cigar firmly clenched between his teeth.

There was a moment of uncertainty, of caution, but I shook it off. 'You damn well mind your manners when you are speaking to the

Yuwaraj of Begwad,' I said, knowing that this was something I had to win; I had gone too far to draw back. I reached out and pulled the cigar from his mouth and flung it out of the window. 'Now get out,' I muttered. 'Out!'

Abdulla Jan stared coldly into my eyes for a few seconds before he turned his back and walked out of the room, slowly, almost defiantly, as though to demonstrate that he was taking his time to get out.

'Here, turn back! ' I called out, and I was surprised how composed my voice sounded, almost like my father's I thought. It made him stop in his tracks and turn back and glower at me, his eyes thin slits of hatred.

I was like a strange man even to myself, cold and deliberate even in the grip of seething anger. Without a word, I picked up the Holland and broke it and inserted two number four cartridges and snapped the barrels home while he stood stock-still.

'Don't you know you can't leave my presence without doing mujra, just like any of the others in the palace?' I asked. 'I will give you both barrels if I see any more disrespect.'

I held the barrels pointed at his stomach, and he must have heard the snap of the safety-catch going forward. I was fifteen years old, nearly as tall as he was, and I was conscious that I was doing what I was doing not for my own sake but for the honour of our state.

I saw his face turn red and then white. Without a word, he bowed to me, bending low as any menial, and touched his forehead three times with his right hand.

'And another thing,' I said. 'I don't care if you are the Palace Officer or the Chief Minister, I don't want you hovering about my rooms or fiddling with my things, understand? I don't want my things touched by filth such as you are. Now get out!'

He did another mujra, just as low as the first one, and turned away. The back of his neck had flushed a deep pink.

I was still fuming, later that evening, when I went to see my mother. 'How thin you've become,' she complained.

'That cur Abdulla has been making free with my gun,' I told her.

My mother was silent for a long time, and there was a hurt look on her face. 'Abhay, you must learn to control your temper, and not use bad words.'

'The nerve! Taking the keys in his charge the moment the season opened. The—!'

My mother winced. This was the first time I had used an oath in her presence.

'My son, I never expected to hear such language from you. Have you no consideration for my feelings?' Her voice was slightly choked and quivering, and there were two thin lines on her forehead. 'I hear that you were shockingly rude to the Palace Officer.'

'I could have killed the son of a bitch.'

Again my mother winced. 'You must learn to forgive,' she said, closing her eyes as though the light was hurting her. 'You must learn to control your temper like … like your father. No one ever knows when His Highness is angry. And Abhay, your language is getting quite shocking.'

I was instantly sorry. 'I am sorry, Maji,' I said. 'You see, I really loved that gun, and I was dying to blood it. He was so insolent too … even if Father might not have shown that he was angry, he would have horsewhipped the man all the same.'

My mother's frown deepened. Her shoulders quivered delicately. 'You must promise not to speak about this to your father, and you must also apologize to the Palace Officer for your rudeness.'

'Apologize! I shall do nothing of the kind, Mother. I shall never do it.'

She stared at me for a long time, and I felt sorry for her. Her face looked so desperately anxious.

'For my sake, Abhay; you've never refused to do whatever I asked you.'

I shook my head. 'No, Maji.'

'How you have changed,' Mother said. Her voice had sunk almost to a whisper.

'And Dada must know,' I said. 'It was he who gave me the gun. He would appreciate how I felt, more than you; more than anyone else. How else is Abdulla Jan to be punished?'

'Punishment, punishment! Is that all you can think of? You and your father. Punishment always rebounds; it grows more and more evil. Punishment is such a primitive way of resolving matters.'

I did not know why she sounded so upset. We were talking on entirely different levels, and I felt helpless and angry. Mother was acting as though somehow it was I who was in the wrong, as though I was making her suffer.

'You must promise you will not say anything about this to your father,' she said. 'That is one thing you can do for me … even if you will not apologize to the Palace Officer.'

I knew she was being unreasonable, and it was almost in spite of myself that I agreed. 'All right, Maji,' I promised. 'I won't say anything to Dada if you don't want me to.'

'Yes, for my sake. You must not say anything to your father. It is all rather unfortunate, whatever has happened. The Palace Officer may have made a genuine mistake … not realized that it was a special gun or anything. We must not forget how useful he has been here, such a comfort to all of us—since your illness. If this … this goes any further, he will only have to go away from here. No, no; he must not go away.' Mother shook her head.

I felt sorry for her and yet I could not understand her concern. There was little I could have done at the time but agree with her, particularly since I had flatly declined to apologize to the Palace Officer. I again promised that I would not report him to my father.

'He will only have to go away, back to his service, if there is any trouble here. You don't know how safe everything is here, since he came.'

I gave her the promise, but I never used the Holland. As far as I was concerned, it had been defiled and was unclean. Perhaps I would have used it if I had killed Abdulla Jan with it, for his blood would have purified it. I shuddered. Where had I heard that blood could purify? Was it some voice from the past, leading me back to the days of human sacrifices? The sort of thing which had provoked the first Abhayraj into cutting off the heads of his victims and decorating the walls of his fort?

The whole night, the gun lay on the sofa in my room, the ugly diagonal gash on the butt like a scar on a virgin's thigh proclaiming her ravishment; and every time my eyes strayed to the gun, I found myself in the grip of a hot shame, a shame and also a searing rage which made my head throb with pain. And when I dropped into sleep, I dreamt of the gun, and in my dream, the scar on it was bleeding. And suddenly the gun was my mother and the scar was bleeding. I woke with a start, limp and covered with cold sweat. The sehnai players at the drum gate were already heralding the dawn.

My limbs felt dead and my eyes were tight with lack of sleep, but my anger was still within me as I dressed. At school I would have worked it off in the boxing ring—the instructors from the British regiments were well able to absorb all the punishment any of us could dish out—or even with a hard game of squash with the marker. Here I burnt within myself. At six, Hamidulla and a syce were waiting for me near the verandah steps, the horses already saddled. I walked up to Sultan, my English-bred chestnut, without acknowledging Hamidulla's mujra. I measured the length of the stirrups with my arm and when I found they were too short, cursed the syce. And when Hamidulla made some joke about my legs having grown longer since I had last ridden. I turned on him viciously:

'Oh, shut up, you bloody fool!'

I pushed Hamidulla's hand away and began to adjust the stirrups myself while he looked on as though he had been slapped in the face, his eyes deep black slits, his mouth a grim line paralleling the rim of his squat helmet; a silent, scornful, dandified figure with the face of an outraged monkey, looking vaguely dignified in spite of the old tweed jacket with the leather elbow patches.

I broke into a canter, not turning my head to see if Hamidulla was following. I went, cantering still, through the empty, early morning roads and over the bridge and through the cremation ground and past the jagged shadow of the hulk of the old fort. Then, as we approached the freshly mown bajra fields and the forbidden territory beyond, I broke into full gallop, the reins free, the knees tight, the breeze like the sound of a beehive in my ears and the wind stinging my eyes and blurring my vision. I rode bent forward, my legs drawn up, almost like a professional jockey in a flat race and not what they called a gentleman rider; on and on in a drunken craving for excess, crashing through the stubble and thorn, accepting the challenge of the fences and the treacherous, twisting watercourses mercifully covered with under-growth. The heavy panting of the horse coming faster and faster like a drum beat and making a rhythm of its own quite distinct from the pounding of the hooves and the lash of the breeze—and all of a sudden the gaping blackness of the nullah, the smooth, sure, powerful thrust, the slow, almost never-ending moment of suspension high in the air, a breathless waiting for the fall, concentrating on the arching, glistening neck of the horse marbled with foam; and then the miracle of landing softly, as on a cushion.

On the rise of the opposite hill we slowed down to a canter and then came to a stop, as though by tacit agreement, the horse sensing my mood and knowing that I had worked off whatever was knotted within me. I felt wrung out but relaxed. And there beside me was Hamidulla, as ever, looking hot and winded but with a look of approval on his shrivelled monkey face.

'We'll just have to let you carry a spear for the next tent-club meet,' he said. 'But that was no way to go about it. You might have broken your neck, and I would have lost my job. I have four children … '

Only a part of my brain was listening to him. He was speaking in Hindi, of course, and he was speaking with the sort of familiarity that none of the other servants would have dared to permit themselves. I was angry no longer, not with him or anyone else. I was beginning to feel a little ashamed of myself.

'I nearly thought you were not going to make it, over the black nullah. It was inches, not more than two inches, I swear. It's a death-trap, with all that undergrowth hiding the real width. I prayed. There was only time to say "O, God!" and then I shut my eyes, knowing there was nothing I could do. That was where—well only about a hundred yards to the left, that your uncle Ashokraj was killed. And he was a skilled rider. He'd won the Central India point-to-point … not a bachha like you.'

I wiped my face and looked at him, the man who had taught me all I knew about riding and horses, and who had been closer to me than any other man. He sat easily in his saddle, as though he belonged on the enormous bay gelding of seventeen hands; the man who, above all, had given me his loyalty—loyalty and, I like to think, his affection too. He sat like a prince for his portrait, with the stubble of bajra fields and the riverside trees making the perfect setting for him. And, far in the distance, the black toy palace which you could hold up on the palm of your hand. This was his element, not mine; here he was the prince and all others commoners his subjects. I felt as a man should in a temple, suddenly solemn and uplifted.

'I am sorry, Hamidulla,' I said. 'I am sorry I lost my temper. I was very angry, but it was with someone else.'

'They are always angry when they do this kind of thing,' he said, almost to himself. 'That was what your uncle was: angry. So he went and broke his neck. They had had a quarrel, your father and him; just one of those brotherly quarrels, I don't know what about. Horses probably, maybe a car or something, even a woman. They were not speaking to each other that morning. We were beating for pig. They both rode after the same one, trying to get the first spear. Your father managed to clear the nullah, your uncle just failed to.'

'What happened to the horse?' I asked.

'The horse had to be destroyed.'

'I am sorry, Hamidulla,' I said again.

'Dammit, you cannot go breaking your neck just because you happen to be angry … remember there is only one of you.' And then he said something which I cherish to this day.

'If His Highness finds out about this, I am sure to lose my job. But it won't make any difference, Bal-raje. You have certainly learnt all that I can teach you about riding and horses. There is nothing more I can teach you.'

I knew even then that I would never know as much about riding as he did, and that I would never even begin to know what he knew about horses; that, measured by his standards, I would always remain a bachha. But he was sincere as he said it, and I looked away from his face to hide the shame in my eyes.

In the evening I had the Holland sent to him, complete with the case. Except for my watch, it was the most precious thing I could call my own. I had no further use for it. I did not know what Hamidulla himself would think of the present, or whether it would be of any use to him. I wanted to give and I gave, and the giving made me happy.

But try as I would, I could not bring myself to forgive Abdulla Jan. My anger stayed within me, like a snake waiting to strike out.

Even though I was in my own surroundings, I felt lonely and confused, troubled by vague longings; not contented and yet not knowing what I was missing. I did not know it was the awkward age, fifteen, and that my problem could be almost wholly ascribed to undirected emotion.

My father was still away, touring the Bulwara district, the wildest and most inaccessible part of our state, inhabited by a race of aborigines, the Bhils, quite primitive and unlettered, for there was not a single school in the whole district. They venerated my father, unquestioningly accepting his divine right to rule them, and he loved them with a positive, possessive kind of love, as a man who was one of themselves. It was a mystic, almost ritualistic bond between the ruler and the ruled, and it was perhaps the only influence that held the turbulent people together. Bulwara was my father's favourite district and it later became my own favourite district, for, however briefly, I too was to become the subject of their devotion. At the time of my holidays, in 1935, few people in India could have been aware of the Bulwara district or its Bhils. Barely fifteen years later, it was to make headlines in the national press and become the subject of a commission of inquiry.

My father was away, and for the first time I realized how much his mere presence in their midst had meant to his subjects, for the capital without him was like a temple without a deity, or as I later came to know, a divisional headquarters without its General. Mr. Moreton had gone back to England. I had no friends in Begwad, or even companions. Charudutt was back for the holidays, but I found that he had been forbidden to enter the palace. My other companion, Ranjit Hazarnis, had been taken to Bombay for an operation. And when I sent word for Kanakchand to come and see me, I was told that he had not come back for the holidays.

But the very next afternoon, when I was doing tight figures of eight all by myself on the polo ground, I saw in the distance Charudutt astride a bicycle, talking to a boy in a brown cap who was walking. For a moment, I wondered who the other boy could be, and on the next turn I looked carefully. It was Kanakchand. Without thinking, I turned my horse in their direction. They were talking very friendlily, and seemed to be laughing a lot, but as they heard the hoof-beats, they looked in my direction, startled. Charudutt said something and quickly pedalled away and Kanakchand began to walk faster as though he wanted to avoid me. I spurred my horse and caught up with him. 'Kanakchand!' I called.

He halted under one of the banyan trees and turned to face me, but there was no smile on his face.

'I did not know you were back,' I said. 'Why did you not come to see me?'

'I don't want to see you,' he said, and his words hit me like a blast of hot wind in summer.

'Why not? What has happened?'

His dark, sullen face broke into a defiant snarl. 'I don't want to see you. I hate you!'

I felt a throb of anger, the urge to lash out blindly at him. And yet there was something holding me back. The crop had done enough damage already; it had turned my only childhood friend away from me. In a way, I could even understand him.

'Why are you so bitter?' I asked 'I did not do anything. It was the white cap that angered my father … '

Kanakchand flung down his brown pillbox cap and pulled a white khaddar cap out of his pocket and put it on. 'And what is wrong with the white cap?' he demanded. 'It is the cap of the people; it is the cap of freedom.'

'Not the cap of the people of this state,' I said.

'State people! State people live in slavery … in chains! Like dogs!' he hissed, and spat on the ground with contempt. 'Like dogs!'

My fingers gripped the crop but I did not hit him. I know my father would have, if only because he would have considered it his duty, for Kanakchand had insulted the people of his state. Who knows, perhaps I felt powerless to hit him because the guilt of his madness was upon me; the guilt of turning a high spirited, ambitious boy into a malevolent revolutionary.

'Well, so long,' I said, and turned my horse. That was what we said to each other at school; 'so long', which, someone had told me, came from the Indian greeting 'salaam'. I thought it was the nicest way to say farewell to a friend. 'So long,' I said. 'Don't let anyone here catch you with the white cap on. You will just be asking for trouble.'

I touched the horse sharply with both heels, and Sultan began to trot. I abandoned myself to the mechanics of trotting, letting myself be jogged up and down, falling in with the rhythm of the pace, and I did not look behind me. But I knew that he was standing under the tree, looking in my direction, until the darkness swallowed me. What I did not know was whether he felt sorry or glad.

7

The Chessboard in Hell

Early the next morning, a message came from Bulwara that my father wished me to join him for the rest of his tour. I left within the hour, longing to be with him again and wondering if this was what I had been missing. At the back of my mind was also the hope that I would now be permitted to see the family treasure in the fort at Patalpat.

We stopped for lunch at the riverside. That was as far as the road went. We had to cross the Kamra in a ferryboat, and as we ate, I could see the horses waiting on the other side, swishing their tails at invisible flies, ready to take me and my servants on the final stage of our journey.

The sun was still high as we sighted the camp in the crook of the hills, a little horseshoe of white tents around a red-roofed bungalow. As we approached, we passed small groups of men and women going towards the camp, all almost naked except for little wisps of cloth around their middles, the men wearing twists of coloured rope for turbans and the women chains of flowers on their heads. They saluted as we passed, folding their hands and saying 'Julay-julay' to me but not bending their heads, for they were a primitive, uncivilized race who took pride in not bending their heads to anyone except their ruler. Their bodies were spare and the colour of weathered rosewood. Their hair was thick and matted in natural hanks like the manes of lions, uncut and uncombed. They walked erect, with their faces set and stern, but quick to break into a grin as I smiled at them and returned their greetings. And all the men, including many of the older children, were armed with thin bamboo spears tipped with steel.

This was by no means my first contact with the Bhils of Bulwara; I had seen them before at my father's durbars, wearing their rope turbans and carrying their deadly-looking spears. But this was the first time I had been in their own country, the first time I became aware of them as a force, as a race of hunters who had barely settled down as farmers and who lived by instinct and emotions and a few tribal laws and were closer to the bronze age than to ours. And it was at this time too that I began to understand why my father had always regarded them as his special responsibility.

We passed through a high arch of bamboos and palm fronds, still fresh and green, and through a long passage of poles festooned with marigold and hibiscus chains. When we came to the gate of the bungalow, the others stopped and dismounted so that I could ride on alone.

My father stood on the doorstep of the bungalow, dressed in khaki hunting clothes and a multi-coloured turban exactly like that of the Bhils, his face wreathed in smiles at the show his people had put on for my arrival. He looked fit and bronzed. He waited for me to do my mujra to him, and then he pulled me up to his chest and after that we stood side by side with his hand on my shoulder, facing the ring of dark bodies.

One of the servants brought up another Bhil turban of rope and my father removed my cap and placed the turban on my head. The Bhils threw their spears high and caught them deftly as they came down.

'Julay-julay!' my father greeted them. 'Julay-julay!'

'Julay-julay!' the Bhils yelled in joy. 'Julay-julay!'

It was a wonderfully serviceable expression. As far as I knew, it meant both greetings and farewell as well as 'all right' and 'thank you' and 'well done', and I am sure it meant many other things besides.

We waited for a minute or two, not saying anything, while the Bhils stared at us, and then my father led me through the house to the back verandah. And suddenly there were no people, just the majesty of the hills. In front of us, the ground dropped abruptly, and the valley beyond was wide and deep, opening out to the west in fold upon fold so that we looked upon an immense, intricate pattern of low, interlacing hills fading into the horizon and now coloured a bright pink by the afternoon sun. It was so sudden and so vast that it made you gasp.

We sat in opposite chairs on the verandah overlooking the valley, watching the view and listening to the jungle sounds; the impertinent clucking of the grey woodcocks and the clamour of the partridges. I felt at once that I was a part of these surroundings, somehow closer to my father than ever before. The servants brought in the tea things, ham and tomato sandwiches and jelebies and chirotees and chocolate cake and chiwada and cheeserings for me and whisky and soda for my father.

I felt slightly artificial, as though I was just someone who had dropped in for tea and had to make polite conversation. 'What wonderful hills these are,' I said. 'Rather like the Western Ghats around Raigarh, but much wilder, of course. And here they are all red.'

'I prefer these hills to Kashmir or the Nilgiries,' my father said. 'So … so unspoilt. The nearest railway is at least a hundred miles away; the nearest place a car can come is at least seven—and that's a private road. No schools, no factories, no lawyers or moneylenders … just the jungles and the hills and the Bhils. Magnificent people, the Bhils, just as unspoilt as ever. This was what Rama may have seen two thousand years ago, during his wanderings—just as we are seeing it today.'

The line of thought was familiar and comforting. He always felt much more at home with the past than with the present.

'And that must be Patalpat,' I said.

My father nodded. 'Patalpat—the Chessboard in the netherworld. That was where we lived in the days of Mahadji, before we went to live in Begwad. Our gods are still there; the gods as well as the jamdar-khana. You will have to be going there some day.'

It lay like a toy fort in the loop of the river, prim as a chessboard, a pattern of grey and brown and green, the fort which was supposed to have a bewildering system of underground passages and which held the family treasure. I had hoped that I was going to be taken to see the jamdar-khana this time. I tried not to show my disappointment.

It was almost as though he had read my thoughts. 'I think it is better to wait. It's only as one gets older that one acquires a better appreciation of the value of things. It is rather bewildering when they first untie the bandage.'

'Why do we have to go in blindfold, Dada. when it all belongs to us?' I asked. 'When the guards can come and go as they please.'

'It has worked very well all these years—nearly two hundred years now. It is perhaps just as well that we should not know the way, that there should be no room for temptation. The Ramoshies, you know, the guards, are bound to us by an oath. There are perhaps not more than a couple of dozen of them. They are the only ones who know the exact place; we can only be sure that it is somewhere within the three square miles that the fort occupies. That is how our ancestors wanted it. It was a wise precaution.'

For myself, I could not see the wisdom of these precautions at all, but I nodded vigorously feeling more than ever like a guest at tea, remembering that I must be polite to the host. I picked up a chirotee and said how glad I was to be there. 'It really is magnificent,' I said.

'And to think that I have just saved it from … from calamity; I and the Bhils between us. We have halted the process of destruction, I don't know for how long.'

'Saved it?' I asked. 'Saved it from what?'

'Do you see where those two hills come together? Just where the vultures are dropping—must be some kind of a kill there. That's where the river runs through a gorge barely three hundred yards wide. They wanted to build a dam there, so that they could make electricity for I don't know how many factories and mills, and also a network of canals just as they have done in the Punjab.'

'And it didn't come off?' I asked.

My father smiled his sly, poker smile and then he threw back his head and tossed down his drink. 'Koi-hai!' he called, and when a servant came out, I pointed to his empty glass.

'Well, they couldn't do it unless they had the whole valley as the catchment area. They offered to buy it.'

'The British?'

He nodded. 'Offered me a whole crore of rupees.'

'A crore!'

'Then they pushed it up to a crore and a half. A lot of money, I know. I can see how their minds worked. There are about twenty-five thousand people in the district, men, women and children; and the area is around a thousand square miles. Four hundred rupees per man or ten thousand rupees per square mile; that seems to have been the basis. You can almost see some finance department clerk in Delhi trying to work out the formula. Yes, a lot of money. Properly invested, it would have brought around eight lakhs a year—just about double the revenue this district brings.'

'And you didn't take it, Dada.'

'No, I didn't. It was tricky to turn it down, of course. I was badly off for money just then, and the Political Department knew all about it. I pulled a long face at Colonel Broom and told him. l did not want the money. Just give me an equal area of land, I asked. I knew the British would never agree to that.'

My father looked into the sunset and chuckled to himself. With the single strand of rope coiled around his thick black hair, his face burnt black with the sun, he looked exactly like some tribal chief, even though he was wearing a shooting jacket tailored by Ranken out of the most expensive imported gabardine.

'Broom didn't like it,' he went on. 'He thought I was a fool twice over; yes, a double fool. First for turning down a crore and a half and then suggesting that I should be given land from British India—quite unheard of.'

My father laughed again, and this time I found myself laughing with him, sharing his triumph, eager to hear the rest of his story.

'The negotiations went on for two years. Broom went away and we got this new P.A., Gibson. Finally they agreed to give me the land, agreed to the principle, that is. They had to ascertain what the people themselves wanted; they did not wish to transfer people from British rule to a Maharaja's rule against their will. They wanted to hold a referendum … '

'But what was going to happen to Patalpat, Dada?' I asked. 'To the family gods … the treasure?'

'Oh, I suppose we could have removed everything to some other place. No, that would have created no difficulty. The British said they would hold a referendum … you know, give a chance to the people themselves to decide; vote for the thing. It certainly was awkward.'

'What on earth did you do?'

'For a time I was in a fix. Then I told them that if the question of transferring land to me from British India was to be decided by the people, then my people too should be given an opportunity to decide whether they wanted to go under British rule.'

He paused while a bearer brought a glass of whisky and soda. He took a sip before going on. 'Of course Gibson did not know my Bhils. "How can anyone elect to live under a Maharaja's rule if given the option of going into British India?" he asked. But I knew I was perfectly safe, betting on a certainty—I knew my Bhils.'

'And they voted to stay back?' I asked.

My father nodded. 'What Gibson was worried about was that the people in the British districts would refuse to come under my rule and spoil their scheme. We agreed on the territory—an equal tract in the Katur district. You may remember that the district belonged to us before the mutiny—was taken away from us—don't you? '

'Yes, Dada,' I said.

'They bustled about taking a plebiscite, asking the people whether they would like to be joined to Begwad. It shook them when they discovered that the majority were in favour of coming over to me—actually, it was only about eighty years or so since we had lost the district. Then they took a vote in this district, all on their own. Their officials went round telling everyone how many schools and canals they were going to be given, how much employment, if only they agreed to the transfer. What do you think the Bhils said?'

I knew what the Bhils had said; knew that they had opted for darkness and squalor when they had the chance to vote for prosperity and light. They had reacted as their ruler knew they would react and between them they had torpedoed the Bulwara dam.

'The Bhils nearly revolted,' my father went on. They went out in processions, boycotted the referendum altogether, and it was all I could do to persuade them not to stage a march on the Residency. They refused even to consider the transfer. The British would not have received a single vote, I tell you, not one. The Bhils would have killed any one who voted for a transfer. The whole idea of the dam had to be dropped.'

'I am glad that the Bhils refused to go, Dada,' I said. 'I like the Bhils.'

'It was an insult, a slap in the face for the Brooms and Gibsons, always going on at us to improve our administration, provide schools and roads. It shook them to see how people from their district were not unwilling to come here, but that our people were determined to stay with us. Remember that, Abhay: remember it whenever anyone criticizes our administration, pities the lot of the people in the states. This must be the only incident of its kind in the field of British and Indian-states relations. We may not give our people prosperity, but we give them roots, perhaps happiness; a cause to live for and die for.

'And remember this too,' my father went on. 'If at any time you need help, after I'm gone, you have only to call upon these men. There are perhaps not more than ten thousand men amongst them, but every one of them will give his life for his ruler. And remember too, the ruler's own responsibility towards these men. They are like children. We cannot let them down.'

Had he not already let them down? I wondered. It was intoxicating to think that there were people who were ready to lay down their lives for you, but how long could they be kept fenced off from the world? Would it not have been better to have persuaded them that their interests lay in agreeing to have the dam built, to go into British India and learn to take their place in the twentieth century?

But we were close to each other that day, my father and I, in spite of my lurking disapproval. I no longer felt a boy of fifteen but a man, a man who was beginning to understand the sort of values that obsessed his father.

'Wonderful people, loyal and brave,' he was saying. 'And they are fighting men. And this is their country, almost as it was since time began. We don't want to take it away from them for the sake of putting up factories and mills somewhere, generating electricity. They would have felt uprooted, sold like slaves—six hundred rupees per head or a patch of irrigated land. I left it to them. The choice was theirs.'

No, the choice was not theirs; the choice was my father's. They were swayed by sentiment alone, sentiment such as a man like my father was capable of evoking in them, both for good or evil, and who could have been guided in the right channels, taught to take their place in a world of factories and mills and electric power. But I did not think so then, for I too was caught up in his exhilaration, sharing his triumph.

'And so they stayed with me, as they will stay with you. It is up to us to see that they go on as they have been living; undisturbed, to enjoy the peace of their valley—who wants a dam?'

Who indeed? Not when you have over ten lakhs a year as spending money and two palaces and thirty odd cars; not when you have blindly loyal subjects prepared to lay down their lives for you. Who wants a dam? No one, I found myself agreeing with him. No one.

The sun was a ball of burning brass falling down with its own weight. The red hills were now washed with gold on top and the valleys had turned from green to blue-grey. The fort below us no longer looked like a chessboard, for there was a thin mist covering its precise greens and browns. Above the faint roar of the river far away, I could hear the evensong of the partridges and the pea hens and the challenge and counter-challenge of the woodcocks.

'Kipling has written a poem saying that a man cannot love the whole earth. He chooses just a small patch. This patch is mine. This,' and he waved his hands at the landscape.

'I like it too, Dada,' I said.

'Just look at the view, listen to the birds! Even if you take a stroll round the bungalow, you will get a dozen shots. That is why I called you here. First to introduce you to the Bhils as my son—their future ruler; and then I thought you would have a wonderful opportunity of trying out your Holland. Listen to that racket!'

The racket? Partridges clamouring, pea hens wailing, the grey woodcocks crowing, the green pigeons whistling, the spur fowls clucking … what else? I found myself trying to distinguish the various sounds.

'What is the time?' my father asked.

I took out my half-hunter. 'Thirty-five past six,' I told him.

'That is a very fine watch, Abhay.'

'Yes, Dada, Maji gave it to me when I was going to school. I always carry it. It's a very lucky watch. I keep it in my pocket even when I play cricket.'

'Six thirty-five,' my father said. 'Well, perhaps it is a little late to go after those birds this evening. Tomorrow morning then, early. We'll try the ridge, both with our new Hollands. They are a pair; made to measure for me, of course, but you are just about my size, or will be soon. I kept one for myself, gave you the other. Mine too is still not blooded. We'll both try them out … '

The Holland! Oh, God, the Holland! Something like that had to come between us now, just when we were so close.

'I haven't got the gun any more, Dada,' I said. 'I gave it away.'

My father, who was gazing into the hills, listening to the jungle sounds with his head slightly cocked, went on looking as though he had not heard me. The late evening sun was full in his face, rugged and handsome as though carved in teak. He had forgotten my presence, because whatever had brought us together must have been brittle and had shattered, and presently I had a feeling that he had even put away the hills and the Bhils from his thoughts, and his mind was far away, getting back its wind. I ached to tell him about the Holland, knowing that he would have understood, but I could not.

'Haibat!' my father called. 'Haibat! Bring the two-two, will you? Let's get some practice in before it gets dark.'

Haibat brought the .22 Remington, already loaded, and my father walked down the steps and stood at the edge of the valley, the sky and the hills silhouetting his tall, spare figure with the ridiculous turban of twisted red and green rope. He took his stance, with his weight evenly on both feet, and Haibat began to throw the copper coins in the air. They went cutting through the blue of the sky in shining disks, one after the other, coming down and flying away again in all directions as the shots cracked.

It was a ritual, a punctuation mark to a moment of stress, a self-imposed test of coolness under strain. As usual, I began to count the hits, half hoping that he would miss, as though his concentration were a measure of the turmoil he was undergoing. He got twelve clean hits, one after the other, and missed the thirteenth, and then he got another eight and missed again. Then he got the next three and missed.

'The light is going,' he complained, during a pause for reloading.

The hills were now purple on top and dark blue in the folds, but he went on shooting until the last hilltop was swallowed by the darkness. He missed five shots in a row. Then he stopped.

My father did not break camp to return to his capital for Dassara as he had planned. He sent me back and himself stayed on in Bulwara. On my part, I was glad to get away from him, for although he was quite his usual self with me, I was filled with a sense of unresolved guilt. While I had perhaps done right according to my own lights, in his eyes I had failed to measure up to the tribal code; I, his son, had let him down in his hour of triumph when his aborigines had demonstrated their loyalty and devotion to him and won him a victory against his hereditary enemies, the officials of the Political Department.

I returned to Begwad, to spend the rest of my holidays riding, fishing and improving my backhand, and was once again in the grip of vague longings. My problems, I now realize, were by and large the problems of every growing boy; the problems of facing up to the process of stepping into manhood, demanding adjustment in my relationship with my parents and friends, replacing the wide-eyed vision of a boy with the ever narrowing one of a man.

I felt the awkwardness of my years; even in the presence of my mother I seemed to detect new complexes in myself, aware that I was no longer a little boy who could break into her privacy as and when I willed, that there were many things I could not confide in her.

And I also became aware of the unhappiness that haunted my mother. I played rummy with her in the afternoons, and accompanied her for her evening drives. It was sad to see what joy these small attentions gave her. My loneliness was nothing to hers; mine was wholly transitory, hers was permanent. Her life was a great emptiness and there was nothing anyone could do about it. One could not do more than feel sorry for her, and play an occasional game of rummy with her, this woman who, although she was a Maharani, was also branded as having the white foot. Cast away by her husband in the first bloom of youth, now grown to maturity with all the fires of her being unslaked, she was if anything looking lovelier than ever, and, almost perversely, more radiant and lively than ever too, full of laughter and happiness.

The tight little world around me was falling apart. I had to find new anchors, fresh objects of love and devotion. But at the time, I could not see what the other anchors were, nor the objects of love.

My father had not returned when the holidays ended. I was eager to go back to school, to the ordered simplicity of Mr. Ludlow's rule, to the taboos of a quite different tribe, to a place where, if we had any differences to settle, we were made to settle them with our fists in the boxing ring and then made to shake hands and smile, and where we did not give a damn about being adjusted.

8

Honourable Scar

I lived happily enough at school, no longer sick for home or parents or childhood friends, finding a fulness in my own surroundings. The days passed in a dizzy succession of sporting events—hockey, tennis, cricket, football, boxing—and the holidays came and went, irritating interruptions that we gradually learnt to live with.

As I have said, it was in the final year at school that Snappy Baindur, the present Maharaja of Ninnore, broke my nose during the finals of the welterweight boxing. I was doing very well against Snappy, and had managed to get a one-two within the first few seconds—left to his face and a right cross to his left ear—that had drawn a round of applause, and then, when he fell back slightly, I had followed through by landing a hefty left hook on his body that had made him reel.

I was doing very well, and perhaps showing off a little, knowing that the championship was as good as in my pocket. Perhaps I had grown a little careless. In the second round too, I had managed to get another classic one-two at him, but after that I must have dropped my shoulder a little too low for another swing at his body and Snappy had found the gap and thrown a right at me with everything he possessed. It exploded on my nose like a redhot flame.

It was some time before I began to taste the salt blood in my mouth, but I did not know that my nose had been broken until the referee intervened and stopped the fight.

'Well done, sir,' I heard the Head say. I thought he was saying that to Snappy who had won the fight, but it turned out he was saying it to me.

In the dressing-room, as soon as they had finished dowsing my head with cold water, I became aware of the school doctor fussing around with tape and bandages and there was quite a bit of blood on the table.

'Does it hurt much?' the doctor asked.

I shook my head and my nose began to bleed all over again.

The doctor sent for ice.

Mr. Ludlow came to see me. 'How do you feel, Bedar?' he asked.

'Fine, sir,' I said.

'You've gone and broken your nose.'

'It was all my fault, sir,' I said.

'These things are no one's fault, Bedar.'

'And please, sir, I don't want my father—or my mother—to be told about it.'

'Oh, really! Why?'

'I don't know what they will think, sir; what my father will think.'

'A boxing scar is an honourable scar, like … like a battle scar.'

'All my fault, sir,' I said again.

'We shall have to see what the doctors say. They may have to operate.'

'I don't want my mother to know, sir.'

'Don't worry, Bedar,' the Head promised. 'I'll see what I can do. We shall have to wait until the doctors have had a look.'

The doctors sent me to the Curzon hospital in the cantonment and there they performed some sort of operation. I had to stay at the Curzon for more than two weeks with a heavy bandage all round my face. When I came out, I was still wearing a thin, aluminium plate as a nose guard, held in place by a bandage.

The first day at school, the Head sent for me.

'How do you feel, Bedar?' he asked.

I told him I felt fine.

'Good! I did what I could. I actually went to see your father, at Begwad. Fine country, you've got there. I explained our attitude to such mishaps to your father, how we like to take these things at the Princes' College,' and the Head smiled reassuringly, 'as scars of honour.'

That was the sort of thing the Head was always doing; that was what made him stand sky-high in the estimation of those who had the good fortune to be his students.

'We talked it over, and I must say His Highness was really most understanding. Between us we agreed that there was no need for your mother to be told … save her all the worry. You know what mothers are.'

'Thank you, sir,' I said.

'The doctors had to send a special report to your father every day, by telegram, and he sent down one of his own specialists from Bombay to take a look at you; a Dr. Ten … Tendulkar.'

'My father is a great one for specialists, sir.'

The Head smiled again. 'His Highness was himself in bed; he had had a fall from his horse.'

'My father is always falling off horses, sir.'

'Hmmm. How long did they say you'll have to wear that contraption?'

'I didn't ask, sir.'

Then Mr. Ludlow told me that my father was coming to see me in the afternoon. 'He wants to have a look at you: quite naturally.'

'Yes, sir.'

'Pity you are still wearing a bandage.'

'Yes, sir.'

'Here is something I have for you,' the Head said a little awkwardly, and he held out a book. It was a copy of *Tom Brown's School Days* just like the one Mr. Moreton had given me.

'Why, thanks, sir!' I said.

'I have inscribed it. Here, read it,' the Head told me, and he reached out and held the flyleaf open:

'The way a man takes a loss is the measure of his Manliness,' Mr. Ludlow had written. 'Thank you, sir!' I said.

When I came out of his office, I went straight to the washroom and threw away my nose-guard. It did not seem to make any difference to the way I felt.

My father was still limping because of his fall, but he was not carrying a stick. He looked at me for a long time before he spoke.

'There is still some swelling,' he remarked. 'How do you feel?'

'I feel fine, Dada.'

'Ninnore,' Father said. 'I nearly married the princess of Ninnore. Must be the young man's aunt. It didn't come off. And now you have to go and get your nose broken by a Ninnore prince. You are going to have a crooked nose. They don't seem to have set it properly.'

'I expect it will be all right, when the swelling goes.'

'You are a brave young man, my son,' my father said. That was the sort of thing that you had to guard against in the Princes' College. I hoped no one was listening.

My father tugged at his moustache and looked into the distance. He did not say anything for a long time. Then he said: 'Is there anything you want?'

'Nothing, Father. I have everything.'

He smiled. It was a sad, almost pained smile. 'Everything,' he said. 'How wonderful. Who can have everything he wants, except perhaps when he is at school? Are you sure you want nothing?'

'A pair of new hockey boots. The Army and Navy Stores have the kind I want.'

'Yes, of course,' Father said. 'A pair of boots. I'll send Haibat to get them for you. I have told Mr. Ludlow that you are not to box any more.'

I was sorry to hear that. 'Not at all, or only till my nose gets all right?' I asked.

'Not at all,' my father said. 'Give Haibat the measurements for your boots.' He came up to me, walking stiffly, and put a hand on my shoulder. In spite of myself, I could not help smiling.

'What makes you smile, Abhay?' he asked.

'Dada, you have fallen off a horse—how many times—twenty times, shall we say?'

'Maybe twenty,' he said.

'And yet I know you will go on riding … '

'They are hardly the same thing,' my father pronounced. 'Boxing and riding are quite different.'

Two months later, we had our farewell parade at school, and the next day I returned home, noticing for the first time the hideous lines and the disproportionate bulk of the palace, and full of forebodings. But inside, I found joy once again, for one of the first things I learnt was that Abdulla Jan had gone back to the Police service in British India.

It was not till many years later that I found out why my father had got rid of Abdulla Jan, but at the time I had no special wish to know why he had gone. For me it was enough to know that he had gone, and my first thought was that now there was no reason why I should not tell my father about my Holland. It was not as though by telling my father about the Holland I would be causing any unpleasantness between him and Abdulla Jan. I felt freed from the promise I had given my mother.

'I am so glad you got rid of the Palace Officer,' I said to my father. 'I hated him.'

'Hated him?'

'Hated him enough to want to kill him. In fact I nearly did kill him once.'

My father's face had suddenly gone pale, almost like the time when I had seen him in a trance in the old family temple. He gave me a sharp, searching look. 'You know you don't have to tell me about it,' he said very softly. 'I would much rather not know the … the actual circumstances.'

'But I want to tell you, Dada; want to explain … explain why I gave away the Holland.'

'The Holland! Oh, the Holland,' my father said, almost absent-mindedly, but I could see the relief in his face.

I told him about the Holland, and he listened as he always did, cocking his head slightly and nodding every now and then. And in the telling of it, my action sounded absurdly churlish and meaningless, for I could not tell him about my horrible, indecent dreams.

'I cannot altogether blame you,' my father said. 'But why did you not tell me before? You know I would not have said anything.'

'Maji had told me that I must not complain to you, and I had given my promise to her. I did not want to break my word.'

'Oh!' Father said. 'Oh, I see. Of course not. But why are you telling me now, breaking your promise?'

'Now I can tell you because you have already sent him away. Maji did not want him to go, because she felt everything was so safe here because of him; if I complained to you, he might have had to go away. Now that he has gone, there is nothing to stop me from telling you.'

My father nodded. 'Yes, of course, you could not have broken your word,' he said, and the hurt look was back on his face. 'Yes. it is all right now.'

I felt suddenly light, as though released from a spell; as though I had recovered something precious in our relationship that had been lost.

'Yes, I can understand it,' my father was saying. 'You did well to throw away the gun. It had been defiled. He had … had defiled something which was precious to you … enough to make you want to kill him. You were quite right to give away the Holland. I understand.'

I could have yelled with joy if I had not sensed that his mind was wrapped up in other thoughts, for he still looked pale and withdrawn and tense, as though he had just received a shock; as though even when he was listening to my outburst with his inherent politeness, his mind was pressed down with its own problems.

'Will you tell Haibat to bring my two-two, Abhay,' he said to me. 'I want to try out the new cartridges.'

I ran out to tell them to bring out his Remington, aware that I had dropped away a burden from my shoulders, and yet conscious that I had not been able to penetrate the doubts in my father's mind, or enable it to dispel its own gloom.

'Oh, what has happened to you?' my mother asked.

'Why, nothing, Mother,' I said.

'Your nose! What have they done to your nose?' she asked in a trembling voice, and suddenly her eyes were bright with tears.

I had almost forgotten about my nose. 'Oh, I damaged it,' I told her, trying to sound casual. 'Busted it while boxing … '

'Boxing! What a terribly cruel thing! To make little boys hit each other and break things. Do they make you hate each other too?'

How could I explain to someone like my mother about boxing and scars of honour. 'No, Maji, we are all friends; very good friends. We just box for fun.'

'For fun,' Mother said. 'Break each other's noses for fun … and they never even told me. Did you—were you sent to a doctor or anything?'

'Oh, couple of weeks in the hospital,' I said.

'But it was such a handsome nose; so straight and sharp. And now look … oh!' and Mother wiped her eyes with the corner of her sari. 'And they never even told me anything about it,' she said again.

She came forward and held my face between her hands, and then she released my head and began to sob in silence.

It must have been a couple of days later. I had gone for a ride in the evening, all by myself, and as I was passing a small, newly-built bungalow with a pink roof, I saw a woman waving to me from the steps. I turned and noticed that it was Amina-begam. It was good to see Amina-begam, bubbling with sheer high spirits, so devoid of fussiness. Now that I come to think of it, Amina was typical of that admirable but fast disappearing class of women, the professional entertainers. One could never apply that ugly word prostitute to them. They were brought up as song-and-dance girls, but they were also masseuses, story-tellers and jesters, companions of a man's leisure hours; it was almost indirectly that they were also mistresses. Most of them ended up as concubines, sticking to one man all through life, almost like a wife without the formality of marriage. They took pride in their profession, and in their ability to make their men forget the cares of the world while in their company.

I turned my horse into the gate. Amina-begam shouted to her Mali to hold my horse and ordered tea. She chatted brightly about her new house and then we both laughed rather a lot over some quite impossible story she was telling me about a fat drumplayer in the court of Akbar, complete with the action and sound effects. Amina was such a natural, gay person, that it was difficult to associate her with sin.

Her niece, Zarina, hovered around the tea table, doing small errands, but not saying anything. Amina told her to come and sit with us and then said to me: 'Don't you think she has grown into a pretty girl? Just think what she will look like in another two years, when you both grow up.'

Zarina was only fourteen then, and of course Amina-begam had said the same thing whenever I had seen her, but now her remark suddenly seemed to acquire meaning. Zarina had grown into a tall, well-built girl, and the way she blushed and turned her eyes away made me think that it was somehow wrong for me to be seen having tea at the house of a concubine, however much I enjoyed being in her company—a concubine with a growing niece.

As soon as tea was over, I rose to go. Amina-begam made Zarina give me a paan but made no effort to keep me. I did not eat paan but I knew it was not polite to refuse. I put the paan in my pocket and rode away.

9

Mainly about Tigers

The treaty between the Bedar of Begwad, as he was then known, and the East India Company, was made in 1803, soon after the battle of Patalpat. On the whole, the British General, John Perkins, gave us very generous terms. Perhaps because we were one of the first among the Padmakoshal chieftains to enter into a treaty with the Company, ours was almost a treaty between two allies, with a clause about mutual aid and respect for each other's territorial integrity. Some of the other princes insist that the Bedars had paid General Perkins five lakhs of gold mohurs for the concessions incorporated in the treaty, and this rumour may have had something to do with the slight unpleasantness that arose between the General and Lord Wellesley, the Company's Governor-General. But according to our family history that my father had had written, there had been no such gifts. General Perkins seems to have been struck by the desperate stand made by the Bedar's army, and his defiance in defeat. The moment the battle was over, the two seem to have met in a spirit of real old-fashioned chivalry, and it is a recorded fact that after the signing of the treaty, both Hiroji Bedar and John Perkins exchanged turbans in token of their close friendship.

For the next hundred years our relationship with the British was marked by a succession of disputes, most of them over questions of privileges. For us, inevitably, they were all losing battles, and as a result we suffered numerous setbacks in our fortunes. During the sepoy revolt of 1857, Sir Edward Burton, the Resident in Padmakoshal, had wantonly blown up the Begwad fort for alleged sympathy with the mutineers, and then gone on to annex our district of Katur. One of my ancestors, the second Hiroji, was deposed because he had had an Indigo planter's moustache shaved off in public for abducting a girl from the Bulwara valley. Another, the first Ashokraj, was declared insane because he had refused to pay a call on the Resident, who had come to visit Begwad, on the ground that, according to the treaty, it was up to the Resident to call on him first.

By now it had become merely an amusing anecdote which officials told each other in their own gatherings; its sting had gone, only the absurdity remained. The day before he was due to arrive, the Resident, Major Gill, had sent a note to my great grandfather:

> 'The Resident will be glad to learn that on arrival in Begwad, the Bedar Rajah will find it convenient to wait on him.'

'And Ashokraj did not go,' my father once told me proudly. 'Instead, he sent a message that he would be waiting in his palace for the Resident to pay the first call. The fool! He lost his gadi. He was declared insane. I would have managed it quite differently. The fool! But perhaps he was a truer Bedar than the rest of us.'

I never found out exactly how he would have tackled such a situation himself. In my father's relationship with the British, there was no possibility of a 'situation' arising. Indeed towards the end he used to be referred to by the Viceroy as being one of the most loyal among the princes. In his time the ritual of the annual visits by the Political Agents, of who was to call upon whom first and walk how many paces to receive him, was firmly established. And if my father never accepted the position of vassal and overlord that these occasions tended to emphasize, he was careful to hide his feelings behind a screen of pleasantries.

I remember the durbar that was held for Colonel Gibson's visit early in 1938, if only for the contrast it provided with an informal visit made by him a year later. I had passed the matriculation examination from the Chelmsford College at Agra two years earlier and was a student at the degree college at Jubblepore which Kanakchand too attended. I was in my eighteenth year and down from college for the winter holidays when the Political Agent came to Begwad.

At the third milestone from the city Lala Harikishore, our Chief Minister, waited for the Political Agent's party, complete with a brass band and an escort of lancers. At the boundary itself it was Harikishore's privilege to welcome the guests and to garland them. From there they were escorted to our guest house. On the guest house itself, they used to fly the Union Jack during the P.A.'s visits, for the time being converting it into a tiny island of British India.

After giving them an hour to settle down, my father and I, accompanied by our principal courtiers, proceeded to the shamiana set up on the lawn in front of the guest house where the British party awaited us. At first the P.A.'s chief of staff, usually a British subaltern with family influence, would distribute betelnut and perfume to our side, taking care of the order of precedence, and whether he stopped with the Dewan and the two principal sardars or went further down the line to include some of the lesser courtiers was a matter of the utmost significance. After that it would be the turn of our own Chief Minister to distribute the paan and attar, taking care to ensure that the courtesies were scrupulously reciprocated.

I remember sitting by my father's side at that durbar in 1938, shivering slightly in my brocade achkan and feeling a little sorry for the Political Agent and his party who were dressed in white cotton uniforms, because it was one of those sharp winter mornings. I felt like a stranger on the lawn of our own guest house and thought how ridiculous it all seemed to be observing the archaic politenesses of more than a century and a half ago.

Only my father looked fully at home, indeed almost as though he were enjoying the formalities; for here, according to him, was a pageant of history, the scene of the first meeting between Hiroji Bedar and General Perkins being re-enacted in all its essentials, the treaty between two allies of equal strength being reiterated.

He loved pageantry, processions, ceremonials, and a Resident's or a Political Agent's visit was an unending round of small and big ceremonials. Even a tennis party or a walk in the garden was invested with an air of formality, with its own, correct, inflexible rules evolved as a result of a century and a half of trial and error, and to beat the P.A. at tennis or to double his wife's call at bridge would have constituted a major social error.

The only other point of contact we had with the British was during our various shoots and sporting meets. At such times there was little or no formality between my father and his guests.

They were all social equals, the rulers and the ruled, the white and the brown, joined together in the brotherhood of blood sport: the riding after pig or the hunting of tigers.

I suppose that it was as much a tribute to my father as to his shikar officer, Hanuman Singh, that the Viceroy had once remarked that our state could be depended upon to produce a shootable tiger.

'The Maharaja of Begwad is the only man in India who can guarantee a tiger,' His Excellency had said to one of his dinner guests. 'I mean really guarantee.'

And that casual remark of the Viceroy had caused a distinct stir among the princes; the competition for Viceregal approbation was always fierce, and His Excellency's singling out my father like that must have caused a lot of heartburn.

But it was quite true about the tigers; we certainly seemed to specialize in them. My father had always taken a quite unreasoning pride in his ability to provide tigers for his guests, and his organization, or what even his most casual visitors had learnt to call his 'bandobast' or just 'bando', was quite absurdly elaborate. He had reduced the business of finding tigers and getting them within shooting range of his guests to an almost infallible science.

'We just have to have something with which to hold our own,' he used to explain. 'I cannot afford a polo team … or a pack of hunting cheetahs.'

And it was well known that none of his guests missed his tiger. 'No guest of mine has ever lost his tiger,' my father used to say with a twinkle in his eye.

The result was that our state had acquired a special importance all its own. We had become recognized as one of the best states for shooting tigers, our reputation rivalling that of Rewa or Gwalior, and every year my father was called upon to play host to at least two or three important visitors from England.

Our state, lost in the depths of Padmakoshal, itself regarded as perhaps the most inaccessible part of India, consisted mainly of squat, serrated hills like crumbling graves in an abandoned graveyard, covered with impenetrable jungle which was once the hiding ground of the Pindaris and Thugs, the professional highwaymen of India; a lean and hungry land with a deceptive lushness given by the dark-green forest, sprawling on the north bank of the Kamra river like a hoary old crocodile lying in wait along a game trail.

Begwad was not one of the major Indian states, but it was an important one, carrying higher prestige and honours than its area or population or revenues may have warranted. Its ruler had a seventeen gun salute and the hereditary title of Maharaja, and both my father and grandfather had been knighted by the British as soon as they had ascended the gadi and also made honorary Colonels of the Awera rifles, whose men were recruited from Padmakoshal.

We had neither education nor industry, no roads to speak of, and only a single track railway line running from east to west. Ours was one of the least populated and the least developed states. Our income, which came mainly from agriculture and forest produce and which was just over ninety lakhs of rupees a year, was nowhere near that of the giants of the princely world, the twenty-one gunners. In the matter of gun salutes and similar honours, we were well down in the order of precedence. Of course, none of my ancestors had ever reconciled themselves to the ranking signified by the gun salutes, and indeed my father had consistently refused to take his seat in the Chamber of Princes in New Delhi because he would have had to cede precedence to some of the princes whom he had never considered his peers.

'What is Tilkatta?—the descendant of a water carrier! And mind you, the Nawab-sahib is a great friend of mine and of course, he is a very fine man; but we must not forget the fact that the first Nawab of Waranda was the Mughal Subhedar's coachman. How can we afford to be seen walking behind him?'

It was all so important to my father—as it was important to every Indian prince—who walked in front of whom. Rather than walk behind some of the others, he preferred not to go to the meetings of the Chamber at all, even though he could not very well decline to join it. He was a ruling prince and he had to become a member, whether he liked it or not; his seat with the crest of the double axe embroidered on the back was always there, waiting for him, placed exactly in the ranking order that the British had accorded him.

We had to have something with which to hold our own, as Father used to say. He had picked on tigers.

The matted jungle which surrounded our state had always been renowned as the tiger-land of India. Shaped like a crocodile, Begwad too had a soft belly and a horny upper crust, for once you got away from the river bed and the lush rice and sugar-cane belt in the Kamra valley, you entered the rugged mountain terrain, the Sattawan or 'fifty-seven' mountains, a thick, evergreen fastness criss-crossed with dry watercourses and studded with low, bleak islands formed by the hills. Even without being told, you knew that you were inside tiger country. It was almost unusual if one could not, on any given evening, hear the roar of a tiger from any one of our three shooting lodges.

And many of our tigers had not just strayed over the borders, they had been enticed into our territory.

My father always had one or two female tigers in his zoo, and during the mating season he would have these tigresses put into wheeled carriages and placed close to the known tiger jungles of our neighbours. Their mating calls would attract any male tiger within several miles, and once a tiger strayed into our forests, it was seldom permitted to leave. It was supplied with prime buffalo calves at regular intervals and kept happy and well fed and undisturbed. We always had at least half a dozen male tigers on hand.

In the light of today's values, such elaborate preparations just to provide a tiger for a visiting hunter must seem quite absurd, and the spending of the large sums of money involved positively sinful. And of course it was slightly inhuman to entice a wild animal through a mating call and then offer it to some casual visitor to shoot. At the same time, it was perhaps the only way in which the ruler of a state like Begwad could keep himself in the race for social recognition: Gwalior could feed five hundred guests on gold plate; Indore had French cooks and a cellar unsurpassed in the east; Jaipur its polo, Kolhapur its cheetah hunt, Bundi its palace fort; other states had their dancing girls, temples, cave paintings. Begwad just had to have some distinctive feature of its own.

'If it weren't for our tigers, we would never have any visitors at all,' my father used to explain. 'That is the only thing that we can give them that the other princes cannot: a tiger. Dammit, even the Viceroy has said I can guarantee a tiger!'

It was almost characteristic of my father that his inherited grievances against the Political Department or his extreme sensitivity in matters of prestige never manifested themselves in his behaviour towards the officials or the guests sent to him by them. Oddly enough, he had perhaps more personal friends among the officials than most other princes of comparable rank. They seemed to accept him at face value, the charming, enlightened prince who spoke English like an Englishman or almost like one, who entertained lavishly, and who, above all, could be relied upon to produce a tiger.

Our European guests were by no means confined to the tiger hunters. Many of them also came to our annual Christmas shoot at Tatwal. At times we had as many as two dozen 'guns' at the Tatwal jheel, mainly from amongst the officers of the Political Department and their wives. They stayed in the Tatwal shooting lodge and in the adjacent cottages for three days, firing at ducks until lunchtime from the camouflaged platforms in the middle of the jheel and drinking champagne every evening until, on 27 December, they trooped off to some other shoot organized for the New Year by some other Maharaja or Nawab.

During the rest of the year, they came in ones and twos. These were the tiger hunters, resolute men anxious to complete their 'big five' of Indian game before going off to Africa, even nursing a hope of getting their names in Rowland Ward's records, for did not Begwad have something of a reputation for the size of its tigers? And they went away happy, having bagged their tigers on schedule and having been treated to what was called a 'state banquet' in their honour, complete with gifts of lengths of himru brocade and Kashmir shawls and ivory statuettes for the ladies and gold and silver cigarette cases for the men.

They came and went, captivated by my father's simple, old-world dignity, his quaint eccentricities, his preoccupation with religion, his fasts in the midst of plenty, impressed by his prowess as a marksman, his skill as a rider, and above all by his clockwork bandobast for their shikar.

'Damn fine bando, Your Highness,' they would pronounce, and they would go back to wherever they came from and write bread and butter letters.

Only occasionally they would also go away shaking their heads in wonder at the sheer physical courage of their host. This was when any of them wounded a tiger. My father always took it upon himself to finish it off.

'It is my privilege—my privilege as your host, and I insist on it,' he used to tell them.

I have never been able to make out whether it was a display of sheer bravado or cold courage. Or was it some inner compulsion making him put his skill as a hunter so lightly to its highest test, this taking on of a wounded tiger? Whatever it was, it used to invest the shoot with a sense of stark drama, as though a game of tennis had suddenly transformed itself into a duel. At times his eagerness to go after a tiger wounded by a visitor, this casual risking of his life for a man of whom he had not even heard a few days earlier, made me wild with anger.

The rest of us would wait in the silent jungle, a small group of shikaris and hunters surrounded by uncertainty, helplessly watching my father go off following the blood-trail. He used to fling away his cigarette, break open the rifle to see that the cartridges were in, and march off, confident, businesslike, never looking back, never giving us a chance to wish him luck. He always got his tiger.

And, of course, the tiger always belonged to the guest, to whoever had drawn first blood—for those were the rules of the hunt.

My father was, without exception, the best marksman I have seen—and I have seen some really fine shots, including the late Nawab of Mansuba and both the Phippses who came to shoot with us from America. He was perhaps one of the half-dozen men in the country who could keep three loaders busy at a duck shoot, managing to get in five shots with three different shotguns, two-one-and-two-again, at each flight of duck. Most hunters consider themselves pretty fast if they can fire off four shots at a low flight of teal, two on the approach and two going away.

And his rifle shooting—it was in a class of its own. I have not seen Donald Ker or Syd Downey shooting at charging game, but I would have been prepared to back my father against either of them, or any of the other professional hunters you could name. Shooting was something of a passion with him, a release mechanism for his tensions, and he would go on firing shot after shot with his twenty-two Remington with the same concentration as I have seen other people display in playing the sitar or the piano, wholly oblivious to the world around him, finding an intense joy in the sheer mechanics of handling the rifle, of working the bolt in and out, of shouldering it and firing it. And the day he had signed the agreement calling upon him to abdicate some of his powers as a ruler, I saw him, without a single miss, hit twenty-three pice coins in succession as a servant threw them in the air.

But there I go, getting carried away whenever I think about my father, as though from a sense of unresolved guilt, as though now that he is dead I subconsciously seek to make amends for my lack of understanding while he lived; extolling what was no more than a facility with the rifle and the shotgun and, of course, the means to spend vast quantities of ammunition; in spite of myself, seeking to endow with glamour his excessive zest in the killing of tigers, his unabashed efforts to curry favour with the officials of the political department.

For, in a sense, even his 'bando' for the winter visitors the Government planted on him was nothing more than a well rehearsed, cleverly stage-managed show, something like the 'American style' wrestling, complete with groans and moans and the sound of tearing muscle and breaking bone, that we were subjected to at the end of the war.

The element of chance had been almost completely eliminated from our shoots, so that at times a visitor who had missed his shot completely found that he had managed to bag his tiger after all. This was, of course, done with great circumspection, so that there would be no possibility of the hunter himself discovering what was happening. My father would announce that the shikaris had seen that the tiger had been wounded by the hunter's bullet and that the trackers had gone off to follow the trail of blood. Then he would despatch Hanuman Singh to shoot another tiger with the same bore of rifle that the guest had been using. Of course all of us, those who were close to my father, knew exactly what was happening, for if the guest really had wounded the tiger, my father would never have permitted anyone else to follow it. It was only when he was convinced that the guest had missed his shot completely or made what was called a 'skin wound' that he magnanimously waived his privilege to follow the tiger.

Hanuman Singh would go off looking suitably glum, and that same day or the next, a tiger would be brought ceremoniously to the camp. Not even the most fussy hunter, the sort who probed the bullet holes in the carcasses, would have any reason to suspect that the tiger was not the one he had fired at.

And there was my father's own characteristic punctuation mark on every one of his tiger hunts, the ceremonial full-stop which, owing to the pictures in the *Bystander* and the *Field*, acquired so much currency that it even found its way into fiction and films: the measuring of the tigers between pegs.

All our guests had read about the various methods of measuring tigers and knew that the only precise method was the 'between pegs' method, which meant the distance between the pegs put into the ground touching the nose and the tip of the tail of the carcass. What none of them could have known was that my father, like several other princes I could name, always used a special hand-made tape measure for the tigers shot by his guests which could be relied upon to add at least an extra four inches to their lengths. After that, it was up to the skinners to stretch the skin to conform to the extra length.

But they were measured between pegs. My father saw to that personally, bustling about energetically and lending tone to the proceedings. He would chat lightheartedly to the guests, hazarding a guess as to the length and shaking his head slightly and saying that it was a pity that for all that length the head seemed a little on the small side.

Meanwhile, the shikaris and the beaters would clear the ground and stretch out the dead tiger and put down the first peg touching its nose. And then Hanuman Singh would come solemnly forward and announce:

'The first peg has been put down, Your Highness.'

'Good!' Father would beam. 'Let us put down our peg before proceeding further.'

The camp waiter would come forward, with ready poured pegs of whisky in little crystal tumblers and carrying bottles of soda water and a jug of plain iced water. Everyone would stand around the tiger and toast it while the photographer took pictures. After that my father would order them to put down the other peg.

'This is the only correct way of measuring a tiger—always between pegs. I have always believed that it adds a few inches to the measurement.'

He would laugh at his own joke, his infectious, childlike laugh, and it was almost impossible for those around him not to join in it. Then he would beckon to the waiter to bring the tape measure, and he would himself bend down and measure the distance between the pegs.

'Nine three!' he would announce triumphantly, or whatever the measurement was. 'Just as I had thought. Well, I was out only by an inch.'

Everyone would be served the second drink, and this time they would drink to the hunter, the second peg completing the process of measuring.

The days of the great shikaris were still very much with us. My father was undoubtedly one of them, a hunter of the Victorian school, the school of Selous and Leveson and Pretorious, obsessed with the idea that big game hunting was a career in itself, and one of the nobler careers at that, like soldiering; that at man's records of tigers, bears and elephants were somehow a measure of his manliness, and that getting one's name in Rowland Ward was as good as getting a new decoration from the Viceroy.

'I shall get there yet,' he used to say. 'I will break Lord Hardinge's record. What do you think, Hanuman?'

Hanuman Singh would shake his head glumly. 'Tigers don't grow to that size any longer, Maharaj,' he would point out. He was always the realist, so unlike the other courtiers.

Tigers were the major landmarks of my father's life. He often spoke of events as having taken place before or after he had shot a particular tiger. I can still hear him saying with that special glint in his eyes, which came on whenever he was talking of shikar or his heritage, that the Bihar earthquake had occurred just the day after he had shot the Ambewadi man eater, or that King Edward VIII had abdicated during the week he was trying to bag the Pilapani tigress.

He had shot his eightieth tiger on his fortieth birthday. The coincidence was too marked for him to leave it alone. He paid a visit to his astrologer and afterwards announced that he would restrict himself to two tigers every year and complete his hundred in his fiftieth year.

'None of my ancestors has lived to be fifty,' he would say. 'And no one has shot a hundred tigers, either. We are a shortlived clan, thank God! But I do want to live to fifty and I must shoot my hundred tigers. I shall break both records in the same year. Then I shall give up shooting.'

It seems that the astrologer had told him that he was not destined to shoot more than a hundred tigers. My father had great faith in his astrologer; at the same time, he did not want to give up tiger shooting altogether.

'Well, I shall just have to pick and choose them from now on; try only for the big ones—just two a year. And I am still hoping to beat the record.'

In the event, he never shot his hundredth tiger, nor did he get his name in Rowland Ward's book of records.

He never consciously tried to induce in me his passion for big game shooting, but all the same I was caught up by it. I am, at best, only an indifferent shot with the heavy rifle, but even today whenever I sit up at a tiger beat, my mouth becomes dry and my nerves tingle and my heart thumps against my ribs. Who am I to run down others caught up in the highest drama of the Indian jungle, the tiger hunt, for I still remember that when Hanuman Singh first brought the news of the tiger we later named the Kolarus Giant, my first thought was wholly selfish: how lucky it would be if it were to fall to my gun! And then suddenly I felt ashamed of myself, remembering my father's lifelong yearning for a record tiger.

We first came across his name early in 1939. It was eight years before he was finally shot.

My father was busy organizing a shoot for Lord Northwick who was what the Political Department used to term a 'Distinguished visitor'. It was said that he was to be the next Viceroy. He had been sent out to India as the chairman of the Minerals Commission to give him an opportunity to see the country before taking up office.

At first there had been an unscheduled visit by Colonel Gibson. He had sent a telegram saying he and his wife would drop in for tea and it had caused a flutter in my father's court. It was most unusual for a Political Agent to invite himself to tea unless he had news of major significance to convey, even perhaps a private reprimand from the Viceroy. What had gone wrong?

It was nearly six o'clock before they came. We received them in the European-style drawing-room on the ground fioor. My father was grumpy, anxious, suspicious. What did the sudden visit of the P.A. signify? I remember he was fasting that day because it happened to be the death anniversary of my grandfather.

'You must forgive me for not joining you,' he apologized. 'But Abhay is here to keep you company.'

This was the first time in three years that I happened to be home during the shooting season. I had received my bachelor of arts degree from the college at Jubblepore and my father was in communication with the Political Department to arrange for me to be sent to some progressive Indian state for training in administration.

'We still haven't heard from Delhi, but I'm sure it will be all right about Travancore,' Colonel Gibson said. 'Where do you want to go, Abbey?'

I was not particular where I was sent so long as I was going away from Begwad. 'Travancore will be all right,' I said.

The servants brought the tea things. Mrs. Gibson, who gushed politely over Tippu, my father's golden retriever, had a very long face and long, grey teeth. I thought she looked rather like a horse. Her husband had the reputation of being absolutely immune to bribes, and as though to underline it, his tweed jacket looked frayed at the elbows and her pearls were patently artificial. 'No milk, just a slice of lemon, thank you,' she told the A.D.C. brightly.

'And would you prefer milk or lemon, Colonel?' my father inquired.

I am sure that what the Colonel would have preferred was a whisky and soda, and that on any other visit he would have asked for it. Today he was being circumspect. He made a face and said: 'Milk will do fine. Never cared much for tea, myself.'

It was a game, stiff and formal, and I never understood its rules. He had said he was coming for tea, and my father was giving him tea. They were both out of their depths. The guest was uncomfortable because he had come to ask a somewhat unusual favour; his host feared that he had come to convey a reprimand from the Viceroy about the unhappy financial position of his state. They were both practised in the moves and countermoves of formal visits, and they both knew the easy familiarity of informal visits. This was a departure from both, an 'informal official visit'. What did it portend? We sat solemnly, sipping our tea with decorum, making small talk and avoiding each other's eyes in the room with the plush-covered Victorian furniture and the portraits of my ancestors in their ornate gilt frames.

But when the purpose of the visit became known, the skies cleared. My father immediately sent for the champagne which he had had kept on ice. By the time they were ready to leave, he was in wonderful form.

'Do tell me what you think of the caviar, Lady Gibson?' he asked. 'Mr. Moreton had it sent out.'

Mrs. Gibson expanded visibly under her tailor-made suit and I had a feeling that she was going to whinny. She fingered her bluey white pearls and sipped her champagne and bit daintily into the wedge of toast covered with caviar. 'Excellent!' she pronounced. 'But Your Highness must not address me as Lady Gibson, though Gladys Broom told me that you had addressed her as Lady Broom the last time they were here, and lo and behold, Percy was knighted in the New Year's list.'

'Your husband too will be knighted, mark my words,' Father assured her. 'They can hardly help giving Colonel Gibson a knighthood when we have given a tiger to the future Viceroy.'

Colonel Gibson had done his sounding and gone, and after that there was a series of letters from the Political Department in imposing blue-crested envelopes and finally one with the red crest of the Viceroy's house, thanking my father for offering to give a tiger to Lord Northwick.

Since Lord Northwick could not spare more than three days for the shoot, it was decided to dispense with the usual banquet and other formal entertainment and take him straight to the lodge at Shiparkota. There were at least three tigers in the Shiparkota jungles. There was no danger of His Lordship not getting his tiger.

It was nearly a year after my tiff with Father in the room with the tiger rug, but I still felt a bitterness towards him. He, on the other hand, was wholly relaxed and as jovial as ever from the very next time we met; for he had an amazing capacity to sublimate his real feelings, to hide his anger and displeasure, his frustrations and disappointments, behind a hard coating of purely artificial bonhomie. I could see that he was making a conscious effort to draw me into his own sphere of activities; as he told me, he was gradually preparing me for my responsibilities as the future ruler. He made me accompany him for his morning drives through the city when anyone who wanted to could stop our car and present a petition, and I had to sit by his side during his afternoon audience when any of his subjects who had a grievance would receive a hearing. I also had to go with him whenever he went inspecting the crops, chatting with the cultivators in their dialect and sharing their quite uneatable meals. Every now and then, we took time off for shikar.

My father was in a jubilant mood. 'What do you think of the Viceroy writing to us for a tiger?' he asked Lala Harikishore.

The old man's clean, catlike face broke into its practised smile and his spaniel-like eyes lit up as he gave my father the answer he expected.

'It is a great honour, Your Highness, a signal honour—quite unprecedented.'

My father beamed and nodded and pulled at his moustache, knowing there was more to come.

'All the twenty-one gunners will be jealous of His Highness,' Harikishore added.

'What do I care?' my father asked. 'I didn't go behind their backs to invite Lord Northwick.'

'And to think that the guest is none other than the future Viceroy himself—a signal honour for His Highness; and also nothing short of a slight to the other rulers.'

'What do you think, Abhay?' my father asked.

The courtiers and I never seemed to think alike, and of late it had become almost a matter of principle with me to disagree with them. 'I don't know, Dada,' I said. 'For one thing, this man Northwick may never become the Viceroy, and a three day shoot is going to cost us at least thirty thousand rupees.'

'Oh, money!' my father sneered. 'What is money? Think of the izzat, the honour! The future Viceroy himself as our guest for three whole days! What is money? The money is there to be spent.'

That was just it. As I could see it, the money was not there to be spent, and although I refrained from reminding my father about it, I turned to the Chief Minister and asked:

'Can you tell us, Lalaji, whether the state can afford to spend money on such lavish entertainments when the revenues are dropping?'

'The Yuwaraj has such an acute appreciation of financial matters,' Harikishore mumbled, bowing in my direction and with another smile on his shining face. He was an out-and-out courtier of the old order, polished, well-fed, oily, as faithful as a dog guaranteed not to bark or bite. He would never allow himself to be goaded into saying anything that would be regarded as critical of my father's administration.

'I can always find the money, Abhay,' my father said with an impatient gesture. 'It is not your money, dammit; not at the moment, anyway. Not until I die and you become the Maharaja.'

'Chhi-chhi!—what is His Highness saying!' the Chief Minister gasped, registering dismay and shock, and he slapped his own cheeks lightly as though to appease a malevolent providence lying in wait for such a challenge. It was a gesture like the Catholics crossing themselves.

My father could always find the money, as what Indian ruler could not? They had so much to offer as security, and were always regarded as fair game by the money-lenders of Bombay and Calcutta. But was it right to borrow money to buy yet another Rolls, or, indeed, to go about in a Rolls at all when the peasants could not afford sandals for their feet?

Money was the one thing he never understood. It was almost as though he had never reconciled himself to either his status or his purse. He seemed to nurse illusions of grandeur, spending money recklessly as though trying to live up to the riches of the Scindia or the Wadiar. He was competing out of his class. Both Gwalior or Mysore could have bought up the whole of our state merely from their reserve funds.

From our revenues of around ninety lakhs of rupees, my father was said to take no more than ten lakhs for his personal expenses. But this was a pure myth, preserved only for the vague scrutiny of the Political Department. In any case, all palace servants and the personnel of the shikar department were not included in my father's personal budget. Throughout the years of the depression my father had steadily borrowed money from the Marwaris, while the revenues dropped by nearly a third; his expenses, on the other hand, had risen considerably, and for some time he had been spending as much as a fourth of our total income on himself. There had even been one or two ominous references to a commission of inquiry being appointed by the Political Department to go into the finances of the state. But before these talks gathered momentum, the national agitation had spread all over the country like wild-fire and the Political Department had become surprisingly lenient towards the princes. There was no question of their making a fuss about the extravagance of a prince who was known to be staunchly loyal.

It was later, during the war years, that the soaring prices of timber and grain restored the prosperity of our state, but at the time of Lord Northwick's visit, early in 1939, our finances were in a sad mess.

It did not seem to distress my father unduly, however, and he bustled about making his 'bando' for Lord Northwick's shoot with his customary zeal. Every other day there were prolonged conferences with Hanuman Singh and the shikaris. My father seemed to regard the forthcoming visit as a sort of test, a challenge to his reputation as a provider of tigers.

As I said, that was the first time that we heard of the Kolaras Giant. He had come across the river from the high forest of Kolaras, drawn, as usual, by the mating calls of one of our tigresses. I still remember Hanuman Singh's expression as he was telling us about the tiger.

'He is the biggest I have seen, a real giant,' Hanuman Singh said. 'I saw the pugmarks about a week ago. They were as big as palas leaves. I know that he must be an enormous tiger. But I did not want to come and say anything until I had actually seen him myself. I did so this morning.'

If I had not known what a simple soul he was, I would have thought he was trying to be dramatic.

'He is a giant all right,' Hanuman Singh went on. 'He should measure up to Lord Hardinge's tiger any day.'

'Is he going to exceed eleven feet?' I asked.

'Nearer twelve than eleven, Yuwaraj,' he told me.

'Between pegs?' my father asked.

'It doesn't matter between how many pegs, Your Highness,' Hanuman Singh said.

'Well, we do seem to have found the right tiger for the future Viceroy,' my father said. 'So you think he will go into Rowland Ward?'

'Maharaj, I am telling you he is a giant. He will not only go into Ward's, I will be surprised if he does not top the list.'

'What fun if Lord Northwick were to break Lord Hardinge's record even before he becomes Viceroy ...'

'I personally don't think we should waste this tiger on Lord Northwick, Your Highness,' Hanuman Singh said. 'Considering that it is going to be one of the biggest. He should be shot by Your Highness or the Yuwaraj.' And he gave me a smile.

That was what I had been thinking. If the tiger was as big as Hanuman said, it was only fair that my father should have a shot at him himself.

'We should not waste him on a guest, Your Highness,' Hanuman Singh said again.

'Yes,' I said. 'Why should you not shoot him yourself, Dada? Now is your chance to beat the record.'

'No,' my father said with emphasis. 'If it is Lord Northwick's nasib to break the record, let him have it. Why should the tiger have turned up just when we're going to have a guest? It is nasib. It is much more important to be giving up a tiger for a guest ... much more hospitable.'

At the time, I did not altogether trust his argument about the demands of hospitality. I suspected that his chief motive was to keep on the right side of the incoming Viceroy so that he could try to secure greater privileges and honours during his regime. Now I am not so sure. He was a great believer in nasib—fate. He must have been torn between his lifelong desire to better the tiger record and the thought of the prestige inherent in giving a record tiger to the incoming Viceroy, and had left the decision to nasib.

Lord Northwick came and went, but he did not shoot the giant ... it was not in his nasib, just as it was not in his nasib to become the Viceroy of India because of the advent of war. But the tiger was in the beat all right during his shoot, and he came right up to the 'stop' machaan where my father and I were sitting. As I saw him, I tingled with excitement, knowing that before me was perhaps the biggest tiger that anyone had ever seen in a hundred years. My father gently tapped the tree with his cane, trying to guide the tiger to Lord Northwick's machaan. The tiger jerked his head in surprise and gave a low, rumbling growl. Instead of changing his direction, he turned right back into the beat, and a minute or so later, we heard the clamour of the beaters as he broke through their line and escaped.

It was eight years before he was to come into our forests again.

We had both seen him, my father and I, and we were both speechless for a time, awed by his sheer size, his magnificent head, his glowing beard, his rippling skin. It was like going into a room and being confronted by a dazzlingly lovely woman, or looking at a painting by a great master. It made you catch your breath.

My father was the first to recover. 'Very jumpy,' he said. 'Must have been fired at before. Pity it is not in Lord Northwick's nasib to break the record.'

But it was not difficult to find another tiger for him. In the next day's beat, he managed to shoot quite a good specimen. Between pegs and measured with my father's special tape measure, it was nine feet and eleven inches, which is almost exceptional as tigers go these days.

10

'Don't Forget the Knuckle Duster'

During the summer of nineteen thirty-nine, I had improved my backhand considerably, practising with Gonsalves whenever I got the chance, and I was all ready for the tournament at Mussorie. After that I was going to Travancore for administrative training under the Dewan, Sir C.P. Ramaswamy Iyer. My father had been very pleased.

'Sir C.P. is the greatest statesman in India,' he told me. 'He is a realist, not a radical like the white-cap wallas whose only thought is to destroy us and devour us—they hate the princes worse than the British.'

For my part, I was looking forward to an interlude at the seaside, surf-riding and fishing off a catamaran or just lying on the white sands under the palms. I have always loved the seaside with the special fervour of the land-locked.

From now on, my future had a regulated simplicity about it. I knew that after finishing my administrative training I would be sent on an instructional tour of India, accompanied by at least two guardians, taking in all the places of pilgrimage, and then a tour of Europe in the company of Mr. Moreton. After that there was nothing to look forward to except to spend my time playing games and riding and hunting until, barring accidents, I became the Maharaja of Begwad.

I was also aware that my father was trying to find a bride for me. He had not said anything to me about it, but from his talks with Lala Harikishore and the other courtiers close to him, I knew that he was running into the usual resistance on the part of the high-born Rajput and Maratha princely families to marrying into our house.

Then came the war, like a world-wide fire alarm, shattering the pattern of living. My father greeted its advent with signs of unmitigated relief. As far as he was concerned, the war could not have come at a more opportune moment, for it rang the death knell of the scheme for the federation of India under which the princes were required to introduce drastic political reforms within their states. Most princes had regarded the federation as an imposition, a betrayal of their treaties. The war had come to their rescue.

For the whole week, as the talk of war gathered momentum, my father had been busy exchanging wires and emissaries with his friends amongst the princes, and between them they had worked out the wording of the telegram they were going to send to the Viceroy the moment the actual declaration of war came out.

I was with my father in the billiard room when we heard Neville Chamberlain's broadcast telling the world that we were at war with Germany. My father sent for his secretary and dashed off the agreed telegram to the Viceroy, ordered another whisky and soda and resumed his interrupted game. As far as he was concerned, he was done with the war: he had demonstrated his loyalty, he had formally placed the entire resources of the state at the disposal of the Viceroy. Now he could shake the war off his shoulders.

What my father had done was exactly what all the other major princes had done. It was no more than a meaningless formality indulged in by the princes as a kind of insurance against the taint of disloyalty: if any one of them had not sent the expected telegram to the Viceroy, it would have singled him out as not conforming to the pattern approved by the Political Department. It was something like a ritual, no more than a display of a hallmark to establish proof of good behaviour.

My own reaction was equally uncomplicated. I lay awake for some time that night, conscious that the war had broken the pattern of my life too, and thinking out my plans. Almost inevitably, I kept asking myself what the Head would have wanted me to do. Before

I went to sleep, I made up my mind to apply for a commission in the army. In the morning, as soon as I was dressed, I drove to Purangad, forty-two miles away, to call at the Residency to see the Political Agent. Colonel Gibson was in the garden telling his mali about weeding the lawn and planting the border. He invited me to join him for breakfast.

There was no talk of war here, no excitement; everything was as it always had been, unruffled. Was it sheer, bovine insensitivity, or a glimpse of the proverbial British phlegm, a show of business-as-usual under stress? I wondered about this as they went through porridge, enormous helpings of scrambled eggs and bacon, toast, marmalade, coffee and fruit. The only reference to the war was indirect.

'The rain has killed all the phlox,' the Colonel complained to his wife. 'But the geraniums have survived.'

'I was worried about the sweet peas,' she said. 'But they seem to be doing all right.'

'And I don't know what Gajanan has done to the lawn, it's full of patches,' the Colonel said, slapping butter on his toast.

'That happened when all those convicts came to do the weeding,' his wife said. 'Trampling all over the place in their boots.'

'That weed-killer we got here is no earthly good,' he said, 'We'll have to get a tin of Higgins's stuff, the same as we did last year. Though how any more weed-killer is going to come out here now that there is a war on … !'

'I think there is still a tin in the go-down.'

'Really! A full tin?' The Colonel beamed. 'Oh, good!'

It was only after he had finished breakfast and lit his pipe and his wife had gone indoors, presumably to look for the tin of Higgins's weed-killer, that I could tell him why I had come to see him. He was genuinely pleased.

'Jolly good show!' he pronounced. 'Jolly good! What do you think, Nancy, Abbey here wants to do?' he yelled. 'He wants to join up.'

'Jolly good show!' his wife yelled back from an inner room.

'You will have to obtain His Highness's agreement,' I said. Colonel Gibson raised his eyebrows and gave me a long stare.

'You mean you haven't told your father?'

'No.'

'Why not?'

'Well, sir, I didn't know how he would react.'

'Hmmm … how old are you, Abbey?'

I had just passed my eighteenth birthday, but if you counted the years according to the Hindu calendar, I was nearly nineteen. 'Nearly twenty, sir,' I told him.

'Oh, I expect it will be all right. I'm sure I'll be able to sort it out with the M'raja. I think he will be very pleased. What regiment were you thinking of joining?'

'I have not given it a thought, as yet. But it will have to be some cavalry regiment—perhaps the Royal Deccan Horse.'

'The R.D.H. Oh, yes, fine regiment, the Deccan Horse.'

'It'll just have to be some cavalry regiment,' I said. 'The only thing I know anything about is riding.'

'Well, you'll have to think about that. No use going anywhere where one can't fit in—it can be murder.' He shook his head reminiscently. 'You'll have to go up before an interview board, of course, up in Simla. Then they'll send you on a course of training.'

'If they select me, sir.'

'Oh, they'll take you in all right,' Colonel Gibson assured me.

Almost surprisingly, my father did not raise any difficulty. 'So you want to go and become an officer,' he said.

'I want to get into the fighting,' I said.

'Oh, I see,' my father said, and I could see the faint look of disapproval on his face. 'The Germans are excellent fighters. It seems such a waste, their being on the wrong side, because we have nothing against the Germans. If one had to fight, one should be fighting the British—the British and the nationalists. Why should you—any of us—get into this war? It is not our war. We can give help. Money, recruits.'

I did not say anything.

'What happens to the succession, to the gadi, if you … if something were to happen to you?'

There were several answers I could have given. Father was barely forty, young enough to have another son. Even if he considered himself separated from my mother, he could always get married again. Or he could have adopted someone, perhaps his own son, Charudutt. But at the time, the problem of what would happen to the succession if I were to be killed did not bother me in the least.

'Well, I suppose you just have to go, if you've made up your mind. I would not have objected … it was not necessary to get the P.A. on your side first. But it's a waste. It is not our war.'

'I am so glad you aren't annoyed,' I said.

'Of course I'm not! If you feel you must join up, I suppose you just have to go. The Bedars have always been soldiers. I don't suppose you can keep them out of a war.'

He paused for a few seconds and then added: 'I am proud of you, my son. I am proud, even if it is so unnecessary for you to join up.'

It was not until March 1940 that I received a call to appear before the interview board at Simla.

I went to Simla a whole week in advance. My father wanted me to stay at the Maharaja of Tilkatta's bungalow on Curtis avenue, where he himself stayed whenever he visited Simla, but when I told him I would prefer to stay at a hotel, he had compromised by booking a suite of rooms for me at the Cecil Hotel.

That visit to Simla, and in particular my staying at the Cecil, changed the entire course of my life. It was at Simla that I met Minnie and Punch.

I went to Simla early because I wanted to order one or two suits from Ranken. Hitherto, at home and even at school and college, I had mostly always worn Indian dress; whenever I had worn

European clothes, it was usually grey flannel trousers and tweed jackets or blazers. I also wanted to get used to the complexities of wearing a hat, for when to take off one's hat and when to keep it on could be quite complicated to someone who had been brought up in a society where to keep your head uncovered in company was regarded as impolite. The only hats I had worn were riding helmets and topees, and although Mr. Moreton had given me detailed instructions about when to remove my hat and when to keep it on, I remembered his instructions only vaguely.

I chose a plain, light-grey worsted flannel for my interview suit and a darker one with a faint chalk stripe for the evenings. Then I went into Phelps to buy my hat. After I had tried out a dozen or so, I chose a dark-brown felt made by Lincoln Bennet.

'It is a fine hat, sir,' the assistant said. 'Aztec brown, the latest shade.'

'I like it,' I told him.

'All it needs now is wearing, to break it in.'

I knew that a hat, even when paid for, does not really belong to one. You have to turn down the brim exactly as you like it and punch the crown just so and give it a special shape of your own before it really becomes yours.

'I'll start breaking it in right away,' I told the assistant. 'No, don't bother to wrap it.'

I came out on the Mall, wearing my new felt hat and carrying my pith topee under my arm and stood on the pavement, conscious for the first time of the snap of spring in the air. The Mall went curving off on both sides until it was swallowed up by the hillside, the bright, glass-fronted, pink-roofed shops merging smoothly into the wet, sparkling landscape. The rhododendrons made poster-red patches in the dark forest; the horse-chestnuts and cherry trees were dripping with blossom; and the blue pines of Simla looked bluer than ever. The mountains were rainwashed, the sky was a bright blue and the air was stiff with the scent of pine and flowers and charged with an almost electric silence broken by the sharp warnings of the rickshaw pullers.

They had gone to a good deal of trouble to preserve the old-world charm and dignity of Simla, for they had banned all motor vehicles and forbidden indiscriminate building. They had succeeded. The British certainly knew all about resisting change. It was spring in the Himalayas, and Simla was exactly as it had been fifty years ago or a hundred, and Mrs. Hauksbee might have been living just around the corner.

I felt a little self-conscious, carrying a spare hat in my hands, and I laughed to myself as out of nowhere the words of the Head came back to me. 'A gentleman never carries anything, except perhaps a walking stick.' He certainly does not carry a spare hat, I thought. I beckoned to one of the hamals loitering on the sidewalk with their enormous bamboo baskets and gave him my sun hat to carry.

I was purely indulging a whim, deliberately letting myself be carried away by a mood that had seized me as I walked along the Mall that spring morning, followed by a grinning Garhwali coolie carrying my hat in his basket, when I became aware of the man and woman passing on two unkempt, donkey-sized tattoos. The girl was mounted on an elderly hack, heavy-boned and coarse-grained, but I had no doubt that it was guaranteed to be sure-footed. I remember thinking that that was the one quality above all she must have prized in her mount, for she looked nervous and insecure, flustered and tight-lipped with concentration. The man with her was square-jawed and blunt-nosed and he had a fierce, orange-coloured moustache. Bare-headed and tweed-coated, he wore a regimental tie, and sat slumped on his overweight chestnut with the clumsy heaviness of a bridegroom on a borrowed-for-the-occasion pony.

'Beauty and the beast,' I remember saying to myself. 'Beauty and the beast riding by on Simla tatts.'

For some reason I cannot explain, I could not drag my eyes away from the girl, for she was by no means beautiful. She sat awkwardly on her pony as though afraid of slipping off any minute, gripping the sides with her thighs and legs and yet showing a lot of light under her knees. Her face was flushed, her nose was shining and her hair was disarrayed. But I could feel that she was somehow a part of the morning, of the verve and vitality of spring, volatile and blooming, and she was slim as a bamboo and fresh as the morning dew. As the sunlight glanced off her corn-gold hair, I went on looking at her, her femininity and helplessness a challenge to my youth. I stared until she happened to turn her face and look straight into my eyes.

I turned my gaze and looked into a shop window. There was a display of Kashmir shawls, furs, carpets and carved wooden trays and tables. In the glass I could also see the two riders now directly behind me, their ponies clop-clopping on the tarred surface of the road. I was bending right down, peering into the design of a carpet when I heard the man give a snort and say to the girl: 'Do you see what I see?'

I did not hear what the girl said, but I heard the man's next remark. 'Christ! A coolie to carry a blinking hat, I ask you!' And he gave another contemptuous snort.

The girl laughed. Her laughter was like the tinkle of sheep bells along a mountain path, but what I felt then was its cutting edge, sharp as a kukri. I turned back in sudden anger and met her eyes again, derisive and mocking. She was laughing with her head thrown back and her mouth had a delicious downward curve and her teeth were strong and even.

I took in the details of her figure, hard, slim, supple, and once again I was hit by that quality in her, the earthy sensuousness, the glow in her dark, half-Mongol face. At the time I did not think that she was either beautiful or appealing. My only feeling was one of anger and annoyance, and yet she must have left a wealth of desire somewhere within me.

Somewhat self-consciously, the man spurred his pony into a laboured trot and the girl followed suit, bending forward and hugging her mount's neck. I remember noticing that her yellow shirt was dark with perspiration under the arms and the way her brown elbows jutted out as she grabbed hold of the mane.

I stared at the pair until they had turned the corner and gone from my view.

That evening I went to see a film and on the way back to the hotel, I dropped into the old Gallico where the Handloom House now stands. The Gallico was a bar and grill of the more expensive variety, with soft music and subdued lighting. I handed my hat to the girl outside and walked in. It was only when I had reached the bar and perched myself on a stool that I noticed the man and woman I had seen riding in the morning. They were sitting on a sofa along the wall, quite close to the bar, and as I happened to look at them, they exchanged meaning glances; the girl smiled and the man twirled his flame-coloured moustache, shrugged and gave a barely audible snort.

I felt a little self-conscious, wondering if they were thinking that I had followed them into Gallico's, but I knew it would have been too pointed to leave the bar and go. I ordered a small bottle of beer and a packet of Gold Flake, and I sat smoking and sipping the cold beer, looking fixedly at the array of bottles in front and at my own reflection in the glass.

And as I sat there, alone and slightly self-conscious, three men in police uniforms came and occupied stools at the other end of the bar. They were talking loudly and slapping one another's backs as though celebrating something. One of the three men was Abdulla Jan, and I soon discovered what it was they were celebrating. Abdulla Jan had been promoted from an Inspector to a Deputy Superintendent.

He must have seen me even before I saw him, for in the glass I saw him nudge his friends so that they both turned their heads to look at me.

'Three double whiskies!' Abdulla Jan ordered.

There was no question of leaving now, for that would have made Abdulla Jan think I was running away from him. I ordered another half-bottle of beer. Only once I glanced at the man and woman sitting close together on the sofa, and I noticed that under the table, he had locked his ankle round hers.

Abdulla Jan and his friends seemed to be talking about me and my parents, for their voices were lowered and every now and then they glanced in my direction. I took time over my beer, and then asked for my bill and paid it. I pulled out my watch and looked at the time. It was five minutes to nine.

In the glass I could see Abdulla Jan's face, with its leer slightly exaggerated by the reflection, and he was telling his friends something which they must have found vastly entertaining. He tossed down his drink and ordered another three double whiskies. Then he dug his hand into his trousers' pocket and brought out his watch and placed it on the counter with something of a flourish. I could not help noticing that it was a large, gold watch, and then with a catch I saw that it was the exact twin of my own half-hunter which my mother had given me.

'Arre, what a fine watch, waah-waah!' said one of his friends. He picked it up and turned it in his hands. 'Was this another present from your Maharaj?' he asked.

Abdulla Jan smiled his crooked, meaning smile. 'No, not the Maharaja,' he told them. 'The Maharani.' And he gave a broad wink.

Both his friends burst into guffaws and slapped him on the back. 'You are a great one for the bibies, arre waah! Even a Maharani,' one said.

'Yes, the Maharani gave it, for services rendered,' Abdulla Jan said, and he gave another wink.

All three of them roared with laughter and their shoulders shook.

I pushed back my bar stool and pounced on Abdulla Jan. I held him by the collar and pushed him away with all my strength. He toppled slowly back, stool and all, and fell into the table behind which the Englishman with the orange moustache and his girl were sitting. The man said 'Christ!' and jumped to his feet, and I saw the quick flush of alarm on the girl's face.

I was still looking at Abdulla Jan, waiting for him to get up, when one of his friends crashed his elbow into my stomach from the side and the other gave me a sharp clip on the temple with the edge of his hand, making me wince with pain.

'Not both of you at the same time, damn it!' the Englishman shouted. 'Not both, blast you!' And he roughly pulled back the man who had hit me on the temple, leaving me to tackle the one who had hit me in the stomach. He was a small, weedy man. I made a neat job of him, taking my time, measuring the distance. I slammed a right and a left at his face and side that would have won approval from the Head himself.

'Attaboy!' the Englishman said.

There was commotion all round. The man with the orange moustache was standing on one side of me and the girl on the other. Abdulla Jan and his friends were glowering at me from near the wall. I knew that they would all have come charging into me if it had not been for the man standing by my side. In the India of the British, no policeman would have dared to attack an Englishman.

'Any more for any more?' my unknown helper was saying, now with a lot of amusement in his voice. 'One at a time, only one at a time!'

The pain in my stomach was like a fire, my left eye was throbbing and I had a feeling that I had had enough. I was thankful that the game had suddenly been subjected to rules with an Englishman to see that they were observed, and I hoped that no one was coming for any more.

'Come on, let's get you out of here,' the Englishman said. 'They won't play.'

He clutched me by the elbow and the girl took my other hand and we marched into the cool night.

'I have to go back and collect my hat,' I suddenly remembered.

'Oh, forget your bloody hat,' he snapped.

'Let's get away from here, first,' the girl said.

'My god, you have a nerve, tackling three policemen in a bar! Come on, let's get somewhere we can assess the damage. Your eye looks quite bad.'

'Let's go to the Cecil,' I offered. 'It's quite close by.'

'Have you a room there?'

'Yes.'

'What did I tell you,' the man said to the girl.

As soon as we got in, the girl put a cold compress on my eye and her fingers felt cool on my face. The man sent to the kitchen for a piece of raw meat. It was good to be amongst friends, even new-found ones whose names I did not know, even with a bunged-up eye and a stomach burning with pain. I lay back on the bed with the raw meat pressed to my eye, while the man and the girl sat smoking cigarettes. Behind them I could see through the open window the moonlit peaks of the Himalayas, from Bandar punch to Trisuli.

'Oh, do please order a drink,' I said. 'Whatever you would like.'

'I should love whisky,' the man said. 'I'll get hold of a waiter. What about you?'

My stomach was aching all over and I was beginning to feel queasy. 'I think I'd like some champagne,' I said. 'That's about the only drink I'll be able to keep down.'

'Is the pain very bad?' Minnie asked, although, of course, I had not begun to think of her as Minnie then.

'It's a dull pain, sort of spread all over,' I told her. 'I'll go and get hold of a waiter,' the man said.

Minnie sat on the sofa, still looking flushed and a little anxious, her teeth pressing her lower lip. I had to prevent myself from staring at her with my working eye, and then I heard her chuckling to herself.

'What is it?' I asked.

'That business about the hat ... getting a coolie to carry a second hat. One for the sun and the other when there is shade, Punch said. He says someone told him you were a prince.' She stopped laughing and gave me a level look, cool and bold, as though she was studying my face. I squirmed at the thought of the red meat stuck to my eye.

'Well, are you?' she asked.

'Am I what?'

'I mean are you a prince?'

'Sort of a prince. The son of one, anyway,' I said. 'But please don't hold that against me—and the other hat was not for the sun.'

'No?' Minnie said and she laughed again. 'Well, it's nice to know a prince—even a sort of one. What do they call you?'

'Abhay-raj,' I told her.

'Abhay-raj,' Minnie said after me.

Punch came back with a waiter carrying a tray with a bottle of champagne and glasses, and Minnie said: 'You were quite right. He is a prince.'

'Oh,' Punch said. 'I expect you have to be one to be able to afford the Buckingham suite in this place. And what are you doing in Simla?'

'I have come to be interviewed by a board for a commission in the army,' I told him.

'You can't go before a board with a bunged-up eye,' Minnie said.

Punch opened the champagne and poured it into the glasses. 'What had those men been up to?' he asked. 'Or is one not supposed to ask?'

'I'd much rather not say,' I said.

'They should have known better than to tangle with someone with a busted nose.'

'A prince with a busted nose,' Minnie said.

'It certainly was a neat job, particularly the little fellow with the blue chin—crack-crack! Look, have you decided what regiment you are going to join, Scrapper?'

My eye was throbbing quite wildly under the steak, and I was getting slightly groggy. But the champagne felt cool in my throat.

'It will have to be a cavalry regiment, perhaps the Royal Deccan Horse,' I said.

'Cavalry!' Punch gave a snort. 'Oh, my God! Why do you princes always rush into Cavalry regiments?'

'Well, the only thing we can do tolerably well is ride.'

'Riding? Horse riding?'

'That's right.'

'Is that why you are going into the R.D.H.?'

'If they will accept me.'

'Then forget it, chum, the cavalry rides horses no more.' And Punch gave a snort.

'No?'

'No. They go to war in little death-traps called tanks. Steel coffins. The bloody cavalry is all mechanized, don't you know? The

Deccan Horse is mechanized. The tanks smell of petrol and grease and burning rubber, and the tracks get overheated every few miles and fall apart and you wait in the middle of the desert like sitting ducks and Jerry comes in the middle of the night and lobs a grenade right down the little manhole and bang!—roast prince in a lancer uniform.'

'Ugh!' Minnie said and made a face.

'And I don't suppose you want to go through the show warming a chair in some H.Q., do you? I expect you want to see some fun.'

'Fun' he had called it, and the war was a 'show'. He looked like a bulldog, tough and ferocious, who got into fights for fun. That was what warfare was to him.

'Oh, I certainly want to see the fun,' I said. 'No chair.' My head was feeling very light.

'Attaboy!' Punch said, and poured another round of champagne. 'Then you keep close to me. You get into the Satpuras, and by Jove, you'll see all the action you want. Already got two battalions in the Middle East.'

He was sounding a little far away, a voice in the distance, ambling away like background music, and I was trying my best not to pass out. 'Why, thanks,' I said. 'Thank you very much. What regiment did you say?'

'The Satpuras. The fighting tigers. Don't tell me you haven't heard of the Satpura Rifles.'

I had never heard of the Satpuras. I shook my head. It was feeling strangely light and I wanted to laugh.

'Haven't heard of the Satpuras—and you want to join the army!'

His voice was getting fainter and the lights were getting blurred. The clout on the head had a kind of delayed action. The pain was now worse than ever in quiet persistent throbs. I made an effort to gather my wits. I gulped down the champagne. It seemed to help, but I still wanted to laugh.

'No, I hadn't but I am going to join the Satpuras all the same. The Satpura Rifles, if you say so, sir, Mr. …'

'Captain Farren, sir, Captain Cedric Farren of the Satpura Rifles, at your service,' he introduced himself with a formal, almost German heel click, and Minnie was laughing her bell-like laugh and heaven was only an arm's length away even though I did not know which was hurting worse, my eye or my stomach.

'"Punch" to his friends, sir,' Punch was saying.

I began to chuckle, as though from some release mechanism, and I could not stop myself, even though I wanted to.

'What's the matter?' Minnie said. 'Are you all right?'

'You two on the Simla tatts, riding by,' I said between gasps.

'Like … like Don Quixote and his wife; Captain and Mrs. Cedric Farren of the Satpuras. "Punch" to his friends …'

I stopped chuckling, knowing something was amiss. I did not know anything about wedding rings in those days; there are no wedding rings amongst Hindus.

'Not Captain and Mrs.,' Punch explained carefully. 'Captain Farren and Miss Bradley, Miss Minnie Bradley.'

'Oh, Miss,' I said. 'Oh, Miss,' and I began to giggle once again.

For the next three days, until Punch finished his ten days' casual leave from his regiment, I saw a lot of him and Minnie, and I must say that although they seemed to be for ever kissing each other at the slightest pretext and holding hands under tables, they did not make me feel like an outsider. We would meet for lunch at Davico's or Wenger's and then we would go for a stroll or see a film. In the evenings they came to my hotel, and after a drink or two in my room went off hand in hand into the night. The nights were their own, and I was careful not to intrude.

'Don't go wandering all by yourself in the dark,' Punch had warned me. 'Now that you have managed to range the Simla police against you.'

I laughed at his fears, but he was quite serious. 'Matter of fact, I had better get someone to speak to the police boss here to see that you're not molested. I'll get Barraclough on the job.'

'Oh, please don't bother,' I said. 'I can take care of myself.'

Punch snorted. 'You don't know the Indian police.'

'Who is Barraclough?' I asked.

'Don't you know anyone in Simla at all? Bill Barraclough is one of the Governor's A.D.C.s. I can even wangle an invitation for you for a Government House party.'

I did not particularly want to go to a Government House party, but Punch was as good as his word about getting Bill Barraclough on the job, and the next time we met he told me that Bill had rung up the police superintendent to see that none of his officials gave me any trouble. 'I told Bill to lay it on thick,' Punch told me.

After Punch went away I was on my own. I knew that Minnie had some sort of a job in a government office and lived in the Miranda House hostel, but I would never have thought of asking her to come out with me. I spent the next two days mostly in my room. By the time the interview came on, I was determined to join no other regiment but the Satpuras.

My left eye was still quite black when I went for my interview, but no one seemed to worry about it. The President of the board, a polite, mild-mannered man with mousy grey hair and a wispy, smoke-stained moustache, talked to me about riding and shooting and asked solicitously how close my father had come to shooting the record tiger, and none of the other members had anything much to say after that.

It was on the evening of the day of my interview that Minnie rang up. I remember there must have been something wrong with the room connection for I could not hear her very well.

'How did the interview go?' she wanted to know.

'Very well,' I told her. 'Oh, very well indeed.'

'They didn't say anything about your eye, did they?'

'What? No, no, they did not say anything about the eye.' Minnie had been a part of the team, and now when she was speaking to me I felt awkward for no reason at all, and slightly disloyal to Punch.

'Well, I'm glad you got through,' she said. 'Just wanted to ring up and find out.'

'I'm glad too,' I said. 'It was nice of you to ring up.'

She laughed. 'No more fights with the police?'

'No, no more fights.'

'I was wondering what had happened to you … if you had actually gone away without even saying good-bye.'

'No,' I said. 'I haven't gone. Leaving tomorrow.'

'Oh, tomorrow,' Minnie said

'It was nice of you to ring,' I told her again.

'Just wanted to find out about the interview,' she said.

'Look,' I said. 'Do you think you could … that is, we could meet somewhere this evening?—have dinner somewhere?' I had not meant to ask Minnie to come out with me, it just seemed to come over me as I was speaking to her over the telephone.

She laughed and then she was silent for a long time. I thought she had not heard me properly. I had hardly given her a thought that day, but all at once it had become urgent that I should see her.

'I was saying, couldn't we have dinner together somewhere this evening?' I said. 'Considering I am going tomorrow.'

'Well, we could,' she said, 'considering you are leaving tomorrow,' and she laughed again. 'Where?'

'What about Gallico's?' I said, 'I have to retrieve my hat.'

'Your what? Oh, my God!' she said. 'Yes, Gallico's will be all right. I will bring my knuckle duster!'

'You will bring your what?'

'Oh, never mind,' she said, and laughed again. I have often wondered if I hadn't already fallen in love with Minnie Bradley.

11

'Come Again, Highness'

I had never taken a girl out before, and I was nervous as I waited for Minnie that evening. And when she walked into the foyer of the Cecil, dressed in a bare-shouldered, almost backless evening dress, her mobile face eager and smiling, the thought struck me that I had no business to be seeing her alone like this, with Punch gone away.

'Would you like a drink?' I asked.

She peered at me with those mocking, light brown eyes of hers. 'You mean down here?' she said.

'Yes, in the lounge.'

'Well, no; no, thank you.' She shook her head and the roll of her soft, corn-gold hair swayed from side to side on her naked shoulders.

'Your eye looks perfectly all right, now,' she said, 'Well, almost. Does it still hurt?'

I told her that it didn't hurt at all. 'Shall we go in rickshaws?' I asked.

'No, I'd like to walk. It's just around the corner. I'd just like to powder. Can't we … can't we go up to your room?'

'Why, certainly,' I said.

The lift man touched his cap and gave me a rather meaning look as he closed the door, and when we stepped out of the lift, the room boy threw open the door of my suite with something of a flourish and disappeared.

We were all alone, in the darkness of my room, with the view of the moonlit Himalayas through the open window. I could smell the perfume she wore.

'Wait,' I said. 'Let me put on the light.'

I went in and groped for the switch and Minnie followed. She stood close to me, her hair brushing my face lightly, and suddenly I did not want to find the switch at all but gather her in my arms and hold her close. But I found the switch all the same, flicked it down, and wondered whether I was right in thinking there was a shade of disappointment in Minnie's expression.

I took care to leave the outer door open while Minnie was making up her face. She came out, looking just as ravishing as before. 'Let's go to Gallico's and get it over,' she said, and her voice had a brittle quality that I had noticed a few minutes earlier.

'I like your perfume, whatever it is,' I said.

'Chanel number five. I had just a scrap left, but I had to wear it—for going out with a prince.'

'Why, thanks!' I said. 'I'll buy some more.'

Minnie looked at me for a second, and I was glad to see that the peeved look on her face had gone. 'I don't know where you are going to get it—there are no imports and all the shops pretend they have run out.'

The lift man gave me a surprised look as he opened the door for us and I gave him a rupee as he left us on the ground floor. We walked through the glass door and stepped on to the cold Mall. I waved the rickshaw boys away and we began to walk to Gallico's in silence. After we had gone a few yards, Minnie hooked her arm into mine.

'Don't walk so fast,' she complained. 'I can't walk fast in high heels.' Once again her perfume was very close to me and her hair was brushing against my cheek.

It was a heady feeling, taking out a girl for the first time, and Minnie's hand felt warm and moist in mine. It was all I could do to prevent myself from stopping and taking her into my arms.

'Did you remember to bring the knuckle duster?' I asked.

Minnie laughed and peered at me in the half-darkness and, prompted by a common impulse, we both stopped. It would have been easy to forget that Minnie was someone else's girl, but I thought of Punch and after a moment's hesitation, we walked on.

The girl at the hat counter gave me a smile. 'We still have your hat, Your Highness,' she said.

The waiters hovered round us, pulling back chairs and the Manager himself came to say good evening and to remove the 'reserved' card. Bill Barraclough certainly must have laid it on thick, I thought, just as Punch had said.

'Shall we have champagne?' I asked Minnie.

'I have had champagne only once in my life,' Minnie said. 'In your room the other day.'

I ordered a bottle.

'Here's to your getting into the army!' Minnie said, holding up her glass.

'Here's to you … to you and Punch,' I said. 'Have you heard from him?'

'Who, Punch? No, I have not heard from Punch.'

'I wish he was here,' I said. 'It would have been such fun.'

'You don't think you're having fun as it is?' Minnie asked.

'Yes, of course,' I assured her. 'Yes, of course.' And then I told her something I had not meant to. 'Do you know, this is the first time I've taken a girl out to dinner.'

Minnie put down her glass and stared at me. 'You mean you've never taken anyone out before?'

I shook my head.

'And how does it feel?'

'Wonderful!' I exclaimed. And then I said. 'But it wouldn't have felt so wonderful with another girl.'

'Oh,' Minnie said, and she laughed. 'You know very well you would have gone away without even saying good-bye.'

That was exactly what I had been going to do, but it seemed so improbable now. 'I did not know how to get into touch with you,' I said.

'It's just as well you are a prince,' Minnie said. 'Otherwise, you might have found life much more complicated.'

I was still trying to fathom the meaning of her remark when the string orchestra broke into soft music and a few couples left their tables and began to dance.

'And I don't suppose you dance,' Minnie said.

'No, I don't,' I told her.

The waiter came and poured more champagne into our glasses.

'I do wish Punch did not have to go away so soon,' I said.

'Do you have to go on talking about Punch?' Minnie asked, but she did not sound the least bit annoyed.

'Well, I do miss him. Don't you?'

Minnie shook her head. 'No, I don't. Just now, I don't miss anyone at all,' she said, 'and I'm getting to like champagne.'

'Ganges water, my father calls it. Have some more,' I said and made a sign to the waiter.

'And where do you go tomorrow?' Minnie asked.

'I go back to Delhi for a day, and then take the train for Begwad, to our state.'

'And then you get swallowed up, never to be seen again.'

At the moment it seemed quite unlikely that we would ever meet again, but I did not want to say anything about it.

'Here's to our evening, short and sweet,' Minnie said. Her voice sounded slightly husky.

I did not know what to say, and for a moment I wondered if my first date with a girl was going sour on me. But just as the waiter was serving us, Minnie held my hand under the table and gave it a gentle squeeze.

'Little boy on his first date,' she said. 'And I keep feeling like your aunt.'

'I shouldn't have told you about it,' I said. 'And you are too lovely and too young to be anyone's aunt.'

'I'm glad I'm the first girl you took out,' Minnie said, and she laughed dreamily as though the champagne had been affecting her. 'The first girl. And how old are you, if one may ask? You look about seventeen.'

I did not know how sentimental girls can go for no reason at all. I told her I was nineteen.

'Nineteen.' Minnie shook her head. 'Nineteen seems such a long while ago—a whole two years. Exactly two years tomorrow.'

'Don't tell me tomorrow is your birthday?' I said.

She nodded. 'This is the last day, the very last day that I shall be twenty. And I'm enjoying it. I am going to treasure it!' And Minnie again held my hand.

'And what are you going to do tomorrow?' I asked. 'Anything special?'

'Special? Certainly. Stay in my bed so long that I shall have to go without breakfast because they stop serving at nine. During the day I shall think of my misspent youth, and in the evening I will go to the pictures with one of the other girls from the office and we'll eat enormous ice cream sundaes at Davico's ...' Minnie stopped abruptly and gave a queer little laugh.

I was surprised that a girl as attractive as Minnie should have to spend her evenings alone in wartime Simla, for I did not know the taboos of British officialdom. An Anglo-Indian girl who had to work for a living was not someone you could take into the clubs and the more exclusive restaurants. In a sense, Punch Farren had been something of a renegade, for Simla society was strictly confined to those who were on the garden-party list at Government House and was still dominated by the spirit of Mrs. Hauksbee.

As I looked at Minnie, in her pearl-pink dress with little blue sprigs on it, I thought of my own birthdays: the music of the sehnais; the booming of the guns at the time of my birth; the salver of silver coins cast away after being proffered to me; the prayers in the temples; the public holiday all over the state; the procession; the garlands; the almost vulgar, senseless extravagance. And here was this lovely girl, living on her own, having to earn her living in a strange, unfriendly town, spending her twenty-first birthday in some desolate government hostel for women.

'Twenty-one is a lovely age,' I said.

'Everything must be lovely when one is a prince,' she said.

'Look, I don't really have to go away tomorrow,' I said. 'I mean I can cut out my day in Delhi without anyone knowing anything about it, and go straight to Begwad. How would you like it if we … if we spent the day together … just you and I? Go down to Kasauli or somewhere by car? Picnic in the woods?'

'Just you and me?' she asked.

'Just me and you.'

'But you don't … I mean, you don't have to, unless of course. you want to.'

'I want to,' I told her. 'Oh, yes, I want to. What about it?

'I should love to,' Minnie said, and suddenly her eyes were moist with tears. 'Oh, I'd just love to.' And she sought out my hand again.

Everything was fine after that, as we made plans for the next day. We enjoyed our dinner: sole meunière and creamed chicken with mushrooms and crêpes suzette, coffee and cognac. And once again the Manager came waddling up to ask me if everything was all right.

'Come again, Highness,' he told me as he held Minnie's chair back for her.

I gave a five-rupee note to the hat-check girl and she gave me a broad grin. 'Thank you, Highness,' she said. 'Come again.'

Out on the Mall, I gathered Minnie in my arms and kissed her.

By then I had stopped bothering whether I was doing right or wrong.

'Really, Highness,' Minnie said when I released her, 'you take my breath away.'

I drew her to me and kissed her again.

That day was ours, Minnie's and mine, and for me it was a day of growing up, of coming of age, almost discovering myself.

We went out in a hired Buick, driving through the dark pine forest, and I had to drive carefully because I could not keep my eyes away from Minnie's face. She wore a silk scarf with a design of bamboos on it knotted under her chin, a man's green knitted shirt, a tight, blue-grey skirt which ended just above her knees, and openwork sandals. Her face looked flushed and radiant, alive with pleasure and anticipation. Now that I look back on it, I must have been already quite deeply in love with Minnie.

We stopped on a knoll, slippery with pine needles and surrounded by tall, upstanding trees, and far below us were the pink roofs of the houses in Subathu or Garkhal or somewhere. I opened a bottle of beer and a bottle of lemonade and poured them in equal proportions into the pottery mug I had brought with me. And I lay on the cool grass, leaning against a tree, sipping my shandy and smoking, listening to the wail of the Himalayan cuckoo and to the breeze soughing through the pines and watching Minnie.

She had busied herself opening packages of curry puffs and sandwiches and cheese and jam rolls and paper plates and setting them down neatly on a rug. She had removed her head scarf and her hair fell in a soft gold wave round her face. She was bending down, almost on all fours, and her skirt was riding high. I was content to go on looking at her, stockingless, her skirt revealing the smooth skin of her legs and accentuating the curve of her hips.

Minnie finished laying out the lunch and looked at me, a little shy and self-conscious, almost as though she were seeing me for the first time. And then she smiled and shook her hair and crawled across to me, still on all fours. She took my face in her hands and kissed me gently on the nose.

'I love the way your nose twists,' she said, holding my head.

'It wasn't always crooked,' I told her. 'I managed to break it.'

'It's a lovely nose,' Minnie said. Then she added: 'Kiss me.'

She was breathless, her voice was a husky whisper, her mouth was half open and he eyes were hall-closed.

I held her head in my hands and kissed her hard on the mouth. I had never imagined that a kiss could be such a searching, revealing, intimate experience. I went on and on as though we were both determined to see who would be the last to draw way. I could feel Minnie's hard, hot body pressing into mine closer and closer, responding to the rhythm of the urges within me, the perfect counterpart to my flaming desires. She made a sound, something between a sigh and a moan, and I knew that it was purely involuntary sound, an index of desire, a reflex of some deep emotional stirring. I pushed her back brutally, as though at a signal, her breath still coming in gasps, her mouth shaped for the kiss, her eyes half closed and slipped my arms around her and caught up the folds of her knitted shirt. I realized with stab of ecstasy that she wore nothing beneath it. She lay still while I had the folds of her shirt in my hands and pulled it over her head with a jerk and flung it on to the grass, and then she was snuggling closer and closer to me, white and feminine, hiding her face flushed red with shame into my chest.

'No, no!' Minnie gasped, and her voice was low, almost inaudible. 'Please, darling, not now, not here.'

But, perversely, I pushed her away from me and held her down with force because I would not be denied full measure; because I wanted to gaze at her in her nakedness, this first woman I was going to possess.

My father did not like the idea of my joining the Satpura Rifles. 'You should be going into the cavalry, the Royal Deccan Horse,' he said on my return from Simla. 'Much more in keeping with our izzat. I can't imagine Jai going into an infantry regiment.'

'Jai is a Maharaja,' I reminded him. 'Also perhaps one of the greatest polo players in the world. I am only a Yuwaraj, and of a much smaller state. For me it is not important …'

My father had never liked any references to the disparity between Begwad and some of the major princely states. 'Polo is not everything,' he scoffed. 'Our ancestors have always been cavalrymen—commanders of mounted troops.'

'The cavalry is no longer mounted,' I said. 'They go to war sealed up in tanks.'

He gave me a surprised look. 'Go to war! You weren't actually thinking of getting into the fighting, were you? Of going to the front?'

'Of course,' I said. 'Otherwise there would be no point in joining up.'

The thought was wholly repugnant to my father.

'This is not our war,' he reminded me. 'Not the war of the Indian princes. I have given five lakhs of rupees to the war fund—much more than any of the other Padmakoshal princes—and we have already sent nearly three hundred recruits. We, Begwad—we have done our bit.'

It is only fair to say that my father saw the war from an entirely different angle, distorted by his own values, conditioned by his own upbringing. He was certainly no friend of the British, and he felt no particular hatred for the Germans. He did not see the war as many of my own generation did, even though our own perspective too had its own distortions. We thought of the war as an adventure, an opportunity to prove oneself, something that a young man could not afford to keep out of. The war was almost an extension of school and college, the training given by the Head being carried forward to its logical, inescapable conclusion.

My father was content to hold back and watch from afar, without anxiety, doing only just what was absolutely necessary to keep his political superiors in good humour.

'The war will be a long one, even longer than the Great War,' he said. 'And both sides will bleed each other to death. That will be the time for the princes to unite and rise: to drive away the British and put down the nationalists and set up our own rule in the country. It is only the princes who can do it. Gandhi and the Congress, the white-cap wallas, will never do it … It is we who will oust the British. That war will be ours, yours and mine, a war in which we shall serve with pride … if necessary lay down our lives.'

Father had lapsed into his favourite dream. There was no way of persuading him that the antiquated, unnatural world of the Indian princes would disintegrate long before the Germans or the British were finished off as world powers.

So I left my father that evening, wrapt in a dream, and went to bed to dream my own dreams. I lay awake in the hot summer night which carried the scent of the mango-blossom, gazing at the star-spangled sky and thinking of Minnie: Minnie who stood as a symbol of conquest, my first successful encounter in the war of sex; Minnie, shy and protesting and passive on the grass, the first woman I had seen naked; Minnie who had proved so deliciously bold later when she spent the night in my hotel room …

My thoughts were cut off by a slight noise, like the clink of glass bangles, and I jerked my head up and saw a shadow disappear behind the long window-curtain draped to one side. I switched on the light, sprang to the window, and pulled the curtain aside.

I nearly laughed. Zarina, Amina-begam's niece, was cowering behind it, her eyes wide and her face white with nervousness. She wore the almost traditional costume of the harem girl, an outrageously low, outrageously brief, sleeveless blouse that would now be compared to the top half of a Bikini, showing an expanse of waist and barely concealing her firm breasts, and voluminous pale blue pyjamas made of negligé material tied up at the ankles. 'Amina-begam sent me,' Zarina stuttered. 'She told me you wanted to see me. She also told me to tell you that the Maharaja knows … that it is all right.'

I felt sorry for Zarina, to whom I had given my sweets when I was much younger, and who had now grown into such a lovely young woman. But I sent her away. It was Minnie who filled my mind; Minnie who had set the standard. I wanted to keep the memory of my day untarnished.

12

'Is Your Journey Really Necessary?'

Soon after my return from Simla, I was sent to the Military Academy at Dehradun. It was almost like going back to school. I flung myself into the work with gusto, even with joy, just as I had done at school. I was rewarded for my efforts by being made a cadet sergeant half-way through the course. During the eight months of training, my father and mother, my horses and guns, my two-litre Lagonda, even Minnie, all fell into the background.

But just before Christmas, when the course was about to finish, I suddenly began to long for Minnie. We were to be given ten days' leave before joining our battalions, but of course there was no question of my going all the way to Simla to see Minnie. I had no excuse to visit Simla and it would have raised no end of complications at home and used up nearly half my leave just travelling. Besides, my father had been sending me a series of telegrams for the last two weeks, laying down the details of my leave. I was going to be home just in time for the annual Tatwal shoot, and my father was keen that I should meet some of the special guests he had invited.

'You must come home on the very first train,' he had said in his letter, 'and do ask one or two of your own friends to the shoot if you would like to. And mind you come straight home.' It was almost as though my father knew that I had been toying with the idea of going to Simla for a day.

I sent a wire to Punch Farren inviting him to our duck-shoot. There was no question of asking Minnie over.

The only way I could have seen her was if she came down to Delhi. My train from Dehradun reached Delhi junction early in the morning, and the Western Mail did not start until the evening. But of course I would never have thought of asking Minnie to come all the way to Delhi just so that we could be together between the trains. I wrote to her, explaining how important it was for me to go directly home even though I would have liked nothing better than to be with her in Simla for a day or two at least.

As it turned out, however, Minnie was going to be in Delhi for the Christmas holidays in any case. She wrote to say that if I told her the train I was coming by, she would meet me at the station.

My train was an hour late and I was sure Minnie must have tired of waiting and gone. But she was there, all muffled up in an overcoat, with her hands thrust deep into the pockets. She was standing under a red neon sign which said, 'Is Your Journey Really Necessary?'

For a moment we were strangers, each looking into each other's eye for the spark of recognition. I waved to her from a distance, and then she rushed up and hooked her arm into mine. I wanted to take her in my arms, but the platform at Delhi junction at eight in the morning was no place to embrace a girl.

'Was your journey really necessary?' I asked Minnie.

'What?' she said, sounding peeved. 'Whatever do you mean?'

'Oh, never mind,' I said. 'Let's get out of this place.'

Minnie clutched my hand tightly as we went out, followed by the red-coated coolies carrying my bags. We did not speak until we were in the taxi.

'You look nice in uniform,' she said. 'Handsome.'

'Have you heard from Punch?' I asked. 'I've asked him over for our shoot. I do hope he can make it.'

'Oh, Punch will make it all right,' she said.

'I do hope he can.'

'And what have they done to your hair—they have cut it so short!'

'That's the Dehradun crop. They don't bother much with hair styles there.'

'And you're as brown as a berry—all sunburnt.'

'You are looking quite tanned yourself,' I said. 'And lovelier than ever.'

She slid closer to me. 'Kiss me,' she whispered.

The taxi was just turning under the railway bridge, and the Sikh driver was concentrating on the road. I held her in my arms and kissed her.

We spent the day drifting around in a hired car and I took her to lunch at Maiden's and we held hands under the table. In the afternoon we walked through Connaught Place, looking at the shops, and I bought Minnie a silver compact and six bottles of Chanel No. 5. On the way back to the station, I had to take Minnie to the Constantia Hall hostel where she was staying because she said she wanted to collect something.

Almost before it had begun, our day was over. Minnie stood on the platform beside my carriage right under the sign which said 'Is Your Journey Really Necessary?' carrying a paper package, neatly done up in pink Government tape, which she had collected from her room. She looked as though she were going to cry.

'You didn't tell me if you ever heard from Punch,' I said.

Minnie shook her head and gave me a tight-lipped smile and her mouth curved downward at the corners. The guard blew his whistle. I wanted the train to start before she started sobbing.

'I'll write as soon as I get there,' I told her. 'I won't be like Punch.'

The train gave a lurch, and all around us people were saying good-byes. I wanted to jump out and hold Minnie in my arms. She came close to the window and shoved the brown-paper parcel into my lap. Then she turned and walked away.

I tore open the package. It was a hand-knit khaki pullover with a cable-stitch pattern.

I leaned out of the window to try and thank her, but already she was quite far away. I could make out her figure, trim and erect, striding into the distance. She did not look back.

The whole palace was bristling with excitement as it always did before the Tatwal shoot. Extra waiters had been brought from Bombay, and the man from the Taj was allotting them their duties. The palace servants were busy cleaning up the glassware and silver and putting flowers in the guest rooms.

The war was remote from Begwad. The 'finest hour' of the British nation had come and gone, Hitler and Mussolini were masters of Europe; but these events were in a world away from my father's. The fall of France only affected him indirectly.

'I don't know what we are going to do about wine,' he complained. 'Phipsons won't take any large orders. I'm afraid we can serve champagne only for the Christmas dinner.'

This year my father's guests were mainly from the army, with the usual sprinkling of the officials of the Political Department. There was General Hinton who was the Director of Military Intelligence, and Brigadier Oswald who was the Assistant Military Secretary. There were two Colonels and three Majors and of course our Political Agent, Colonel Gibson. Most of them had brought their wives, although I never really found out which one was whose. They all arrived on the twenty-fourth, in ones and twos, the men wearing old tweed jackets and grey flannel trousers and the women tailor-made dresses, cackling, excited like children before a picnic and complaining of the petrol shortage.

Charudutt, my half-brother, was also down from the Police Training College. He had grown into a stout and heavy youth who took himself very seriously. I found that I had even less in common with him than before. He went about as though he had a chip on his shoulder, always grumbling about the way he was being treated. It seemed he had not been given a room in the palace itself or one of the guest houses, but had to live in the town with his mother, and hadn't even been allotted a special car. On the day of the shoot he was so upset because the butt allotted to him was even lower than Hanuman Singh's that he went straight back without firing a shot. It is, of course, possible that he had a genuine grievance, for of late my father had tended to neglect him altogether, but at the time I only felt irritated with him.

I was glad to get a letter from Punch saying that he was coming, for I was anxious to get this thing between us over before I went to join the regiment. I did not know what he would think of me after I had told him about Minnie and myself. From what little I had seen of him, I liked Punch and wanted him to like me. I took special care about the arrangements for his stay. I had him put up in the room next to mine in the palace itself, otherwise they would almost certainly have sent him to the number two guest house. I went to look at his room before his train was due and told the servants to light a fire, to put a bottle of whisky in the cupboard and to put flowers in the vases and writing paper on the desk. And when I found that he had not brought a gun, I lent him one of my own Purdies. I had a lot to make up to Punch Farren and I was anxious for him to think well of me in spite of all that had happened.

We were in the sitting-room, late in the evening on the day of his arrival, and I knew that this was the time to tell him about Minnie and myself, but I did not know how to set about it. We had drawn our chairs close to the fire and he was asking me something about Brigadier Oswald.

'That's the chap to get on the right side of, dammit,' Punch was saying. 'Assistant Military Secretary. Give you any posting you want. What's he like?'

'Punch, there is something I have been meaning to speak to you about,' I said. Now that I had begun, I did not want to go on. And yet I knew it was important to have it out. I was hoping he would take it well and not think too badly of me.

'And General Hinton, the D.M.I. I've arranged to travel back in his car.'

'I saw Minnie after you left,' I blurted out.

'Minnie! Oh. Did she bring Tony along?' Punch asked.

'Tony?'

'I expect he was still on leave,' Punch said. 'So you saw Minnie.'

'I took her out to dinner, the day of my interview. And the next day we went for a picnic.'

'Oh,' Punch said. 'Picnic.'

I almost wished he would show his displeasure in some way, that he would say something that would reveal his real feelings instead of treating it all as a kind of joke.

'What butt has the old boy drawn?' Punch asked.

'Who?'

'Never mind about Oswald,' I said.

'Brigadier Oswald.'

'I was just thinking that if our butts were close together, we could go up in the same car.'

'I'll tell them to put you in the same car,' I said.

'Thanks. You were saying something …'

'I was telling you about Minnie and me going on a picnic.'

'Just the two of you?'

'Yes.'

'Well, well,' Punch said.

'You see, it was her birthday,' I explained.

'Oh, yes, of course,' he said and gave a mild snort. 'Birthday. Good for you, Scrapper.'

'I hope you don't mind.'

'Oh, no,' Punch assured me. 'No, I don't mind. I only hope you had a good time.'

'Yes, I did have a good time; we both did,' I said.

'Well, well.'

'We had a wonderful outing.'

'Hmmm … Now, who'd have thought …' Punch stopped abruptly and began chuckling. 'Perhaps a picnic in the woods with someone like Minnie was just what you needed. I do hope you were not … not disappointed.'

This was not going the way I had anticipated at all, and I was puzzled by his reaction. He was concealing his feelings very well, for I knew how fond he and Minnie had been of each other. I wished he would not go on pretending that it did not mean anything to him. I was getting a little fed up with the stiff upper lip of the British.

'I saw her again, two days ago; just before coming here,' I said.

Punch stopped chuckling. 'You mean you went all the way to Simla?'

'No, we met in Delhi. We met at the station and then I took her to lunch.'

'Oh, lunch, not another picnic. Not much percentage in a lunch, I shouldn't think. Couldn't you have laid on another picnic, somewhere beyond the Kutab?'

'Minnie said you never wrote to her.'

'No, I didn't write,' Punch said. 'I do hope the picnic was … was all that you wanted. I hope you enjoyed yourself.'

'I found her most charming company; most understanding,' I told him. He was taking it very well, all things considered.

'I am glad you're not annoyed,' I said.

'No,' he assured me. 'I'm not annoyed. Relax, Abbey.'

'I'm so relieved. I did not want this … this thing to come between us, and I was so hoping that you would understand. Now I know you do.'

'Of course, I understand,' Punch said. 'Minnie! Wonderful company. What I would call a hot little number … and not so little as all that, either. No, sir—full measure, in fact.'

'I know how you must be feeling, Punch,' I said. 'But I do wish you wouldn't refer to her as a hot little number. It … it doesn't sound decent.'

'What's that? Christ!' Punch began to chuckle again. 'No, no, Scrapper. I won't say anything like that, now I know the score. You haven't fallen in love with Minnie or anything like that, have you? … I mean, I hope she's just a girl you like to take out to a picnic in the woods.'

'I don't know, Punch. I don't know myself.'

'Christ!' Punch said again. 'Look, Scrapper, don't get me wrong, but you just have to learn how to take a girl like Minnie. Take them and leave them; that about sums it up. The leaving part is just as important as the taking part—possibly much more important.'

I knew how bitter he must have felt, and I was glad he had taken it so well. I did not tell Punch any more, though. I did not tell him that after the picnic in Simla I had taken Minnie to my room in the hotel, that she had spent the night there. I was relieved that we were still friends. 'Would you like a drink, Punch?' I asked. 'I told them to put a bottle of whisky in your room. Black Dog.'

'Of course, we'll have a drink, Punch said. 'Black Dog would be just right. And Abbey, you won't forget what you said about putting me in the same car as Brigadier Oswald when we drive out to the jheel, will you?'

Our Tatwal shoot has always been a popular annual sporting event, almost on a par with the Dipalpur and Bharatpur shoots. The Tatwal lake, fanning out into the folds of the Sattawan hills, makes an enormous figure of eight of water and reeds and thorned hyacinth. Dotted all round and hidden by the surrounding babools and lantanas growing on the banks, were the permanent platforms built on stilts, the butts or blinds for the duck-shoot. There were twenty-six of these blinds, and my father always saw to it that we were never short of the requisite number of 'guns'. Most of the better blinds were in the direct path of the flights and it was only a stray flight that would miss going over one or other of them. The ducks usually began to rise while it was quite dark, so that in the beginning you could only hear the whirr and whistle of wings overhead, and see nothing but swift shadows in the sky. Exactly at first light, when the first curt shot of the shoot was fired by my father, they would rise in great flocks and come flying faster and faster in neat geometric formations, as though eager to play their part in the game, faster than you could shoot, so that in no time at all the chill had left your bones and the gun was smoking in your hands.

One could call it a highly organized form of slaughter. The ducks were lulled into false sense of security because no one was permitted to fire a shot in the vicinity of the Tatwal jheel before the shoot or to snare the birds. These birds came to our country in their millions and to our state in their scores of thousands, seeking sun and shelter, fleeing from the frozen lands of their birth beyond the Himalayas, from Tibet, the Ukraine, Siberia, the tundras of Asia and Europe. And each year they came, back to their own favourite jheels as though drawn by a spell, forgetful of the slaughters of the previous years, sacrificing themselves to the rhythm of migration.

But in those days I never remember pausing to give a thought to the rights and wrongs of duck-shooting or of any other form of blood sport. For me it was enough to have a favourite shotgun ready in my hands, a loader who was quick, a team of diving boys to do the retrieving and, of course, the ducks flying overhead. I was transported to a different element, a part of the morning and the mist and the honking of the geese; I was no longer a human animal endowed with the powers of reasoning, of distinguishing between right and wrong, cruelty and kindness. The sight of a bronze and green mallard corkscrewing down to the earth in slow spirals because a spark of his being was still alive, still struggling to carry on his suddenly-interrupted flight, did not touch a chord in me; the thwack of a bird dead long before hitting water was music to my ears, and getting a right and left with teal, both birds killed cleanly in mid air, was very heaven.

For me, a morning duck-shoot will always remain an interlude of pure ecstasy, an experience with strong physical overtones, of sights and sounds and smells and nerves and muscular exertion. I would wait for the flighting to begin, my senses sharpened to needle point, taking a voluptuous pleasure in my surroundings—the night passing into day in sharply drawn phases, the crispness of the early morning, the mists curling thinly out of the black water, the waiting in the cold stillness of the dawn while listening with tingling nerves to the commotion in the reeds and the whisper of the wings overhead, the colours slowly coming back to the sky and the earth, and then in one sharp, unbearable jab, the quick erupting into action, the first explosion of the shells and the acrid gun-smoke and the first killing of a bird, bringing an acute awareness of fulfilment, a joy almost barbaric in its intensity.

I was good that day. I shot sixty-eight duck and thirteen geese. Father and his special guests, occupying the prized butts, of course did much better. Only Punch did not seem to have much luck. In all he shot only seventeen birds and nine of them happened to be coots which were regarded as unshootable.

We never told Punch about the coots. He was enjoying himself so much, the typical, easily pleased guest, full of the glow brought on by the outdoors and by having participated in a blood sport; the friendly bulldog, fascinating in his ugliness, gnawing at his bone contentedly in front of the hearth. He made a wonderful guest at a house party, full of life and eager to be useful, pouring drinks, lighting people's cigarettes and making up bridge fours with elderly ladies.

It was a wonderful Christmas, that Christmas of the year nineteen hundred and forty. We had champagne for dinner that night, and the table sparkled with silver and crystal, sparkled too with the talk of men and the laughter of women. The war was so very far away that day, and the freedom of India merely a forlorn hope in the minds of people spending their days behind prison bars. And we, the Indian States, were at last coming into our own, so my father said, in a far stronger bargaining position with the British than at any time since our conquest.

The guests had left. The ducks and geese had been dressed and packed in ice and sent off to friends. The party was over and the palace wore an empty look. It was at such times that its extravagant proportions began to press down on its inmates.

I ached for Minnie, knowing that with her around there would have been no loneliness for me. I tried to picture her in the palace, in my own surroundings, sharing my life, walking hand in hand through the dark corridors, looking at the trophy room and the room with the tiger rug and the two reception rooms and the Indian-style dining-room where we had to remove our shoes because we sat cross-legged on the paats, and the durbar hall with its stained glass windows; and, inevitably, I pictured her in my own rooms, lying in my bed, naked and shy as she had lain beside me at the picnic, and later in the privacy of my room, naked and wanton and desiring and demanding. I went to the writing desk and wrote a letter to Minnie.

When I read over the letter, it sounded crude and callow, like a schoolboy's letter to his girl friend. I added a postscript, asking her to send me a photograph of herself, and then I made a bold cross below the postscript. I put the letter in my pocket because I wanted to post it myself. I did not want anyone at home to find out about Minnie. I did not know that my father already knew.

I was still at the desk, thinking of Minnie, when Siddoji, my bearer, came and told me that Lala Harikishore was waiting to see me.

I had never cared much for our Chief Minister, but of course there was no question of keeping him waiting. I got up and went in to the sitting-room.

Lala Harikishore rose to his feet and did a very stiff, very formal mujra. As usual, he was carrying a sheaf of papers, tied in red dust-cloth.

I acknowledged his mujra and sat down. He cleared his throat apologetically.

'I have, hmmm, a delicate mission to perform,' he said.

'Is it so delicate that you cannot even sit down to speak about it, Lalaji?' I asked.

He smiled, his smooth, hairless cat-face breaking out into his practised creases. 'Thank you, Yuwaraj,' he said, and sat down on the opposite chair.

'Now perhaps we can get down to it,' I said.

'His Highness has entrusted me with a difficult, rather delicate mission …'

I waited for him in silence. I had no wish to help him out. I had a feeling that his mission had something to do with my marriage.

The chiming clock hummed wheezily and struck the half hour. It was three-thirty. The sound of the gong hung trembling in the air.

'I am, of course, honoured by the confidence that His Highness has reposed in me in entrusting me with this, er …'

'Difficult, delicate mission,' I suggested.

The trace of smile on his face vanished. 'It is about the Yuwaraja's marriage,' he said. 'His Highness has asked me to have a … a frank and open talk with the Yuwaraj, and to let him know'.

'There are two proposals,' Harikishore went on. 'Both, er … both equally desirable in their own ways. Highly eligible.'

'Oh,' I said. 'Both eligible, in different ways.'

He gave me a quick look, turned his eyes away and cleared his throat delicately. 'One is from … hmmm … the Raja-saheb of Akheti. The other is from the Jagirdars of Kurdalli, the Puranwad family.'

'Oh, yes?' I said. I put my hand in my pocket. Minnie's letter was still there.

'I was told to … to ascertain from the Yuwaraj … an indication of his preference.'

'Both these families have made these proposals? On their own?' I asked.

The Chief Minister had never liked awkward interruptions, but if he frowned, it was a delicate frown, just the dipping of an eyebrow by a hair's breadth. 'Well, it is we who made the … er, initial proposals. They, so to say, have reacted favourably.'

'I see.'

'And His Highness has directed me to ascertain from you an indication of your preference. That is, which of these two proposals would be more in line with the Yuwaraja's wishes.'

'So I gathered,' I said. All my life, I had known that some day I would be confronted with this particular problem. And yet, now that the time had come, I was wholly unprepared for it.

'The Puranwads, of course, belong to the thirty-seven families, even though they are—they are just land-owners. The Raja saheb of Akheti, well, is a Raja; a salute prince.'

I ran my fingers over Minnie's letter and thought of the way her lips curved downwards when she smiled.

'I have brought the photographs,' he was saying. 'Photographs of both the prospective brides. If the Yuwaraj will permit me.' He opened his red dust-cloth bundle and brought out a large, cream-coloured envelope.

'Please leave them on the table,' I said. 'And thank you very much.'

Lala Harikishore bowed his head slightly; the seasoned courtier's practised salutation in acceptance of dismissal. His face was entirely blank. 'And when,' he asked, 'may I call again to … to ascertain the Yuwaraja's preference?'

'I'll send for you,' I told him. 'I'll send for you when I have something to say.'

He bowed again. 'Have I the Yuwaraja's permission to leave?'

He was always the perfect courtier; cool, syrupy, unruffled.

'Yes, of course. And thank you for coming.'

Throughout the afternoon, the packet of photographs lay on the coffee table beside the previous day's *Statesman* and the latest issue of the *Strand* magazine now shrunk to pocket size because of the paper shortage. When I went for my evening ride, wearing the new sweater that Minnie had knitted for me, I could not put it out of my mind. It was after I returned from my ride, having posted Minnie's letter on the way, and Siddoji had pulled off my boots and gone to draw my bath that I happened to pick up the packet and open it.

As Harikishore had said, there were two photographs. I looked at them, at first with resentment, and then with a growing curiosity. Each had been taken with the floodlight full on the face of the sitter and no doubt they had been heavily retouched. I remember thinking that both must have been taken by the same photographer. Both girls had pleasant, nondescript faces, and I would not have called either of them good looking. Compared to Minnie's liveliness, they had a drab quality, as though the photographer had gone to some pains to efface their characteristics rather than bring them out; as though they were behind some kind of purdah even in their photographs. I was amused to see that there was no writing of any kind on either photograph, so that there was no way of telling which was the daughter of the Puranwad Jagirdars and which the princess of Akheti. I remember thinking that if I really did have to make a choice, I would not know which family she belonged to unless I sent for Lala Harikishore and asked him.

And with that thought I went to have my bath and change for dinner, the problem of the day still unresolved.

13

'Always Is So Long'

My mother was in the glazed verandah which opened out of her sitting room, playing rummy with two of the palace officials' wives whose faces were only vaguely familiar to me. Now that it was dark, they had rolled up the chits behind the windows, and you could see the line made by the lights curving along the drive and the line of their reflections in the pond. They were all squatting close to the fireplace, each with a small pile of coloured counters before her, and when I entered the verandah, the two women jumped to their feet and stood looking down, holding their cards in their hands. I told my mother I wanted to talk to her, and the two women shuffled out of her presence, taking care not to show their backs, still clutching their cards.

'I rather thought you were going to come to see me early this evening,' Mother said, and there was a glint of laughter in her eyes. 'Would you like anything to drink?'

'Could I have a little whisky?' I asked.

'Yes, of course,' Mother said. I was glad that she had not shown any surprise, for this was the first time I had asked for an alcoholic drink in her apartment. She called one of her maids and ordered her to get hold of a servant.

'I see that you are winning, Maji,' I said, pointing at her pile of chips.

'I never win,' Mother pouted. 'Those are all one-anna chips. I never seem to have any of the blue chips, the rupee ones.'

'Oh, the blue chips,' I said.

'I saw you go out riding, along the drive,' Mother said. 'Wearing a hideous khaki pullover. I didn't think you would have bought yourself a khaki one.'

I had always gone in for colourful sweaters with my riding clothes: electric blues and canary yellows, lime greens and strawberry reds. Most of them had been hand-knitted by my mother.

'To go with my uniform, Maji,' I explained.

'Yes, of course, the uniform,' she said almost absent-mindedly. She too had not got used to my joining the army.

A servant came in, white-coated and pink-turbaned, carrying a tray with a glass of whisky and soda already poured out, just as my father was used to having. It was too strong for me, but I did not mind.

The maid had gone, the servant had gone, and my mother and I were face to face, squatting on a carpet in front of the spluttering fire. The preliminaries were done with. Now the play could begin. I wanted to tell Mother about Minnie, but I did not know how to begin.

'Well, what did you decide?' she asked.

'Maji, I don't want to get married,' I said.

'Oh, none of us wants to get married. I never wanted to.'

'And look what marriage has brought you,' I said. 'Not a day's happiness in your life.'

'Happiness!' Mother said, and shook her head. The two tiny furrows on her brow had deepened. 'One has to live with one's destiny. The world has to go on. It doesn't run on happiness.'

I felt we were talking on vastly different levels. 'But there is a lot I want to do,' I protested. 'Go to the war, see life, go abroad, to Europe and America, before getting tied up with marriage.'

'It would all be in the wrong order,' Mother said. 'You can do all that … all that you want, only after you have … after you have made provision for the succession. There is a duty, an obligation.'

She was talking almost like my father. It was no use telling her that now, in the twentieth century, you could not think of marrying a girl just by looking at her photograph; at least not when you were in love with a girl like Minnie. There was such a thing as love, you had to love the person you married. But the subject of love was taboo. I felt weak and without a valid argument. What was love against duty? I gulped my whisky and was comforted by its fire.

'But I haven't even seen either of the girls—just their photographs. And from the photographs I am supposed to choose a companion for life ...'

'Remember that the girls don't even get that much of a say—they are not even shown a photograph. They are raised in the strictest purdah, secluded, sealed off from the world, not knowing anything—anything at all about the facts of life. And it is all so heartbreaking. One day she is playing with her friends and the maidservants begin to giggle mysteriously and then her mother or someone comes along and tells her she is to be married ... tied up for life to someone she has never seen.'

'Marriages don't have to be like that,' I said. 'They are not like that in western society. There the men and women mix freely and everyone is left free to choose their mates.'

It was almost as though she were not listening to me. 'The first time I saw your father was during the wedding ceremony itself,' she said. 'When the priests stopped chanting their verses and removed the curtain that had been held between us. And then I only saw his feet because a girl cannot raise her eyes to her husband's face during the ceremony itself. That is what marriage means to a girl: being tied to a pair of feet.'

She was looking at it from the point of view of the bride; I was thinking of myself. Somewhere at the back of my mind, I was also thinking of Minnie, comparing her, lively and gay and bold, to a Hindu girl who would not raise her eyes to see what her husband looked like.

'But I don't know either of these girls,' I said. 'How can I be expected to love a person from a photograph? Love, honour, cherish?'

'Love, honour, cherish,' Mother repeated the words in a dry, flat voice. 'Where do you get such notions? There can be no love without marriage. Love only comes after marriage—sometimes after many years. Love comes with maturity. It cannot be there in the madness of youth …'

'Is there always love in marriage?' I asked, knowing that I had no right to ask such a question of her.

My mother gave me a long, searching look but there was no sign of anger on her face. 'Not always. There are exceptions … unfortunate exceptions. But one does not take them into account. Marriage doesn't have to have love; not our kind of marriage. Our marriages are not our personal affairs but matters of duty. Look what happened in England—even in England where you say the men and women are free to choose their mates. The King was not free to marry the woman of his desire—not while he still was King. The rules are far more stringent here.'

I was amazed at how much my mother seemed to know of the outside world even though she lived in purdah.

'There are rules,' she was saying. 'Rules for husbands and rules for wives. You live by the rules.'

'Always?'

She shook her head and placed her hand on mine, ever so gently, like a butterfly landing, and I remember looking down and thinking how shapely her hands were, small and firm like the hands of a dancer, the slender fingers with their satiny skin and hardly noticeable joints tapering smoothly to the shell pink nails.

'Always is so long,' Mother said. 'And men and women are not … not made of stone. They are creatures of flesh and blood, of hatred and passions and desires; and sometimes they find that … that always is too long. But it is important to begin with honour, to observe the rules as long as you can; until you find it quite impossible to do so.'

I had a feeling that our talk was running off its rails, that it was only bringing home to my mother the painful inadequacies of her own life. 'This whisky is too strong for me,' I said.

'Married … tied to a pair of feet,' Mother went on in a low, flat voice, 'and afraid to raise her eyes to the face of her man; and yet, knowing deep inside that at the merest sign of kindness from him, her fear will turn into a flood of love. But sometimes it doesn't work out that way. The feet you clutch kick at you—kick at you on the very first night … the night of love.'

'Is that what happened, Mother?' I asked.

She nodded. 'She grows up, but things die within her. She grows up while a jeering world points a finger at her … the girl with the white foot, discarded by her man, left alone like a leper. She grows up into a woman, pining for the experiences of womanhood, longing, above all, to be loved … Love, honour, cherish, these are not for her. She grows up, watching the women of the streets brought into the house and showered with what is hers. And sometimes, sometimes, the desire to set fire to everything, to get away from it all, nearly drives her mad. She wants to break through the bonds of convention and go away. She wants to go where there will be affection and love—yes, physical love, violent and abandoned—before there is the final ebbing away of desires, before the fear of old age, before the creeping hand of death. To go … to go and live the life of a normal woman. But there is no remedy. The end can come only with death.'

Her face was dead white, and her voice was dry as the rustle of straw. And I could feel the anguish of her mind like a hot flame.

'There's always a remedy, Mother,' I said. 'There is always a time to break away. Break away before it is too late. Now.'

'It is already too late, my son.'

It must have been the strong whisky I had drunk, and of course there was the emotional impact of my mother's words, but I still cannot find justification for what I said to her.

'Maji,' I said, 'Go away from here. Go somewhere and live a life of your own. You have your own money, your own houses. You can't go on living here, the way you are living; shut away, forgotten. I have always pitied you, felt for you …'

'I've never spoken about it to anyone, Abhay, not even to my parents when they asked me if I were happy. My mother cried when I told her I was happy because she'd heard the truth from my maidservants. But I felt you had a right to know. You must know how things were, because whatever happens, I don't want you to think too harshly of me. You can ask me any questions you like, anything at all, for you have a right to know.' And she braced herself, preparing for my questions. Her face was white and her lips pressed firmly together, as though to keep them from trembling.

But I shrank away from knowing more. I had a feeling that I had already transgressed, as though I had been sitting at a confessional, a fear that I might stumble upon facts that might be even more unpalatable. I did not wish to probe further.

'We were talking about the undesirability of my having to get married,' I said. 'Not marriage in general.'

'And I was telling you what it is like for the girls. But this doesn't mean that all marriages turn out like mine. They are very careful to match the horoscopes of the bride and the bridegroom and to see that all the stars are in the right places at the time of the wedding. But sometimes a star slips, unnoticed by anyone, and then everything turns sour. I hope the stars will stay firm for you, and I hope you will be able to play the game by the rules—that you will make whoever you marry very, very happy. I shall pray for you.' And Mother turned her face away.

I could see past her profile into the drive beyond, the curving line of the lights and their reflections trembling in the dark pools, and I longed to say something that would assuage her sorrow. But I could not think of anything to say. I had a feeling I had already said far too much. I sipped the strong drink which was now lukewarm in my hands, grateful for the burning sensation in my throat and stomach as it coursed down.

The clock on the tower began to chime and it broke the silence of the night. It was nine o'clock. It was time to say good night to my mother and go down and join my father for dinner.

My father was still in the billiard room, and when I went in, I was glad to see that Hanuman Singh and two other people were with him. They had just finished a game. The marker was putting away the cues in their cases and one of the servants was handing round a tray of drinks.

'Ah, here is Abhay,' Father said, almost as though they had been talking about me before I entered. 'Would you like a drink, Abhay?'

This was the first time my father had offered me a drink. 'No thank you, Dada,' I said.

'Hanuman has been telling us about the giant; you know, the Kolaras tiger.'

'Oh, the giant,' I said. 'Is he around?'

'Tell the Yuwaraj about the giant, Hanuman,' Father said.

Hanuman Singh began to tell me about his efforts to follow the activities of the Kolaras tiger. He must have seen hundreds of tigers in his life, more tigers than perhaps anyone else, and yet whenever he talked about some special tiger he was trying to outwit, his eyes would light up and his voice would take on the earnestness of a confession. Listening to him, it was so easy to forget that, as soon as dinner was over, I would have to talk with my father about more serious matters. And then I found myself thinking that, as far as my father was concerned, there were few things more serious in life than the shooting of tigers.

Hanuman Singh and the other two men stayed on to dinner, and throughout dinner we talked alternately about the Tatwal shoot and the Kolaras giant.

We ate in the Indian-style dining-room, which had no carpet because the floor was swabbed after every meal. We sat on hard wooden paats placed along the wall, our legs folded under us, with the taats and waties of food placed before each of us on individual chaurangs, barely a foot high. I ate without appetite, leaving the taat with the Indian food severely alone and keeping to the lighter western dishes. I had clear soup, baked pomfret and an orange jelly. My father, who never ate much, made his usual pretence of eating through the entire menu, both western and Indian, the quails in aspic, the Mughlai partridge, the lamb pallav, the curried pintail, the puries and the papars and the chutneys, the pulses and the curds, pressing his guests to try one or the other dish, and asking the table boys to put out some special preserves prepared by the cooks.

'Let's have some of the wild-boar achar,' he would say. 'It should be fully cured by now.' Or 'Hasn't the pickled fish-roe arrived yet from Bombay? I must remind them about it.'

It was long past ten when we finished dinner, and Father washed his hands in a silver bowl brought to him by one of the servants. 'Don't forget to tell the Dewanji to order some fish-roe from the Tata Industrial Home,' he ordered the butler.

In the verandah, the guests did their mujras and sought his permission to leave, and he joked with them as they said good night. After that we walked in silence to the room with the tiger rug, and he squatted in his accustomed place, close to the bolster and yet not leaning into it. It was cold, since there was no fire, and the Bacarat chandelier threw a cold light and somehow accentuated the stillness of the room. The hookah-burdar came with the hookah already glowing, placed it by my father's side and handed him the pipe.

'For people in our position,' my father began, 'a marriage is a sacred thing. It is not a private, purely personal matter at all, but an affair of state, as it were. Even the Political Department has an interest. There is a duty, an obligation, to marry someone suitable. Someone whom the people will one day have to accept as their Maharani.' And my father picked up the hookah pipe.

It was almost as though he had been reading through a prepared speech, choosing his words with care, pausing for effect.

I looked at him, smoking his hookah with extreme concentration and almost felt sorry for him, for he himself was so singularly vulnerable. I could have told him that I had just left a Maharani, his own wife, on the verge of tears, a woman who might have been happily married to some humble soldier or clerk, a woman whom I had advised to go away and find a new life for herself. What was the point of making a girl a Maharani if you were going to treat her as an untouchable?

The gurgle of the hookah stopped. 'Look at the King of England,' my father said. 'Look what happened to Edward VIII.'

My mother, too, had mentioned the King of England, and for a moment I wondered if my father and mother had been talking about me. I did not want to say anything about the King, knowing my father's views on the subject of the abdication. For my own part, I have always held that the King was served shamefully by his Government, and that the abdication was one of the noblest acts of man.

'But in the twentieth century,' I said, 'to choose a wife, a wife who would become a Maharani … just by looking at a photograph. It seems quite fantastic. Supposing, just supposing that she has some sort of … some sort of infirmity that a photograph cannot reveal? Supposing she stutters?'

My father put away the pipe carefully in its stand and shook his head. 'All that has been seen to,' he explained. 'At first there were the sardars, trusted noblemen, going round and making inquiries, both direct and indirect. They went and saw at least twenty young ladies, all from the best families. After that, their womenfolk took over, making the most careful inquiries. Then the horoscopes were matched, the blood-lines scrutinized …'

'Like buying a horse,' I said.

'What? Oh, yes, very much like selecting a horse,' my father said. But he was not laughing as he said it. 'Just as one would not think of buying a horse that had not been certified sound in body and limb and did not possess the looks and other attributes … why, even with a horse, the astrologers have to sit down and make sure that the stars are propitious. Who would buy an ill-starred horse? And of course there are the blood-lines. Breeding is most important … far more important in men and women than in horses.'

'But what is the special hurry? Why can't it wait … for a couple of years? Until the war is over?'

'I've already waited longer than is customary in our circles. Besides, it is most important to get this thing all settled before … before you do anything rash. It is important to make provision for the succession. We cannot always think in terms of our inclinations. We have a duty, a sacred obligation to our gadi, to our people. "I shall be true to the salt of my ancestors," we say in our prayers. No, Abhay, I'm afraid it will not be possible to wait.'

'I was not prepared for this: I was given no hint when I was asked to come here,' I protested.

'Besides there are these young ladies. We have to give a definite answer. After that, if necessary, the marriage itself can wait for a year or so. They … their parents, must have an answer. They cannot afford to wait. Girls in our kind of family must be betrothed before they are eighteen. I can assure you that they are thoroughly accomplished girls, selected for looks, education and upbringing … and neither of them stutters.'

My father smiled and picked up the stem of his hookah pipe, and for a time there was silence except for the rhythmic gurgle of the water in the bowl. I had a feeling that our talk was over and that we were exactly where we were. I wanted to assert myself, make it quite clear to him that I was not prepared to be rushed into marriage.

'It's not as though you have become fond of any girl, have you?' my father asked, and I was startled by his voice, for I was getting used to the silence that hung between us.

This was my opportunity to open my mind, but again I shirked. I did not want my father to know about Minnie. They lived in different worlds.

'That girl you took out in Simla, the station-master's daughter,' my father said. 'You haven't got involved with her in any way, have you?'

I was too taken aback to say anything. I did not know that my father had received a report from the Simla police about my friendship with Minnie. In a way he seemed to know more about her than I did, for I had not known that Minnie's father was a station-master.

'Now, that sort of girl … a girl who does not object to … to being together with one. That's certainly not a girl a man can think of marrying … not in any class, and certainly not when it means elevating her to rank of Maharani.'

'Why not?' I asked. I was hurt more than angry. 'Why not?'

'Well, look at it in this way. In a few years, this … this young lady who has to make her own living, I understand, by taking a clerk's job in the military accounts department, what will she be like in ten years from now? Like Mrs. Hinks. Remember Mrs. Hinks, your nanny?'

Yes, I remembered Mrs. Hinks, poor Mrs. Hinks with the faded mother-hubbards, the flat-soled shoes, the yellow, wrinkled face, the nervous giggle, the scaley hands. It was not fair to talk of Mrs. Hicks in the same breath as Minnie; honey-coloured; fresh and firm and radiant.

'Mrs. Hinks came from the same sort of background. She was, if I remember right, a Customs Inspector's daughter, deserted by her husband. But of course she always made out her husband had died.'

'Miss Bradley is quite different from Mrs. Hinks, quite different,' I said.

'You have not seen of this … this Miss Bradley, since you were up in Simla, have you?'

'We met in Delhi, when I was coming down this time.'

'Oh, in Delhi. By previous arrangement, I presume?'

'Yes.'

'I see. That means you've been writing letters.'

'Of course I have been writing,' I said,

'Oh!' my father said, and there was a worried frown on his face. 'I had not realized it had gone any further than … than Simla. Compromising letters?'

'Compromising?'

'Letters that Miss Bradley could … you know, letters that could be used for blackmail.'

The thought of Minnie, tearful and erect, her face pale, turning away before my train left because she was afraid to break down, using my letters for blackmail was quite preposterous. The implication made me burn with anger.

'She is not that kind of girl,' I protested, reminding myself that this was a time to keep cool. 'Miss Bradley is a wonderful girl, and I'm in love with her,' I told him.

'Oh, in love,' Father said, and I did not know whether there was a sneer in his voice.

'Yes.'

'Does that mean you were actually thinking of marrying her?'

'Yes, sir.'

'You didn't say anything about this in your letters, did you?' he asked with a touch of anxiety.

'No,' I said. 'But that was merely because I have still to ascertain her feelings—whether she loves me.'

My father was silent for a long time, and he was not smoking either, for the fire seemed to have gone out of the hookah and the stem lay cold in his hand.

'Remember that with some kinds of girl … well, it is not always necessary to marry them even if you do happen to be in love … if love is the correct word.'

'You mean keep her as a mistress?'

'Yes. Now that I think of it, it seems I made a mistake in … in not keeping to the customs of our class in seeing that you were introduced to someone who could have ensured that you did not fall for these … these wayside temptations.'

In spite of myself, I could not help thinking that he had spared me many of the inflictions that he himself had been subjected to. The thought of someone like Bibi-bai being installed in a dark corner of the old palace for me to work off my youthful appetites on was quite revolting.

'That would seem to be the solution,' my father said almost brightly. 'And I can tell you there would be nothing objectionable in such an arrangement. You make up your mind which of these two proposals is acceptable to you, and then continue by all means, your … friendship with this girl in Simla. But please don't write any more letters to her, Abhay. One does not write letters to one's mistresses. It can be quite dangerous.'

I felt so disloyal to Minnie, discussing her like that, and yet I felt almost sorry for my father whose ideas were so hopelessly out of touch with the times.

'And if there is any … any issue, you can always make some suitable agreement …'

'Issue?'

'Well, children.'

Children whom their schoolmates would call bastards and whore-sons and who would grow up into bullies, hating the world from sheer self-defence. Again I thought of Bibi-bai and Amina-begam and Sherawathi, tucked away in dark corners, living in the smothering world of the concubines, only to be visited after the hours of darkness.

'No, Father,' I said with determination. 'I don't think Minnie—Miss Bradley—is that kind of girl at all. I love her and I mean to make her my wife, not my mistress.'

'If she is willing,' my father said very softly.

I did not reply to that. Somehow I had always felt that Minnie would not turn me down.

'I am sorry to hear that,' my father said. 'Your mother will be most unhappy. It is not easy to make a decision like that and keep it. Not in our sort of circle. Convention is far too strong. You cannot flout it—cannot swim against the current and hope to survive. You will find too many people ranged against you, and too many forces.'

There was no suggestion of threat in his voice, only disapproval. I almost wished that he would lose his temper, shout that he would disown me as they always did in books, so that I could have come out with all the pent-up fury of my own rage against him for sullying Minnie's name. I wanted an opportunity to bring out the chaos of his own private life, expose the hollowness of his values, the shameful treatment of my mother; I wanted to bring his make-believe world tumbling down around him. But he was not making things easy for me. He was being the Maharaja again, not the kindly, anxious father having a man-to-man talk with his son; he was taking command, as he always did, confident, assured, even arrogant.

'To be born to rule, to rule six lakhs of men, to come into the wealth and prestige of a seventeen-gunner Maharaja—that has its privileges. Privileges and almost absolute power. But remember, my son, that the position also calls for tyaga—sacrifice. It sometimes makes cruel demands, demands that one is convinced are beyond one's powers of giving. In the olden days, before the British conquest, it even called for the giving of life itself—for how many of our ancestors, yours and mine, have laid down their lives for the sake of our heritage? Now often involves the giving up of … of things one wants above everything else. And one has to give, give as gracefully as one can, whatever suffering it may involve. There is no other way. It is odd how these things seem to fall into a pattern. Your grandfather was confronted with the same sort of situation: private desires against the dignity and welfare of the state, the continuation of the line in the traditional way. I myself …'

'You!' I could not contain myself. 'You, Father!'

But he did not take umbrage at my tone. 'Yes, Abhay,' he went on, quite evenly. 'I, too. You will never know how much I had to give up—how suddenly—when my brother was killed and I was called upon to marry the girl who was to be his bride: your mother. I had to make a sacrifice which I then thought was quite beyond me.'

Sacrifice! The most fortunate thing that could have happened to my father was his marriage to my mother, and he was talking of sacrifice. I wanted to tell him so; tell him to count his blessings and make his peace with my mother before it was too late. But his face had a sad, faraway look, as though he was reliving a part of his past that had called for sudden sacrifice and suffering. And again I caught myself feeling sorry for him. It certainly did not make things easy for me.

I had an impression that our lines had been said, that there was nothing more to add. I waited for a few minutes as though for some sort of signal from my father, and when I found that he was wholly absorbed in his own thoughts, I rose to my feet and did my mujra.

'You will cause a lot of unhappiness, my son; a lot of unhappiness to all those who love you, if you go on with this foolishness,' my father remarked and his voice had a slight edge. 'That is, if Miss Bradley is willing. There is still that "if". We shall see.'

Perhaps he was right, but then I had my own happiness to consider, and as I came out into the cold air, I was aware of a sense of achievement, even of triumph, a feeling that I had broken through the clammy web of antiquated taboos that surrounded me and that I was a free man in a free world.

We had decided nothing, and yet we had not left things as they had been, and as I walked down the gloomy corridors, I did not feel towards him the same bitterness that I had felt earlier in the evening. I was glad that Minnie's name had cropped up and that I had made it clear that I was determined not to give her up. But knowing how strongly my father held to his beliefs, I found myself wondering what his next move would be.

In my room, the two photographs were still there, lying face down on the rosewood table. Without looking at them, I tore them into little bits and threw the pieces into the waste-paper basket.

I was leaving next morning. My father had gone out fishing for mahseer and I could not find him to say good-bye. My mother looked pale and tense, as she often did in the mornings, and gave me the impression that she was trying to be brave because she was convinced I was going to the wars. I thought it was really considerate of her not to ask what had happened in my talk with my father the previous evening.

'There is something I want to give you,' Mother said. 'I don't know how long it will be before we see each other again. It is for your bride.'

I did not tell her that I had decided not to marry either of the two girls who had been found suitable for me.

She unclasped the rope of pearls round her neck and handed it to me. 'I would like you to give it to her from me, whoever she is.'

The pearls fell with a smooth rattle, and they felt warm and hard in my hands. Even in the dim, early morning light, they shone bright and pink.

'And I want you to know they are mine,' Mother said. 'Mine to do what I like with ...'

'Why, Maji, everything that you have is yours.'

'No.' She shook her head. 'Not everything. Only what I came to this house with—nothing else.'

I slid the pearls into my bush-shirt pocket and stood awkwardly, towering over Mother, while she put a dab of curds on my palm in the traditional gesture of farewell. 'Bless you, my son,' she said. 'And don't think too harshly of me whatever happens.'

I did not know what she was referring to. 'Nothing is going to happen, Mother,' I assured her. 'Don't worry about anything.'

Almost for the first time in my life, I was glad to get away from home, to shake myself free from the weight of personal problems, and I looked forward to the hard work that lay ahead; to the ordered simplicity of regimental life.

My first posting was to the Satpura Regimental Centre at Raniwada. As I reported at the office, one of the clerks gave me a registered package. It was a large, mounted photograph of Minnie. I was sharing a room with another newly commissioned officer, a sullen, taciturn man called Barber who had a crop of large purple pimples on his face and body and who slept with a paperbound copy of Plato's Dialogues under his pillow. I felt a little self-conscious at putting out such a large picture on my tiny desk. Compared to it, the postcard-sized snapshots of my father and mother in their double leather frame looked ridiculously small. But it was nice to have Minnie's photograph in the room, bare-shouldered and with her large, lustrous eyes caught with just the beginning of a smile. The first evening I was allowed out, I bought the most expensive silver frame I could find for it. Lying in bed after a hard day's work, I used to find myself gazing at Minnie, often comparing her to the two girls with saris so decorously draped over their heads whose photographs I had torn to pieces.

It was while I was at Raniwada that I heard my mother had left Begwad and gone to live in her family house at Jhansi. At first there were rumours, beginning with a vague report in one of the Hindi papers which someone had read in the bazaar—for those were the days when no Hindi papers came into officers' messes—and then there was a letter from my mother herself. It was sent from Jhansi, telling me that she had decided to leave my father, and again asking me not to think too harshly of her.

Even though I had myself advised her to go, I received the news with a sense of shock and with the numbness one experiences at feeling that something that cannot be remedied has taken place. I kept asking myself: had I interfered without justification?

It seemed that my mother had set out as usual for her evening drive, and when she had failed to return for dinner, they had sent out search parties. It was not until the next morning, when Lala Harikishore received a telegram from her, that they knew she had left for good. She had gone with only a small suitcase containing her personal belongings and taking her own chauffeur and maid with her.

'Only what I came to this house with,' I could hear her telling me when she had given me her pearls. 'Nothing else.'

For what she had done, I felt my heart go out to my mother. It must have taken great courage to break away, to steel herself to do what she should have done long ago. I sent her a telegram, wishing her well, and afterwards a letter telling her I would never misunderstand, that I would never think harshly of her.

But I was wrong. The very day I wrote to her, I received a letter from Charudutt; after I had read it, I was not sure that I would ever be able to forgive my mother for what she had done.

Charudutt had stayed on in Begwad after the duck-shoot and he had had his leave extended because there was some talk about my father arranging his marriage. I had not heard any mention of Charudutt's marriage then, but I knew he was in Begwad because I had seen his name mentioned in press reports of cricket matches;

and once, when he scored a century in the Indore match, they had printed his photograph.

As I opened Charudutt's letter, I was overcome by a sense of foreboding. I knew that he had never liked me and would not have taken the trouble to write except to give me news that would be hurtful. But even so I was not braced for what was to come.

His letter contained no reference to my mother until the very end. It was all about cricket and tennis and his century in the Indore match. He even said that the cricket team was missing me, which I remember thinking it was very good of him to have mentioned. But in the postscript he came to the real purpose of his letter:

> 'I hear that Her Highness, your Mother, is well. She is living in her family mansion at Jhansi, as you perhaps know, and I understand that Mr. Abdulla Jan, who was once the Palace Officer here, has taken on the job as her estate manager.'

I noticed without seeing, as though I were looking at someone else, that my hands trembled and my knuckles had gone white, and there was a buzz within my ears as though something was about to explode.

You could not forgive a goddess who had gone wrong. In anyone else, you could overlook a blemish; not in someone you had always regarded as perfection itself.

I was not conscious of a pain so much as an overpowering numbness. I caught myself wishing that my mother had died; that somehow her death would have been more bearable than the crushing humiliation she had brought upon us. Until a hundred years earlier, it was customary for a Bedar Maharani to perform sati at her husband's death by throwing herself on his funeral pyre. The satis sacrificed themselves and became goddesses; their names were added to the family shrine. Now a Maharani had taken a lover. She had desecrated the shrine of the satis she had worshipped; she had blackened the name of the Bedar women for all times.

All my childhood hallucinations came snarling back at me in a new garb, the garb of truth. A part of myself could even rationalize—the young woman cast on the dustheap in the full bloom of youth, growing to the verge of middle age with all her womanly desires still unslaked, rebelling, refusing to spend the rest of her life shut away in a dark palace, a volatile bundle of yearnings tearing herself away from the shell of conventions. There was something pathetically heroic about it.

And yet there was another part of me that would never be able to condone it; that would carry this humiliation to my death—and that was my real self, as I was beginning to find out, as I grew more and more deeply rooted in the abstract values of the princes.

The hateful, leering face of Abdulla Jan leaning over the counter of Gallico's bar, whispering to his companions, showing off his watch and bragging about having received it from my mother for services rendered …

'Steady, old chap; you've knocked over my drink!' someone was saying. 'Anything wrong?'

I shook myself, and for a moment I wondered where I was and what I was doing. Then it all became clear. I was in the regimental mess of the fourth Satpuras, and we were just about to go in to dinner.

14

Stripped for Action

In the Regimental Centre, we were still three stages away from the war. We were given rifle drill every morning, saluting drill twice a week, guard-mounting duties on Saturdays to teach us ceremonial drill, and every Sunday there was a cricket fixture with one of the local clubs complete with a shandy lunch. And in the mess too they kept up a pretence of peacetime routine, with regular mess nights and drinking toasts to the King—we even had a ladies' night once every two weeks.

After six weeks in the Regimental Centre, I was posted to our training battalion in the Fourteenth Division in the Chindwara jungles. Here we dispensed with all the frills and frippery of military life. We lived under canvas, 'stripped for action' as our General never tired of telling us. We moved from place to place at the double, always carrying our light packs with us, and we began to sleep with live grenades under our pillows, next to our service revolvers, so that we could get used to their feel. We gave up wearing shirts altogether except after dark, for we were being toughened for battle, and by merely looking at a man you could tell how long he had been with the division by the degree of sunburn on his shoulders. All of us acquired sharp patterns on our backs and chests made by the equipment, large crosses on the back and broad stripes running down from shoulder to waist in front. For days on end we had to subsist on hard rations and water at the rate of one bottle per day, which included what we used for shaving. We lived in minute, single-flapped tents, but mercifully each of us had a tent to himself, and I felt relieved to be separated from Barber who had left Plato behind and acquired a pocket volume called *The Teachings of the Great Philosophers*. I had to take Minnie's photograph out of its frame, for all the furniture in our tents consisted of a low canvas bed and an all-purpose table hardly two feet by two, and what with my shaving things and other belongings, there really was not much room for photographs.

But it was nice to have the photograph in the tent, all to myself, away from Barber's disapproving gaze; a link with a civilized, sophisticated world which was growing more remote every day. I would drop off to sleep looking at the photograph and dream of Minnie.

My impressions of the days in the training camp were overshadowed by an awareness of a total breaking away from my roots. It was almost as though I were a fugitive, leading a new life under a new name, a second-lieutenant Bedar of the Satpura Rifles. My father had not written to me since I left home, and after a few weeks I too stopped writing to him. My mother wrote regularly, at least once a week, but I tore up her letters unopened. My only contacts with home were occasional letters from Hamidulla and Gonzalves, all about horses, tennis, cricket and fishing. I willingly, almost eagerly, surrendered to the daily fatigue of mind and body, thankful for the merciless pace of the training, the quick, unnoticed turning of day into night, the instantaneous surrender to sleep after dinner.

It was from the training camp that I wrote to Simla for Mappin and Webb's catalogue. From it I selected a gold and rhinestone clasp in the shape of a heart with an arrow running through it. I sent them a cheque, with instructions to have the clasp delivered to Minnie on her birthday, the twenty-third of March.

For the first few days, my skin was a mass of flaming itches, from the jungle tick and mosquito bites, from the long tears caused by the thorns and from the sores made by the brass ends of the equipment burning into it during the heat of the day. But at the end of six weeks all the scars had healed, my skin had become impervious to the bites and I was proud of the rich brown tan I had acquired with the equipment straps neatly marked out on my back and shoulders.

One day at the end of March, I was delighted to be told by the Adjutant that I was being sent to the Holding Battalion, from which to be posted to one of the active battalions of the regiment. I was sure that I would get the posting of my choice, for the Adjutant of the Holding Battalion was none other than Punch Farren. Punch was beaming as I went in to report my arrival. I saluted and stood stiffly to attention.

'Ah, Scrapper, here you are at last! I was beginning to wonder when you were going to turn up,' Punch said.

'I am glad to be coming to you, sir,' I told him.

Punch gave me a hard stare. 'Sit down, damn you, and stop being so damned G.S. You've certainly come at the right time. Big things cooking. Don't speak about it to anyone, of course, but it looks as though we shall be sending a few chaps to Malaya—the other end of the world. Operation EMU, you know.'

I did not know anything about Operation EMU then. It was only later that I found out that it was the code word for sending a brigade to Malaya in preparation for the Japanese threat.

'Or again, there's the usual draft going to the Middle East; well, bigger than normal, I should think. Warming up for a big scrap there too. Old Rommel just has to be slung out of Egypt, y'know. There's talk of big changes in command. Oh, a hell of a big do coming on in the desert. You're in a damned lucky position, Scrapper. One of the few people who can choose wherever he wants to go.'

'It's very lucky for me you're here, Punch,' I said.

Punch gave a snort. 'EMU or the Middle East, you just have to give the word, old boy. And I don't mind telling you, you've come with a damn good chit from the Training Div. The Adjutant there has graded you as "Outstanding".'

I was glad about this, for no one there had told me I had done well.

'I would like to go wherever you're going yourself, Punch,' I said. 'I'd like to be in the same battalion.'

Punch frowned. 'I'm afraid that's not going to be so easy, old boy,' he said. 'The C.O. here's not going to let go of me. They were in a hell of a mess here, until I took over—the admin work all gone to pot. And since I was able to put it into … into some kind of order … Well, it's just one of those things, Scrapper. He wants me to go on doing Adjutant here.'

'Oh, I'm sorry to hear that, Punch,' I said.

Punch shook his head from side to side and tugged at his moustache. 'Unless, of course, they pull away the C.O. himself … give him a brigade or something. Otherwise there's absolutely no chance of my being able to get away from this hole,' he said ruefully. 'But, of course, I'm trying like blazes to wangle it.'

I knew how sick Punch must be at the thought of being stuck in the Holding Battalion, almost next door to a theatre of war, but as usual he seemed to be taking it very well.

'That's tough luck, Punch,' I said.

'Damned tough,' he said. 'But there it is. That's the army all over! If you are any good, they won't let you go.'

'In that case, I don't mind where I go. There is just one thing …'

'Yes?'

'I'd rather not be sent to the same battalion as Barber.'

'Oh, Barber!' Punch snorted. 'Master Barber,' and he began to chuckle to himself.

'We have sort of tended to haunt each other; sharing a room at the centre, and then a basha here.'

'Oh, yes, we can lay that on all right. Now let me see. Look, I personally don't think there's going to be much chance of your seeing any fun in EMU—bloody waste of time. I don't think the Japs are going to risk getting into this war. So we'll put you down for the desert and detail our friend to go to Malaya. OK?'

'Thank you, Punch,' I said. 'I would like to go where the fun is.'

Since the battalion sent to Malaya was in action against the Japanese before the year was out, and since not a single one of the officers of the 8th Satpuras in that particular action was ever heard of again, I have often wondered whether I was personally responsible for sending Lieutenant Barber to his death.

Life was what we had learnt to call 'cushy' in the Holding Battalion, and the work, as far as the officers were concerned, mainly administrative. We had to build up the drafts required for going overseas, so many men, so many N.C.O.s and so many officers; a matter of fitting individuals into the columns of the establishment tables. We hardly did any drill and spent our mornings at the ranges, practising with rifles and light machine-guns. Once a week we went for short, easy route marches. We were on a wartime scale of rations, generous, even sumptuous, and entitled to N.A.A.F.I. facilities—we got our Scotch at six rupees a bottle. Hot water for our baths was plentiful, and the mess had a wonderful cook. There was abundant time to think and brood, for suppressed longings to return, for old wounds to open up.

The only major inconvenience was our lack of accommodation. We lived in minute basha huts, flimsy erections of bamboo and straw, and were accommodated two to a hut. My bed was so close to Barber's that we could shake each other's hand while lying in bed. Because of the restricted space on my bedside table, I had to trim the edges of Minnie's photograph. That was how I would have to carry her picture to the wars, trimmed down to the edges and without a frame.

'Stripped for action', I remember thinking to myself; and if I let my mind wander, it was so easy to think of Minnie as having no clothes on at all, for the photograph only showed her head and shoulders and the shoulders were quite bare.

I was in the Holding Battalion for nearly three weeks. On a Monday in late April, while I was at the miniature range, an orderly came to tell me that the Adjutant wanted to see me. I knew that my posting orders had come.

'You are not going to like this,' Punch said.

'Why? EMU?' I asked.

'No, old boy. You've been selected to go to the Intelligence School at Karachi.'

'Karachi!'

'There is a silver lining of sorts. Your promotion to Lieutenant has come through. You can start wearing your second pip.'

'But Karachi, Punch!'

'Well, it's a bit of a feather in your cap, really. The "I" course is usually meant for really promising officers, mostly Captains.'

'But I don't want to go on any damned course, for Captains or Majors! I want to go to the Middle East!' As I have said, it was late April in the year 1941, and all eyes were turned to Egypt where Rommel had just been checked in his audacious push through Cyrenaica.

Punch gave a disapproving snort and shook his head. 'It's not going to be any good getting all het up, Scrapper,' he said. 'I seem to discern your old man's hand in this.'

'My father!'

He nodded. 'I got the C.O. to make a call to G.H.Q. and find out what was at the back of this posting, right from the Holding Battalion … most unusual. Quite unheard of, dammit! The C.O. had his ears pinned for his trouble. It seems that the Chief of Intelligence himself, General Hinton, has asked for you by name to be sent on the "I" course.'

'Hinton?'

'That's the old boy who was chief guest at your father's duckshoot, don't you remember? I got a lift back in his car to Delhi.'

Yes, I remembered the mild-mannered man with cold grey eyes who had sat next to me at Christmas dinner and talked to me about riding and fishing the whole evening.

'There can be little doubt that your Pa has been doing a certain amount of really high-level wire pulling. You can chalk up one for the old man and start thinking of a suitable way to christen your second pip,' Punch said.

We christened the second pip in the mess that evening and we all got mildly drunk. It was while Punch and I were still in the mess, after the others had gone, with an almost empty bottle of Old Angus on the table before us, that I asked him:

'Do you think I could get a few days' leave?'

'Before a course? Not bloody likely,' Punch said. 'Going home?'

'No, I just wanted to go up to Simla for a day.'

'Oh,' Punch said. 'Oh, I see. Sort of getting your own back on Papa.'

'I want to see Minnie, Punch,' I said.

'Have you heard from her lately?'

'Well, not lately, but you know how erratic letters are through the Field post office,' I explained. 'It's odd, but she hasn't even written about something I had her sent for her birthday.'

'Maybe she doesn't want to write,' Punch said. 'Tony Sykes must be back in Simla. He's on the staff there.'

'Is he in the regiment?'

'Oh, rather. He's a Satpura officer, all right; terribly pucca.'

'Do you think I can get the leave, Punch, just a day or so?'

Punch laughed. 'My God! Just shows how green you are. Don't you know anything about joining time?'

'You mean the time for getting to Karachi from here?'

'That's right. Now, whenever an officer is transferred from one place to another, he gets what is known as joining time. Works out to around one day for every two hundred miles, with the Sundays excluded. So Karachi being, let us say, a thousand miles from here, and since it's not going to take more than three days to get there, there's no reason why you should not nip off to Simla for a day and not saying anything to anyone about it. Only, don't get found out, for Christ's sake … raise no end of a stink.'

'Why, thank you, Punch! Thank you very much,' I said. 'No, I won't get found out.'

'Personally, I should strongly advise you against going up to Simla … at this juncture.'

'Why, Punch?'

'Let's kill the bottle,' Punch said, 'and get back to our bashas. Christ, it's past one!'

I poured the remaining whisky equally into our glasses and topped the glasses with water.

'Why not, Punch?' I asked again, after I had handed him his drink.

'Why not, what?' he said, and his voice was quite blurred.

'Why do you advise me against going to Simla?'

'Because, old boy, it's in the middle of the bloody season there, don't you know, and you might be spoiling a lot of fun for a lot of people.'

But Punch had had a lot to drink and I realized he did not know what he was talking about.

I arrived in Simla on a Saturday evening, driving up from Kalka in a hired car. The Cecil had no room for an army Lieutenant and I certainly had no wish to tell them that I was the Yuwaraj of Begwad, having sneaked off to Simla without leave. I got a room for myself at the Continental and signed the register as Lieutenant Singh.

There was no telephone in my room, and I had to go down to the reception desk to ring Minnie. I gave the clerk the number of the Miranda House hostel and waited for the call to go through. It seemed a long time before Minnie came to the telephone.

'Here you are, sir,' the clerk said and handed me the receiver. I was so excited that my hand shook.

'Minnie!' I said, and my voice to myself sounded surprisingly high-pitched.

'But Tony,' Minnie said, 'It's not nearly eight and ...'

'Minnie, it's me, Abhay,' I told her.

'Who? Oh, Abhay,' Her voice had a sharpness that was unfamiliar to me, 'Where are you speaking from?'

'Here ... Simla. I've just arrived,' I explained. My heart was beating fast, 'How are you, Minnie?'

'What? Oh, I am very well, thank you.'

'I want you to come out to dinner,' I said.

'This evening, Abhay? But I can't. Not this evening.'

'Why not?'

'I am … I'm in the middle of washing my hair,' and Minnie gave a nervous laugh.

'But I must see you, Minnie. Can't I see you later? It's only half past seven.'

'Oh, Abbey,' Minnie said, and her voice was like her old self again, soft and purring. 'A girl just can't come out when she's washed her hair. I am sorry, Abhay, really sorry. But you should have given me a little warning.'

I had a sudden longing to see her as she was. I could picture her bending over the phone, perhaps wearing an old dressing gown, and her hair lank and glossy from the washing and her face without make up, looking nervous and helpless and appealing because she wanted to come out and could not.

'Minnie,' I asked, 'What are you wearing?'

'What did you say? What am I wearing?' Minnie said, and again her voice sounded slightly peevish.

'Minnie, aren't you glad that I'm ringing up—wouldn't you like to see me?'

'Of course I want to, Abbey; but of course I'm glad you are ringing up! It's just … it's just that I simply cannot come out this evening.'

'Well, tomorrow then,' I said, trying to hide the disappointment in my voice. 'What about tomorrow, Minnie? I was thinking we could go out in the car.'

'Oh, tomorrow?' Minnie said, and there was a slight pause. 'Well, I'll have to see about tomorrow. Can I ring you up, later?'

'Yes, of course,' I said. 'Please do. You must come, Minnie. I have something, something really important to tell you …'

'What's that?' she asked.

'Something I want to tell you.'

'Oh, I'll give you a ring,' she promised. 'The Cecil?'

'What? Oh, no; not the Cecil. The Continental. And Minnie …'

'Yes?'

'Ask for Lieutenant Singh,' I told her. 'And please, you must come. Please.'

'I'll try,' she said. I'll certainly try to make it.'

After dinner, I went to see a film, and sitting in front of me was Lala Harikishore, our Chief Minister. Even in the darkness, I knew I had not made a mistake: the tight-fitting churidars, the neat, knee-length achkan, the angocha draped primly around the shoulders, the oversized round pagri of the Poona brahmin. He was so close that I could have tapped him on the back by reaching forward. For a moment I wondered what Harikishore could be doing in Simla, and if my father had come up with him. And then I got absorbed in the film, a Betty Grable extravaganza with a South Sea background.

When I got back to the Continental, the reception clerk told me that there was a message for me. I waited impatiently while he fished it out from a drawer. Minnie had rung up to say that she could go out with me next day.

15

A.W.O.L.

I wore my uniform with the khaki pullover that Minnie had knitted, although I knew that it was not in conformity with regulations, and I was pleased to see that Minnie was wearing the gold and rhinestone clasp that I had had sent for her birthday, pinned at the V of her sweater. Her face looked pale and drawn as though the breeze had been too cold for her, and for the first time I thought that she looked very beautiful.

We sat huddled close to each other in the car, not saying much, and I drove straight to the spot where we had picnicked a year earlier. I had brought a lunch basket from Wenger's with the same things we had had to eat before. It was roughly the same time of the year too, but I had a feeling that it was not going to be the same. Nor was I wrong.

There were big grey woolly-elephant clouds in the sky and the sun came out only in patches. When I stopped the car, I found that our private patch of grass was in the shade. As we got out, I held Minnie close and kissed her. I felt her shoulders tremble in my arms.

We lay down on the grass, close to each other, my arms cradling her head. For a long time we did not say anything. Then I asked:

'Why did you sound hesitant about coming out this morning?'

'Sunday,' Minnie explained. 'For once I wanted to go to church.'

'Oh, church,' I said. 'Sunday, of course. I had not realized.' It was the wrong note and it lingered in the air. I found myself thinking of my mother's preoccupation with the household gods, the shrine of the family satis, the noisy ritual of my father's poojas. I wondered if there was a church in Begwad. I had never seen a church in our state.

I looked at Minnie, wearing a short skirt and quite unconcerned about showing her knees as she sprawled beside me, at the tight orange sweater, the neck quite bare of jewellery, the forehead blank as a widow's, the scarlet nails. For a fleeting moment I became aware of how deep my roots went into a Hindu past, and how we seemed to belong to separate compartments. Minnie's world was different from mine, the world of the occasional visitor to the palace, not of its inmates. I tried to drive away the thoughts of our difference from my mind because I knew they were disloyal to Minnie.

'Have you ever tried wearing a sari?' I asked.

'Only once or twice, for a fancy dress dance. It kept coming off.'

'You must look lovely in a sari,' I told her, and yet I found it difficult to picture her in Indian clothes. 'And bangles,' I said. 'Bangles and a pearl necklace ...'

'Real pearls?' Minnie said.

'What? Of course, real pearls. You couldn't wear false pearls with a sari.'

'Yes, I should love a pearl necklace,' Minnie said dreamily, and her eyes were wide. 'Necklace, but not bangles. Bangles don't go with dresses and high heels.'

I lay back, smoking a cigarette and watching Minnie's face and wanting to take her in my arms. And suddenly I thought of the string of pearls lying in my uniform box. 'I want you to give it to her, whoever she is,' Mother had said. They would look lovely around Minnie's throat, I thought, and then I shrank from the idea. They were Mother's pearls, tainted pearls. Did strings of pearls carry their influence as diamonds were said to do?

The clouds overhead drifted away, and their shadow went flitting from our patch of grass. 'What are you thinking about?' Minnie asked.

'You.'

'There is something I wanted to tell you,' she said after a pause. And the way she was looking at me, I knew that it was not going to be pleasant for her to tell me whatever it was she had on her mind.

'What is it, Minnie?' I asked.

'A man called Harikishore has been to see me. He says he is the Chief Minister of your state. He said your father sent him.'

'Oh, Harikishore. I saw him at the Plaza last night. What did he have to say?' I tried to sound casual even though I had a sudden sense of foreboding.

'He was a perfect old dear, of course, perfectly charming in a bowing, scraping sort of way … you know what I mean.'

'But what on earth did he want?'

'He said he had been sent to tell me that your marriage had been arranged with some girl or other—a princess of the blood, as he put it. He wanted to make quite sure that … that there would be no difficulties on my account.'

'The cheek! The damned nerve! Did he … did he try to threaten you with anything?'

'Well, only perhaps just a veiled one. But he offered me money, quite a large sum, if I promised not to see you again.'

'The bloody little cat-faced swine!' I said.

'There was something else. He also wanted me to pass on to him all the letters you had written … that's what the money was for.' Minnie gave a nervous laugh. 'Your letters—oh, God!'

'Why did you laugh, Minnie?'

'Why, what could anyone be worried about, with your kind of letters? I don't think there can be more than a dozen in all. And oh, they're all so … so innocent; like a schoolboy's letters to a girl in the same class … a girl he doesn't know very well.'

'I'm sorry, Minnie. I was never much of a letter writer,' I said.

'He went on as though they were love letters, highly intimate and compromising. That's right, compromising was the word he used.'

So that was what they had been up to, my father and Harikishore. No wonder Minnie had sounded so cool over the telephone.

'And what kind of threats?' I asked.

'Well, that if you were to get involved in any way—he meant with someone like me, of course, but he was too indirect to say it outright—if you got involved, your father would disinherit you. I didn't know such things could really happen.'

'They do, in the Indian states. We are still in the middle ages in the states.'

'He hinted at a settlement. A generous settlement, he called it.' Minnie laughed again.

I was glad she was taking it like that. 'I hope you told him to go to hell,' I said.

She shook her head. 'Ten thousand rupees, just for those letters, and the promise not to see you again. It's a lot of money. Things you have longed for all your life suddenly becoming yours. A car, jewellery, dresses, bottles and bottles of perfume, a house … no, one couldn't buy a house with ten thousand. Perhaps just a wee one.'

I did not like the hard gleam in her eyes. It was as though she were calculating, working out the best way to use up ten thousand rupees. But I was instantly ashamed of myself. What did I know about going without things? About not having a car or a house of one's own?

'Minnie, I love you,' I said.

Her look softened. She leaned on her elbows and peered at me as though she were studying my face. 'I love the way your nose twists,' she said.

'You have told me that before, Minnie. I love you. Will you marry me?'

She went on staring at me for a long time, not saying anything. Then she said: 'Give me a cigarette.'

I held out my case and then lit her cigarette. Minnie took a deep puff and exhaled the smoke through her nostrils.

And again there was the wrong note, the needle-sharp prick bringing out the gulf between our backgrounds. My mother would never approve of a daughter-in-law who smoked, I kept thinking; she would not be permitted to enter the shrine of the satis. I must warn Minnie not to smoke in my mother's presence. And then it came back to me that my mother would not be there.

'But, darling, have you thought of the consequences?' she said.

'You mean my father creating difficulties?'

'Yes.'

'To hell with that. I can always make a living somehow. If it comes to that, I can keep on in the army.'

Minnie was looking at me anxiously, as though she wanted me to go on. After a time she asked:

'Hadn't any other way occurred to you?'

I shook my head. 'What other way can there be? If they won't let me marry someone I love—to hell with them. I don't see how Father can disinherit me, but I would be quite prepared to risk that.'

I knew that it must have sounded trite and slightly melodramatic, but Minnie did not seem to think so.

'Darling, you say the nicest things even if you are such a babe.' She crept closer and kissed me gently on the forehead. 'Your Mr. Harikishore had an alternative suggestion, as he put it: that I could go on living with you as your mistress. But oh, he was so delicate about it. "A sort of unsanctified marriage" was the way he described it, and because I didn't know what that might mean, he told me. He told me I could be one of your concubines.'

Minnie began to laugh softly to herself. '*One* of your concubines. Darling, how many do you mean to have?'

'I'm dreadfully sorry about this, Minnie. I'm ashamed of everything that he said to you.'

'Concubine,' Minnie said, 'Such a lovely word, concubine.'

'I am sorry, Minnie,' I said.

'And yet you have been so sweet. And thank you for not saying what you didn't—for not suggesting that I should be one of your concubines.'

'I want you to be my wife. Will you?'

Instead of giving me an answer, Minnie flung her cigarette away and crawled over to me and pressed her lips to mine.

I held her close. 'I want an answer,' I told her. 'I want an answer now.'

Minnie kissed me again and then held my face in her hands. 'I don't know,' she said. 'Oh, I don't know, and please don't press me, please … not now. You are so sweet, and you don't know anything about how the world goes round at all. Just a big schoolboy with a broken nose he got fighting the cops.'

'But I love you, Minnie.'

'Darling, you don't know what you're saying,' Minnie said softly, and her eyes were closed. 'Love. Taking you away from all that is yours. We are so different, so far apart, how can we come together without losing so much that is ours, that has grown with us …'

'Tell me you love me, Minnie,' I implored. 'It's so important for me to know. It is … it is everything.'

'It's so difficult not to fall in love with someone like you,' Minnie said. 'But love is not everything … it just makes things complicated …'

She broke off abruptly and turned her head away. It was a most unsatisfying answer, but I had to be content with that. Her eyes had suddenly filled with tears and she pushed herself away from me and turned her face.

I reached out and pulled her to me and held her close, nuzzling her hair.

'Minnie, who is Tony?' I asked.

Her shoulders stiffened slightly in my arms. 'Tony Sykes,' she said. 'Captain Sykes. I thought you knew him. Belongs to your regiment.'

'Are you in love with him?'

Minnie raised her head with a jerk. 'Love! I loathe the man. Love!'

'Is he in love with you?'

Minnie shook her head and gave a dry mirthless laugh. 'No, I don't think he is the type of man who falls in love … not Captain Sykes,' she said with a touch of vehemence and turned away from me.

I reached out and pulled her back to me with force, and I cupped my hands against her breasts and buried my face in her hair.

'Darling, your hair smells lovely,' I said.

'That reminds me, I must wash it today,' Minnie said.

I released my hold gently, and suddenly I felt a prick of jealousy for a man I had never met: a man called Tony Sykes.

And then, as though the fact that Minnie might be in love with another man had made her all the more irresistible, I pulled her towards me, and this time she did not resist.

My days in Karachi were spent in a daze, a state of bitter-sweet intoxication that only comes from being hopelessly in love. The Intelligence School was in the old Government House, and bore a plaque to the effect that Sir Charles Napier had built it. It was a house in the grand colonial style, and what had once been the formal reception room, a room with rosewood flooring and enormous French windows opening out onto a lawn, was our main class room. The garden had ornate fountains and glass-houses and a bandstand, and I often used to picture Minnie and myself walking hand in hand in the garden or sitting behind the shrubbery as lovers must have done when the British governor lived there.

Minnie's photograph, complete with a new mount, was back in its silver frame on my dressing table. I sent her Mother's pearl necklace, and wrote to her at least once a week, and no one could have called my letters schoolboyish any more. I sent her other presents, taking special delight in choosing things that were difficult to get: a hand-embroidered Kashmir shawl, silk stockings smuggled by Sindhi merchants, a gold and enamel dressing set, a book of Byron's poetry sixty years old.

Minnie was the centre of my world, her portrait with the naked shoulders and the look of helplessness on her face a constant spur to my longing to be with her. I had no problems except the minor one of winning Minnie away from Tony Sykes, and that was something in the nature of a challenge that I accepted with confidence. The fact that she was someone that other men wanted gave an added sharpness to my desires.

I tried to tidy up my affairs. I wrote a perfectly polite but firm letter to my father explaining my attitude, taking care not to show any resentment at his having sent Harikishore to Simla with an insulting offer to Minnie, but telling him how determined I was to marry her and how futile it was to expect me to change my mind. I also told him how annoying it had been to discover that I had been posted back to Karachi when I was on the point of going on active service.

I also wrote a postscript that if he stopped sending me my allowance, I would understand perfectly. All these months, my allowance of two thousand rupees a month had been regularly paid into my bank.

I had no wish to hurt my father, still less to cut myself off completely from him, but I wanted to be true to myself. At times I felt sorry for him, alone in the vast palace and brooding over the past. But nothing I could do would lessen his problems, and I always ended up with the reflection that my father was not a man one could pity.

He reacted just as I expected. He wrote telling me that my allowance would continue, and he assured me that in future there would be no interference on his part in my career in the army. Of Minnie, there was no mention at all.

I went through the 'I' course with almost single-minded concentration, absorbing a good deal of what they had to teach about the organization and tactics of the Germans and the Italians. We learned nothing about the Japanese army because even at the 'I' school, no one really took Japan seriously at the time. Almost as an afterthought, they gave us precisely one lecture on the Japanese army. We were shown a drawing of a Japanese light mortar and given some figures about the rate of fire of the Meigi machine gun, which was always said to be jamming in any case. We made jokes about how Japanese gunners had to lay their guns by inserting graduated blocks of wood under the barrels, and about how the whole race was too myopic ever to make proficient marksmen.

At the end of the course, the Commandant sent for four of us. I was the first to go in.

The Colonel looked up from his papers and said, 'Ah, Prince, do sit down,' and shoved his files to one side.

He was a jovial, red-faced man with bushy eyebrows just going grey, and he wore a brand-new M.C. ribbon.

'Just the customary chat,' he explained. 'Now that the course is nearly over.'

'Sir,' I said.

'You've done well on the course—damn well. In fact, you have managed to get a "D".'

I knew I must have done well, but I had hardly expected a 'D', which stood for 'distinguished' grading.

'I doubt if we have given half a dozen "D"s since the school opened here, and never to a lieutenant. My congratulations!'

'Thank you, sir.'

'Now, it is customary to discuss with those who have done well here, the sort of posting they would like to go to. But, of course, we only make the recommendations; the M.S. branch usually respect our recommendations—as far as possible.'

I did not say anything to that.

'It is not easy in your case, Prince, because … because we usually have Captains on this course, and if they show any special aptitude for "I" work, we send them out as Intelligence Officers to Brigades and Divisions. You know, I.O.'s or G.3's.'

'I would appreciate a posting back to my battalion, sir.'

'Oh, but we can't have that!' The Commandant shook his head. 'Easier if you hadn't done so well. Then we could have returned you to the unit. But we can't R.T.U. you now … perfect waste of a trained I.O., to be sent back to regimental duties.'

'I am sorry about that, sir, but I have no particular liking for "I" work, and as you say, sir, for the usual sort of appointment, I haven't the seniority.'

I cannot, to this day, explain my urge to get into the fighting.

It may well have been a quirk of bravado, but I can only say that it was wholly sincere. I had no visions of winning a decoration, nor did I seem to feel very strongly about the outcome of the war. Possibly it was only a desire to be doing something that my father, from a misguided view, had forbidden me to do, like riding in the scrub beyond the old fort. It is also possible that it had something to do with the compulsions and ideals left over from my schooldays; certainly it had nothing whatever to do with family tradition, with the fact that my distant ancestors had lived for soldiering and that most of them had died fighting. I had no conscious desire to forge a link with dead traditions; in fact, I hardly gave a thought to our history in those days.

The Commandant was looking at me with raised eyebrows, as though slightly shocked, and for a moment I wondered if I had overstepped the mark. I knew it was contrary to the customs of the service for a lieutenant not to show complete agreement with whatever line of thought his commanding officer had indicated. But there were certain privileges attached to being a Maharaja's heir, as I was beginning to discover.

'I do appreciate your keenness to get into the fighting, Prince,' Colonel Strang said. 'Perhaps we can get you a posting as a battalion I.O., just for a couple of months, and then you can be sent to a division as a Captain … unless you would like to come back here as an instructor?'

'No, sir,' I told him flatly. And then I added: 'Of course, I realize what a great compliment it is.'

He cocked his half-grey eyebrows again, but he was smiling.

'Well, well; we'll try to get you in as a battalion I.O.'

'That would be perfect, sir—in a battalion serving overseas.'

'Or a battalion just about to go overseas?' the Commandant suggested, and there was a twinkle in his eye as though he had made a joke.

'Thank you, sir.'

'We shall have to see about that. I don't know if G.H.Q. have anything special in mind for you. It may not be known to you that your posting to the course here came directly from G.H.Q.; from the D.M.I. himself, General Hinton.'

I did not tell the Commandant that I knew how my posting had come about, but I assured him that this time G.H.Q. were not likely to have anything special in mind for me.

'No?' he raised his eyebrows again.

'No, sir.'

'Oh, good! I don't mind telling you that we tried to dig our toes in at their sending a lieutenant on a course, just because he happened to be a Maharaja's son. When there were others with the necessary seniority, well, clamouring for vacancies. But you have … you have belied our fears.'

'Thank you, sir,' I said.

In spite of the mischievous gleam in the Commandant's eyes, I was sorely disappointed when, a few days later, my posting order was handed to me. It said that I was to report for duty to the 9th battalion of the Satpura regiment stationed at a place called Mundgad.

I had never heard of the 9th battalion; nor had I heard of Mundgad. The clerk in the Adjutant's office took a long time finding the place in the railway guide, and then it turned out that it was some thirty miles from Jalna, in the heart of the Deccan.

In the next three days, I changed trains four times. It was the middle of June, and a scorching loo blew most of the time like the air from a blast furnace. All day long, as I lay on the railway berth, the fans only disturbing the dust in the carriage, the sweat poured in little runnels from my bare body. I kept closing my eyes and thinking how cool it would be in Simla, seven thousand feet high, how pleasant to lie under a tree with Minnie in my arms, her body cool and fragrant.

It was nearly noon on the fourth day when we reached Mundgad station. An army truck had been sent to meet me. I sat beside the driver, squinting my eyes against the glare and the loo, the heat of the engine seeping through the soles of my boots, and tried to pump him about my new unit. From what little he knew, it seemed that the 9th battalion was being raised from scratch, by what was called 'milking' other units of the regiment, but the men and equipment had not begun to arrive. In fact, he told me, I was the second officer to report for duty; so far, only the Adjutant had arrived, and he had brought with him his own Jemadar, a man called Dongre. The driver seemed to think very highly of Jemadar Dongre.

I could see the tented camp from quite a distance, shimmering in a blanket of heat in a treeless waste, the tents dazzling white in the noonday sun. When the truck came to a halt, I stamped my feet to shake off the dust caked on my boots, wiped my face with my handkerchief and adjusted my cap before going into the Adjutant's tent to report my arrival.

He was sitting at a folding table, his long legs crossed underneath, and he was smoking a cigarette in a long black holder. His blouse with the Captain's stars was starched and crisp, his elegant boots polished a perfect dark tan. He looked businesslike, poised, alert, and although his face and arms were tanned a dark brown, he even looked cool. He glanced up from his work and his sharp blue eyes gave me a quick, purely professional going over from head to foot.

'So you're the I.O. Welcome to the Ninth,' he said. 'My name is Sykes. Anthony Sykes.'

Our Commanding Officer, Colonel Appleton, who had been called back from the Middle East to take command of the newly formed battalion, did not show up for another three weeks. By that time we had already reached full strength and were ready to go into training. New drafts arrived every day, and so did crates of equipment and stores and ammunition. The officers came in ones and twos, both Indian and British. Every day, from dawn to dusk, we were in a continuous whirl of activity, and we only stopped working at nightfall because we had no lights other than hurricane lanterns. We worked till our hands blistered and our bones ached and we even forgot the heat and the dust. Throughout these weeks, the Adjutant's tent was the centre of our world, for there sat Captain Anthony Sykes, efficient, unruffled and looking cool, a professional in the midst of clumsy amateurs, knowing the answers to everyone else's problems, a human slide rule, always available, any time of the day or night. And from the jumble of weapons and ammunition, boots and mosquito nets, blankets and buckets, bundles of barbed wire and great mounds of canvas, we began to grow into a fighting unit.

By the time the C.O. turned up, we were ready to go into training. We went on long route marches both by day and by night, carrying full packs and our own water, and then we carried out battle drill, complete with smoke and mortar support. By the middle of September we were doing embarkation drill, shipwreck drill and air-raid drill. The officers were given sand-model exercises on some of the recent battles in the Middle East, and evening lectures on the Do's and Don't's of life in the desert. The men were given talks on the high incidence of venereal diseases amongst troops in the Middle East and lurid warnings about the red-light districts of Cairo and Alexandria.

We entrained for Bombay on a misty February morning, an infantry battalion fully trained and ready for action, and equipped for warfare in the Western Desert with all that was best in what India Command had to offer.

Only, when we did embark, it was not to the Middle East that we went. We went to Burma.

16

Patrol Report

The transition from peace to war must have been too abrupt for it to have made any deep impression on my mind; there was no time for any anxiety or fear or even any real excitement to build up. In the morning, as our ship crawled into Rangoon harbour, we were eating soya-link sausages on deck and idly speculating about the pall of smoke that hung over the city. We did not know that we were entering a city which our Generals had already decided to abandon, and that the smoke came from the burning oil refinery which had been set on fire in preparation for the evacuation.

As soon as each company disembarked, we were formed into platoons and put into lorries and rushed half-way to Pegu where the Japanese had cut off the road. By the evening we were attacking the Japanese position astride the road. We had to do a bayonet charge before it was cleared. That night our first battle was already behind us, with our first casualty reports just coming in.

Early next morning we had our first experience of a quite unopposed air attack, when planes with brilliant red circles on their wings made leisurely passes over our positions at tree-top level, and when they had done with us, their artillery took over. There were rumours of heavy enemy troop movements on both sides of the Pegu road, but we saw no enemy troops that day. What we did see was a steady, unending stream of our own troops falling back through our positions and long grim convoys of lorries carrying back our wounded. The same evening we received orders to abandon our position, and ourselves became a part of an army in retreat.

The next few weeks are a blur on my memory, a patchwork of events and impressions and of purely reflex action, of hurry and swearing, remorse and anger, hunger and fear, frustration and the quick dehumanization of war. We occupied new positions, only to abandon them a few hours later; we 'spiked' our own guns; destroyed our own stocks of petrol and liquor; set fire to our own lorries. We tried to rally the spirits of our men, broken not so much by their rude baptism of fire as by the shock of being witnesses to the shattering blows inflicted on something that they had been taught to regard as inviolable. Was the Empire doomed?

And the man who stood as a living refutation of all doubts about the inviolability of the British Empire was Tony Sykes, still unruffled and cool, even elegant, still smoking cigarettes in his black holder, displaying no more than an air of bored contempt for the enemy.

Throughout our eight months in Burma, we were hardly ever out of contact with the enemy for more than three nights at a time. We were in headlong retreat, with the Japanese in full pursuit. The roads were jammed with unending columns of refugees, and death was everywhere. We lived in its shadow, getting inured to its sight and smell.

I remember living wholly in the present, more distressed about having to go without today's breakfast than about tomorrow's river-crossing. Clearing a road block that confronted us or finding a way round it was far more important to me than the overall progress of the war or the future of mankind.

And yet sometimes, when I wrote the regimental diary, I would feel a lump rising in my throat, for death was one thing when you saw it in the streets, but quite another when you came across it in your own shelter, in your own trench. I discovered for myself what many fighting men have written about, that you can take love to a war, nursing it, magnifying it, even making of it a shield round you and believing yourself immune to the bullets because of it, but you cannot take hatred.

My longing for Minnie formed a background to all my thoughts. I loved and desired her with a passion I had not known I was capable of, and yet my time was so fully occupied with the tasks of the moment that I could not write to her as often as I would have wished, and during March we were being kept so much on the move that I completely forgot her birthday.

Our mail service was totally disorganized and I did not get a single one of Minnie's letters. In fact, I don't think I received more than a dozen letters all the time I was in Burma. At least half of them were from my mother. In one, Mother enclosed a copper tait which she had obtained from the head priest in Benares and which she wanted me to wear round my neck to protect me from harm. But I was not touched by my mother's anxiety for my safety. I did not hate my mother; I just did not want anything to do with her. I threw away the tait and never wrote back to her. My father wrote only once, asking if I wanted anything. Now, even more than when I was at school, I wanted nothing. He would hardly have understood. I even got a letter from the Head, telling me how proud they all were of me at school and that I must visit them and talk to the boys when I next went home on leave.

I discovered that I no longer had any hard feelings towards my father, nor did I dislike Tony Sykes as much as I had expected. Now that I think of them together, they seemed to share a number of traits: disdain for danger, a capacity for coolness under stress, an unfailing readiness to take responsibility, and above all, a stubborn, almost stupid refusal to bend under pressure.

As the Adjutant and the Intelligence Officer, Tony and I had a good deal to do with each other. We called one another by our first names, and even today I feel slightly elated when I remember that I was the only junior officer on a first-name basis with our Senior Captain. I cannot say I liked Tony, but, in spite of myself, I came to admire his professional brilliance and to rely upon him more and more. It was only occasionally that I doubted whether my aversion to this man, who almost certainly had been Minnie's lover even before I met her, had vanished altogether or whether it lay dormant somewhere deep within me.

It was particularly when he and I used to go over the regimental diary which I kept that such doubts came to me most forcibly. As I read out the fresh casualties, I could hardly keep my voice from cracking. He, on the other hand, sat completely unperturbed, his long legs twisted under him, the ash on the cigarette in his holder getting longer and longer, not showing by a flicker of his eye or an inflection in his voice whether the deaths of the men with whom he had joked and laughed the previous day meant anything more to him than a column of figures. And for an instant, only for an instant, I used to be filled with an almost uncontrollable rage, wondering whether his aplomb was not just a total absence of any finer feelings, even pure callousness, his glamour just a part of professional competence. At such times, my feeling of hatred would surge back and catch me completely unprepared. And yet, even at such times, I was aware at the back of my mind that my rage had nothing to do with my love for Minnie, that it was roused by a sense of inadequacy, at finding that I detected in him a quality which I admired and found wanting in myself.

We were in the vicinity of a place called Ettaw. The entire Burma army was converged on the road along the Chindwin river about twenty miles to our west—the Burma army as well as the throngs of refugees. We were the end battalion, guarding the flanks against a surprise penetration by the enemy. We had been out of touch with our pursuers for nearly a week, even though their aircraft had never left us alone for long. What we had to discover was exactly how far the Japanese had penetrated to our east.

Two of us were going on the patrol, Jemadar Dongre and myself, and the Adjutant was briefing us in his shelter which was made up by draping half a dozen groundsheets over a low branch.

'Between here and here,' Tony said, drawing a neat circle on the map around the Ettaw-Kilin road, 'we've got to make sure if that patch is clear—just in case. As a sort of escape route.'

We peered at the map, at the track shown by a faint dotted line. The idea of an entire army having to withdraw along that track was preposterous, but Tony seemed to know what he was talking about.

The Jemadar shook his head and clicked his tongue. 'You don't really think we will be pushed that far—so that we have to use this track, saab?' he asked.

'Only in an emergency, saab,' Tony explained patiently. 'The evacuation is planned to go along the Alon road. But if we are thwarted … what is it, saab?'

'Along the Alon,' the Jemadar said grinning. 'Along the Alon.' His teeth gleamed white in his coal-black face.

Tony gave a nervous laugh and flicked the ash off his cigarette. It was just as well that the Jemadar had caused a diversion; the thought of what would happen if we were thwarted in our attempt to escape was too grim to entertain.

'Well, as far as we know, that track is still free of any Japanese soldiers,' Tony went on. 'The Japanese are concentrating their entire strength on a main assault on the Alon road.'

I remember thinking that he must be the only officer in the Burma army who did not call the enemy the 'Japs'. I looked at the map again, at the double black line of the Alon road that was to be our escape route going roughly north-west, between the railway and the Chindwin river, and then at the Ettaw-Kilin emergency track.

'You know, of course, what sort of report I want?' Tony asked.

'Jee, saab,' the Jemadar grinned. 'The nearest enemy position; a six-figure map reference; strength, weapons, equipment …'

'Buss-buss!' Tony said in mock irritation. 'You know damn well, Jamadar-saab, that I would much rather you brought in a report that there are no Japanese in the Ettaw-Kilin area than all your six-figure references …'

'All right, all right, we'll bring you an all-clear report, if that is what you want,' Jemadar Dongre grinned again.

They had joined the regiment on the same day, six years earlier, and when Tony had been posted to the newly raised battalion, the only man from his old battalion that he had made a special request for was Jemadar Dongre. There is always at least one Jemadar Dongre in every battalion, crude as they come, bursting with raw humour, but hard as nails, full of guts and a soldier to his fingertips.

'And we, or one of us, must get the khabar back to you by midnight tomorrow,' the Jemadar concluded.

I looked at the Jemadar's coal-black face, wondering at the strange bond between the two; the elegant, fastidious, haughty Englishman and the heavily built, earthy, rough-tongued Maratha. A respect for each other's professional ability? For each other's character and courage? Could they also be friends? I asked myself whether a man like Tony could ever have a friend amongst the non-commissioned Indians—whether he had any friends anywhere?

Tony looked at his watch. 'What about a cup of char, saab?' he asked.

The Jemadar rose to his feet and gave me a broad wink. 'That means the Adjutant-sahib wants to talk to you alone, saab,' he told me. 'I can take a hint.' He grinned affably and strode out.

'And don't you drink it there, you surly old devil,' Tony yelled after him. 'Get a mug each for Mr. Abhayraj and myself.'

'Achhi-baat, saab,' the Jemadar yelled back.

'You heard, Abhay,' Tony said.

'Yes.'

'And of course you appreciate why I am sending out two of you, both trained in "I" work.'

'So that at least one of us gets back with the gen.'

He inserted a fresh cigarette into his holder. 'You'll have to promise absolutely, Abhay, if there's any kind of trouble, neither of you must indulge in heroics—this is really vital. Your primary duty is to get the information back here. Brigade H.Q. must have it.'

I remember thinking how I had learnt to call it 'gen' and that Tony still called it 'information'.

'I know it sounds melodramatic,' Tony said. 'But the entire evacuation operation may depend on this. Is that quite clear?'

'Of course, Tony. No heroics; the gen must get back.'

'And I've told the same thing to Dongre. That if you bump into any trouble, he is not to waste his time but make his own way back.'

We looked at each other with no particular sense of foreboding. We had gone on patrols before. More often than not, we had bumped into trouble. We were still alive.

The Jemadar came back, followed by an orderly with three steaming mugs of tea. We drank it, checked up on our grenades and the rounds for our very pistols and donned our rubber shoes. Rather self-consciously, we took out our wallets and papers and handed them to the Adjutant, who put them into separate envelopes and passed them to his clerk.

'Don't let them pinch my money, saab,' the Jemadar made the standard joke. 'My money or my love letters.'

'Money!' Tony said. 'Love letters! Bills, most likely—and threatening letters from outraged husbands.'

They had known each other for a long time, and they both laughed as they shook hands and patted each other's shoulders. I felt almost like an intruder.

We had marched for nearly three hours, and were at least six miles away from our camp, perhaps getting a little careless, when we stumbled on a Japanese position. We must have been crunching the dry leaves as we walked, when we heard a dog bark. It was the frightened kind of yelp of a pie-dog, and we both froze in our tracks. I could feel my heart thumping. We were quite certain there was no village anywhere near; the barking dog could only mean that we were close to an enemy position. The Japanese had been known to tie dogs up near their positions, kept permanently hungry, to raise the alarm at any unusual sounds in the jungle.

There was an almost-full moon. The jungle was giving out a steamy, stifling heat, and the faint breeze was laden with the strong, almost pungent scent of mango blossom. I wanted a drink from my water-bottle, but checked myself just in time. I was much younger than Dongre, and was certainly not going to give in to my thirst before he did.

'Must be quite close, saab,' Dongre whispered. 'Have we been spotted?'

For an hour by my watch, we lay and listened. There was no further alarm. The dog had apparently gone to sleep. After that we had a whispered consultation and then it was up to me to give the orders, for I was the senior even though he was the professional.

'So you stick here,' I told Dongre. 'I'll go scouting further along the track and find out if there are more positions. By the morning, I'll come back and lie in wait on the other side of the track, somewhere near the top of that hill. We will observe them by daylight—you from here, myself from the other side. It is just as well to keep separated. Clear?'

In the light of the moon I could see the flash of his teeth. 'Achhi-baat, saab,' he said. 'And thank you for offering to go over the remaining length of the track. You are a much younger man, younger and thinner.'

'You are much stronger,' I said.

He grinned again, and his laugh was reassuring. 'Well, heavier certainly,' he said. 'And we meet here tomorrow evening.'

'As soon after sunset as we can make it,' I told him. 'I'll join you here. Then we go back to camp. We should be able to make it by nine.'

'And then we get a hot meal. Adjutant-sahib is bound to have one waiting for us.' He smacked his lips. 'I'm feeling hungry already. You know what I feel most like eating, saab?'

'No,' I said. 'What?'

'Cornmeal roti and mustard-leaf curry as only my wife can make it—the bread dripping with white butter.' And he smacked his lips again.

It was odd talking about cornmeal roties and white butter in the midst of the Burmese jungle, but I was aware that we suddenly had been brought closer together.

'And I always dream of Mughlai partridge and saffron rice,' I told him. I had never expressed my special wartime longing for food to anyone before.

'Mughlai partridge. Who makes it?'

'One of the cooks at home. He is from Hyderabad.'

'I have never eaten Mughlai partridge,' he said. 'Or any kind of partridge.'

'You come to my place, saab, and we will have partridge every day.'

'That's a deal,' Dongre said. 'It would be wonderful to have partridge every day—four fingers of rum and partridge. But you must try the corn bread and mustard curry in my house some day.'

We clasped hands in the moonlight and I left him.

After that the jungle was alive with Japanese soldiers all along the track. I could hear faint noises in the dark and the sound of laughter, and once I saw a light, just a flicker, as though someone had lit a cigarette. I kept on going, making careful notes of my bearings, and I was beginning to think that I had cleared the screen of enemy positions when I stumbled right into another post. There was a sudden sharp challenge from hardly thirty yards away, followed by silence. I hit the ground and lay still for a long time before I crawled away.

The Ettaw-Kilin track was bristling with enemy troops; it was not going to serve as an escape route. I decided to get back to the position I had allotted myself on the hill opposite where I had left the Jemadar. When I got there, I had the usual feeling that I had missed my way in the night and was on some strange hill, miles from anywhere. But the first light of day was reassuring. It showed that I was in the correct position, with the Ettaw-Kilin track right below me, dipping down in the bed of the chaung. From where I lay, I could observe the cart-track for a stretch of nearly three hundred yards. I had stumbled on a wonderful observation point.

I did not have to wait long. Even before the sun came up, I could see the green-clad figures coming out on the track and getting down to work. I counted thirty of them, but the way they were milling around, it was difficult to keep track of their numbers. I remember thinking that with a Bren, I could have picked off most of them neatly. The distance could not have been much more than two hundred yards. I knew I should have had to crawl forward for another hundred yards or so to make it absolutely fool-proof, and then a long, steady burst with a full magazine ... it was a mouth-watering thought.

But, of course, I had no Bren with me, only a very pistol with green and red flares and six sixty-three grenades fitted with four-second fuses. And in any case, it was not our business to kill the enemy, but to keep hiding and take back a report of their whereabouts.

Through the binoculars I could see their faces, grim and purposeful, as they worked in silence. They were digging shallow trenches right in the middle of the track. I could see the yellow-topped mines being placed, two to a trench, and even the trip wires. I watched the green figures with fascination, for they looked like mechanical toys, working in quick, jerky movements, and I had a feeling that they would stop working as soon as the springs became unwound. In no time at all, they had put down their A.P. mines, and laid several strands of wire along the track. After that they shovelled back the earth and the dry leaves on the road to make the surface look undisturbed.

By nine they had finished laying the mines. Then, leaving two sentries on both sides of their position, they got down to digging their own slit trenches on my side of the track. Now that they were off the road and in the jungle, they were almost totally hidden from my view, but I knew that they would be more clearly visible from where Dongre was sitting. They worked methodically. Every now and then, two or three of them would come loping on to the road and put their heads down and point out the undergrowth that obstructed the field of fire from their machine guns.

Their purpose was only too clear: they would sit in their fox-holes, guarding the track, and ambush any of our troops that happened to come along it.

I had ample time to make my notes. Even though the track was not likely to be of any use to us now, I wrote down the usual information about strength and weapons. I put down the compass bearings for my return to camp. I worked out the six figure map reference of their position and noted that they had four to six light machine guns and six Japanese-type light mortars. I even put down the dog, the thin, pale yellow and liver mongrel.

By an odd coincidence, it was just as I was writing about the dog that I heard it howling. It had been quiet all morning, lying in the sun tied to a stake planted right in the middle of the road. Now it was yelping. I put up my binoculars and saw a puny Japanese soldier taking swipes at it with an upraised spade. He missed twice, and during that time, the dog kept up its terrified yelping, and then when the spade came down squarely on its skull, it fell limply on the ground and lay twitching silently for a few seconds before it became absolutely still.

There was a clammy, choking feeling in my throat, and I found that my teeth were on edge. I watched as though spellbound while the little green man dragged the dog's body away and two other men shovelled earth on the track to obliterate the blood-marks. I remember wanting a drink of water. It took a long time to unbuckle my belt and loosen the bottle from its harness because my hands were unsteady. I brought the bottle clumsily to my mouth and recklessly drained away its contents. The sight of the dog being finished off in that brutal manner somehow revolted me far more than many other things I had seen in the war.

And yet I could see why the dog had been killed. It was a two-edged weapon: an excellent, wide-awake sentry when you were not quite ready for the enemy, but equally capable of giving away your own position by barking at the wrong time. If you happened to be lying in wait for the enemy to walk into an ambush you could not afford to have a barking dog around.

By the time I had emptied my water-bottle everything was quiet once more, and the meandering red line of the cart-track looked peaceful and deserted. Even the sentries had been withdrawn, leaving a brooding silence around me, a silence heightened by the din of the jungle insects and the smell of the mango blossom.

We had accomplished our task, but we were going to take back unwelcome news: the Ettaw-Kilin track was alive with the enemy. I felt bitter as I waited for the sunset when I could rejoin Jemadar Dongre; I knew how anxiously Tony Sykes would be waiting for our return.

But it turned out that the Adjutant was not waiting. The general position had got worse and our Commanding Officer had been ordered to give an immediate report on the feasibility of using the Ettaw-Kilin track for evacuating an entire brigade.

To this day I think that the Adjutant should have waited for our return, however frantic the orders from Brigade H.Q. But then again, knowing Tony, I could appreciate why he had not waited.

He had decided to send out another patrol, not a reconnaissance patrol, but what is called a fighting patrol, for a quick, hit-and-run raid in case they bumped into any enemy, and he had obtained the C.O.'s permission to lead the patrol himself. I could picture Tony giving the orders to the patrol, crisp and unhurried and enlivened with a joke or two that the men would laugh at: rations, torches, binoculars, one very pistol for every two men, one Bren with six magazines for one man in six, everyone carrying six hand-grenades each and wearing rubber-soled shoes. It was a no-nonsense, business-first sort of patrol, and before setting out he must have handed his own wallet to his clerk to be sealed in an envelope and kept behind, just as we had done.

But of course I knew nothing of this as I waited that afternoon on the hill overlooking the track, looking at my watch every few minutes and feeling faint with hunger. Suddenly, as though they had sprung out of the greenery, there came into my vision three men in olive green uniforms with British-type helmets, proceeding along the track below me. By the time they came into my view, at the turn of the road, they were already well inside the killing ground prepared by the Japanese troops. They were moving with caution, watching both sides of the road and keeping dispersed, and then I saw behind the three leading men at least another ten strung back along the track. Even without the binoculars, I could recognize Tony Sykes's tall figure in the lead.

I had to do something instantly, even if it meant giving away my own position, for the Japanese were obviously waiting only for the main body of the patrol to come into the stretch of the road before opening up. If I acted quickly, I could save at least some of them from being slaughtered. I pulled out my very pistol and fired a red flare into the sky. I could have yelled with joy when I saw Tony and the two leading scouts throw themselves on the ground.

Then the bullets started flying and kicking the dust around the three men lying prone on the track, and I could see that it was just a matter of time before they would be riddled. Almost in spite of myself, I put up my binoculars and watched.

I heard a yell from the opposite hill and saw Jemadar Dongre break cover and rush out into the open jungle along the track, shouting obscene Marathi curses. I realized that he was trying to create a diversion, trying to save his friend by drawing the fire upon himself, and I remember thinking how futile and utterly stupid it was.

Close to where the dog had been killed was an anthill. I saw the Jemadar fling himself behind it and yell: 'Go back, sahib! Go away—I'll deal with them!' I could see him pull the pin out from one of his grenades and hurl it expertly across the track in a perfect arc; from the sound it made, not a bang but a dull crump, I knew it had exploded right inside one of their trenches. I saw him chuck two more grenades, and the bangs they made were much louder and longer—bang-whistle … bang-whistle. As he was about to pull the pin from his fourth grenade, I saw him lurch and fall forward on his face, and the grenade drop from his now powerless hand and roll away. I flinched, purely by reflex action, thinking it was going to explode in his face, but the pin must still have been in and the grenade did not explode.

The fire was concentrated round the anthill now, and Tony and the other two men looked safe for the moment and should have made a dash for safety. For even as I was watching, there was Jemadar Dongre again, looking more enormous than ever, rising to a crouching position behind the anthill and yelling: 'Go back, Sykes Sahib—go away, you ulloo-ka-bachha! —there are fifty of the —s dug in there!'

Through my binoculars I saw his shirt redden, and the blood squirting out of his shoulder in thick little gobs. I saw him biting the pin out of another grenade with his teeth and throwing it across the track with his left hand, shouting: 'Take that, you dog-killing ——s!' And this time too the grenade made a delightful smothered crump, having found its mark.

And then I saw Tony rise to his feet and run criss-cross at a loping, head-down run into the dust rising from the bullets which raked the road near the anthill. I saw him run right through the screen of dust quite unharmed, and I heard the Jemadar cursing the Adjutant in anguished swearwords. 'Hato-bacho, you damnfool Sykes sahib—bloody Bhag-jao ekdum!'

I saw Tony pick up the Jemadar, sling him across his shoulder and begin to run. I saw him stumble and fall, then rise heavily and run another ten yards or so. And I saw him stumble a second time, fall down again and lie in a heap in the dust of the track in the bed of the chaung. And as I continued to watch more and more bullets hit the two prone bodies, making their limbs twitch with each hit.

It felt almost indecent to be opening the two envelopes. But I was the new Adjutant of the battalion. The formalities had to be gone through if only to ensure that the 'effects', as we had learnt to regard them, were duly sent to the next of kin.

Jemadar Dongre's wallet contained neither bills nor letters from indignant husbands. But besides some money and a visiting card from a Poona fortune teller and one or two other papers, it did contain a love letter, if one could call it that, because it was from his wife. It was written in Marathi, a neat, bold hand, and even the few words that cannot help registering themselves as you put away a letter were enough to show what kind of a letter it was. It was written by a devoted, orthodox, old-fashioned village woman and it was written in the third person, as though to a total stranger. The letter had a short postscript in English which I did read. It was written in an unformed, childish scrawl, and all it said was:

'Darling Daddy what time you coming back?'

'What time,' I kept thinking to myself, not 'when'. It was signed 'Seeta'. I must go and see Seeta and her mother when I get back, I told myself.

It was Tony's wallet that contained the two bills. One was from his London tailor for twenty-nine pounds, seven shillings and sixpence, the other from the Army and Navy Stores, Bombay, for a pair of silk stockings sent to Simla at his instructions. I looked at the date. The stockings had been sent for Minnie's birthday. There was also a letter from a Marwari money-lender in Meerut reminding Tony that with the interest for the past six months, he now owed them exactly two thousand, one hundred and fifty rupees.

In the inner compartment of his wallet was a three-page letter from Minnie written on bright blue paper, and with it a snapshot of her. Even though I had somehow known I would find Minnie's photograph in Tony's wallet, I was not prepared for its discovery. I knew that I had stumbled upon something Tony himself had taken care to keep hidden from me. But I am ashamed to say that I felt compelled to read a part of the letter, not because it came from Minnie, but because, as I put it back, I saw my own name in it.

'Tony, my Darling!' Minnie had written.

> 'I was so desolate because you had not written for so long, and then your lovely birthday gift came—exactly on the day—and I knew that everything was all right. Now I am miserable again, not knowing if everything really is all right. Darling, how can I be sure unless you tell me so, again and again, tell me that you love me. I love you, I love you, I love you—I want to go on saying it to you, and I want to lie in your arms. And it is no good telling

> me there are no postal facilities wherever you are, because I have received three letters from Abhay. I only hope, my sweetheart, that you are still not annoyed with me about the pearls. All I know is that I am crazy about you and how many times have I told you that Abhay means nothing to me and the necklace means nothing to me and the moment …'

That was where the page ended, tantalizingly, and I held the letter in my hand for a long time but I did not turn the page. I was already overcome with a sense of guilt at having read even so much. I wrapped it round the snapshot, and put it back in the wallet, just as I had found it.

Tony had also left his Dunhill cigarette holder behind. I put it in my pocket. Somehow I felt that he would have liked me to take it, I kept the bills and the letter from the Meerut moneylender to myself, stored Tony's wallet away and tried to put the whole thing out of my mind.

Oddly enough, it was of Tony that I kept thinking, not Minnie. He had never once given me an indication that he was in love with her or even spoken about her. Nor had he ever shown any ill-will towards me. Ours had grown into a clean, purely professional relationship, untainted by rivalry. It was hardly fair, I kept thinking; dunning letters against a prince's resources, silk stockings against a pink-pearl necklace. And yet I was aware that Tony did not lack resources, for he was a man complete in himself; he was the prince, not I. And if he was in love with Minnie and she with him, it was exactly as it should have been and it was I who was the outsider, the third man. I felt no bitterness.

I sat for a time, overcome by the aura of humility which death leaves in its wake, holding Tony's black cigarette holder in my hand. It still smelt of tobacco. Even though I had never consciously done him any harm, Tony's death had left a feeling of guilt within me.

I wondered a long time whether I should write and tell Minnie that Tony had died. It would have been a difficult letter to write, now that I knew how she felt about me. Couldn't I say it was Tony himself who had told me how she felt about me?

But I was spared the decision. While I was still sitting on the footboard of the lorry, trying to make up my mind, direct orders came from Corps Headquarters to move with all possible speed towards Alon. The enemy was already advancing on our flanks in large numbers.

I almost welcomed these tidings of disaster, for I forgot about Tony and Minnie and Jemadar Dongre as I busied myself with the tasks of the moment. Even as our rear companies were pulling out two hours later, we could already hear the familiar stutter of Meigi machine guns in the jungle behind us.

17

Salt and Milk Don't Mix

It was in Karachi, in the winter of the same year, 1942, that I received the 'Dear John' letter from Minnie Bradley. I was an instructor on the staff of the Intelligence School then, and had been promoted Captain.

I had just given my final talk on the Japanese Triangular Division to a class of students who seemed only half awake after an all-night exercise the night before. I went back to my tiny office and there was the letter, lying on my desk.

I had not learnt to call them 'Dear John' letters then, and now that I look back on it, it was hardly true to type except that it began 'Dear Abhay' and ended 'Yours sincerely'. For one thing, it lacked the stamp of sincerity, the urgency of a letter written by a young woman torn with emotion and suffering from a sense of guilt. Indeed, even as I read it, it gave me the impression that Minnie was getting over a somewhat unpleasant chore which she had kept putting off, but that now that she was getting down to it, she was anxious to make a neat job of it. Her letter looked as if it had been composed with care, with every punctuation mark in its proper place, just as though she had made a rough draft before copying it neatly on to blue writing paper.

She had thought and thought about us until she thought she would go crazy, Minnie wrote, for every time she looked at the lovely necklace I had sent her, she could not help remembering everything I had said when I had seen her in Simla. But at last she had been compelled to conclude that we could not be really in love with each other. She had first suspected something had gone wrong, Minnie said, when abruptly and for no reason at all, I had stopped writing to her; she could not imagine what could have made me do so. And the more she thought about it, Minnie said, the more she realized how callous men could be, but even then she had decided to wait until she saw me, for she was sure that in all fairness I would at least try and see her as soon as I returned from Burma, to explain. But though more than four months had passed since my return, I had neither visited her nor troubled to write a single line. I could never realize, Minnie pointed out, because she had come to the conclusion that all men were selfish, what a great sacrifice she had been on the verge of making when she thought she was in love with me; it would have meant the flouting of all conventions and spending the rest of her life in a strange environment with someone who belonged neither to her race, nor to her religion. Lastly, Minnie hoped that we would always remain good friends, since, while it had been a hard decision to make, it was in both our interests. There was also the usual bit about not feeling too badly about her and the ardent wish, as Minnie put it, that I would always be very, very happy.

I remember feeling only slightly dazed, neither sorry nor glad. It was as though a chapter had ended and I was going to put away the book for the night. As I was reading the letter, I kept thinking of Tony Sykes. Where would he have fitted into all this?

In my room late that night, as I re-read Minnie's letter, I realized how right she had been in much of what she wrote. Perhaps I had never really been in love with her, I kept telling myself. Otherwise I would not have this feeling of relief and freedom, as though the chapter had closed at the right place and on the right note.

It must have been nearly a week later that I read in the 'Personal' column of the *Sindh Observer* that Captain Christopher Dudley Osbert Farren, A.D.C. to the Governor of Bombay, and Miss Minnie Bradley of the Railway Colony Tinapur, had been married at All Saints' Church on Malabar Hill. I was a little hurt that Punch had not sent me an invitation to his wedding, but sent them a small silver salver as a wedding present. I had not known of Punch's appointment. It was odd how quickly one lost contact with one's brother officers during the war. Remembering how much he had always longed to get into the war, I thought how disappointed he must have been to find himself posted as an A.D.C. to a Governor.

It was almost exactly two years since I had been home, but in the train I experienced my usual exhilaration at returning there, almost as though there had been no interruption in the pattern. I felt light and free, already caught up in my own surroundings.

My father was on the lawn outside the back verandah, shooting at copper coins. As soon as he saw me, he stopped, handed his rifle to the A.D.C. and came and put his hands on my shoulders.

'Back from the wars,' Father said. 'Our conquering hero!'

He looked slightly older, for there were a few strands of grey in his moustache, and one of his teeth had a new gold capping, but through the thin cloth of my uniform blouse, I felt the strength of his grip.

'Hardly a hero, Dada, and certainly not conquering,' I said. 'We ran away from Burma.'

'But they gave you a Military Cross. The British don't throw their M.C.s around.'

'That is just the customary decoration for all officers,' I told him.

'A most beautiful decoration, the M.C. The D.S.O. has the wrong colours—the British never did understand colour combinations. The V.C. ... well, the V.C. reeks of a touch of bravado—of being a thruster. The M.C. is the most appropriate. I am proud of you.'

It was no good throwing salt in his cup of milk, as he would have said; no use telling him that I had got my M.C. for bringing back the patrol after Tony Sykes and Jemadar Dongre had died, and for my part in the quick evacuation of the Ettaw position; not for bravery, but instinctive caution and a habit of mind. I wanted to steer him away from the war.

'Anyone special coming this year for the Tatwal shoot?' I asked.

'Anyone special?' my father said, and his eyes lit up. 'Yes, very special. You, my son.'

What are the birds going to be like?'

'Well, I don't know; I really don't know, though Hanuman says they are better than last year. The war has even affected the ducks,' Father complained. 'Are you asking anyone?'

'No, Dada.'

'What about that delightful young man with the very respectable moustache?—Captain Farren, that's right. Charming man, charming. Sent me an invitation to his wedding. I sent him a silver salver.'

That was how Minnie's name came into our conversation, Minnie Bradley who was now Mrs. Punch Farren, but somehow I knew that it was only his way of telling me that it was all over; that everything was just as it had been.

'I wanted to talk to you about that, Father,' I said. 'That and other things.'

But Father was not inclined to talk of serious things. 'You had better have a chat with Harikishore,' he said. 'He has something to give you.'

'I'll send for him this evening,' I told him.

'Well, with the blessings of Ambica, you are back home, after that dreadful campaign—quite shockingly mishandled ... disgraceful! But you are home, and that is all that matters. Is there anything special you want to eat?'

'Mughlai partridge,' I said. 'Mughlai partridge and saffron rice. That was what I seemed to want most whenever we had to go without food.'

'Were there many occasions when you had to go without food?'

I knew that he could never have understood the importance food assumes during a military debacle, and about men like Dongre trying to save a friend's life by giving their own. I was still trying to keep the salt from mixing with the milk. 'Off and on,' I said. 'Not often.'

'We'll go and shoot partridge in the evening. We shall have partridge every day. How long will you be here?'

'Ten days.'

'I thought your leave was for fifteen days.'

'I want to go to Poona,' I told him. 'I have to see a woman there.'

'A woman?' Father said, but his face did not register either surprise or disapproval.

'A woman and her daughter, a girl called Seeta. Her husband was my Jemadar, and he died doing something which was not really in line of duty. When he need not have died. I have to go and see them. I promised myself.'

'Yes, of course,' Father said. 'Yes, of course. At least you came—better than not coming at all. But I suppose the young have to have their way—get things out of their blood. And I wanted to tell you that I'm sorry I tried to keep you back from the wars. I should have known better, that we Bedars have always tended to be headstrong. But you are back home now.'

'Yes, I am back,' I agreed.

'We are going after partridge in the afternoon,' he said. 'We'll try the Sanchiwalla drive, beyond the bridge. Plenty of birds there.'

'I'll be ready,' I told him, glad that he had taken it for granted that I would go shooting with him. 'The Sanchiwalla drive would be just right.'

I know we had not said much, but when I left him, I had a feeling that the air had cleared.

I rushed up the stairs, three at a time, hardly noticing that the stair carpet had been removed, that the blinds were pulled down and the bamboo curtains rolled up. It was only when I was on the landing that I realized this part of the house was empty; my mother no longer lived in the palace.

I missed a lot of birds in the beginning, but once I got into my swing, I was shooting as well as ever, even though I had a feeling that my father was leaving me all the easier shots, himself taking only the overhead ones. We returned from the shoot soon after sunset, and as soon as I was back in my room, I sent a servant with a message for Lala Harikishore. Then I went for my bath.

From my mother's cupboard, I had brought down a nearly full bottle of bath salts, and emptied a generous portion of it into the tub. I don't know how long I lay in the bath, turning the taps alternately with my toes and enjoying it.

The crisp white churidars felt soft and light around my legs; the Jodhpore jacket had become tight around the shoulders. In the mirror, I looked at a stranger burnt black by the sun, but I liked the new leanness of my flanks and the overall impression of hardness. I was whistling as I came out into the sitting-room and then suddenly remembered about Lala Harikishore.

He must have been waiting outside for quite a while, but was of course too polite to say so. He came in, wearing the correct gradation of a smile on his face, and did a mujra. As usual, he was carrying a bunch of papers tied up in red dust-cloth.

'Welcome back, Yuwaraj,' he said. 'And may the blessings of Shiva keep away all shadows.'

'On you too the blessings of Ambica, Lalaji,' I said, reminding myself that I was back in my own world, back to the frills of conversation and manners of the Indian states.

It was no use offering him a cigarette or a drink. That would have been almost an impertinence. 'I understand you have something to deliver to me, Lalaji,' I said, 'Or am I mistaken?'

'No, sir.'

I laughed. 'Does that mean, Lalaji, that I am not mistaken or that you have nothing to give?'

He permitted himself a smile. 'I meant that the Yuwaraj is not mistaken,' he said.

'Letters?'

'Yes.'

'Well, let's have them.'

He untied his red cloth bundle and produced a stack of letters neatly tied up in Government red tape and bearing seals on all sides and handed it to me.

Minnie was always neat, I kept telling myself. She must have made a wonderful secretary.

'I do hope you haven't been having a peek at them,' I said.

The old man stiffened slightly, and there was a suggestion of reproof in his voice. 'Does the Yuwaraj mean I have been reading them?'

'It was only a joke,' I explained.

'They are sealed, Yuwaraj. I … er, insisted that the young lady should put her own seal on them.'

'It is the Government of India's seal,' I said. 'And Government sealing wax and Government red tape.'

But Lala Harikishore was not prepared to fall in with my mood. He still looked slightly annoyed. 'There could have been no other seal handy,' he explained.

I turned the packet in my hands, again thinking how methodical Minnie had been, keeping all the letters in their original envelopes, almost as though she knew that they would have to be returned.

'Was there anything else, Yuwaraj?' Harikishore asked.

'No, thank you, Lalaji. And thank you for all this.'

He rose to his feet and did a mujra.

'How much did they cost?' I asked.

He hesitated for a moment. Then he said: 'Fifteen thousand rupees, Yuwaraj.'

'At one time I understood that they were only going to be about ten thousand.'

He took his time with that one. 'That was so,' he said. 'At one time.'

'Oh.'

'And after that there were … er, more communications. Communications of somewhat higher sentimental value.'

'It is so easy to be sentimental in the midst of war,' I explained.

'I have no experience of warfare,' he told me.

'And one always has to pay for sentiment.'

'That is so, Yuwaraj.'

'Thank you for everything, Lalaji.'

He left after doing his mujra and walking backwards the customary three paces, still with a hurt look on his face.

She always had an instinct for business, Minnie, and I could not help admiring the way she had handled this; a complication of life neatly turned into a profit. For fifteen thousand rupees she might just get a small house in some cantonment town. Minnie always had a cool head, so inconsistent with her hesitant, helpless air. She had come out very well out of this, all things considered.

And I was also beginning to feel a lurking admiration for Lala Harikishore too, and the way he had handled his assignment. Fifteen thousand rupees was cheap; yes, definitely so.

18

With the Blessings of the Gods

My marriage to Kamala took place in the spring of 1943, when I had finished my tenure of duty on the staff of the 'I' school and had taken four weeks' war leave. I had given my consent by letter, without even asking to see a photograph. When I went home, the whole town was preparing for the wedding.

Kamala was the eldest daughter of the Raja of Akheti, one of the two girls whose photographs I had thrown into my wastepaper basket. To this day, I do not know which of the two photographs had been Kamala's.

As things turned out, it was lucky for me that when I did agree to get married, the other girl, the daughter of the Kurdalli Jagirdars, had already been disposed of. Kamala was thus the almost automatic choice. Her parents had apparently run into difficulties over her marriage, because the news that I had turned her down had leaked out. My father, who had his own code in such matters, had offered to help by getting Charudutt to marry her, but Kamala's parents had flatly declined to have their daughter married to an 'up-raja' son.

So everyone was pleased when I declared that I would have no objection to marrying whatever girl Father chose, and he and Kamala's father soon worked out the details.

Though ours was a purely conventional Hindu marriage, a family alliance brought about by the pandits matching our horoscopes as much as by the conventions of caste and prestige, it has turned out to be a happy one. When I reflect on this, I wonder whether there might not, after all, be something to be said for our deeply rooted customs, evolved after generations of trial and error; mine is certainly not an unusual example of how love can flow as a consequence of marriage, living together and the begetting of children.

I first saw Kamala during the actual wedding ceremony, when the curtain held between us had been drawn away. She stood with her head lowered, wearing her red bridal sari draped over her head and looking fixedly at my feet. I remember noticing that her eyelashes were slightly wet and that her face looked damp and smudged as though she had been crying. She looked as all Hindu brides must look, nervous, flushed and resigned, and I remember thinking that her colour went well with the red of the sari and the bridal ornaments. I was conscious of my own emotional detachment, knowing that I was going through the ceremony as a sort of penance. It merely emphasized that I was now back within the fold, aware of my obligations to my inheritance. I was taking a wife because a future Maharaja must have a Maharani, but I knew that no other obligations, such as love or marital fidelity, were imposed.

Today, nineteen years afterwards, Kamala looks entirely different from the girl I married, for she has learnt to make the best of her looks, and the years have given her features more definition and a look of refinement. In a certain light, she might even be called beautiful. Washington Bond, the society photographer from *Home and Outdoors* who came to India to do a series on the homes of the Indian princes, has posed her with her face turned slightly upwards and to the left and called her one of the loveliest amongst the Maharanis—not that Kamala is any longer a Maharani.

In spite of the war, there were the usual festivities, with the usual somewhat tasteless display of wealth and extravagance inseparable from weddings in India. My father had a glorious time organizing the accommodation and the receptions for the other princes; seeing to the lighting and the decorations, the arrangements for the banquets, the feeding of the poor and the elephant procession; and evaluating the wedding presents so that gifts of equal value could be returned to the givers on suitable occasions. He was immensely proud that my regiment had sent a party of officers to form an archway of swords and that there were more 'salute princes' present at my wedding than at any other during the year. The festivities went on for a whole week, and after that Kamala and I went to live in the old riverside bungalow known as the 'Captain's Lodge' where the first of the Agents of the East India Company used to live and which had been renovated for our use.

My mother neither attended my wedding nor sent me a present or a message of blessings, but I thought this perfectly understandable in view of my own attitude towards her. What I thought odd was that Charudutt stayed away and gave me no present; it was only when I happened to mention it to my wife that I learnt what good reason her father's attitude had given him to avoid the festivities.

I saw a lot of my father during those days. I went riding with him every morning, before the heat of the day, and once or twice a week we would invite some of the officers from the Aweda cantonment for an afternoon of tennis followed by billiards. Perhaps it was as well that the shooting season was over, otherwise I would have had little time to get to know Kamala. In the evenings she and I would go for a drive, and afterwards I would leave her in the bungalow and stroll down to the palace along the river path to join my father for a drink.

I had been so deeply immersed in the state of bliss which follows even a good many Hindu marriages, the delightful experiment of two complete strangers discovering each other in all their intimacy, that I did not realize my father had something on his mind.

We were having a drink one evening in the room with the tiger rug. His hookah was going nicely when he complained, 'I don't like the way things are going at all.'

'But we have driven Rommel out of Africa,' I said. 'And everyone knows that the tide has turned—at last. Did you know it was the Fourth Indian Division that captured Van Thoma? I actually knew the chap …'

The look on his face made me stop in mid-sentence. Clearly, we were not thinking of the same thing.

'Things may be going well in Africa,' Father said, waving the stem of his hookah impatiently, but I don't like the way the paramount power is behaving in this country. It looks as though they would be quite prepared to sell us short.'

'To the Japanese?' I asked. 'Quite unthinkable.'

'No, no, to the nationalists.'

'Oh, the Congress!' I almost laughed with relief. 'You mean the Cripps mission. But it was a failure … it misfired.'

'Yes, but it was a close call. I offered a mahapooja as soon as I heard that Cripps had packed up and gone—a mahapooja and a gift of twenty cows to the brahmins. But it was touch and go.' And father gave a sigh of relief.

All over the country there had been acute disappointment at the failure of the Cripps mission, and here was my father offering gifts to his gods. But I had caught up with his trend of thought now. I did not want to confront him with unpalatable truths. I wanted the white cloth between us to remain white.

Sir Stafford Cripps—must come from a good family. And yet they say he's a socialist. I offered to get him here for a tiger shoot. The Political Department seemed to fight a little shy. 'Koi hai!' my father called out. 'Koi-hai!'

A servant came with a tray of drinks and the hookah-burdar put a new bowl on the hookah.

'Aren't you having a drink?' Father asked.

'No, thank you, Dada. I'll skip this one.'

'The Political Department rather gave me the impression that they wanted nothing to do with Cripps,' Father said.

'I was away during all that, Dada,' I said. 'I was in Burma when Cripps was here—somewhere near the Yenanyaung oil fields.'

It must have been the persistent scent of the mango flower in the summer breeze more than my casual mention of the Burmese oil fields that set my mind off at a tangent again, for the next moment I was thinking of Tony Sykes and Dongre and how lucky it was that I had put down all the compass bearings for the return march.

'… actually thinking in terms of revising our treaties!' my father was saying. 'How can they? What right has anyone to change a treaty? Guaranteed by Queen Victoria and every successive monarch. The treaties are inviolable!'

The treaties were, at best, makeshift arrangements, hoary with age, and many of their provisions were quite meaningless. For instance, it was laid down that our state had to provide free fodder for the company's elephants whenever the company's army was passing through our state. The East India Company no longer ruled India, and its successors, the British Government, had no elephants in their army. But it was pointless to tell all this to my father. To him as to the rest of his order, the treaties were the bedrock of their prestige and power and wealth, their very existence. They were the gods of the Indian princes.

'The Cripps mission only gave an impetus to the undesirable elements in the country—local goondas calling themselves nationalists. There were demonstrations in many of the states. Even here … can you believe it? I had to be firm. I arrested the leader—that fellow Kanakchand—and I've forbidden him to enter the state for five years.'

'Five years!' Even the two years I had been away had seemed so long.

'That's right,' Father said. 'You know, the boy I whipped. He was busy trying to organize a cell, right here in Begwad.'

'A cell?'

'You know, an underground group, trying to incite our own people to rise against us … demand that the treaties be scrapped.'

I had to take a firm grip on myself; drag my mind away from the Burmese jungle and bring it back to the room with the tiger rug and the old swords and shields.

'But what is happening now?' I asked.

'Now? We—that is the Chamber—have demanded a categorical assurance from the Government that our rights will be safeguarded.'

I was a little surprised by my father identifying himself with the Chamber of Princes, since he had always tended to hold himself aloof from its activities.

'And that is exactly what I don't like,' Father said. 'They took six months to reply and now they say that the treaties must be interpreted in relation to the changing times.'

'I expect some sort of adjustments will be inescapable if they do mean to give self-rule to India,' I said.

There was a frown of disapproval on his face. 'We cannot tolerate any talk of adjustments; we just cannot afford to. The treaties are inviolable, so long as the sun and the moon go round! Not a word can be changed.'

The white cloth between us was still spotless, but I knew that any moment now, a shadow would fall over it. It was time to do my mujra and go.

'The way the Government has begun to suck up to the nationalists is absolutely shocking—the nationalists who have never co-operated and have openly called upon the British to quit. We, on the other hand, are their staunchest allies. Without us, the Princes, there would be no such thing as an Indian Empire. We have offered everything—all our resources—to the war effort.

The Congress has only obstructed it. And yet the British would be prepared to sell us to the Congress. That is what makes me furious—that there should be no justice.'

No, there could be no justice, I was thinking, if the bodies of men who had died for the sake of their values were to lie bloating in the summer night for a feast of vermin.

'Even in Burma you get the scent,' I said.

'What scent?' Father asked, suddenly alert.

'Mango blossom. You get it all the time, even in the jungle.'

'What has that to do with what we were talking about?'

'Only that in Burma too there was no justice,' I told him.

'There is no justice anywhere,' Father agreed. 'How can there be any justice when a man like Churchill sends out a socialist to solve the problems of India? Churchill himself should have come. I'm sure he could have found the time to come out here for a tiger shoot. You need a man who knows the country—has lived here.'

'A man who knows the scent of mango-blossom,' I said. 'Anyone who cannot be carried away by the scent of the mango flower does not know India at all.'

My father looked at me for a long time. There was a gleam of amusement in his sharp, coal-black eyes. And then he began to chuckle to himself.

'I expect there is a lot in what you say,' he said. 'The scent is quite strong. One gets rather used to it here. Are you ready for a drink?'

I had a drink and left him, left him with a feeling that the whiteness of the mattress between us was still without a blemish.

19

Prelude to Standstill

I spent the remaining years of the war as a staff officer at General Headquarters, New Delhi, a gaberdine swine, as the rest of the army used to call us. I was in one of the sections of the Intelligence Directorate which dealt with internal security, first as a Staff Captain, and later as a Major. I was happy in my job and I think reasonably proficient, otherwise it is hardly likely they would have kept me in G.H.Q. for so long.

I took up the trappings of military life with proper seriousness. But even people who usually made fun of the G.H.Q. shields and the red and black arm-bands cast an envious second look at my M.C. ribbon.

It is, of course, quite possible that after a few months at G.H.Q. I could have got myself an operational posting, but by now I was an old enough soldier to have learnt to take my soldiering as it came, content to go where I was sent but careful not to give cause to be regarded as a 'thruster'.

Besides, New Delhi was an exciting place to be posted in, in those days. The talk of India being given her freedom was daily gathering momentum, and I felt I was in a ringside seat, watching history in the making.

My father had arranged that I should be given a wing of 'Tilkatta House', the New Delhi residence of the Maharaja of Tilkatta in the Princes' Park, and there I set up house with my wife and my own servants, glad to have no part of the rough and ready Officers' Messes of wartime Delhi.

And it was here that our marriage began to make a groove for itself, falling into the pattern of all marriages which were supposed to be kept together in their early stages by the bonds of convention and in which love and even happiness were guaranteed to follow as night follows day.

But I cannot deny its rewards: the ecstasy of bringing out the bodily responses in a young woman as sheltered as Kamala was; the uncushioned, almost abrupt falling into intimacy; the inhibitions, fear, shame, the agony of failure and frustration; and then the gradual growing together, the adjustments, the drawing out, the teaching and learning and the sheer joy of mutual discovery.

These rewards were there, in full measure. And just as I was beginning to take them for granted, discovering within me an entirely new range of passions and fire, a kind of pagan completeness in the very act of marital relationship, Kamala became pregnant.

I knew that it had to happen, and yet I felt bitter and let down at thus being suddenly cut away from the life of the senses into which I had plunged; and it brought home to me more forcibly than anything else could have done, that there was not a single spark of love within me for Kamala. I began to wonder how a union worked out by the matching of horoscopes and initiated by putting a young man and a young woman to bed together in the hope that their bodily urges would do the rest, could ever be blessed with happiness. As I watched Kamala's body grow heavy in pregnancy, I found my thoughts constantly straying away to other women; to Minnie, slim, bold, deliciously wanton; to Zarina in a transparent gauze dress, Zarina who had been assiduously trained in the art of making herself agreeable to men, and who was being brought up as a concubine for me.

It was in Delhi, on a cold afternoon in December 1944, that our daughter was born. I can still recall the quick flicker of disappointment that crossed my father's face when the nurse came and broke the news.

But, as always, he was quick to recover. He sent instructions to the waiting pandits about showing him the horoscope as soon as it was ready so that he could initiate the customary religious ceremonies. Then he called for the champagne which, all unknown to me, he had had put on ice.

'Never mind,' my father said. 'Here's to the girl.'

As it happened, I did not mind. But if only for his sake, I would have liked my first child to have been a boy. My father was a much worried man in those days, and it would have given him great joy to have discovered that the succession to the gadi had been made secure. I had a feeling that he had ordered champagne to be kept on ice in order to drink a toast to his grandson, and that now, in having it opened, he was just making the best of things.

'Well, cheer up,' Father said. 'How does it feel to be a father?'

'Wonderful, thank you,' I told him. 'Just wonderful.'

As far as I was concerned, it was 'wonderful, thank you' all the time I was in Delhi, but I knew that that was not how my father had been feeling lately. He had come to New Delhi for one of the numerous conferences the princes were having at this time. My father was one of their most indefatigable workers behind the scenes.

'What happened at the meeting today?' I asked. I did not want him to feel that I took no interest in his activities.

His face fell. 'The Viceroy disallowed the motion,' he said. 'Quite absurd! All we wanted was an assurance that there would be no decision concerning our future without our consent.'

'Does it matter very much if we don't get such an assurance?'

He gave me a startled look, as though he found it unbelievable that I should not know the main facts about an issue which was so vital to our order. But the champagne was working nicely, and I was feeling finer than ever, thank you, because I had become a father, and his look did not damp my spirits in the least.

'Before we go on,' I said. 'Let's have some more bubbly, I haven't had any for months.'

'Bubbly?—what a thing to call Moet et Chandon,' he protested.

'Fine stuff. Let's have a little more. But you've still got some in your glass.'

He tossed his drink down and we held out our glasses for the bearer to fill. 'Well, how does it feel to be a grandfather, Dada ?' I asked.

'Why, wonderful,' he said. 'Just grand!'

He certainly did not look as though he was feeling grand. 'What happens now?' I asked. 'Now that the Viceroy won't play?'

My father looked over his glass with narrowed eyes, and his face broke into its poker smile. 'We meet privately now,' he said. 'And we are going ahead with the formation of the third force. You must have heard of the third force?'

Of course I had heard of the third force which the princes were hoping to set up as a counterweight to the Congress and the Muslim League, the two main political parties. There were rumours that the Political Department was actually instigating the rulers in their efforts to set it up.

Knowing the Indian princes as I did, I was convinced that no third force was likely to emerge. I knew about the deep-seated internal jealousies amongst the rulers, I knew how every single one, however small his state, felt about preserving his own frontiers and his powers and prestige intact. It was out of the question that they would ever pool their resources and offer a common front against the nationalist elements.

My father evidently had great faith in the emergence of the third force, and I had no intention of arguing the point with him. It was just as well that at this moment the nurse came out, her face wreathed in smiles, holding a small bundle swathed in white cloth. Almost involuntarily, I held out my hands and took my daughter into my arms.

I was so moved by the inert, weightless bundle that was my daughter, slightly nervous about supporting her head properly and wanting to go on hugging her close to me, that I hardly noticed my father go out and come back with some sovereigns in his hand. He gave them to the nurse and asked her whether she would not like to join us in a glass of champagne.

He always had the instincts of a prince.

I was too excited to go to bed, and as my father had to attend some after-dinner meeting the princes were holding in Bikanir House, I offered to drive him over. After leaving him there, I went to what in those days was called the Imperial Delhi Sports Club.

As I was parking my car, I happened to notice that there was something familiar about one of the others parked nearby. When I passed it, I realized that it was my mother's Daimler, complete with its dark-blue purdah windows and with the blind on the rear window. But there was no flag on the bonnet and the Begwad red number plate had been replaced by an ordinary black and white one.

I had not thought about my mother for a long time, which shows I had been so completely absorbed in my own doings that my brain had been able to shut out the memory of the humiliation she had brought on us. But at that moment I was aware only of a sense of pleasurable excitement that my mother was somewhere in the Club and all I had to do to see her was to go in. I also felt a twinge of self-reproach at having broken off all contact with her for four years. I wondered how much she would have changed, and whether, never having been out of purdah before, she would feel out of place in mixed company. The champagne had brought on a mood of elation and I could hardly wait to tell Mother about my baby, and take her to my house.

There was a dance at the club that evening, with the usual crowd of onlookers around the dance floor. I thought to myself how shocked Mother would be to see men and women who were not married holding each other in their arms. I walked through all the rooms looking for her, but without success. Then, as I was standing near the dance floor, idly watching the dancers, I suddenly saw Abdulla Jan and my mother.

They were dancing. She wore a green sari, an off-the-shoulder choli and high-heeled shoes. Her hair was waved and fell on her shoulders. She was laughing at something he was saying, and looked entirely self-possessed. In spite of myself, I found myself working out her age. She must have just passed her fortieth birthday, and yet she looked trim and supple. No one would have referred to her as a middle-aged woman.

I slunk away. I had not known what to expect, but what I saw was curiously humbling. Out of purdah, wholly at home in the westernized social atmosphere, dancing; all these might have been bearable if it had not been for the air of radiance, even of happiness that she bore. It was so starkly inappropriate, somehow almost vulgar, that a wanton woman should be holding her head high, as though proud of her sins.

I went into the main bar and ordered a drink, telling myself that there was always a shaker of salt around whenever one's cup was full of milk, to remind one that happiness could never be unadulterated. I must have been so lost in my thoughts that I did not see two people come in and occupy the stools beside me until one of them spoke.

'Hullo, there! A penny for your thoughts!'

It was Minnie and Punch. Both were laughing and looked genuinely glad to see me.

There was a quick moment of caution, even of suspicion, in my mind, and also a flicker of resentment that I had been caught unprepared. But in a moment I was laughing with them.

'Minnie! Punch! What do you know? I am a father!' I announced. 'A girl—eight pounds and three ounces.'

I ordered a round of drinks and we drank to my baby. Minnie was wearing my mother's pearls; she looked just as lovely as ever, and seemed genuinely friendly.

'We saw you standing by the dance floor, and we were both waving away, but of course you were just glowering at that chap. You know, the one you knocked down in Simla,' Minnie said.

'I didn't knock him down. I just pushed him,' I said.

'My word, that was a scrap,' Punch said.

Punch had finished his posting as the Governor's A.D.C. and for two months now had been working in the Quartermaster General's branch in G.H.Q., but I had not seen him in the club before.

'We don't belong here, y'know,' Punch explained.

'Well, not yet,' Minnie said. 'We're on the waiting list, though.'

'Must get together; see something of each other,' Punch said.

'Of course! You must come over and have a meal,' I said.

We had got over our initial exuberance and we were trying to break the remaining ice.

'We're not going to have a rumpus here tonight, are we?' Minnie asked. 'I just like to be warned.'

'Rumpus?' I exclaimed. 'Why not? Of course we can have a rumpus. One is not a father every day, dammit! What sort of rumpus had you in mind?' I was certainly learning to handle conversation, now that I had been in New Delhi for nearly two years; meaningless, insincere, but light. You had to keep it frothy, that was all that mattered.

'She means the sort we had in Simla,' Punch explained.

'I saw you looking daggers at that chap,' Minnie said. 'And I said to Punch, oh-oh, here we go again, any moment now.'

'No,' I said. 'Afraid we can't have that sort of a rumpus here, in the Imperial Delhi Sports.'

'What this club needs *is* a damn good rumpus,' Punch said.

'I couldn't agree with you more,' I told him. 'But not today, I'm afraid. Not when one has just become a father.'

'Oh, stop showing off,' Punch said.

'Here's to our getting together,' Minnie said.

'Of course,' I said. 'Here's to all of us.'

'Why, look at Minnie in all those pearls!' yelled someone from the other end of the bar. Minnie was still, I could see, as popular as ever.

Minnie and Punch waved back to their friend and the friend came up and joined us. After a while he took Minnie off to dance.

For a moment I felt uncomfortable because I wondered if Punch was going to bring up anything from the past. But I need have had no fears.

'I say,' Punch said, and he gave his moustache a tug. 'Are you still chummy with anyone really high up in the M.S. branch? You know, someone like Oswald?'

'Who is Oswald?' I asked.

'The chap who came to your shoot, of course. The Assistant Military Secretary.'

'He's gone,' I said. 'And I can't think of anyone else in the M.S. branch just at the moment, Punch. What do you want done?'

'They've gone and posted me to the Chindits. I ask you! —Just as I was beginning to get dug in here. You know, getting a flat, being lined up for a Club membership and all that. And the Chindits, can you beat it?—just when the war's being wound up. They … they're not allowed to take their boots off at night and they're made to double from place to place and grow beards …'

'Who?'

'The bloody Chindits.'

'But don't you want to go, Punch?' I asked. 'Wouldn't you like to go and take a crack at the Japs before it is all over?'

'You know I do, Scrapper. Dammit, you know how much I want to get into it. Lord, the efforts I've made all these years to wangle a posting to an active battalion! But this happens to be a particularly inconvenient moment, old chap, and I was wondering if I couldn't just … well, dammit, it hardly seems decent going overseas at this stage.'

'And no baths,' I said. 'And no change of socks except once a week and …'

'My God, what are you talking about, Scrapper? Who doesn't have baths?'

'The Chindits. And they're allowed no doctors. If you fall ill, the others dose you with stuff, and if you don't respond, they just leave you by the roadside and press on …'

'Ghastly!' Punch cried with a shudder. 'But of course, ordinarily one wouldn't mind a posting even to the Chindits, dammit! It's just that I'm in touch with some of these Johnnies in Imperial Metals who have promised me a job. You do see, old chap, why I didn't want to leave until it was all tickety-boo, what?'

'But naturally, Punch,' I said. 'It just doesn't seem right.'

Punch gave me a long, quizzical stare as though he thought I was pulling his leg, and then grinned affably and patted me on the shoulder. 'And also, old boy, we've just bought a piece of land off Ratendone Road and we're building a little place of our own. I want to settle down here as soon as the shooting stops and everything rather depends on this job coming through. Plenty of money to be made in this country if only one has the right contacts—oh, oodles. And contacts is one thing I don't lack, what?'

'You certainly have the right ones, Punch,' I said.

'And then there's the house coming up. Dammit, I can't leave the old girl alone to look after the construction and all that. Poor Minnie will be quite lost in New Delhi.'

'You mustn't worry about that, Punch. I expect she will be able to find her way back,' I said. 'I am sure Minnie can always find her own way back.'

'What are you two talking about?' Minnie said, coming to rejoin us.

'Abbey has been saying you can always find your own way back,' Punch told her.

'You bet, I can,' Minnie said. 'I'm right back here, all on my own, and I didn't miss the way once.'

20

'So Long as There Is Grass'

There was little I could have done to help Punch get out of his Chindit posting because G.H.Q. had become very strict about such things since the Chester case. In fact I made no attempt to do so and Punch's own efforts failed, since I next heard from him when he rang up to tell me he was leaving next day for the Chindit training camp.

'Just a week from Christmas too,' he complained. 'Can you beat it?'

'It really is tough, Punch,' I said.

'Of course it is. Still, I can take it, damn it,' he said, with a defiant snort. 'Someone's got to go and do the fighting so that others can sit on their arses in New Delhi.'

On the whole, I thought he was taking it very well.

Early in the New Year, I ran into Minnie one evening on Queensway and offered her a lift. But as she was not going anywhere in particular, I took her for a drink to the Criterion instead. And two drinks later, when Minnie's ankle touched mine under the table, I knew that it was not by accident. It was reassuring to know that Minnie no longer held anything against me.

Kamala had taken the baby to her parents' place where my daughter's naming ceremony was to be held. She was to be called Shakuntala, after Kamala's grandmother, a name which both Kamala and I liked, and to which my father had no particular objection. She was going to be away for nearly two months in order to remain with her parents until Holi. I was at a loose end in New Delhi.

By now I have come to accept the fact that whatever else the Bedars may claim as a family, celibacy was certainly not a pronounced trait of our character. At this time, however, I was still feeling a little shocked at myself for taking pleasure in another woman's company when my wife had barely left the house.

But my sense of guilt soon vanished. Sitting beside Minnie in the dark cocktail lounge of the old Criterion, my only doubt was how best to come out with what I had in mind. I even vaguely wondered how my grandfather or my father would have handled such a situation.

I studied Minnie's face and figure with a curious sense of detachment. Marriage had given her an air of prosperity, but otherwise she had hardly changed. She had grown her hair long, and the way it fell over her shoulders added to the earthy sensuousness of her face, and also to that air of helplessness which had always seemed to me to be her most compelling attraction. She had thinned down a little and was wearing a quiet blue-grey dress which fitted her well. Her make-up was subdued, her nails the palest of pink, her perfume discreet.

I knew that the air of helplessness was no more than a feminine weapon of attack, that it merely cloaked an inner core that was tough cowhide, that the wide amber eyes were restless in their search for the main chance, pausing only long enough to put a mental price tag on anything they thought worthwhile.

And yet I had no hard feelings towards Minnie that evening, for at the back of my mind I was aware that she was the first woman who had drawn me out of myself, offered me her body for me to prove my manhood. I have always acknowledged that debt with gratitude.

As I looked at Minnie, I thought of Tony Sykes and how she had loved him, and I wondered if, in whatever I was about to do, I was being loyal to Tony. It was odd how I never gave a thought to Punch.

'Say something,' Minnie said. 'Don't just go on staring. It makes me feel self-conscious, as though my nose is shining.'

'No, your nose is not shining,' I told her. 'But I wasn't saying anything because I didn't know where to begin.'

'Sometimes one can begin where one left off,' Minnie said.

I was glad at the way she seemed to be playing up, because cocktail talk came easy to me in those days. I ordered two more drinks.

'Were you doing anything special this evening?' I asked. 'Going anywhere?'

'Doing nothing, going nowhere,' Minnie said. 'Just a grass widow at a loose end.'

'How do you do, grass widow,' I said. 'Meet the grass widower also at a loose end.'

'You too!' Minnie said. 'Oh, so much grass.'

'We'll have to do something about this,' I assured her.

'About what? Being a grass widow or being at a loose end?'

'Both,' I said. I liked the way she was reacting, taking the game a step further every time she said something. 'Sort of long-term planning,' I added.

'Well, well,' Minnie arched her eyebrows. 'Wouldn't that be a little … a little ambitious?'

'Not if it is a co-operative effort.'

'You make it sound so much like—so much like a business proposition. Or is that what it is?'

Was it getting a shade crude?—I wondered. But I had gone too far to turn back. Of course, I did not wish to turn back.

'Well, it is, sort of,' I said. 'A kind of joint venture.'

'Oh,' Minnie said, and she did not say anything for a long time. 'And how long do you think this … this joint venture should go on?' she asked.

'Only so long as the grass is there,' I said.

'Darling,' Minnie asked, 'are you asking me to be your concubine?'

'Well, not anything so permanent,' I told her. 'Just an arrangement that might be of mutual advantage.'

'That's something, anyway,' Minnie said. 'Well, so long as it is only during grass and so long as it is going to be … of mutual benefit.'

I have always admired Minnie's forthrightness in such matters, as well as her business instinct.

'Mutual benefit sounds even better than mutual advantage,' I said. 'Much less ambiguous.'

'Don't be cruel, now, and don't spoil it,' Minnie said. 'There is something else to it, too, as far as I am concerned, that makes it so attractive.'

'What is it, Minnie?' I asked.

She took her time to answer. '*You*, darling,' she said, looking at me level-eyed and her mouth slightly open.

As I have always said, Minnie had a wonderful head for business. I was aware that these effects had been put on for my benefit, and the husky-voiced '*you*, darling' meant nothing at all. But I could not have wished it otherwise. I wanted to take her face in my hands and kiss her mouth.

Things worked out very well, and I am glad that I was able to help further with Minnie's house off Ratendone Road. We were careful to observe the rules; we never mentioned Tony Sykes in our talk later that evening, nor during any other evening in the next two months. Nor did we mention the name of Punch Farren.

For me, it was a singularly rewarding experience. It was good to know that the ways of the world had not changed so very much from the times of my grandfather.

I particularly remember those days of my reunion with Minnie with strong overtones of nostalgia because they were a sort of idyll, an indelible punctuation mark in my growth to manhood. There was no deep emotional involvement and no tearing apart of live tissue when it was over. It was mature, complete in itself, even perfect. It was like another chapter coming to a close on the right note and leaving behind just a suggestion of remorse, as though to emphasize that no book has any business to go on being preoccupied with unmixed contentment, a sort of lingering in the land of the lotus eaters, for too long.

No shadow of sin hung over us, nor a sense of guilt. It was as though whatever we were doing was merely a compliment to our respective married lives. It was, above all, an experience which wore away the barbs of intolerance that lay like thorns buried deep within me for all these years. It taught me that my father and mother too were not sinners, but merely helpless human beings caught up in the irresistible urge for fulfilment; that it was just that they were not as fortunate as I was. I could even think of my mother's taking a lover as being something understandable, perhaps even inescapable. But that was as far as I could go. At some stage, the claims of family pride took control and made it impossible for me to condone her folly. It was one thing to go astray, but quite another to be proud of one's sin and look the world defiantly in the face. I could understand my father perfectly, but as far as my mother was concerned, it seemed somehow indecent that she should find it in her to be happy. It was like a sati who had gone wrong and was gloating in her sin, this queen who had shamed her predecessors and still contrived to look like a queen.

21

War and Peace

Kamala returned to New Delhi at the end of March. By a curious coincidence, Punch returned from the Chindit training camp during the same week. He had dislocated his knee while going over one of their specially designed obstacle courses, and after a medical board he had been put in lower medical category for six months. He had been posted to Calcutta as a member of the Housing Board.

There was a week of rather dizzy farewell parties for Punch and Minnie. After that they went off to Calcutta, Punch complaining bitterly that the doctors should have 'boarded him out' just when the Chindits were going to be dropped into Burma. 'I could have told the medics there's nothing wrong with my knee, dammit. But you know what medics are.'

I could sympathize with Punch, for there really didn't seem to be anything seriously wrong with his knee. At a party I gave for them at the Tavern, he spent most of the evening dancing the newly-introduced samba and putting poor Kamala through its paces without any visible signs of discomfort. It was odd, watching Kamala dance the samba with obvious enjoyment, Kamala who, until a year earlier, had spent her life in purdah.

'Well, never mind, Punch,' I said. 'At least you're going on promotion. Why don't you look at it that way?'

'There's that, of course, Scrapper,' Punch said. 'But it's damned unfair, to be pulled back just as we were going in.'

Punch was still on the Housing Board in Calcutta when the war was over. It was nearly three years before I was to see him and Minnie again.

The years of war were drawing to a close, giving place to those of great political upheavals. Khaki and jungle-green uniforms would soon be put on the dust-heaps; the new garb of power was the white cap and the loose knee-length shirt of the Indian Nehru and the other leaders were released from jails and talk of transfer of power to India reached fever heat.

As though in sympathy, Delhi was having one of its cruellest heat waves. The wet khas tatties on our doors and windows hardly cooled the inside air for more than a couple of minutes at a time. Our rooms were noisy with the whirr of the overhead fans and dark, damp and heavy with the scent of khas and the reek of locked-in humanity. Outside, the plain quivered under the brassy glare of the sun and the loo blew in scorching dust-laden swirls. The nights were never cool enough or long enough for the buildings of New Delhi to throw off the stored-up heat of the long summer days.

'You must take Shaku to some hill station,' I told Kamala. 'It's cruel to keep a baby here in this kind of weather.'

'I have just returned from home and the little beast seems to be thriving in the heat, as you can see,' Kamala said. 'I don't want to leave you alone—not in this heat.'

'But I can't get any leave just yet,' I explained. 'Isn't your father going to Mussorie this year? Or you could go to Kasauli. I'll get father to open his bungalow.'

'No,' Kamala said with determination. 'We will all stay here. I don't like the idea of your being all by yourself.'

'But, darling, I don't mind being alone,' I said. 'I can look after myself all right … perfectly happy.'

'That's just it,' Kamala said. 'I don't like the idea of your being quite so … so capable of looking after yourself, when I am not around.'

The way she said it, made me think that she suspected something about Minnie; women have an instinct for such discoveries. But I was not altogether sorry. If Kamala did not know that ours was purely a marriage of convenience, it was time she woke up to the fact.

I looked at Kamala, who had had her hair waved by Julian and who no longer wore her saris draped over her head; at the woman who had been maturing under my guidance, learning to wear clothes with a flair and to do the things I liked her to do. I had even had her taught to dance, and I liked to take her out, now that her figure had gone back to its normal slimness, into the kind of westernized social life that I was getting used to. At times I even felt proud at the way she carried herself, gracious and dignified or sparkling and lighthearted as the occasion demanded, it would have been nice to have her as a girl friend, I kept thinking. But I had not married her for love, she was not capable of causing any great emotional stir within me, even though she could be the subject of a purely proprietary pride.

In the end, I did not press the point. We stayed on in Delhi all through the summer of 1945. And it was convenient having my wife to run the house for me in those days, for my father had taken to visiting the capital frequently, and did not make a very easy guest.

It must have been a few weeks after VE day that I saw my father's name mentioned in one of a series of files on the political unrest in the country passed on to us for information by the Police Bureau. It contained a report from the Central India Agency.

Begwad, it said, was a state in which there was growing likelihood of unrest, particularly among the aborigines of Bulwara, who had begun to agitate against the prospect of the Bulwara hydro-electric dam being taken in hand by the Government as soon as the war was over.

> 'While the movement in the rest of the state is directed against the Maharaja's misrule, it is believed that the agitation amongst the Bhils has been instigated by the

ruler himself. The ruler is actually said to be supplying arms to the Bhils.'

I first read the report with more amusement than interest, but then, as I remembered my father's views about the prospect of integration with the rest of the country and about the Bulwara dam going up, this gave way to a feeling of distress, even of vicarious guilt.

The report itself was based on a series of complaints received from the President of the Begwad Praja-mandal, and copies of some of these complaints were enclosed. They were all signed by a man called K-C. Gaur. The name did not mean anything to me then, nor did I know that this was the first shot in a battle that was to last for more than three years, ending only with our extinction.

My father was in New Delhi a few days later. I mentioned the report to him.

'Completely fabricated,' he assured me. 'There is no agitation of any sort, anywhere.'

'It says that you have been secretly supplying arms to the Bhils to resist the building of the dam,' I told him.

'Nonsense!' Father announced airily. 'Rubbish. That the British police should even countenance such a suggestion … who could have sent it, do you think?'

'I'm not supposed to tell you, Dada. It's a secret report. But I am going to. It is based on complaints made by the President of the Praja-mandal in Begwad—a man called K-C. Gaur.'

'Oh, K-C. Gaur!' Father gave a contemptuous snort. 'That boy I had to whip.'

'But he was Dhor,' I pointed out. 'Kanakchand Dhor.'

'Changed his name. Dhor rather stamps him as an untouchable. So he now calls himself Gaur—the scoundrel!'

'He also happens to be President of the Mandal,' I said.

'There is no such thing as the Praja-mandal in Begwad. I have banned all political parties, including your Congress. And as to this man, I have forbidden him to enter our state. I don't hold with this nonsense about people's movements!'

'But the way things are going, Dada, wouldn't it be safer to permit some sort of representation of the people?'

'And suffer people like this Dhor, or Gaur, to dictate terms to me? Never!'

'People like him can do a lot of harm, and it might be quite easy to win them over.'

'Never!' Father said again. 'I have forbidden him to enter Begwad. How can he profess to represent the people when he cannot even enter the state? What people? And why should the police send on such complaints to the Government, even if they do receive them?'

'Where is Charudutt these days?' I asked, almost without thinking.

My father raised his eyebrows. 'Charudutt is in Agra. You don't really think it could be him?'

I shook my head. It was unthinkable that Charudutt should be sending such false reports against his own father, and yet … and yet, the coincidence was far too marked to be ignored. It was in Agra that the police had their Central Agency, and it was the Agency that had forwarded the report.

'And who in his right mind is going to believe such nonsense? Not the British, certainly. And as to the nationalists … the Congress, I don't care what they believe. They can go their own way. I shall go mine. We are enemies. "Lunatics, knaves, fools", that is how Nehru refers to us. We'll show the Congress.'

'Does that mean there is some truth in the reports, Dada?' I asked, suddenly suspicious.

He gave me his poker smile. 'Well, there is certainly some talk in the state, as there is in all states, of a people's movement. But I won't have it. As to the Bulwara people … well, they are my own men, mine and yours. If they are provided with arms … if, I say … we can be sure that they will never be used against us. Only to help us. And mind you, there may come a time when we might have to make demands upon their loyalty and devotion. If that time does not come, no harm will have been done. A man has a right to carry arms, a birthright. That is the very first amendment in the American constitution.'

'But, Father …' I protested.

'And it is their right to agitate against building the dam. Are they to lose everything they possess just so that the Government can build a dam? To have their forefathers' lands submerged for the benefit of others? It is everyone's right to agitate. Gandhi himself has taught the people to agitate. Why exclude the Bhils?'

I was too shaken to say anything. I could see there was no longer anything in common between his outlook and mine.

'And who is going to take notice of reports sent by such riffraff?' Father asked. 'Certainly not those who govern.'

'The trouble is, Dada, that there's a very good chance that people like Kanakchand will become the people who govern,' I said.

'I won't live to see that day, thank God!' Father replied. 'I want to die before anything like that happens.'

The summer went the way of all summers, leaving behind a feeling of disbelief, of coming out into the open and finding that the grass was still on the ground and the trees still had their leaves. The first rains brought their own miseries; the smell of rotting vegetation, the myriads of insects exploding against the lights, the clogging of drains, the foul vapours rising out of the earth.

And then the turning point of the year, September, with the first unbelieving symptoms of coolness, and after that the quick-healing breath of winter, transforming an abandoned dust-heap into a landscape of abundance, of lush green grass, of birds and flowers days that you want to catch and keep, of early sundowns and long, fireside evenings, the 'Season' of New Delhi, the gift the Gods for the forgotten penance of the summer.

I wanted to leave the army soon after VJ day, but much to my surprise my father asked me to stay on for a few more months.

'It is good to have you here, right in the Secretariat. A sort of listening post,' he said.

I had no particular feelings of loyalty towards the Government, and I would have unhesitatingly passed on to my father any bit of information that came my way if I thought it would be of any use to him. All the same, I did not relish being regarded as a listening post.

My father was worried about the prominence the British had been giving to the Congress leaders. The Congress party, he was convinced was out to liquidate the princes. The princes were now openly advocating the 'third force'.

'I've always said that we should be prepared to meet the threat of the Congress by force,' he told me one day, 'instead of depending wholly on the promises of the British.'

'But have the British given any indication that they might welsh on their promises?'

'Welsh?' Father asked.

'Well, go back!'

'We don't know. It's rather disturbing that a party which calls itself the Labour party should be in a position to form the Government in England. It just doesn't bear thinking about.'

My father shrugged his shoulders in a gesture of revulsion, but I felt that his attitude somehow symbolized the current of fear that had run through the princely order at the Labour victory in England. The structure of their world was beginning to show cracks, and it was becoming clear that they would do themselves no good by trying to hinder India's attainment of self-rule. The nationalists who would succeed the British were not even prepared to recognize the rights of the rulers to speak for their own states.

'They want elected men,' Father sneered. 'If the British let us down, we will just have to raise troops and fight for our rights and for our territories. Let the Congress just try and take them from us.'

'But what about the treaties?' I asked. 'Has the British Government said anything to cause you alarm?'

'They keep making promises, and then they keep hedging, giving in to the Congress. Why should they have let them out of jail in the middle of the war? If the British would only keep their political agitators where I keep mine, India would be a peaceful place.'

There was no use arguing with him that the release of the political leaders was an act of wisdom, that many of them were great men and that it was criminal to keep them in prisons for their patriotism. But I could protest against their determination to go to war.

'How can anyone, anyone at all, justify a war? A war against our own people?' I asked.

'We shall not be making the war. It is the British who will be compelling us to go to war in self-defence. If they let us down, we shall have to take up arms against the nationalists.'

'Are the British going to let you down?'

'We can't be sure. I hope we shall get a clear idea tomorrow.'

'What is happening tomorrow?'

'The annual session of the Chamber,' he said.

I think that that meeting of the Chamber of Princes on 17th January 1946 must have been the very first of its kind that my father attended. It was a historic meeting if only for the false sense of security it projected among the princes.

I had just returned from the office and we were in the sitting room. Kamala was pouring out tea and Shakuntala tugging at the ribbons on my battle-dress jacket when I heard my father's quick footstep on the verandah. Kamala pulled her sari over her head and was about to leave the room, when he walked in, beaming. He picked up my daughter, threw her into the air and caught her just as he had with me when I was small.

'No, no, don't go away,' he told Kamala. 'I would like a cup of tea.'

I could see that things had gone well at the meeting and that Father was bursting to come out with it.

'Everything went off perfectly,' he said. 'But what a shock to the Congress-wallas! You'll see it in the papers tomorrow. Long leaders … everyone fuming. I'd no idea His Excellency was going to be so positive—so firm! Wonderful man, Wavell. Must try and get him over for a shoot.'

I was pleased for him as well as for myself, for I wanted to share in his joy.

'This girl of yours is most irreverent,' he complained. 'Kamala has not brought her up to show respect to her elders.'

Shakuntala was pulling at his moustache and snatching at the cake he was trying to eat. Kamala put out her arms to take her away from him.

'Oh, let her be,' Father said. 'Let her be. She's no trouble.' He fished inside his pocket and brought out a paper and handed it to me. 'That's the address HE gave,' he said. 'Just read the bits I've underlined. Read them out aloud.'

'… no change in the relationship of the princes with the Crown,' I read, 'of the rights guaranteed to them by treaties and engagements would be initiated without their consent …'

'Well, what do you think?' Father asked.

'That seems definite enough,' I said.

'Of course it is. My god, it will burn up the white-cap wallas!'

'I think this calls for champagne, Dada,' I said.

'It certainly does. I'll get Haibat to go and find some. Or have you any stocked up?'

'Of course, Dada,' I told him. 'I always keep a bottle or two handy so that it's there for celebrations.'

'Very wise,' Father said. 'A most wise precaution. I shall have a case sent to you as soon as I go back.'

I called to the bearer to bring out the champagne and the glasses. It had not been kept on ice, but of course it was cold enough not to matter.

'Have some champagne, Kamala.' My father offered her his glass.

I had never offered Kamala a drink. 'Don't tell me you are going to drink that?' I said.

'How can I refuse if Dada-maharaj offers it?' Kamala said. Her eyes were bright with happiness.

'Champagne is always a good drink for the ladies,' Father declared, 'It is tirtha—Ganges water. Let's give the little one a spoonful. Infants thrive on champagne.'

'So long as it is only a spoonful,' I said.

My daughter squealed with delight and polished off her share like a true Bedar.

'You don't know how Abhay used to lap up my drinks at that age,' my father told Kamala.

'I wonder what Nanny will have to say to all this?' Kamala complained

'Nanny! Why, send up a glass for her too,' Father said. 'I expect you have another bottle?'

'Yes, Dada,' I replied.

'Good boy,' he said. 'Well, here's to all the good boys! When are you going to have yours?' he asked Kamala.

She blushed a deep pink and turned her face away, for she was already two months gone with child.

'You had better make this one a boy,' I said to her.

'I'll send you two cases,' Father said. 'One for you and one for your son.'

It was long past Shakuntala's bedtime and Kamala left us, carrying my protesting daughter. My father and I sat on over our drinks.

Now that the Viceroy had strengthened their hand, he said, the princes would not give an inch of ground to the nationalists. 'We need not pay any heed to the Congress or the Muslim League. We are going to be the third force, far more powerful than either the white-cap wallas or the dadhi-wallas. Powerful because we have the resources, the money and the arms.'

The Viceroy's assurance had whipped up their enthusiasm for the third force. 'We shall have a separate India, the India of the Princes,' he explained. 'Powerful, solid, deeply rooted in tradition; six hundred independent states merging together to form a princely India …'

'Independent states?' I asked.

'Of course, independent. The moment the British go, we become wholly independent.'

This disquieted me all the more because I knew my father was not alone in advocating the third force; his attitude was precisely that of the majority of the princes. They were going to join hands and oppose the nationalists—even if it meant civil war.

It was pathetic to see how desperately they clung to their illusions. Panic had been replaced by wishful thinking. A glance at the map would have shown them how impractical the idea of forming a union of Princely States was, for the states were peppered all over the landscape of India and even in and out of each other. But even if geographical contiguity had existed, such a creation would still have been out of the question, because all history had shown that the princes were incapable of uniting. Their internal jealousies had made it possible for the British to pick them off one by one. The compulsions that governed them now, two hundred years later, were still the same. Without British protection they would have been finished long ago. Now the British were going, leaving them to their fate. It was incredible that they could not see the writing on the wall.

They were like ripe mangoes in late May, all ready to fall, and some were downright rotten. All it needed was for someone to come and give the tree a shaking. They would all drop off—good and rotten alike.

But my father's mind was still in the Chamber of Princes, savouring the day's victory, dreaming his own dreams. And knowing the nature of his dreams, I was sad for him. He was drinking champagne now, and he had a right to his dreams; but the champagne was running out, and the time of dreams coming to an end.

22

Number Account

Many people say that the Naval mutiny in Bombay accelerated the process of the British quitting India. The time for leisurely round-table discussions was over, and things began to move with speed. A British Cabinet Mission came to India charged with the task of setting up the proper machinery for the transfer of power into Indian hands. In his announcement, the British Prime Minister had expressed the hope that the princes would not act as a 'positive veto on advance'.

A shock like an earth tremor passed through the princely states. Alarmed, the princes rushed to New Delhi to seek assurances from the Mission, only to discover that it was not open to business on the usual terms. There were to be no prolonged discussions with anyone who had a view to put forward; indeed the Mission restricted its interviews to only a few selected representatives of the princes.

At last the princes woke up to the fact that they were being relegated to a position of unimportance; that their insistence on the sanctity of treaty rights was being recognized for what it was: intransigent.

On 16th May, they must have become aware of the first whiff of the scent of defeat. The Mission had announced that there would be no continuity of relationship between the princes and the British crown after the transfer of power into Indian hands.

'Are we to be left at the mercy of the rest of India?' the princes groaned, but in the convulsions of the Hindu-Muslim riots in Calcutta and Lahore, no one heard their wails. The Chancellor of their Chamber wrote a pathetic letter to the Viceroy, asking whether His Majesty's Government intended to leave the states as a 'sort of no man's child'.

But the Viceroy was in no position to help. The princes were being suddenly orphaned; the mango tree was not only being shaken but it was being cut down. Now, if the princes wanted to participate in making the new constitution, they could do so only by joining the Constituent Assembly.

From inviolable treaties to a back-seat in a constitution-making body was a great fall. Spurred into activity, the princes held a number of emergency meetings to devise ways and means to safeguard their positions. My father, who had been touring the Bulwara district, came rushing to Delhi for these discussions and for consultation with the eminent London K.C. some of the princes had invited to New Delhi.

'It looks as though we shall just have to fend for ourselves,' my father said to me as he was getting into the car to go and see the barrister. 'Let's see what Sir Ronald Meakins has to say. Are the princes to be thrown on the streets for a picnic of crows?'

Sir Ronald Meakins was being paid five thousand rupees per day in addition to his expenses, but he had nothing reassuring to tell my father and his other consultants. He explained to them that on the day of the transfer of power, all the states would be sovereign independent states.

'That, of course, is the legal and constitutional position,' he emphasized, 'How Your Highnesses protect your sovereignty, how you guard your independent status, is left to yourselves.'

The princes held more emergency meetings. The time had come to face the issues. Were they going to participate in the Constituent Assembly and thus throw themselves on the mercy of the nationalists whom they had always distrusted? The only other way was to forge the third force, stick together and refuse to join the Assembly; if necessary, to fight it out.

'At a time like this, you should be where you belong—with your own,' my father said to me.

I was myself beginning to feel bored with my life in New Delhi. 'Do you want me to leave the army?' I asked.

'I want you to be with me. We could—who knows, we might have to make use of your knowledge of training and warfare.'

Even though I knew something of what had been in his mind, it came as a shock to me that my father was actually thinking in terms of military action in the state.

'Your presence would be a great help to me,' he added.

I wanted to help him, but even more to save him from rashness, so I was pleased at the way he had put it.

'I will leave as soon as the baby is born,' I said.

'Yes,' he said. 'You'll have to remain here until the baby comes—the future Maharaja. I am offering a mahapooja for it to be a boy.'

Would my unborn son ever become a Maharaja? Or would everything have been lost even before he was born? I found myself wondering. And in the wake of that doubt, as though the future of a generation yet unborn had cleared my mind and given me an additional stake in the heritage of my forefathers, I was touched by a spasm of anxiety and thanked him for having offered the mahapooja.

As always, his eyes had lit up at the thought of religion. 'They will go on with the yadna for seven days and nights without a break, seven pandits chanting the guru-pooja in relays, with the Head Priest from the Durga-math himself presiding. Couldn't you come for it?'

My mind shrank from the thought of a religious orgy. 'It is hardly likely,' I said. 'I'm doing two jobs now—officiating for my G.I.'

'Oh, that friend of yours came to see me—the one who came for the Tatwal shoot once,' Father said.

'Punch?' I said. 'Punch Farren?'

'That's right. Exceedingly bright man. Full of ideas.'

'Was Punch on leave?' I asked. 'Or had he wangled a tour of some kind?'

'He's not in the army any longer. Some kind of a job in Bombay. But he is leaving his job, he told me. Wants to start on his own.'

'Did he bring his wife with him?' I asked.

My father gave me an amused look. 'Oh, yes, Mrs. Farren came too. I thought that you knew about their visit—kept in touch.'

'What did Punch want?' I asked.

'Oh, I expect he just wanted a holiday—wrote to me asking if he could come. We discussed a little business too. He has some very bright ideas.'

'Punch was always full of ideas,' I said.

'He has a wonderful grasp of the way things are shaping here … and how to be prepared. He even offered to act as a kind of middle man, you know, in case I wanted to send any jewels for safe keeping. He also told me he could lay hands on as many dollars as I would care to buy—four rupees a dollar. Evidently that is the thing to do, buy American dollars. He certainly knew what he was talking about. And Abhay, you must look into this …'

'Did you buy any dollars, Dada, or give him any jewellery for sale?'

'No, I had to rush off here. I'm hoping to get hold of him soon, though, when things are a little more settled. It is not selling, mind you, unless you want to. Evidently he takes it abroad for you and keeps it in a bank. Seems to be doing work for several rulers. Most enterprising man … knows Rosenthal and Harry Sumner personally. But what was I telling you about?'

'Something I must look into.'

'Now what … Oh, yes. Major Farren said that the safest way to keep money these days is to open a number account in a Swiss bank. You know, so that …'

'What is a number account?'

'He explained it to me. You send the money or jewels out of the country with Major Farren, and he deposits it for you in a bank in Switzerland. Safe as houses and no one the wiser. The account just bears a number. No names, no packdrill, as they say in the army … if they still say it.'

'It sounds illegal to me,' I said.

'Nonsense! Why should we not look after our own money; keep it somewhere safe? Just enough for an emergency, at least. A few lakhs, not much, in a bank in Zurich or somewhere. And if there are people willing to help—friends, it would be foolish not to take advantage. If there was a lot to be transported, he even hinted at being able to charter a plane. Old Tilkatta was quite taken with them. He even …'

'I didn't know Punch knew the Maharaja of Tilkatta,' I said.

'Why, I gave him a letter of introduction myself. They've been all over … he and his wife. Tilkatta, Joida, Ninnore … exceedingly bright young man.'

'I hope they are not breaking the exchange regulations,' I said.

'If you ask me, we have a perfect right to protect what is ours. All the big princes seem to be doing it. His Highness has—even sent out his state jewels.' Father mentioned the name of one of the highest ranking princes.

'Oh, my God!' I said.

'Something like that has just got to be done. And where else would we get someone like Major Farren, a close friend of the family, as it were?'

'I still don't like it,' I said.

My father gave me a long, questioning look. 'Isn't Farren still a friend of yours?'

'Of course he is,' I assured him. 'But what he's doing does not sound right at all.'

'You're still not … not enamoured of that girl, are you?'

'Who, Minnie? Certainly not!'

'Then I can't see any reason why we should not take advantage of Major Farren's kind offer. Everybody is doing it.'

We left it at that, and my father went back to Begwad, determined not to take part in the Constituent Assembly or to sign away his rights. At least it was something to be thankful for that he did not make a public boast of it. Some other princes openly threatened armed opposition. 'We will fight, if need be,' they thundered.

But no one was sufficiently interested even to feel outraged. The papers gave little prominence to the pronouncements of the princes. All eyes were pinned on the communal conflict that raged throughout the country. There had been mass killings in most of the major towns. The process of dividing the country, of tearing apart what had grown together and taken deep roots, was already taking a toll. The road to freedom was red with blood.

The princes had been relegated to a position of extreme unimportance. After a century and a half of hot-house living, they found themselves suddenly abandoned on the doorstep of the Indian National Congress. Some of them were determined to keep their independence.

Matters were coming to a head. I could no longer remain a mere spectator. If there was going to be an open split, I would stand by my father, right or wrong. But I hoped against hope that the split would not occur, that somehow things would arrange themselves in a way that would be acceptable to both the princes and the nationalists.

On a rainy day in July, my son was born. We named him Ashokraj, after my uncle. My father came to New Delhi for the naming ceremony and offered another mahapooja and gave away twenty-five cows as a token of thanksgiving. He also gave a party at the Tilkatta House for his friends and mine. I was surprised at the number of princes that came to the party, for I had never thought that there would be so many in New Delhi. They seemed full of laughter and talk that day, though all of them must have realized what was going to happen to them. A race that was doomed, waiting in the hospital lobby to be told just how long they had to go on.

Two weeks later, I resigned my commission.

23

The Tinkle of Glass Bangles

My father wanted us to take my mother's wing in the palace, but I preferred to go into the Captain's Lodge, near the elbow of the river, which Kamala and I had occupied when we were married. I felt that our children should grow up as far away from the atmosphere of the palace as possible, spending most of their time with Kamala and their Nanny.

Kamala made a diligent housewife and mother, and I had come to depend more and more on her and to share my thoughts with her. At times I would think that we were more like two friends in our attitude to each other than a husband and wife, and I could even see our marriage sliding smoothly into one of those staid Hindu marriages that go on and on with only the tight bonds of convention to hold them together. I was a little surprised to see that Kamala seemed to feel far more distressed at the way things were going politically than I was, and then I realized that with the birth of our son, she too had a vital stake in the future of the state.

I kept myself very busy in Begwad, keeping to the G.H.Q. office hours and working in the Administrative building, going through the files. Most evenings, I used to be present when my father held his audience chamber. After that there were usually various matters that had to be discussed, and some evenings I was held up so late that I stayed on in the palace, in the same apartment I had as a bachelor.

Within two weeks of my coming to Begwad, my father and I went to Bulwara. And on my first evening there, I rode down the valley to the fort of Patalpat, the stronghold of my ancestors.

At last I was going to see the Jamdar-khana, the family vault.

I was all by myself in the small room above the entrance gate in the fort that so far I had seen only from above. I was sitting in a carved chair which smelt faintly of sandalwood.

It was nearing dusk and the room was almost dark. As I sat, I could hear the little unidentifiable noises in the darkness around me, the whispers and creaks and faint stirrings of an aged fortress.

It seemed a long time before the two men entered the room, their feet making small scuffing sounds on the carpet. They stood silently on both sides of me. Without raising my head, I could see that they were carrying swords. I knew it would not have done to raise my head and look at their faces.

One of them produced a black silk sash from his pocket and held it before me. 'Please shut your eyes, Bedar-son,' he said softly. Even the accent was quaint, as was the mode of address, as though it belonged to another age and had not been softened and civilized by contact with the outside world.

I closed my eyes and the man tied the length of black silk over them. After that the other man put another bandage over the first. The second bandage felt like wool.

'I hope it is not too uncomfortable?' he asked.

I shook my head.

'Come, Bedar-son,' he said, and he held me by the hand.

I rose from the chair, allowing myself to be led. The other man must have been walking just a step or two ahead of us, for he kept telling me to bend my head for a low door-frame or warned me when we were coming to a flight of steps. I did not know where I was going, but I had a rough idea of what I was about to see.

We went down what must have been a long staircase; even without counting the steps, I was aware there were at least a hundred of them. After that we took several sharp turns to right and left, but I suspected that this was only a move to make me lose my sense of direction in case I had been trying to memorize the way. At intervals we halted and there was the sound of keys being fitted and doors turning on squeaky hinges. The old fort, as one could see from above, was a vast labyrinth of communicating buildings, surrounded by a deep moat. It was part fort, part prison, and part residence. For a long time we seemed to be going through a low, closed-in passage in which our footsteps rang hollow and the air was musty, like an underground cave inhabited by bats.

I was beginning to develop an itch under the bandage on my right temple, when we stopped. I was gently guided into a seat. There was the sound of a key being fitted into a lock and turned. Then they took off the bandages.

I blinked my eyes and saw in the dim light of a flickering flame in a bowl of oil that I was facing a low, solid-looking door.

'The door is unlocked, Bedar-son,' one of the men said from behind. 'But it will be locked again as soon as the Bedar-son goes in. Please knock when you wish to come out. We shall be waiting here.'

'And, of course, there is no need to tell you that only one article is permitted,' said the other. Even their voices sounded alike.

I nodded my head. That was the limit imposed on our avarice—by whom? I wondered. We could carry away only one article at each visit. There could be at the most three visits during a life-time: once as a Yuwaraja, once as the Ruler, and once in case of emergency.

I had always ached to learn the truth behind the legend, for over the years I had almost ceased to believe that there could be such a thing as the treasure of the Bedars guarded by trusted family retainers who permitted no one else to enter, and even that the Bedars themselves could enter but three times in a lifetime.

I hesitated. It was too much like the three boons offered by a revengeful God; there was always a catch to each one. Suddenly I did not want to make a wish; I wanted nothing. Why should I not hold back until I really wanted something?

I was prodded by the charged silence behind me. 'Is there a light … inside?' I asked.

'The diwas were lit, Bedar-son, just before we came out to escort you.'

The door opened smoothly to my touch, without a squeak, and I walked into the family vault. As I pushed back the door and waited, trying to get a grip on myself, I heard the faint click of the key being turned behind me.

I was in a long, low-ceilinged room with no windows. The roof seemed to be supported by a series of stone arches. The flames of the oil lamps in the niches along the walls were dead straight. There was a faint odour of dead roses, but the room did not smell musty.

On my right, there was a large, high-backed chair made of some dull metal, and I sat down on it. The seat felt cold and the arm-rests in the shapes of lions were scratchy with decoration, being inlaid with little green and red stones gleaming dully, like the eyes of dead animals. I jumped to my feet with a sudden start, knowing that I had just been sitting on the golden throne of Murad, Aurangzeb's brother, who had had it cast in anticipation of becoming the Mughal Emperor. Murad had been murdered by his brother. His golden throne had been renowned in history as the unlucky throne. In the mood I was in, I thought there was something ominous in my resting on the seat of a man who ended his life wearing heavy golden fetters. Almost without meaning to, I looked under the seat for the fetters. Of course, they were not there.

On the other side of the door was an elephant howdah, and because it was kept where it was, I knew that it too must be made of pure gold.

Along the walls were the copper hundas, vessels large enough to heat bath water in. I threw open the lid of one. It was full to the brim with gold coins, crude, uneven, heavy, and shining dully as though with a life of their own. There were eight other hundas, all in a row, but I did not look into the others.

There was a chest full of swords, with intricate work on the hilts and scabbards, and another containing match-lock and wheel-lock guns and pistols with exquisite workmanship on their butts and barrels. There were shelves of figures of gods and goddesses, shivas, elephant-gods, buddhas, vishnus, and other unknown ones, all robbed from the temples of the rich in the days when might was all. A series of camphor chests were full of old garments, exuding the scent of roses with which they must have been impregnated two hundred years ago: silk and velvet and himru, lying crumpled in unidentifiable twists, the crumbling flags of some forgotten ruler, the saris and lacy petticoats of some harem favourite, voluminous satin robes, iridescent brocade woven by sightless men, blinded at birth …

In a great black chest as high as my shoulders, there were precious stones and ornaments reflecting the light from the oil flames in a riot of colour. There was a ruby as big as my thumb set within a circle of smaller rubies and provided with a clip to be worn as a turban clasp, and I knew without being told that they were all what were called pigeon-blood rubies. There were clear white stones, pale blue stones, stones of green, amber, azure, and many other colours I cannot describe. In a small compartment of its own was a pearl necklace such as I had seen only around the neck of the Maharaja of Baroda, and of which the pearls were reputed to be virtually matchless. I think the Baroda necklace had seven strands, ours had only three. Each strand had about two dozen smooth pink pearls, the size of small marbles, so perfectly matched that only by the way the strands fitted one within the other, could one tell that they could not all be of the same size. There were ornaments I could not describe and did not know the use of, and a jumble of minor pearl necklaces, amulets, nose-rings, ear-clips, bangles, turbanclasps, anklets. There was even a baby's rattle made of gold and studded with gems.

I did not open all the drawers of the blackwood chest, nor did I look into any of the other boxes. I was suddenly overcome by a feeling of revulsion, a nausea brought on by the realization that the garments and ornaments, the baby's rattles and the golden thrones, once belonged to living men and women. It was as though the owners had left a part of themselves hovering behind over their belongings. The vault with its dark stonework arches could have been a mausoleum. And as though affected by my thoughts, the flames in the oil diwas gave a quick little flutter, making the shadows move along the walls like soldiers drilling.

The treasure of the Bedars had been put together as the result of five generations of plunder, things taken from their rightful owners by force, by the killing of men and the capture of their women. And it was all ours, mine and my father's, but only for an emergency. For ourselves, we could carry away only whatever bauble we fancied twice during our lifetimes. But if there was an emergency, the whole treasure was ours, ours to do as we liked.

It had never been valued by experts, but my father once told me that his father, who knew a good deal about jewels, had estimated it to be worth between five and six crores of rupees. The crore during my grandfather's time was something like five crores today; but whether in his day or mine, five crores of rupees in negotiable trinkets would have sufficed for any kind of emergency.

Had there been no emergencies? What about the time when my great grandfather had been deposed? Could he not have bought off the wrath of the British Resident by the gift of a turban-clasp made of pigeon blood rubies instead of spending the rest of his life in prison? What about that other one, who was declared a lunatic? Could he not have persuaded the doctors to certify his sanity in exchange for a throne made of pure gold and studded with precious stones?

And what about my father himself, whose extravagance had brought our state to the verge of ruin during the depression so that the Political Department had hinted darkly at setting up a commission of inquiry? Did not his plight, too, constitute an emergency?

Thoughts flooded my mind, like unhappy ghosts restless with unrequited longings. Who kept a record of all that was valuable in the vaults? What guarantee was there that everything was as it had been before? How trustworthy were the Ramoshis, who guarded the treasure? And how could one remain honest in the midst of daily temptations? How could one ever test, if one was allowed to enter only twice or at most three times in a lifetime, whether everything was in its place? Would I myself remember exactly what I had seen when I came back? And when would that be? In twenty years' time?

Brought up as I had been, I realized it was almost sacrilegious to doubt the trustworthiness of the Ramoshis, the men who had guarded the treasure for more than two hundred years. They were bound down by the curse of Ambica. They and their descendants would be condemned for all time if they were so much as to covet what they were charged to protect.

And what about the other curses, those of the victims of the plunder? Of the kings, the concubines and the terrified children who were put to death by the dreaded men with double axes swooping down on their encampments in the middle of the night, cutting off their tent-ropes, setting fire to their grain and fodder and rummaging for gold, heedless of the curses of the dying and the screams of the wounded?

The oil-flames gave another flicker, as though disturbed by a breeze, the shadow-men doing drill leaned forward and then back again. I shook my head and took a deep breath. There were beads of perspiration on my forehead.

I wanted to take nothing away. I had no use for the pearls and diamonds of the dead, nor for a copper hunda filled with goldmohurs of the Mughal emperors. I had a sudden feeling of claustrophobia. I wanted to get out, away from the room in which were stored the clothes, the ornaments and the curses of men who had been ghosts for two hundred years. I opened the chest nearest to me, the one with the pistols and guns in it. I picked up a wheellock pistol from its velvet case. It had swirls of yellow and blue engraving on the lock and barrel, a design as intricate as an old Kashmir shawl. The butt fitted snugly in my hand as though it had been made for me, and the barrel was almost weightless, so perfectly balanced it was.

I knocked with the butt of the pistol on the door, feeling it would never open, that I was locked in for life, for my bones to lie buried with other people's trinkets.

As I waited, there was a moment of sheer panic, and I had to fight a desire to bang against the door with all my might and to break it down. But then, with startling noiselessness, the door swung open. I stumbled out and sat on the chair.

One of the men began to tie the bandages round my eyes while the other made a note in some register about the pistol I had brought out.

I had gone in burning with curiosity; I came out feeling I had desecrated a tomb.

As I expected my father never asked me what I had brought out. It would have been interesting to compare notes with him, to find out what he himself had brought out, and how he had felt. But when I saw him the next evening, I refrained from saying anything about my visit to the Jamdar-khana.

My father looked tense and preoccupied, a man confronted with a harsh decision. He reminded me of a hard-pressed general during a back-to-the-wall campaign, but also of one who had lost his way, for he was working at something doomed for failure: the formation of the third force.

'I wish we could be more certain of this man Mountbatten,' he said to me after dinner. 'What is he going to do?'

'He is about the most brilliant military commander of the times,' I told him.

'Yes, and he has the right background too,' Father said. 'Queen Victoria's grandson—or is it great-grandson?'

The fact that the new Viceroy was related to the royal family counted far more with my father than his military brilliance.

'We are still waiting for a clear-cut statement of policy from Mountbatten,' my father said. 'Exactly how do we stand when power is transferred? We want guarantees.'

'Perhaps the Viceroy is not in a position to give any guarantees, Dada. What happens after the British have gone will have to be settled with their successors. And it would hardly be in the interests of the country if the work of framing a constitution had to be held back because of the princes.'

He gave me a pained look. 'You, too,' he said and shook his head. 'But of course you have always been somewhat leftish in your views. I, on the other hand, am old-fashioned. To me the interest of my state is paramount—sacred above all, I cannot change now. And as to self-rule, we have always had that in the states. When the English leave, we will be completely independent. Why should we join the Constituent Assembly when we know that the nationalists are only out to finish us?'

'If we join now,' I said, 'we can at least escape being branded as traitors … hostile, as Nehru has declared.'

'That is just an idle threat!' he fumed. 'Are they going to have a hundred wars on their hands? We can defend ourselves. We can even carve out bigger territories for ourselves.'

I was distressed by his vehemence, even though I was aware that he reflected only the general attitude of the princes—to preserve the heritage of their forefathers at all cost. I could understand his feeling that it was necessary to seek reassurance from someone whom he loved and trusted—myself—that what he was doing was right. But to me it was all too clear what an unbridgable gulf separated him from the wave of nationalism sweeping the country and erupting in the states just as the princes were organizing their precious third force. Almost overnight there had sprung up all over the states political organizations calling themselves Praja-mandals, or peoples' assemblies, and they had begun a virulent campaign of slander and falsehood against the rulers.

'Sir Arbuthnot himself feels that the third force is not only feasible, but the most sensible solution,' my father told me.

As Colonel Gibson, Sir Arbuthnot had been our Political Agent until the end of 1940. He was now one of the secretaries at New Delhi. I could understand why Sir Arbuthnot should favour the third force idea. He was one of those older British officials who had always regarded the nationalists as their arch enemies and had never reconciled themselves to the liquidation of the empire they had helped to rule. Theirs was merely the anguished cry of the last-ditchers in the face of progress.

'Gibson is just an old koi-hai,' I said.

'Koi-hai?' Father asked.

'Army slang for the pukka-sahibs,' I explained. 'All the officials of the Political Department are old Koi-hais.'

'Then give me a koi-hai every time. I can understand them. I don't think that I will ever be able to get on with the white-cap wallas.'

But the whole idea of the third force went up in smoke on a hot day in June, when two of its most ardent protagonists declared that, as soon as the British went, they would set themselves up as independent sovereigns.

My father took the news very hard. We heard it on the wireless at lunchtime but, composed and confident as ever, he went on eating as though nothing had happened, making small talk to the people at the table.

But we talked about it later that night, sitting in the verandah of his bedroom. The lights had been switched off, and the moonlight fell between the tall pillars.

'So the third force is dead,' Father said. 'Killed by those who set it in motion.'

'Perhaps it is just as well,' I said. 'Now at least we know where we stand.'

My father laughed. 'And where do we stand, Abhay?'

'We stand with about five hundred other princes who have not declared themselves independent.'

'It is difficult to reconcile oneself to what is in store for all of us now. As I see it, the only way open to us is to join the Constituent Assembly and see what the Congress has to offer.'

Even in his anguish, I was thankful to hear, he did not think of perpetrating the final absurdity of declaring himself independent. An independent state had no chance of survival.

'The nationalist leaders have given us all the assurances that anyone could reasonably demand,' I pointed out.

'You trust their assurances, Abhay. I don't. But I do hope that I am wrong and you are right. And thank you.'

I did not know what my father was thanking me for, but I was aware that at that moment I was closer to him than ever before. I longed to comfort him, shake him out of his gloom, and suddenly I thought of the pistol I had brought out of the Jamdar-khana. 'It's a magnificent piece,' I told him. 'Wait, I'll go and get it.'

I ran to my room and brought the pistol, and once again I was struck by its beauty. My father held it in his hands for a long time without saying anything. The moonlight shone blue and silver on the butt and the barrel.

'It's a duelling pistol,' he said, and his voice was very soft, almost as though he was talking to himself. 'And it is one of a pair. Philippe Cordier Daubigny made them, in the seventeenth century—made them for the King of France, Louis XIII, I think. You can see the arms of the King on the butt-plate.'

'I like the engraving,' I said. 'The boar's head hammer, the gold-work on the butt, the blue of the barrel. I did not know it was a special pistol.'

'Very special,' Father said. 'And one of a pair. I brought out its twin when I went in as a young man. I did not feel like taking anything else. Now you have got the other … it is amazing how these things seem to fall into a pattern.'

'It is perhaps natural, Dada,' I said, 'It just shows how like each other we must be.'

But I had the impression that he was not listening to me. His head was still bent as though he were studying the markings on the pistol. I noticed that his shoulders sagged slightly.

'Now we have both of them,' Father said. 'You and I. We could have a duel … at twenty paces apart. We'll have no seconds, for we don't need them. You will fire first. The one who survives will have to carry on the burden.'

His words sent a finger of ice running down my back, but I forced myself to laugh. 'Oh, no, Dada,' I said, 'You are much the better shot. I just won't have a chance. It would be …'

'It would be absurd to have seconds,' my father went on, and I was struck by the way his words fell into the silent night like pebbles rolling on a carpet. I peered at his face to see if he was really serious. But it was too dark to see his expression. 'A most honourable way of settling problems, duels,' my father said. 'Only gentlemen were permitted … it was almost a privilege.'

'I'm going to bed,' I said, 'Here, give me my pistol.'

'Yes, of course,' Father said. 'Your pistol. I'll need my own. It is in the bottom drawer of my sword box.'

I took the pistol and crept out of the verandah of his bedroom. The moonlight made ghostly shadows along the walls as I walked.

It was a warm and humid night and it was far too late to go back to my bungalow. I decided to spend the night in my rooms at the palace. After a while I heard my father's car go off whispering along the gravel drive, and I wondered if he was going to Amina-begam or to Sherawathi.

It must have been an hour or so later. I was still sitting up in bed in my pyjamas, again holding the Daubigny pistol in my hands when I thought I heard a slight noise behind the door which opened into the courtyard. I was no longer thinking of ghosts. I rushed to the door and threw aside the curtain.

There was a woman behind the curtain, trying to hide her face with her sari. I took her by the shoulders and pulled the sari away from her face.

It was Zarina, Amina-begam's niece. She was trembling with nervousness but she did not look frightened.

'I have come again,' Zarina said. 'I have come, knowing you were alone.'

I went on gripping her shoulders, harder and harder, my fingers digging into the flesh. Her face became white with pain and her eyes filled with tears, but she did not wince. It was almost as though she were challenging me, defying me to hurt her.

'Who sent you?' I asked.

'No one sent me, Raje. I came myself. I came because you were alone. I came because I wanted to. Please don't send me away.'

Her lips trembled, her eyes smouldered, her chest heaved. Her youth and beauty were like a glowing fire. My fingers loosened their grip. I put my arms around her and crushed her to my chest.

'Don't insult me again, Raje. Please don't send me away.'

I did not send her away. After that, I began to spend most of my nights in the palace, only going to the bungalow for breakfast with Kamala and the children before rushing off to my work. As the days passed, I seemed to grow into the new pattern of my life, with its separate compartments for sex and family life, each lived with a new richness and fullness. And I had a feeling that Kamala too had fallen into her role of the ideal Hindu wife, completely wrapped up in managing the household and bringing up the children, serene and dignified. Sometimes I even wondered if she was trying to prove that it was unworthy for a wife to show herself aware of her husband's waywardness.

24

The Instrument

The Government drew up a formula for the acceptance of the princes which was called 'The Instrument of Accession'. Under it, the princes were required to hand over to the Government control only defence, foreign affairs and communications within their states. There were categorical assurances that their other powers would not be interfered with. 'The Congress,' the Minister for States had declared, 'are no enemies of the Princely Order.'

The offer could hardly have been fairer. In actual fact, the new government was asking for nothing more than the British had controlled throughout their rule. Now that the British were going, all that their successors demanded was that the states should formally surrender powers which in practice they had never exercised.

The difficulty was that many of the princes would not accept the nationalists' assurances at face value—my father among them.

'It is all a matter of interpretation,' he told me. 'They are all clever lawyers. They can do anything they like under the guise of these concessions—take control of our states at any time, on any pretext. Just by making out they are protecting us from attack.'

'Attack! Attack from whom, Dada?' I asked.

'Anyone at all, even an imaginary one. Or they can always engineer one—I wouldn't put it past them. Why, they can always say they are protecting us from an internal rising. They have always hated us. The vengeance of sheep can be a terrible thing.'

I laughed at my father's apprehensions, for they seemed so far-fetched. But he did not join in my mirth and time showed he was justified. Two years later, not a single princely state was left.

The transfer of power was to take place on the 15th of August. Three weeks beforehand, the majority of the rulers had still not formally accepted the Instrument of Accession.

Throughout July most of the princes and their Dewans sat in New Delhi, talking interminably, getting nowhere and dividing into two frantically opposed groups. At one extreme were those who had declared themselves independent and who now realized that unless they could persuade a majority of the rulers to do likewise their own stand would look absurd. Opposed to them were the princes who had co-operated with the authorities right from the start, those apostles of caution and commonsense who were bringing pressure on their friends to accept the Instrument.

The princes and their advisers hung on in New Delhi, confused, dejected, tense, torn between personal pride and commonsense, between vague, undefined loyalties and their survival, between facts and wishful thinking, while the time for decision was drawing to a close.

Almost as though to force the pace and bring the princes to a decision, the Viceroy called a meeting of their Chamber on 25th July, just three weeks before the date of the transfer of power. I accompanied my father to New Delhi. In the train we talked about what Lord Mountbatten might have to tell the princes at that stage; I could see that my father still nursed a hope that he would come out with some dramatic solution that would give them all a fresh lease of life. But in the capital itself, we found the atmosphere charged with despondency. The princes sat as though they were waiting for a great king to die. We made the usual rounds, my father and I, visiting the different groups, the Rajputs and the Marathas and the Muslims, all sitting in their tight little circles, suspicious of each other, surrounded by gloom and making heavy jokes about their own extinction.

'We are just like the oysters invited to attend the tea party of the Walrus and the Carpenter, as the Nawabsahib has said,' one of them remarked.

'There is nothing we can do but sign the instrument of destruction,' another said.

I thought 'instrument of destruction' was a really dreadful way to describe it.

From my seat in the gallery I saw the historic last session of the full Chamber of Princes, and in spite of myself I must have been moved by the solemnity of the occasion. The princes sat in rows, looking like oysters arranged on a salver, some fat and plump, some old, some younger than myself. Not one of them was dressed as Indian princes were supposed to dress. Most of them wore white cotton jackets and pastel safas or caps. Admittedly there were one or two smears of colour, a flash of brocade or silk, but the accent was on simplicity, even austerity.

At another time I would have perhaps been impressed by the gathering itself, the sombre dignity of the hall, the Viceroy in his dazzling white uniform, his almost theatrical good looks. I counted the eleven rows of decorations on his chest. He spoke without notes, confidently, serenely, almost disdainfully unaware that he was the central figure on the stage of history. The gathering humidity of the air-conditioned room, the faint smell of furniture polish, the dark panelling of the walls, the crimson curtains, the circular rows of velvet seats embroidered with the coat-of-arms of each Prince, were only background impressions, like the soft music in a suspense film. My eyes were pinned on the alert figure in the chair with the crest of the double axe, wearing the purple cap and the dead white achkan, sitting forward and listening with rapt attention, looking, from where I sat, so pathetically eager.

And I was listening to the ringing words of the Viceroy, the crisp, military prose, the sincere, well-modulated voice, the cultured accents of the British aristocracy.

'Your Highnesses cannot run away from the dominion Government which is your neighbour any more than you can run away from the subjects for whose welfare you are responsible ...'

They were told what they already knew too well, what they had discussed threadbare amongst themselves: that they must accept the facts of geography, that the concessions they were now being called upon to make were concessions which they had never enjoyed, that they could not stand as little or big pockets in a vast land ... and suddenly I saw they were all leaning forward, craning their necks so as not to miss a single word.

Lord Mountbatten was defining the limits of their concessions, telling them that their acceptance of the Instrument would leave them all the 'practical independence they could possibly want', that in other matters there would be 'no encroachment on their sovereignty'.

I could sense more than hear the combined gasp of relief, the sudden shudder of release from tension. What the Ministry had been telling them again and again for the past few weeks and what they had never wholly believed now gained their implicit trust because of the man behind the words: Mountbatten.

We returned to our capital in a far less dismal frame of mind than we had set out, and it was in this mood that a week later my father signed the Instrument.

I was with him, sitting by his side, when he put his signature to the document. Then he laughed and said:

'When God fails to provide for you, then he is giving the signal of retreat.'

I did not know what he was talking about, and I knew better than to ask him, being long familiar with his habit of bringing out obscure and, as far as I could see, quite irrelevant quotations.

Once Lala Harikishore had taken away the paper he called for his A.D.C. and told him to bring out his Remington. We went onto the back lawn and he took his stance beside the fountain. I watched in spellbound admiration as he shot down the copper coins thrown into the air by his bearer. Shooting twenty-three times without a single miss, he broke all past records.

'I am still good with the old two-two,' he said proudly. 'I can still handle it as I used to. The only thing that remains with a man as the years roll on is his personal prowess with such small things. It seems so childish, but that is all a man can be really proud of.'

I was aware that I was in the presence of sorrow; a grief deeper than when his brother had died, a humiliation far more wounding than when his Maharani had taken a lover.

The bearer loaded his rifle and handed it to him. He began to shoot once more. I watched him like a mother, hoping that he would miss before long.

25

'This I Swear'

Looking back on those days, I see the inescapable logic of events. The fate that overtook the Indian Princes was ordained; it was a mistake ever to have believed that their order could withstand the forces of disruption unleashed in the country.

Within a few weeks, those who had believed that by signing the Instrument they had entitled themselves to what the Viceroy had described as 'all the practical independence they could possibly use' were disillusioned. And yet, in all honesty, I cannot say that the blame lay with those in authority. No one could have foreseen what chaos in the states would follow in the wake of freedom. The authorities had to do what was best suited to the overall interests of the country according to their rights, even if it meant retracting step by step the solemn pledges given to the Princes. Wholly absorbed in stemming the tide of anarchy, they had no time to shed tears over the fate of oysters, however docile they had now become.

Nor can I bring myself to blame my father and the others like him, those who accepted the pledges given to them as constituting guarantees, believing that the Instrument they had signed had merely replaced their treaties with the British Crown.

The day of our freedom, what Nehru had referred to as our tryst with destiny, had come and gone. The whole country rejoiced, forgetting, in the advent of freedom, the great communal conflict raging all around them. The rumblings of the long war for self-rule and its accompanying evil, the vivisection of the country, went on unchecked as though through a chain reaction. For the next thirteen months within the Indian states there was neither the old order nor the new democracy, only a mounting chaos. The most natural targets of the people's still unappeased hunger for universal liberation were the pockets of states ruled by the same old princes, virtual relics of British imperialism in the land of the free.

It was I who prevailed upon my father to declare an amnesty on all past political offenders, but the removal of the ban on wearing the white cap was almost automatic. We could not very well ban the headgear of the party that ruled us.

But in Begwad the white cap had already gone out of vogue. Its place had been taken by the blue and white cap of the state Praja-mandal. Everyone seemed to be putting up their blue and white flags and wearing their caps as though anxious not to be caught out with the wrong kind of headgear. On 18th August, Kanakchand, or K-C. Gaur, as he now called himself, entered the city in a triumphal procession and was received in the main square with a public address of welcome.

With his return the activities of the Mandal began to take on an increasingly militant turn. Within a few days Kanakchand had carried out a tour of the entire state, addressing meetings everywhere and calling upon the people to put an end to feudal rule. Batches of volunteers went round writing slogans on the walls, and every few days there was a fresh crop of expensively printed pamphlets, each more virulent than the last, alluding to my father's private life: his extravagance, his drinking, his concubines, and even to the fact that the Maharani had run away with a Mohammedan.

My father was convinced the ruling party itself was egging Kanakchand on and helping with funds.

'How can he have taken a new house?' my father asked. 'Where does the money come from? And how can a nobody like him get a jeep when I can't? When I wanted to buy one, they told me that all surplus jeeps had been frozen by the Government.'

While I was not prepared to believe that the ruling party could have been helping the various state Praja-mandals, I had little doubt that its sympathies lay heavily on the Mandals' side.

We had signed the Instrument, thus reaching friendly accord with the Government as well as with the ruling party. But the Mandal did not consider itself bound by any Instrument. Quite evidently its sole aim was to bring our administration to a standstill. As though to render the task of administration still more difficult, there was a growing crop of complaints against us from the officials of neighbouring territories, alleging that large quantities of sugar, rice and kerosene were being smuggled across from our state. Smuggling liquor was also causing our neighbours a good deal of distress. In Begwad we had no prohibition; indeed, in some of the more backward parts of the state, the villagers were permitted to distil their own liquor. The moment total prohibition was imposed in the neighbouring areas, the number of distillers in our state shot up; Begwad rum flowed steadily into the adjoining districts.

For our part, we felt the complaints reaching the Government were magnified out of all proportion. They were mostly made by a crop of overzealous officials suddenly promoted to positions of responsibility and desperately trying to curry favour with those in power. But we could not get the authorities to appreciate our point of view.

My father's attitude was characteristic. 'I cannot change my laws to suit my neighbours,' he told me. 'How can I suddenly introduce food rationing when there is plenty of grain here? And why should they charge so much duty on kerosene and sugar? They always call us extravagant. If we can manage with three per cent, why should they find it necessary to charge fifteen?'

'They have to find money for major projects, Dada. Canals, roads, aerodromes, dams ...'

'I don't want any of their dams. Let them just start putting one up at Bulwara. They'll certainly get a rude shock.' And my father smiled his sly, poker smile. 'And anyway this business of smuggling has been absurdly exaggerated. Nothing new in it. There has always been smuggling between Begwad and the bordering districts. The British never complained.'

I reminded him that an enterprising carpenter in town had diverted his entire staff to manufacturing nothing but wooden barrels.

He only laughed. 'That just shows Begwad rum is more popular than Ankola or Chendia. I cannot help it if our rum is better than the others. Who asked them to enforce prohibition? Sheer madness. The people don't want prohibition!'

At the time I was irritated by his flippancy. I realize now that he was being wholly natural. The alert, efficient General, busy with his plans, had vanished; in his place there was a man who had shed all inner uncertainties and was ready for whatever the future might hold. I, on the other hand, was bewildered and unsure, thoroughly alarmed at how things were going, really concerned for the first time for what we were about to lose.

I carried out a tour of the border areas to ascertain the truth behind these reports and to increase our officials' vigilance. It was alarming to see the growth of Praja-mandal activities. Wherever I went, I found a new spirit of ferment against my father's rule, and at one place I was actually received with a black-flag demonstration and posters of 'Down with Tyranny' and 'Jai, Praja-Mandal!'

Only when I reached the Bulwara district did I find everything as it had always been. The Bhils were completely unaffected by the Mandal agitation. They were not only fiercely loyal to the ruler, but were indignant at the Mandal's attempts to subvert them. I was received in every village I went to with their customary solemnity and crowned with the rope turban. I found the atmosphere charged with suspicion and distrust of the people from the cities. Was it true, their leaders asked me, that the state was going to be liquidated? Was it true they would have to surrender their lands for building the new dam? That was what Gaur-babu had told them.

I tried to pacify them with soft words, but they wanted an unambiguous answer. 'If there is danger to the ruling family or any likelihood of the dam being constructed, we are going to resist,' they declared. 'We will fight.'

It was a heart-warming experience to be in the midst of the primitive tribesmen who knew no other king except the Bedar of Begwad and whose loyalty, even if it was blind, could never be subverted. And I felt a touch of slightly malicious pride when they told me:

'And when that Gaur-babu came here with his jeep-gadi, we told him to go away unless he wanted trouble. He went quietly, but next time he comes, we shall beat him up properly.'

'Just as Maharaj beat him with a cattle-whip when he was a boy,' one of them jeered. 'How he squealed! Like a pig!'

'Please don't let us have any of that,' I warned. 'We must avoid clashes with our own people.'

The Bhils just laughed as though I had told them a joke.

'Are we to keep quiet then, when people come and say things against your father and mother?' one of them asked.

'Have we started wearing bangles?'

'We will show those wakils and baboos.' The words had a startlingly familiar ring. My father had always called the politicians 'wakils and baboos'—lawyers and clerks.

'We'll teach them a lesson, let them come!' And all the Bhils sniggered again.

I returned from the tour more confused and disillusioned than I had set out. Behind the Bhils' resentment, I could see my father's hand. They were a volatile, easily roused people. What would happen if there was a clash between the Praja-mandal and the Bhils? Would not the Government consider this just cause for intervention and take control?

On my return, I found that my father had withdrawn himself even more from the tasks of administration. He went out riding every morning as before, but no longer stopped to talk to the peasants or to share their breakfasts. He would go galloping into the jungles beyond the old fort where his father had forbidden him to ride and where he himself had forbidden me to go. When he came back, his horse frothing with sweat and his own clothes ringing wet, he would take a quick shower and then disappear into his temple for pooja and would not emerge until lunch-time. In the afternoons he would spend hours in his bedroom verandah, inspecting his guns, fishing rods and hunting spears, training his golden retrievers and waiting for his shikaris to bring him some sort of khabar, when he would dash off to the jungle for a pig or jungle-fowl drive.

It was distressing that my father should be so indifferent to how things were going and giving his detractors more ammunition than ever by his preoccupation with poojas and blood-sport. It was almost as though he were making a special effort to live up to the standard of decadence and extravagance of which the Mandal agitators accused him.

When I went to see him on the afternoon of my return from my tour, I found him sitting on the balcony outside his private room. There was a slight drizzle outside; dressed in his hunting clothes, he was sitting intently examining his duelling pistol. He gave me a look of surprise, as though I had caught him doing something wrong, and followed it by a quick smile of reassurance.

The fresh daub of vermilion on his forehead showed that he had already done his pooja.

'Do you think it will fire?' he asked. 'It looks in perfect order.'

'I had never thought about it,' I told him. 'I only liked the workmanship. It's like a piece of jewellery. And the balance too.'

'Yes, it is a beautiful weapon. But surely it was not made for looks alone? The main thing was that it should fire a ball true and smoothly. But of course the workmanship is something to be proud of. It was made for a King. Fit for a King to duel with and die. I was just thinking; if you had to die in a duel, wouldn't you rather be finished off with something that had been made by one of the greatest craftsmen in the world—something like this?'

I did not answer his question. Instead I asked:

'I understand you are going out on a shoot on Monday.'

'Yes. I have asked Hanuman to get me a shot at a really good tiger. I am in my fiftieth year—must shoot my hundredth tiger. Why don't you come too? I'll give you the first machaan.'

'Do you really think it is wise, Dada, at this juncture, with all the complaints against the administration mounting up …'

'It is most important to me that I should shoot my hundredth tiger before my fiftieth birthday,' he said a little peevishly. 'And no amount of agitation by the riffraff of the state is going to stop me. Not that we can do anything to stop the agitation.'

'But things cannot be just allowed to go on unchecked,' I protested.

'They will go on whatever we do. Don't you see, Abhay, that we are all going to be finished off soon? We might as well spend whatever time is left to us in doing the things we enjoy, for they will not be with us for long. What I should most like to do is to shoot the Kolaras Giant. That is what Hanuman has promised me for my hundredth tiger, so that I can get my name into Ward's.'

'Is it so important to get one's name in Ward's, Dada?'

'Who knows, Abhay, in a few years the only place where our names will find honourable mention will be in the pages of Rowland Ward.'

'Frankly, I don't like that attitude, Dada. I hate to hear you talking as though everything is already over.'

'Everything is already over, my son, and it is no use shedding tears over it. All we can hope to do now is to spend the rest of our days with izzat …'

'But what about the guarantees? What about the Instrument?'

My father shook his head sadly. 'The Instrument was only the beginning. What they did when they got all of us to sign on the dotted line was to line up the oysters all in neat rows, ready for the feast. "And all the little Oysters stood and waited in a row." '

'It has stopped raining,' I pointed out.

'Oh, good! Now I can go and try to spear a croc.'

' "Now if you are ready, Oysters dear, we can begin to feed." I have always adored Lewis Carroll.'

'It has stopped raining,' I told him again.

'Try to what, did you say?'

'Crocodile. Run a spear through it. Bharatpore does it quite regularly. I had a go at one myself, last week. Most exciting … much more thrilling than pig-sticking.'

Crocodiles are tough, horny animals, and they take a lot of killing, even with a high-velocity rifle firing a solid bullet. I had heard that some Maharaja or other made a habit of killing them with a spear. He was said to creep close to a crocodile and plunge a spear into its neck. It was sheer madness, of course, because a single lash of the tail from a crocodile was enough to break a man's legs in two.

'You have to be most careful, absolutely silent, as you creep up to it. And then, after you have driven the spear home, it is most important to jump back because if the flick of the tail catches you, you are finished. Getting away is the more important part of it, as in so many adventures of life.' And my father laughed at his own joke.

'But can a spear go into a crocodile's hide?' I asked. 'It might easily slide off the horny part. I have known even a soft-nosed bullet break into fragments on hitting the neck without doing the slightest bit of damage …'

'No, no, not on the neck, Abhay,' Father explained patiently. 'On the side, really, just where the yellow skin shows. That's where you aim, and then you must jump back, quick as you can. I've been trying to work out the timing. If the animal is longer than twelve feet, you should get as much as a full second. For seventeen feet and more, the real monsters, you get slightly longer, but of course, the distance you have to cover to get out of range is longer too. You really have to move like lightning.'

I did not want to remind my father that his days of moving like lightning were long over. I don't know how many riding accidents he must have had in the past fifty years. 'I don't like it at all,' I said. 'If you have to go and get killed, I'd much rather you were not mangled by a crocodile, Dada.'

He rose to his feet, laughing, full of confidence and good humour. 'No, I wouldn't fancy being done to death by anything so repulsive either. Perhaps by a good tiger. Maybe by the duelling pistol which Louics XIII owned. But don't worry, I am not letting any croc get the better of me. Why don't you come and see the fun?'

'Yes,' I said. 'I would very much like to come and do that. It was always fun whenever Father was out on a hunt.

'Then will you please tell them to bring my shikar van, Abhay? I will meet you in the porch.'

I lay on a sandbank. The ground was steaming and slightly wet with rain. Through binoculars, I was watching the other bank. I saw the khaki-clad figure creeping closer and closer to the greenish log of wood in the middle of the reeds that was the crocodile. My eyes kept straying to the jagged comb of its tail, and I found myself trying to calculate its length. But of course there was nothing near which I could use as a measure of comparison. Nearer seventeen than twelve, I decided. About two hundred yards behind the reeds on the opposite bank was the shikar van, an open Dodge with its doors removed. Hanuman Singh and the driver stood beside it. Hanuman Singh too had his field-glasses trained on the patch of reeds.

My father seemed to be taking a long time getting within range. It may have been my imagination, but I thought I saw the crocodile give a nervous flick of its tail just as he was about to get into striking position, as though conscious of danger. And as my father poised himself to plunge in his spear, a film must have come over my eyes, for although I could hear the sudden wild thrashing of the crocodile's tail on the opposite bank, and the scrabbly sounds made by the pebbles rolling down, I could see nothing. And then through a blur I saw the green of the reeds spattered with red. But it was a few seconds before my eyes focused and I could make out the shape of the crocodile writhing and the reeds snapping all around it. My father was waving to me from hardly twenty yards away from his victim, and then he lit a cigarette as the Dodge began to crawl forward …

Later that evening I drove to the house Kanakchand had taken in the city. He was in the verandah, talking to two men in Prajamandal blue and white caps. All three looked resentfully at me as I approached, and none rose to greet me.

There were glasses on the table between them, and a tin of cigarettes. Under the table was a bottle of brandy.

I took a chair uninvited. 'I want to talk to you,' I told Kanakchand. 'Alone.'

He hesitated for a second, and then he motioned to his friends to leave us.

'Hadn't you better take your glasses with you?' I said to them.

'We were just talking, not drinking,' Kanakchand said.

I waited for the two men to go. Then I said: 'Look, Kanakchand, have you no gratitude, no feeling of friendliness towards those who have been kind to you?'

'What are you talking about?' he asked. 'Throwing me in the school pond or horsewhipping me in public?'

'You know it was my mother who paid for your education, right from high school and all through college.'

'That was merely to salve a guilty conscience. Am I to grovel before you all my life just for that?'

'What is it that you want, Kanakchand?' I asked.

'I want nothing, nothing for myself. I stand for the people, the downtrodden people of this state, for their birthright ...'

'That is all nonsense, and you know it,' I said.

He was quiet for a while, but his eyes smouldered. 'Yes, I suppose I do want something for myself. I want revenge. I want to wash away the insult of poverty ... the shame of untouchability.'

'But what has that got to do with us? What is it that has made you so bitter against us?'

'The shame of my mother not being allowed to draw water from the well because it would pollute the supply, of brahmins washing themselves if my father's shadow fell on them, of temples being barred to us, of tea-shops refusing to serve unless I took my own cup and plate . . . Do you remember the wedding in your Dewan's house? When Harikishore's daughter was married?'

I did not answer his question, and he went on:

'I remember standing with my mother and father near the dustbin on the road at the back of the house, watching the feast in the courtyard. Hundreds of fat brahmins gorging themselves on jelebies and ladds … We waited for the feast to end, knowing that whatever was left uneaten on the plates would be thrown into the dustbin. And then the scramble around the dustbin! All the untouchables within miles had gathered there, squabbling amongst themselves, pulling things from one another, shouting filthy abuse so that the Dewan sent his policemen to drive us away from his backyard. We did not succeed in collecting a single morsel, though we had waited three hours for it. We were beaten by the police, dispersed. That was our wedding feast at the house of your Minister, Harikishore.'

'But we did not create these conditions. They have come from the ages. If anything, we have always striven to eradicate them.'

'No, you did not make me an untouchable. Not you. You are untouchables yourselves, you Bedars; killers, robbers, the worshippers of obscene gods. But your father happened to be a Maharaja, a prince, and you who should have hung around dustbins with the rest of us, lived in a palace. To you, we were just a dirty word: the untouchables!'

I realize now that his mind had been so warped by the iniquities of the circumstances in which he had been brought up that it was useless to talk to him; he had found an outlet for his rage and would not be denied. But at the time I tried to buy him off. 'You are well-educated. You can easily find a job. I can find one for you … Or is it money you want?'

It was the wrong approach. He gave me a mirthless grin, just a baring of his dead white teeth, but his eyes retained their rage against the world. 'No,' he snapped. 'There is nothing you can give me. Nothing!'

He had a thin nose and flaring nostrils and lips the colour of coal, and the way the light fell on his face, I could see what my father had meant when he had likened it to a jackal's.

'Then why the vehemence?—the agitation?' I asked. 'You are only making things more difficult for us.'

'That is exactly what I want,' he told me. 'To see the end of your rule here—the rule of the Bedars. This I have sworn.'

The words were like barbs poisoned with hatred. I could feel my control slipping. 'Then let me tell you this,' I said. 'I too have an obligation. I would go to any length to honour it. I would die for it, but equally so, I could kill.'

He drew back his head in recoil, as though to avoid a blow. His lips curled viciously like a wild animal's when cornered. His breath was coming in fast gasps.

'That's just an idle threat,' he sneered. But I knew that he had been shaken.

I pushed back my chair and rose to go.

'The days of the princes are gone,' Kanakchand said with a new surge of malevolence. 'You are finished, and you know it. All you princes are like impotent cats, pretending to snarl, knowing you can do nothing. I shall do anything I want, understand!—anything. Say what I want, do what I want. No one can stop me. Neither you nor your father. Where is his horsewhip now?'

'I can see, Kanakchand,' I said, surprised at my own calmness, 'that what stung you most was that public whipping. You howled like an animal. That is why you find it impossible to forget. My father did not shame you, but made you shame yourself. And I promise you, as I stand here, that if you go too far, I shall myself flog you before everyone. I now realize that that was something you deserved …'

'Those days are gone … nothing will bring them back,' he shouted. 'Nothing!'

'The days may have gone,' I said. 'But you are here and I am here, and I am warning you. You can do all the agitating you want. But if you make my father suffer any public dishonour, I shall flog you. This I swear.'

He was scowling, spluttering at the mouth, trying to find words when I left him. I did not know whether I had subdued the vehemence of a demented man or merely prodded a cobra into greater vengeance.

26

For the Record

The inevitable happened. The Bhils clashed with the Praja-mandal workers. My father seemed to be far more surprised than I was.

It seemed that Kanakchand had organized what the Mandal described as a 'grand rally' of the cultivators in one of the villages on the borders of the Bulwara district, and some Bhils who had come to the gathering got into an argument with him. In the clash that ensued, three of the Mandal's workers were injured and had to be taken to hospital, and Kanakchand's jeep was destroyed by fire.

Further clashes seemed imminent. In order to ease the tension, my father issued a proclamation banning all political gatherings for ten days and appealing to the people to refrain from violence. Privately, he also sent off a stern reproof to the Bhils.

In itself, the clash was only a minor incident as such things went in those days. But the Praja-mandal organization, which by now had spread its tentacles in most Princely states, possessed an impressive publicity organization. The incident was magnified and distorted out of all proportion. It was alleged that the Bhils were the ruler's hirelings, deliberately sent to break up the meeting, armed with rifles and spears. The casualties, according to the Mandal, were 'more than fifty' and three of them were said to be in a serious condition. The state police, they complained, had turned their backs as the Bhils were dancing round the burning jeep.

The next morning's papers carried prominent headlines. 'Outrage in Begwad State' was one of them. 'Ruler's Goondas Attack

Cultivator Rally' was another. There were leaflets and slogans, calling my father a 'Dog of the Imperialists' and his administration 'Drunken Tyrant's horsewhip rule'.

In the afternoon we received a telegram from the Chief Political Officer who had replaced the Political Agent, ordering my father in no uncertain terms to retract his ban on political gatherings.

My father did not even read through the whole of the C.P.O.'s telegram. He held it by the corner, as though he were holding a dirty handkerchief, and passed it on to Harikishore. 'It only proves what I have always maintained,' Father said. 'The Mandal is nothing but an offshoot of the Congress. Please read it aloud, Dewan-saheb,' he requested Harikishore.

'It is regrettable and also surprising,' Harikishore read out, 'that such a major breach of law and order should have taken place without any attempt on the part of the state police to intervene. This office cannot but view the situation with alarm. In the face of the incapacity of the administration to preserve law and order in the state, the undersigned feels compelled to insist, as a first step, that the ruler should make a request for adequate police help from the Western Province. It is recommended that a force consisting of one officer of the rank of superintendent and a hundred policemen should be requisitioned. The cost of such additional force may be charged to this agency.'

'Truly magnanimous,' my father said, as Harikishore finished reading.

I was struck by the restraint shown both by my father and his Chief Minister. But I knew that it was no use feeling enraged. By now we had come to realize that to point out to the Political Officer that the casualties were only three slightly wounded men and not over fifty as the papers had reported, or that the Bhils had not come in a body and did not carry rifles, would have been quite useless. And it would have been almost sacrilegious to tell him that the practice of putting a temporary ban on political gatherings in order to forestall the danger of violence was quite common all over the country.

'They are all one and the same,' Father said. 'The Mandal and the Congress. Whatever the Mandal says, the Congress will believe.' And then he began to recite the Oyster poem:

> '*"But wait a bit the Oysters cried.*
> *Before we have our chat;*
> *For some of us are out of breath,*
> *And all of us are fat!"*

'Wait a bit! That's all we can say. But how long will they wait? How long will they give us before they send us another telegram saying:

> *'Now if you're ready, Oysters dear,*
> *We can begin to feed."'*

I was irritated by his levity, by his almost stoic calm. 'Would you mind very much, Dada, not reciting that poem?' I said.

'No, of course, not,' Father said affably. 'Let us proceed with the task in hand instead. Make a *request* for the police force. I like the way they phrase it: "as a first step". Such disarming candour. The first step. I can tell you that this first step is nothing but the foot in the door—the foot in the door.'

'Where on earth did you get hold of that?' I asked.

My father laughed. 'From some Americans who came to shoot. Before the war, that was. You knock on the door, and when they open the door a crack, just to see who is knocking, you wedge your foot firmly in. I like the way the Americans have of expressing things.'

'But don't you think we should at least send a report direct to the Government giving the facts of this incident?' I asked.

'The Instrument of Accession does not call for any such report. Our internal troubles have nothing to do with the centre.'

'But since they are getting these completely distorted complaints from the Mandal side, Your Highness,' Harikishore said, 'it might be just as well to send them our version—just for the record.'

'You mean the correct version, Dewan-saheb,' Father pointed out.

'Jee, Maharaj.'

'Yes, of course. Let's do that, just for the record. Another useful little import from the States: just for the record.'

'And I suppose we'll just have to ask for the police force,' I said.

'Oh, but that is mandatory. Oh, no, we cannot possibly fail to take advantage of so much kindness, so much generosity. Mark you, they are being given to us at no cost. Such generosity!'

'Begwad Ruler Compelled to Accept Outside Police,' the headlines screamed. But in spite of Charudutt and his men, the disorders in the state grew steadily worse. We soon found out that the police force had come imbued with a healthy respect for the Mandal, and we even began to suspect them of conniving at the Mandal's misdemeanours.

I have often wondered whether there was any special significance in Charudutt being sent as the officer in charge of our extra police. My father could not have liked the appointment, but had raised no objections. It would certainly have put him in an awkward position if he had protested against his own son being sent to his state.

Now that he was in Begwad, on deputation from his service, as it were, we did not wish to make his job difficult for him. My father offered to put him up in one of the guest houses, but we understood perfectly when he declined and went to live in the Travellers' Bungalow. He was aloof and formal, which was perhaps as it should be, considering his role, but I was a little taken aback when, on first arrival, instead of doing a mujra to my father as was customary amongst us, he gave him a stiff police salute.

After that first visit, he never came to the palace except on official business. It was clear that he was maintaining an official aloofness, and, on our part, we left him severely alone, even though the growing activities of the Mandal had begun to cause us a good deal of anxiety.

In December, the Praja-mandal held its plenary session, and at it Kanakchand openly declared that they were resolved to take over the administration and set up the Mandal's rule in the state. I thought it was time I went and had a frank talk with Charudutt.

He had grown heavy and his stomach bulged slightly on both sides of his uniform belt. He reminded me of his mother, for he had the same heaviness of bone and coarseness of feature, and his finger joints were thick and his mouth flesh-coloured, just as Bibi-bai's had been. It was surprising how little his face resembled my father's.

Charudutt received me in his office, without a smile or a word of greeting. When I explained how anxious we had begun to feel at the way the situation had deteriorated, he looked quite surprised.

'How exactly has the situation deteriorated?' he asked.

'Look at the increase in the activities of the Mandal. The things Kanakchand has been saying.'

'Saying is not doing. There is no violence involved. That is what we are here for: to check violence. But people must be free to say what they like.'

'But can't you see where all this is leading? His only aim is to discredit the ruler and invite the centre to step in.'

'I am afraid I cannot take sides between the Mandal and the state,' Charudutt said.

'The state is functioning under the sanction of the Central Government,' I reminded him. 'Under the guarantees of the leaders and on the strength of the Instrument of Accession. As such, those who agitate against the administration must be firmly put down by those who have the authority to do so.'

'I cannot take sides,' he said again. 'I have to carry out my duties in an impartial manner.'

'But you are hardly being impartial, Charudutt. You know there is not a grain of truth in the Mandal's allegations. And it's no use saying no violence is involved, because there is constant incitement to violence. Let Kanakchand go and make his speeches in the Bulwara valley. See what happens.'

'Oh, but the Bhils are pampered. They hardly represent the general run of the people here.'

'But how can you and your men sit back and refuse to take notice of their threats—they have made an open declaration that they're going to overthrow the Maharaja's government and take control.'

'Look here, my dear fellow,' Charudutt said. 'The right of the people to wish to form their own government is an inherent right.' Again I thought how much his face reminded me of his mother's, for he had a habit of half-closing his eyes every now and then. And he sounded exactly as though he had been quoting from one of Kanakchand's speeches. 'An inherent right that cannot be snatched away,' he went on. 'That is exactly the sort of government that is running the country now, in the provinces and the centre both—a people's government.'

Our talk was getting a little too official and I had to make a special effort to curb my annoyance at his addressing me as 'my dear fellow'. I reminded myself that I was not a prince talking to a bastard half-brother, but an administrator discussing the problems of our state with the representative of the paramount power. 'Why don't we run across to the club and continue this discussion over a drink?' I said. 'Or would you care to come with me to the palace?'

'I don't drink,' Charudutt said. 'And I don't offer a drink to anyone. There is total prohibition where I come from, and we, the police, are there to enforce it.'

'Do you mean to say you really believe in all that nonsense?'

'It is not for me to believe or not believe. My duty is to enforce whatever is enacted.'

'Christ!' I said. 'Oh, my God!'

His hooded eyes closed in a self-righteous grimace. 'Duty is duty,' he said.

They certainly had managed to indoctrinate him thoroughly—or was brainwashing the right word? Almost guiltily, I returned to the business at hand. 'Look,' I said. 'You know as well as I do, that this is just the agitation of a few trouble-makers … disgruntled goondas like Kanakchand. People crazed with undefined hatreds wanting to hit back at those they think have wronged them—you, for instance. You threw Kanakchand in the pond. He must hate you like poison.'

For a split second, I felt the satisfaction of having drawn blood, for his eyes flinched momentarily. But he recovered almost immediately. 'We're very good friends now,' he said.

'So it would seem,' I said. 'But of course you could not be showing any leniency to the Mandal just because of your friendship with Kanakchand—or could you?'

'Of course not!'

'You know as well as I do that, by and large, the people here are loyal to the ruler. If there were to be a plebiscite, the Mandal would get hardly ten per cent of the vote.'

'The Mandal is agitating, the others are not,' he said. 'The ten per cent are the ones who matter because they have united.'

'But you won't let the others unite or agitate,' I protested. 'As soon as there is any kind of opposition to the Mandal you come down on them for breach of the peace. The people here don't want the Maharaja's rule to end, dammit!'

'So that they can go on getting richer by smuggling and manufacturing rum,' Charudutt jeered. 'But what the people here want or don't want is not my concern. I am here to see that there is no undue oppression against the people in the legitimate expression of their grievances…'

'But is that really what you are here for?—to protect the Mandal from the administration? I thought your job here was to see that law and order were maintained. How can you wink at those who incite the people to overthrow the Maharaja's rule? The rule here cannot be overthrown except with violence.'

There was a sulky, defiant expression on his face. 'My terms of reference were not given to me by the Begwad state,' he said in a cold, official, slightly belligerent tone. 'I was given the fullest instructions at headquarters how to act when I got here.'

Did the mask conceal a deep-seated hostility, something that had been smouldering from childhood days? Or was it just a sense of vocation, the result of regimentation and brainwashing? How did human beings become insignificant parts of a faceless hierarchy? What was it that killed all your emotions, leaving you a bundle of dead nerves activated by a set of outside impulses, guided by a book of rules—servile, subservient, soulless?

And yet he was typical of the mind of bureaucracy, in India and everywhere else. I felt as though I were in the presence of something in which the soul had been deadened and what remained was a covering of scar tissue.

'Were your instructions really to wink at the activities of the Mandal?' I asked.

'I cannot discuss my terms of reference with anyone. They are confidential.'

'But have you no feelings of loyalty towards the state … to Father?'

Charudutt sat staring vacantly in front of him for a long time, saying nothing, his thick, double-jointed fingers clasping and unclasping a glass paper-weight. He looked like a malignant god, thinking out his curses. Then he shook his head from side to side, slowly, and his flesh-pink lips parted in a smile.

'Neither the state nor the Maharaja have exactly a right to expect my loyalty,' he said.

I was glad when I came out into the fresh air, as though I could breathe freely once again. I was determined not to say anything to my father about my interview with Charudutt, but now I at least knew how the land lay.

27

Without Thought of Reward

It is not amusing to look back over a dozen years and discover how callow one's thought processes used to be. At that time I had firmly believed that there was still a place of honour for the princes in their own states and for the states within the union. I was convinced that all the princes had to do was to pass on the actual administration into the hands of the elected representatives of the people as speedily as possible, and themselves remain as purely constitutional rulers.

I had not realized that it was already too late for us to catch up with the times; that the times had rolled on, leaving the princes gasping for breath like fishes left by the floods on the sands of the Kamra. For us there was no way out except total extinction.

The princes were hard-pressed. On the one hand they were harassed by the local revolutionaries whom they were quite powerless to control, because that would have been inviting a charge of suppressing the natural aspirations of their people. On the other, if the preservation of law and order really broke down, the Centre had every right to intervene.

All this I did not know then. But my father had a much better appreciation of the plight of the princes. It was as though he could see the end and had given up worrying about it. 'We can only do our duty by our lights,' he told me. 'Do our duty without thinking of rewards.'

I did not tell him that lately he had not been paying much attention to his duties either, that most of his days were spent in hunting and fishing or pooja and his nights in the company of

Amina-begam or Sherawathi. I was impatient with his apathy. I wanted to do something, find a way out.

'It is most important that we stand fast by our values,' my father went on. 'Then at least it will be said we went down with all our guns firing.'

'There is no need to go down, Dada,' I told him. 'Even with our guns firing.'

He brought out one of his quotations: 'When the sky itself begins to tear, it is futile to attempt to patch it.'

'Well, the sky is still intact,' I said. 'There are still a lot of things we can do before it begins to show a tear.'

'Well, do them, dear boy,' Father said. 'Do try and save whatever you can. It is all going to be yours, anyway, some day. Don't let it be said that I stood in the way.'

I think we did everything that was possible. My father agreed to hold elections and to transfer power to the elected representatives. We set about preparing electoral rolls. My father sent for the prominent Bhil leaders and warned them that they must stop the counter-agitation they had begun. He also sent for all his sardars and other supporters to pass the word around that the people all over the state should avoid clashes with the Mandal. My father's only stipulation was that there should be no announcement about the elections until the Mandal on their part gave an assurance that they would stop their agitation. 'If they really want the people's rule, here is their opportunity,' he said, 'Let them contest the elections.'

But when I asked whether he would see Kanakchand and put forward our proposals to him, he declined.

'Let Harikishore handle him,' he said. 'You can be present, if you want to. I don't want to have anything to do with the man. I don't want to discourage you, but I don't think you will get anywhere. His type doesn't listen to reason.'

And again my father was right.

Lala Harikishore and I interviewed Kanakchand in my father's conference room in the Administrative building. We had also asked Charudutt to be present. I let Harikishore do all the talking.

From the very beginning, I had a feeling that we were not going to get anywhere. You could almost touch the bitterness and distrust around the green baize table with your hand. There was no common ground between the Mandal and the state, and the meeting only brought out how starkly opposed our aims and objects were.

I could not help being struck by the oddness of the characters. At the head of the table sat Harikishore, the high-caste brahmin, chaste, haughty and erect, sitting with a permanent sneer of contempt on his pale, metallic face, wholly at ease in his own surroundings, the room with the thick Kerman carpet and the velvet curtains. Opposite him sat Kanakchand, cocky, suspicious, touchy, slightly ill at ease and yet conscious that he was the star turn of the show. Next to him sat Charudutt, the police officer, his finer feelings deadened by servility, his values corroded by brainwashing.

And lastly myself, growing more and more uncertain of my own place at such a gathering, conscious that I had nothing to contribute.

'This is all just a waste of time,' Kanakchand declared with a sneer. 'Nothing but a plot to put us off with promises and kill our movement. How can we trust your assurances that you will hold elections?—transfer power to our representatives?'

'We shall be making an announcement,' Harikishore explained. 'And we shall inform the Central Government that we would transfer power to the party which secures the majority.'

Kanakchand shook his head. 'Ours is a spontaneous movement. When the people rise against oppression, there can be no need for elections.' He paused and stared directly at me, defiant, challenging, and his voice rose slightly. 'The oppression of the rulers. Too long have we been ground under the heels of the princes—no more. No more.' He took out a packet of Gold Flake, lit one and flicked the still-burning match on to the carpet.

Harikishore was looking down at his notes. Without raising his head, he gave a gentle tap on the bell, just one light tinkle on the shining brass dome, and his chaprassi came running in, wearing the green and gold livery of his office.

'Please put an ashtray on the table before the babuji,' Harikishore ordered, still peering at his notes.

I found myself wishing he had not referred to Kanakchand as babuji; indeed, it was perhaps the time to address him as 'sahib' really, but I could not altogether bring myself to blame Harikishore. There was a silence until the chaprassi had brought the ashtray and gone.

'But if yours is a popular movement, Mr. …er … Gaur, then why are you reluctant to face the electorate?' Harikishore asked, waving his hand delicately to fan away a wisp of smoke that had drifted towards him. 'An election would be the most effective way of introducing a democratic form of government—the only way. It would have the sanction of His Highness as well as of the Central Government.'

'Sanctions!' Kanakchand snapped. 'I do not recognize the authority of the ruler. I have the fullest sanction of the people. They are all behind me. I don't need the sanction of—of outsiders!'

'You are not afraid, are you, that your, er … yes, the Prajamandal, would be defeated at the polls?' Harikishore asked. His voice was syrupy as ever, but you could feel the weight of the contempt it held. This was certainly a different man from the fawning courtier I had always known; the embodiment of saccharine, cloying courtesy, of repetitious bowings and meaningless grins. Instead, this was the Dewan of the state, impeccable, haughty, sharp-witted, doing his business. He was doing it very well.

Kanakchand reacted exactly as I expected. He was being put in his place, being told that his agitation was not as popular as he would have liked us to believe, that it would not survive the test of an election. He did not like it. It was also as though the brahmin was creating an invisible shell of untouchability around him, telling him that if he wanted to appease his hunger, he would have to grub around the dustbin at the back of the house, that he would never be invited in for the banquet. It was like watching a spider wrapping up the victim in his web.

'Afraid!' Kanakchand retorted. His coal-black lips curled back in a snarl. 'I am not afraid. It is you who are afraid of me. Elections! You know you can rig the elections; you and your damned aborigines—the Bhils. The forces of reaction and the forces of ignorance joining up. You have coddled them, bribed them to take sides against us. And then you talk of popular elections! No, no, no! We cannot agree to elections at this stage!'

'In effect, what you want is that the Maharaja should quietly abdicate his powers into your hands,' Harikishore said, suave as ever. 'Is that right?'

Kanakchand turned from him to me, and crushed his cigarette on the ashtray. 'That is exactly what I do want. And bear this in mind, we are not going to sit patiently for you to hand us power. We are going to come and take it ourselves, understand, take it!'

I looked at Charudutt's face. He was chewing paan with extreme concentration, and his lips had acquired a crimson stain. He was looking out of the window with half-closed eyes. I looked past his face. There was a lone raven sitting on the lamp-post outside, and a single silver cloud, a faint white streak running the entire width of the window, gave the impression of a rent in the sky.

What was happening in Begwad was happening everywhere else in Padmakoshal and in most Indian states. But we carried on, paying no heed to the ominous rumble around us, to the unrelenting clamour of slogans. We carried on from day to day, patching and mending as best as we could, trying to persuade ourselves that it was not already too late, not realizing that you could not hope to mend a tear in the sky itself.

And then, in the third week of December, came the shattering news that the Government had 'merged' a whole group of princely states known as the Chhatisgarh and Orissa states into their neighbouring provinces and had pensioned off their rulers.

Those of us who had pinned our faith on the guarantees given by the successive Viceroys, as well as on the assurances of the nationalist leaders that there would be no change in the status of the princes without their consent, were stunned. How could an entire group of states be abolished at one stroke? How could all the rulers have agreed to surrender their states voluntarily? Above all, was this what was going to happen to the rest of the states?

And as the papers came out with the details, we began to feel that the merger had not been accomplished without pressure. It was said that the government had been getting apprehensive about the internal disorders in some of these states, and that they would have been compelled to step in and take over the administration if the situation had warranted it. The impression we gathered was that if the government had had to step in to restore law and order the rulers would have been summarily divested of all powers and left to fend for themselves. As it was, in agreeing to the merger they had managed to secure a few benefits: they had been given pensions and permission to retain some of their residences and private estates. It was clear that if they had not agreed to the merger when they did, they would have done themselves out of these benefits.

And the situation which resulted in the wholesale liquidation of these states had a close parallel with our own. All of us were having our own difficulties, created almost entirely by our respective Praja-mandals, in maintaining law and order. It looked as though the government could not fail to step in.

My father was busy with the arrangements for the annual duck-shoot at Tatwal when we received the news. 'They have chosen the little ones first,' he commented.

'You are not going to quote Lewis Carroll again, are you?' I said. 'And remember they are not all little ones. They have even merged Bastar—bigger than ourselves in area.'

'No, this is hardly the time to be quoting Lewis Carroll. The Geeta, perhaps. I am sorry about Bastar, though. It was always rather unlucky. No ruler seemed to last long … such long spells of minorities—and of course, the best tiger shooting in the world. Such a pity! And Patna too. A most civilized man, a true prince. But then we shall all be going, one by one:

> *"The moon shall have a ring*
> *And the peacock wail*
> *The King is gone,*
> *Long live the King."'*

'Where is that from?' I asked.

He shook his head. 'I don't know; don't remember. I only know that there will be no new kings to take the place of the ones who are gone. Now do you agree, Abhay, that all we can do is to wait until they are ready?—and I am not quoting Lewis Carroll.'

'No,' I said. 'We can actually learn a lesson from this. Why can't we do what Mayurbhanj has done?'

He raised his eyebrows. 'What about Mayurbhanj?'

'It's the only one of the group that has been left out. The reason is that it had already conceded responsible government to the people. The ruler was merely a constitutional head. If a state already has a popular government, the Centre can have no cause for intervention.'

'And how do we proceed to establish a people's government in the face of our present troubles?'

'Couldn't we put our problems before the government itself?' I said, caught up with my own enthusiasm. 'We will tell them: "Here we are, ready to hold elections and to hand over power to the people. All we ask is that it is made possible for us to hold elections." They can hardly refuse to help, even with a military force, if necessary, to keep the Mandal quiet for a little while.'

'A stern warning from the Minister will be quite enough for all the Mandals in the country,' my father said. 'Personally I don't think they will listen to us, but it is certainly worth trying out. I think we should ask some of the States Ministry officers over for our duck-shoot, so that we can at least talk things over, see how the land lies.' And he again shook his head.

He was convinced that everything was already over; I still retained a faint hope. We wrote off to the Ministry, putting-forward our proposals. We also sent invitations to some of the senior officials asking them for our Tatwal shoot.

No one from the Ministry came to our shoot, but we did receive a reply asking us to come to New Delhi on 1st January for discussions. I remember with what high hopes I regarded this laconic communication, reading things into it that were clearly not intended, trying to convince myself that if the government were prepared to discuss things with us, they could hardly deny to Begwad the consideration they had shown to Mayurbhanj.

The shock-wave had come and gone, but we knew that other waves were to follow. Now that everything looked lost, I became eager to preserve it. All of a sudden, it was important to try to save our state in some recognizable form, to resist being torn away from what had become a part of myself.

But the Praja-mandal were determined not to give us the necessary breathing pause, almost as though they had a clear idea of what we proposed to do and wanted to make sure that our talks should not succeed. Just three days before we were due in New Delhi, they occupied the Administrative building and hoisted the flag on it. Early in the morning a few of them overpowered the two night watchmen, broke the locks, opened up the building and let hundreds of their men swarm in.

I was wakened in the morning by Haibatram rushing into my room to tell me what had happened. I spent a few useless minutes trying to telephone Charudutt before I realized that the line had gone dead. It was then that Haibat told me that my father, who had been about to set out on his morning ride when he received the news, had mounted his horse and galloped off towards the city.

I pulled on some clothes and we ran out of the room. We jumped into Haibat's car which stood near the porch. 'The fool, the bloody show-off,' I kept muttering to myself as Haibat tore down the drive. And suddenly, from nowhere at all, the thought hit me: was I going to be the Maharaja of Begwad in the next few minutes? Was I already a Maharaja?

As we approached the city we could see small gatherings of people hanging about the street corners, and from quite a distance I saw the blue and white flag of the Mandal fluttering from the mast on our Administrative building.

Towards the centre of the town, the crowd was getting thicker, most of them sightseers rushing to the scene of action. I think they saw a performance that day that they will remember all their lives.

In the central square, flanked on one side by the three-storied Administrative building, was a gathering of between five and six thousand men, with a thin line of the Mandal volunteers in their blue and white caps guarding the sides and the gates of the building.

My father was riding towards the gate, as though conscious that they were no longer looking at the flag or at the building, but at him, wondering when he was going to be struck down. As he passed the crowd made just enough room for his horse to go through and then closed again behind him.

I had never imagined that anything like what I was seeing could be possible. It was the pitting of sheer force of personality against a hostile crowd; leadership stepping smoothly into its own, putting other men in their place; the challenge of courage against the uncertain temper of a mob.

Haibat stopped the car at the edge of the square and opened the door, wanting to jump out and rush to my father's side. Something I cannot explain made me reach out and hold him back. He turned on me with a scowl, his face contorted with anger and suspicion.

'Do you want him to die?' he snarled.

'Don't be a fool!' I told him. 'This is his show. Let him play it his way. We will only spoil whatever chance he has.'

My father went on, riding past the great equestrian statue of his father, looking oddly like a statue himself, slim and erect, sitting easily in the saddle, holding his horse at a slow walk without once turning his head. He looked trim and professional in his pulled-down golfing cap, his riding boots, his tweed jacket. I had a feeling of drama, as though the deep silence of the crowd, the hair-trigger tension, the light clop-clop of the hooves, were only stage effects.

He stopped at the steps of the main doorway and dismounted, easily, lightly, giving the impression that he might have come for some routine visit to his secretariat. Almost without looking, he tossed the reins to one of the blue and white capped men standing by. I held my breath for a moment, but the man clutched the reins, giving in to some inner impulse, indeed, looking slightly as though he had been singled out for special favour.

My father mounted the steps, slower than he normally did and with greater deliberation, and it was only when he reached the wide platform at the top that he turned.

'My people,' he said in Hindi. 'I propose to go into this building and remove the flag which does not belong to us. But this does not mean that I shall in any way dishonour the flag. A flag is a flag to me, a symbol of honour, and we never subject a flag to any abuse, even an enemy's flag. I am going to take it down merely because it has no business to be where our own flag should be. I am going to haul it down and bring it here and deposit it here, on this wall, so that those who cherish it can take it away.'

'Hiroji Maharaj ki Jai!' someone yelled from the crowd.

My father held up his riding crop in acknowledgement of the lone greeting. Then he went on:

'After that I shall expect the police to guard this building and see that the normal functions of the officials are not interfered with. And I promise you, as I stand here, that if I find that those who are responsible for maintaining law and order cannot protect my officials, I shall myself lead the troops of the state here. Let us hope, for your sakes and mine, that the police who have come from outside do not force this course upon us.'

It was then that I realized that not a single one of Charudutt's police was within sight. Our own police, of course, had been sent way to the rural districts after the arrival of the outside force.

My father again waved the riding crop at the crowd in a friendly gesture and turned. In the doorway there was a line of the Mandal's volunteers holding lathis in their hands, and one of them tried to bar his way. But he went on, without so much as flexing his muscles, just pushing the stick away firmly with his body, and then he disappeared from view.

I had the same feeling, of an invisible hand clutching my heart tightly, that came over me whenever he went into the jungle after a wounded tiger, always without looking back; a mixture of paralysis and hypnosis, of sheer anxiety mixed with anger—anger because it was all so unnecessary. And yet, behind it all, there was an almost grudging glow of admiration for the bundle of sheer physical courage packaged neatly into flawless riding clothes—the man that was my father.

Once again there was the pin-drop silence, getting deeper and deeper as the minutes passed. I waited, as the crowd waited, hardly daring to breathe. I could see the agitated blue and white heads bobbing in the windows of the building, like bees in a hive someone had hit with a stone. And then at long last there was a great, audible gasp from the entire crowd as the flag came slowly down.

'Long Live our Maharaja! Hiroji Maharaj ki Jai!' someone yelled.

The purple flag with the yellow overlay of the double axe went up once more, and within a few moments my father was in the doorway again, with the Mandal flag tucked under his arm. He placed it on the parapet with something of a flourish and then stepped back and began to come down the steps. The man who had been holding his horse brought it forward.

He mounted in one springy movement, turned the horse round and waved his crop. Then he walked his horse away, slowly, like a prince in a procession, and the crowds lining his path parted to let him pass.

Anyone could have thrown a stone at him, charged the horse, pulled him down. No one did. Instead, people began to cheer as he passed them, and in a moment it had spread all over the crowd so that the whole square was cheering. They went on shouting louder and louder, and the roar of their cheers boomed back and forth between the four sides of the square:

'Hiroji Maharaj ki Jai! Long Live our Maharaja!'

I felt weak with excitement, and my bones felt as though made of rubber. For the first time in my life, I offered a prayer, a prayer of thanks. It was only later that I learnt that Kanakchand himself had been in the building when my father went in.

As we drove away, Charudutt was leading his men up the steps of the Administrative building.

28

'Who Else is Equal to Me?'

The occupation of the Administrative building by the Mandal, though only for a few hours, was like the last stroke of the axe which sets the tree toppling over. The section of the press that was hostile to the princes pounced on it with gusto. Both the *Observer* and the *Gazette* gave it two-column headlines. Even the usually somnolent regional radio made a reference to it and applauded the police for their timely intervention to save an explosive situation. The *Awaz* went completely overboard with a banner headline captioned 'Praja-mandal Takes Control', and wrote a scathing article calling upon my father to pay heed to the voice of the people and transfer power into the Mandal's hand before the situation deteriorated further.

On the very next day, my father received another telegram from New Delhi, reminding him of the date fixed for our discussions. I had a feeling that the time for discussing with the Ministry ways and means of introducing responsible government into our state had already run out, that all that was left for discussion was the formula of merger.

My principal reaction was an overwhelming awareness of personal inadequacy. We had proved unequal to the task of protecting what had been entrusted to our care, and what the others before us had kept intact for nearly two hundred years. A heritage immeasurably greater than the wealth and power inherent in it was being wrested from us, and there was nothing we could do. Had it not been for the Mandal's precipitate action in occupying our Administrative building, I was convinced we would have been permitted to carry on, on the pattern of Mayurbhanj state. Little did I realize then that Mayurbhanj itself would last not much more than a year as a semi-independent state.

Both Harikishore and myself accompanied my father to New Delhi, and on the first day of 1948 we were all sitting in a small and dim waiting-room in the Secretariat, heavy with the fumes of spices and stale grease emanating from a cafeteria next door. We were waiting to be shown into the presence of a Joint Secretary with whom we had an appointment. My father stood looking out of the window towards the geometrical blocks of the Jantar-Mantar in the distance.

Without turning his head, still gazing at the Jantar Mantar buildings, my father said:

'The Resident will be glad to learn that the Rajah will find it convenient to wait on him.'

'What Resident?' I asked.

'Don't you remember, Abhay? My grandfather getting the note from the Resident …'

'We are perhaps a little early,' I said.

Our appointment had been for ten. At five minutes past, my father looked pointedly at his watch. 'The British, I feel, would have handled it with much more finesse. They would have been civil even as they were putting us on the block—civil as well as punctual,' he said. He looked at his watch once more and then walked out of the Ministry, never to return to any of the meetings there at which his fate was being discussed.

It was another fifteen minutes before we were sent for. The Joint Secretary was a dark little man with bulging eyes and a frog-like expression to go with them. He was just putting away his cup of coffee. On an empty plate before him were the crumbs of samosas and the remains of a red sauce. He shook hands with us solemnly. There was neither smile nor apology for having kept us waiting—only the tray with the dregs of breakfast. I was glad that my father had gone away.

The little man spoke in officialese. He told us how his Ministry 'viewed the situation in Begwad with growing alarm' and that they were afraid they might have to consider taking over control even without the ruler's consent. He told us how the Ministry might 'view with concern' the fact that the ruler himself had not come for the meeting.

'His Highness was here,' Harikishore pointed out. 'He was … he was suddenly taken ill. Something in the air.'

It was now 'highly desirable', the little man went on, 'in view of the alarming activities of the undesirable elements in the state' for us to merge with the other states in Padmakoshal 'without any further delay'.

'There has been no delay of any kind on our part, sir,' Harikishore pointed out. 'Ever since the signing of the Instrument we have been endeavouring to transfer power into the hands of the people through elections.'

There was no question of thinking in terms of holding elections 'at this stage', we were told curtly.

I am convinced that it was largely due to the tact, unfailing courtesy, occasional firmness, innate good humour, and the almost inexhaustible patience that Harikishore displayed during that and the two subsequent meetings, held in somewhat more elegant surroundings with somewhat more amicably disposed officials of the Ministry, that we were able to obtain such terms as we did. I myself would have been hopelessly out of my element, and my father would have fallen out with the very first Joint Secretary.

As it was, we did not fare so badly. The ruler's privy purse was fixed at nine lakhs of rupees per year and he was permitted to keep the two palaces in Begwad, the three shooting lodges and some of his personal estates. He was also given unrestricted shooting rights in the jungles of the state. The jewellery was to be divided between state property and personal property. All jewellery worn by the Maharaja or the Maharani during ceremonial occasions and anything handed down from my grandfather's time was to be regarded as State jewellery and handed over to the government.

Over the question of the Patalpat fort, however, the Ministry gave us a curt 'no'.

'No, no, we cannot permit military installations to remain in private hands,' the Joint Secretary told us.

'Patalpat has not been a military fort for more than a hundred years, sir,' Harikishore pointed out. 'More like a ruin really.'

'In that case, it would fall into the category of ancient monuments. Besides, it will go under water as soon as the Bulwara dam goes up. And then we shall have only given you a handle to claim compensation.'

I was almost a spectator, watching the two brahmins playing their hands with skill, vaguely wondering to myself if either of them knew that hidden in the fort was that enormous hoard of gold and precious stones, the treasure of the Bedars.

Harikishore took the rebuff in his stride. 'It was the ancient family seat, sir,' he pointed out almost without a change of step. 'The family gods are there. When the capital was shifted to Begwad, the family gods were left behind.'

'Then you will have to shift the gods, remove them to some other place.'

Harikishore laughed, an almost noiseless laugh, just a pure brahminic symbol for the mirth of common men. 'Gods cannot be displaced from their seats, sir. They have to be installed in their temples with proper ceremony, and once they are there, they cannot be moved. You can remove kings—you cannot shift gods.'

The Joint Secretary looked at Harikishore as though he were offended by his joke. He shook his head. 'No, we cannot make any more concessions,' he told us.

On the 5th of January we were back in the train, headed for Begwad. That very morning the papers had published the news of our forthcoming merger. I felt as though we were returning from the funeral of a near relative.

My father sat staring out of the window; the only sign of dejection one could read was the way his shoulders sagged. I did not know what to say to him. I had remained with him, as he had wanted me to, and gradually he had come to lean on me more and more heavily, doing whatever I asked him to do even when he was not entirely in agreement with my views.

We had failed. Now there was nothing more for him to do as ruler of Begwad; all that remained was the formal act of surrender, first signing the Instrument of Merger that the Ministry was drawing up, then the actual ceremony of transferring power to the successor administration.

'I am not going to do it,' my father said. 'I shall never put my name to that paper. I shall remain true to the salt of my ancestors.'

I turned my head towards him to say something in reply, and then I realized that he was not talking to me. He was still staring blankly out of the window, sitting hunched up in his corner. I crept out of the compartment, taking care not to disturb him.

That evening, however, while we were having a drink before dinner, he seemed to be in a talkative mood, and I brought up the subject of Patalpat.

'Is there no way of shifting the ... the boxes and things to some other place?' I asked.

'I had never thought about it,' he said. 'Personally, I would hesitate to do so. I have always felt that there is some sort of curse on the thing. It is most odd, but do you know that none of our family have ever taken out anything of real value.'

He paused while the train gave a long, mournful whistle. Then he added, 'What has been kept by our forefathers must remain as it is ... unless of course, there is an emergency.'

'Is this not an emergency?' I asked.

'I don't know, Abhay. What is a real emergency? It is all so relative. Besides, remember that anything that came to us from our forefathers would be classified as State property ... it would only fill their coffers. I hate the thought. But it will be up to you to make the decision whether this constitutes an emergency. Thank God that in my time I never encountered what I regarded as an emergency.'

'The decision is still yours, as the ruler—you are the Maharaja,' I reminded him. 'We are here only to implement your decision.'

My father laughed, and for once his face looked actually sad when he laughed. 'That is my greatest regret at this moment. I have at least had my full innings, perhaps more than full, for none of us has lived beyond fifty. You … you will be losing everything before ever getting to know what it means.'

'But perhaps that is something to be thankful for, Dada. It is easier when one has no idea what the loss involves.'

'Better to have loved and lost,' Father said, and there was still a trace of that sad smile on his face. 'Better to have ruled and lost, for it is a great feeling—being a ruler. Not just the ruling part, perhaps, but somehow being a part of an unbroken past. There is a verse in the Geeta that describes it. I cannot remember it all at the moment, but the beginning is:

"I am rich and well-born; who else is equal to me?

Who indeed? And I could find it in me to give an honest answer, Abhay, any time that verse came to my mind. Who else is equal to me? No one. No one. I must try and remember the other half of that verse. It has, well, I think it has an appropriateness.'

We were silent for a minute or so after that. Through the soundproofing of the carriage, one could hear the soft, rhythmic jiggelty-jolt , jiggelty-jolt, of the wheels, and the sparks from the engine went flying past the black window in long red streaks.

My father shook his head. 'Can't remember it,' he said.

It was sad to see his reaction, and I know that had anyone else been around, he would not have allowed his guard to drop. I knew that next morning, when we reached Begwad, no one would be able to discern, merely by looking at him, that he was a prince who had just lost his throne.

'Oh, look,' said my father, as the train slowed down. 'There is Hanuman waiting on the platform. I wonder if that means he has got some khabar of the Kolaras Giant?'

As soon as we alighted, we found that that was exactly what Hanuman Singh had to offer. The tiger was in the Piladole block, and had made two more kills in the past three days. Hanuman Singh was only waiting for my father's return to organize a beat.

'Why not tomorrow?' my father said. 'Yes, tomorrow.'

His face was radiant and his eyes were wide with excitement. I could not help feeling that it was unseemly for him to display so much joy at the prospect of getting his record tiger when the papers were full of the news of the merger of his state. I had not seen him in such high spirits for a long time. He greeted those who had come to receive him effusively, beaming all the time. It was exactly as though, instead of returning from the capital with dismal tidings of failure, we had come back victorious.

As we were walking to the car waiting in the station porch, we saw a group of a hundred or so Praja-mandal demonstrators holding up a banner and waving black flags. They waited for all our party to come into the main porch, and then Kanakchand stepped forward from their ranks and yelled:

'The tyranny of the Bedars has ended!'

'The Bedar raj is dead,' the others cried.

'Dead, dead, dead, dead,' the others took up the cry, clapping their hands in unison. 'The raj is dead, the raj is dead, the raj is dead …'

I held my father by the arm and guided him to the waiting car. For a moment, just for a fleeting second, I felt his muscles tighten under his sleeve. Then we got into the car.

As the car began to move, the demonstrators' cries became louder and louder, punctuated by handclaps. They seemed to acquire a dreadful rhythm of their own: 'The raj is dead-clap… the raj is dead-clap … the raj is dead-clap…'

That, I thought, was the one thing I would never forgive Kanakchand. He was hitting at a man who had already fallen but was putting up a brave front. He was humiliating someone who still held that he had no equal among men. That, truly, was the vengeance of sheep, as my father had said.

The station building was now far behind us, but we could still hear the cries of the demonstrators. And looking back, I could still see the group of men gathered near the porch with the agile, gesticulating figure of Kanakchand standing out.

'This I swear,' I said to myself.

'Were you saying anything?' my father asked.

I shook my head. I could not tell my father what I had been thinking.

In the evening, we talked only of the next day's shoot. My father had ordered Hanuman Singh to put up two machaans, one for me and one for himself.

'We must both try our luck,' he said. 'If it is in your nasib to shoot the record tiger—why should you be deprived?'

'But I don't want to shoot a tiger,' I protested. 'I don't want to get into any records. I want you to shoot him. I will sit with you and take pictures.'

But he could be so exasperatingly stubborn at times. 'Nonsense!' he said. 'I insist. There is no use trying to be noble about these things.'

I was not being noble. I genuinely wanted him to get the tiger, and I wanted the tiger to be the biggest ever shot, for that was something he valued. I wanted his nasib to give him something capable of compensating in a very small measure for losing everything that had made him feel that he had no equal among men. But I knew it was useless to protest.

He was sitting, leaning against the bolster covered with pale blue Hyderabad brocade, dressed in his purple cap and white jacket, his legs folded under him, and with the cold light of the chandelier falling straight down on his face. He looked at peace with himself, as though the uncertainties of his mind had been resolved, a man who knew precisely what he had to do. 'Who else is equal to him?' I said to myself.

And as though there was some kind of affinity between our thoughts, my father gave a sharp little exclamation and looked into my face.

'I have just remembered it,' he said.

'Remembered what?'

'The rest of the verse I quoted to you yesterday, the one from the Geeta.' He leaned forward in his eagerness and began to recite:

'I am rich and well-born; who else is equal to me?
I will sacrifice, I will give; in that I shall rejoice.'

Something in the way he was looking at me made me think that he was not referring to the tiger he was trying to give me, for there was a look of ecstasy on his face, as though he had just found the answer to something that had been troubling him. For a moment I found myself wondering that he could be so carried away by the little triumph of having remembered the full verse from the Geeta which had been eluding his memory.

'There is a divine appropriateness about it all,' my father said:

'I am rich and well-born; who else is equal to me?
I will sacrifice, I will give; in that I shall rejoice.'

He picked up his hookah pipe and began to smoke. The look of rapture was still on his face when I said good night.

29

'In That I Shall Rejoice'

I sat for the tiger beat as I had sat for a dozen other tiger beats, wholly captivated by the atmosphere and trying to keep my mind from wandering. I sat alone with my thoughts, in a cage of green leaves high up on a platform in a tree, listening to the weird music of the beat that had suddenly replaced the frightened stillness of the jungle: coo-ees and catcalls, the curt, nervous yells of har-har-har, the snatches of song, the sounds of coughing—the indescribable, unmistakable concert of shikar.

Then the sudden break in the pattern of sound, a new theme introduced by a gentle, barely audible, tap-tap-tap of wood on wood somewhere close on my right, setting up an almost unbearable rush of blood through my veins and quickening my heartbeats. It was a signal telling a definite story. It meant that the tiger had been sighted by one of the stops on my right, that any moment now, he would emerge before me.

I had never wanted a machaan to myself. All the same. I found myself being caught up in the drama of the hunt, this most prized hunt of India, the tiger beat, in which the art and science and the cunning of man combine to kill the noblest and handsomest of all beings in creation.

You take your seat on one of the artfully camouflaged platforms called the machaans that are put up in the trees, and wait in the brooding silence of the jungle for the beat to start. You are the 'gun'—the hunter. On both sides of the guns are the 'stops' also sitting up in trees, and it is their business to guide the tiger to the guns. Then comes the signal, the shrill sounding of the horn for the drive to begin, and the thin line of men waiting a mile or so away begins to creep forward, keeping within sight of each other, and yelling all the while to drive the tiger to the hunters. The whole thing is something like putting a wayward bull into a pen, only it is intended to bring a tiger to its death.

Was it murder? I have often asked myself this. Perhaps it was. And yet I am convinced that a hunter has not really lived unless he has sat up for a tiger in a beat.

And this was a special beat for a very special tiger, the hundredth tiger of a man who was going to be fifty. And even if he was not going to be the biggest tiger anyone had ever shot, we were quite safe in assuming that he would find a place in the book of records.

My father's machaan was on my left. The tiger was coming from the right, which meant that he would come to my machaan. I cursed the fates. Was his nasib going to deny him this last niggardly favour? I felt a twinge of anger at the perversity of things. Why should I meekly accept what was denied to him. Could I not act as a 'stop' myself and by making a slight noise guide the tiger to my left, so that my father could get a shot?

There was a rustle in the bamboos which faced me, and then I could see the orange head, enormous and bearded, staring at me from hardly thirty yards away. I did not know how long he had been there before I saw him. Even though I had seen him before, his bigness made me catch my breath. I could see only the head, peering at me through the bamboos, and I had my sights trained on it. I could have shot him clean through the head at that range. But I waited for that last split second of indecision. Should I take him or send him away?

My heart stopped thumping, and I knew that I was nervous no longer but cool and deliberate. I held the 450/400 by Healy and Lock pressed firmly into my shoulder, the safety-catch pushed forward, finger on the trigger.

It was the tiger who made up my mind for me. Some movement behind him made him start and leap forward—a great, springy bound that caught me off balance—and then he began to go off in a quick run, head held low, stomach to the ground, a vivid flash of orange through the waist-high green of the wild turmeric. Once again he was breaking out of the beat. I swung the barrels with him, held the bead just ahead of the front leg and squeezed off.

He gave a short, curt roar and bounded high into the air with the shot and fell on his side, thrashing out with all four legs, and my second shot clean missed him and crashed into the bamboos. As I was loading again, he managed to get to his feet and went bounding away out of sight into the dense matted jungle behind my machaan.

According to custom, we stopped the beat from coming on and warned everyone to climb up a tree, for now there was the danger of a wounded tiger attacking anyone who came close. Within a few minutes, my father and Hanuman Singh came up to my machaan and all of us went and examined the ground where the tiger had been when he was hit.

A good deal of thin, light-red blood had splashed on the leaves and grass where he had fallen, and a trail of blood showed the direction he had taken. Hanuman Singh followed the trail for a few yards and brought my father some leaves with blood on them.

'He has been hit quite badly. Your Highness,' said Hanuman Singh. 'More in the stomach than in the chest,' he pronounced. 'The bullet has gone clean through.'

My father examined the leaf with almost professional detachment. 'Yes, in the belly,' he said. 'What about the other one?'

The second shot was a miss. 'Your Highness,' Hanuman Singh said, 'It has made a clean furrow in the ground and then rebounded into the bamboos.'

I knew I had missed my second shot, but I had not realized that my first one had caught him so far back.

'Must have been running quite fast,' my father said.

'Well, he was fast,' I told him.

'Did you have a good look? Is it really the giant?'

'Yes, Dada,' I said, 'there can be no mistaking him.'

'We will give him half an hour,' my father said, looking at his watch, 'By that time, if he's got it bad, he'll be too stiff to do any damage. If he hasn't, then we owe it to him to finish him off.'

The general rules were that a wounded tiger had to be tracked and finished off, but you could give it half an hour so that it would stiffen wherever it might be lying up. After that, you went and finished it off. You sought the tiger out and killed it, not so much because it was going to be a danger to the villagers or to show how very brave you were, but because you owed it to the tiger not to leave it in pain.

There were local variations to the rules concerning the business of finishing off a wounded tiger. The safest method was to put a herd of buffaloes in the patch of jungle where the animal had disappeared and follow them. The buffaloes would scent out the tiger and become restless when they came close; then the tiger would usually attack the nearest buffalo, giving the hunter a good opportunity to shoot it. In some places it was up to the hunter himself to finish his tiger. He could take a professional tracker with him to follow the blood trail and lead him up to the tiger, but it was his business to keep the tracker covered.

Our local rule happened to be that it was the privilege of the host, my father, to go after all wounded tigers.

We talked in subdued voices at the foot of my machaan. The sudden return of silence to the jungle after the cacophony of the beat was oppressive. The bearers brought out oversized thermoses of tea and arranged orange-coloured bakelite plates and yellow and blue tea-cups on a canvas sheet spread on the ground. We sat down and sipped the tea and munched the biscuits mechanically. I had a feeling that Hanuman Singh was avoiding looking at me.

Both Hanuman Singh and myself knew perfectly well that it was no use trying to prevent my father from going after the tiger, but we both pleaded to be allowed to go with him.

'It is a one-man job,' Father explained. 'Two might botch it, and three is quite dangerous. Only when the shikari is not himself able to do the tracking, can he take another man with him, but then it always adds to the risk. When the man with the gun is also the tracker, it is absolutely fool-proof—as you know.'

We did know. He was not showing off, but stating a fact. He had always gone after wounded tigers alone, and he had always managed to get them, unless of course, they were too lightly wounded and had escaped. If they were lying in wait, they were as good as dead. There was no denying the fact that with him doing both the tracking and the shooting, it was absolutely foolproof as he had said.

And if he went after wounded tigers, you did not feel that he was flaunting his courage, but that it was because he knew how dangerous the game was and knew that he could do what had to be done better than anyone else. He was that rare combination, both the marksman and the shikari, the man who could drop a running black-buck at three hundred yards and who could also tell the age and sex of a bison by a hazy hoof-mark in the dust and judge the span of the horns within a couple of inches. He was not just a man who had made a habit of shooting down falling coins to soothe his ruffled nerves; he could tell by the track of a snake whether it was poisonous or harmless, could call up a tiger by answering its roars, making them a challenge or a mating call according to its mood; he could even call up a jungle cock by clucking like a hen. He could read a game-trail better than his most experienced shikaris; a blood-drop, a bent leaf, the droppings of animals, a blade of grass springing back into shape, were like signposts to him.

My father was the only one who helped himself to two slices of chocolate cake and asked for a second cup of tea. Then we all lit cigarettes again. By the time I had finished mine, I knew that the half-hour must be drawing to a close, but I did not want to look at my watch.

Father crushed his cigarette into the ground and stood up. 'Well, that's the half-hour,' he said.

He broke his rifle, the big .465 double by Rigby, inserted two cartridges into the chambers and snapped the barrels home. There were four more cartridges in the loops of his jacket and perhaps another half dozen in his pockets. He tucked his rifle under his arm and walked away, without a word as always, quick and slim and erect, the cool professional who had so nearly reached his century of tigers, trim and business-like in his junglegreen golfing cap and his gaberdine bush-jacket with its pattern of leaves.

Just before he disappeared into the bamboos, he turned and waved to me. Then he was gone.

There was the usual feeling of something pressing tightly down in my chest, and my fingers as I lit a fresh cigarette were like ice. It was long afterwards, when I had finished the cigarette and thrown away the butt, that it suddenly struck me that all those other times I had seen him go after a tiger he had never paused to look back and wave. I was about to remark on this to Hanuman Singh when we heard the quick, coughing, grunting roar of a tiger's charge, like canvas tearing or a saw biting into hard wood.

Hanuman Singh and I looked at each other for a second of eternity, keyed up to hear the roar of my father's rifle, and then, without a word, we grabbed our rifles and ran into the jungle.

There was a film of sweat running over my eyes—or were they tears?—and I could not see very much as I went running forward in the hunter's crouch, tearing through thorns, wild turmeric and bamboos, blindly following Hanuman Singh's back, keeping close behind him. We had hardly gone a couple of hundred yards when I saw him drop on one knee and bring his rifle to his shoulder.

The magnificent orange and black head with the orb of snow white beard was there again, rising as though out of the earth, coming towards us with a spellbinding slowness, as in a dream, and there was that deadly sound of the quick, tortured grunt. I saw the muzzle of Hanuman Singh's rifle lift in recoil and heard the roar of the shell going off. And then I was firing my own Healy and Lock, both barrels hitting true and solid into the orange mass of shoulder and head from hardly twenty yards away. The tiger stopped rising, stopped without ever beginning the spring that he was preparing for, and fell back and lay with his great white forelegs stretching straight out in a patch of spurting blood, side by side with the body of my father.

We dashed forward, not even bothering to make sure that the tiger was really dead. But before we came to where they were lying, I found Hanuman Singh's hand holding me back and turning me round, and he stood blocking my path with his body, shielding me from the sight.

'Don't go on; you must not look,' he told me.

I brushed away his hand and pushed him aside. I wanted to look. This was my show more than his, and I did not want to shirk the punishment. I wanted to see for myself how my father had met his death, he who now lay there with his face mangled out of recognition, his shooting jacket limp and shapeless and wet with blood and covered with a mess of oozing intestines.

I picked up the rifle which lay close to him. The barrels were clean and blue and shiny. I broke the rifle. It was just as I had thought. There were no cartridges in the chambers. He must have extracted them as soon as he was out of our sight.

Hanuman Singh took off his own jacket and covered my father's body, while I busied myself with the details of the rifle. I pulled out two cartridges from the loops in his jacket. The blood still felt warm on them. I wiped them clean with my handkerchief and inserted them into his rifle. I put the rifle to my shoulder and fired both shots in the air. I did not want anyone other than Hanuman Singh to know that the Maharaja of Begwad had committed suicide because he had made up his mind not to sign the document of merger. I did not want to give his enemies a chance to speculate whether it was an act of bravery or of cowardice on his part to have taken that way out.

'Come, Your Highness,' Hanuman Singh said very gently. 'I think we have done whatever is necessary.'

And it did not seem odd to me that he had addressed me as 'Your Highness'.

We did not measure the tiger. I did not want him to be stretched and pulled about and humbled, his pink, de-skinned carcass left for a feast of vultures. In my mind, he was no longer a tiger but something of a divine instrument sent to aid my father in his hour of need, something that had made it possible for him to realize his wish that he would not live to see the end, made it possible, too, for him to die in the way he would have wished.

I gave instructions for the tiger to be cremated where he lay, in a high pile of sandalwood. The giant of Kolaras did not go into a book of records, but he had suddenly become something of a god.

30

I Go as I Came

I was ruler of Begwad for exactly forty-nine days. As soon as the customary thirteen days of mourning had passed, there was the ritual of my ascending the gadi of the Bedars, all quite ridiculous since I was going to have to abdicate within a few weeks. But this was what everyone seemed to want, and I submitted without protest. At the accession durbar, I was duly proclaimed by the court heralds to be Valorous as the sun, the Chosen of Ambica, the Source of all light, Wazir-e-farzand, Intezam-e-daulat, Sar-e-sarband, Prithwi-naresh, Sena-dhurandar, who held undisputed sway over the territory from the Kali to the Nashi, His Highness the Maharaja of Begwad, Abhayraj Bedar III.

For forty-nine days I was all that, but I expect it was too short a time to give me the feeling that I was above all men. There were too many things to do, most of them unpleasant, and there was so little time to do them in.

On the 25th of February Begwad was to be merged in the Union of Padmakoshal, which was to be formed by joining up four 'A' class states, Tilkatta, Begwad, Aweda and Ninnore, and eleven 'B' class states. The capital of the new union was to be Begwad. The administration was to be in the hands of a council of seven ministers, one each from the four 'A' class states, and three in all from the 'B' class states. Kanakchand Gaur was the unopposed choice from Begwad. Indeed, for a time it was believed that he would become the Chief Minister, but towards the end there was a rift among the Mandal leaders and he was made the Education Minister.

As I said, I had much to do in the time at my disposal. I carried out a tour of the entire state, stopping at every single village, and tried to explain to the people what was happening. Wherever I went, I had to answer the same round of questions. Yes, the state was going to be finished off within a few days, I told them. There was no use mincing words. I had myself got used to the idea of merger, but sometimes, when I saw tears in the eyes of some of the people who had come to greet me, I used to be caught up in their emotions. I did not tell them it was all for their own good, because I have never really believed that it was. For my part, I felt sorry for them because they had not been consulted and were being passed over from one authority to another without any attempt to ascertain their wishes.

I had no solutions to offer, only soft words, and I would not have cared whether they received me with black-flag demonstrations or garlands. But there were no black-flag demonstrations. On the other hand, I was overwhelmed by their kindness and enthusiasm, and the things they said about my father. They were awed and bewildered by the future. The changes were too abrupt and too drastic for their comprehension. What they could see and feel for was the break from the past, knowing that they were being torn away from something they had not just learnt to live with but had begun to value.

My task was particularly difficult and exasperating in the Bulwara district, for here were the people I had been brought up to regard as my own. I had a special obligation towards them because they were almost childlike in their ignorance and also in their range of emotions. They had known no other master than the Bedar, and he too had been only half a king to them because he was also their god. They were like animals caught up in a game-drive, bewildered and suspicious, conscious of being led where they had no intention of going.

Yes, the Bulwara dam was going up, I told them, but they must understand how it was going to benefit the rest of the country, harnessing an immense amount of electricity and bringing water to dry lands hundreds of miles away.

They would shake their heads and look at me sullenly. Then their leaders would begin to argue. 'Yes, but our own land will be going under water, they say to the depth of seven bamboos. We neither want canal water nor bijli-batti. Why should we be made to give up what is ours for the sake of those who live hundreds of miles away? Was it for the Marwaries to make lakhs of rupees by running mills and factories? Even the topiwalla sarkar, the British, gave in when we protested.'

In a way I could understand their bitterness, for they stood to lose everything that was dear to them, their lands and their homes which had been saved for them from the British by their Maharaja. I, their new Maharaja, could do nothing for them.

I gave them what answers I could, feeling the inadequacy of my explanations, wondering if I had the necessary hold on their affection to make them believe that whatever was happening was for their own good merely because I was telling them it was so. I told them that they were bound to get a fair compensation for their lands and houses, and possibly even alternative holdings.

They would nod their heads as though they understood, and for a time they would remain quiet. Then they would start whispering amongst themselves and come right back to the beginning. Was there no way of resisting? Why not make protest marches against the Residency as they had planned to do when the British had threatened to put their land under water? Could they not resist with force? Should they not go on sit-down strikes, refusing to leave their homesteads as Dada-maharaj had advised them to do?

No, no, no, no! My head would begin to spin, and I had to remind myself to be patient, knowing that it would never do to lose my temper with them.

'Remember that what you are going to lose is going to be a gain a thousand times over to the country.'

'What country? The Bedar's state?'

And again, no.

'It is that Dhor-babu's doing, the Dhor is the villain. We will burn his effigy, we will set the churail to haunt his sleep. We are not going to let him enter our district. That was Dada-maharaja's wish.'

'No, that was not Dada-maharaja's wish. He had changed his mind lately, as you know from the advice he gave your leaders before going to Delhi. He told you to call off your agitation, remember? Things have changed, you do not realize. Kanakchand is going to be a big man ... a Minister ... possibly the Chief Minister, with more power even than the Maharaja had. He could do much harm. Don't give him cause for offence. There is the question of compensation for your lands. How much you get will depend on how you behave towards him now ...'

'Oh, we are not afraid of that bit of dirt and his men–eunuchs who ran away from us. We are only afraid of what you will say.

'We were sure that Dada-maharaj would never have got angry with us ... we are not sure of you. If you tell us to resist, we will resist; we are not afraid. We were not afraid of the sahibs, and we will not be afraid of ten governments! Let them kill us before they take away what has always been ours ...'

I did not know how my father would have handled this situation, and the thought went fleeting through my brain that he had perhaps taken the easier way out. We talked in circles, late into the night, and in the end I could only appeal to their loyalty; I told them they had to accept the coming of the dam as a personal favour to me, that they were not to offer any resistance if only to hold up the honour of the Bedars in the eyes of the world.

I said my farewell to them with my head still in a whirl, not at all sure that I had been able to convince them, distressed by the knowledge that they would have to suffer much before they could be brought to accept the inevitable.

The next afternoon I visited the Patalpat fort, right down on the floor of the valley, hugging the sheer wall of the mountain on one side and with the river making a loop on three sides. There I had to face the issues squarely all over again.

I had heard the voice before, but I had not seen the face. Now he stood before me, tall and wiry, in a costume that was a relic from some indeterminate past, his beard a metallic white, his eyes bits of coal, his face a teak mask. He was the head of the Ramoshi clan, the hereditary guardians of the fort.

'There is talk of the whole valley being put under water to the depth of seven bamboos. Surely that is not true?' he asked.

I told him it was true.

'Who can flood the Bedar's fort in the Bedar's land?'

He was still in the middle of the eighteenth century. I explained as simply as I could how neither the fort nor the valley belonged to the Bedars any more. 'It belongs to the people,' I ended up. 'Not to any ruler. It belongs to all of you.'

'All of us don't want the dam to come.'

'It belongs to the Government, then; the sarkar from Delhi wants it.'

'The white badshah from Bilayat?' he asked.

'No, the King from Bilayat is gone. We have our own king now.'

'Has the Mughal Badshah come back?'

'No, it is the people's raj, the people are the Badshah. Neither the Mughals nor the British, but the people … you.'

He cocked his head slightly and looked at me morosely, just like a dog who does not understand what it has done wrong.

'Then what happens to what is in the fort?—the jamdarkhana.'

I had to go carefully with that one. I had rehearsed it in my mind.

'It was my father's wish that everything should be left. Left where it was. That was what Dada-maharaj told me. Two days before he died. It is my wish too.'

It was like dropping a coin in a slot and waiting for the mechanism to act. The teak mask that was his face was incapable of registering emotions. He took some time to react. Then he said:

'Cannot any arrangements be made to remove everything to a place of safety? They say it was brought on the backs of thirty-two elephants.'

'Perhaps it could be done. But we … both Dada-maharaj and myself, decided it would be best this way. We have given up all rights to it. It should be left as it came to us.'

But he seemed to be well-versed in the rights and wrongs of this particular issue. 'This is not proper. It is not the Maharaja's own treasure … not yours or Dada-maharaja's. You may give up your right, but your son has a right too—and his son and his son; whoever happens to be the Bedar king.'

'My son and his son will never be rulers. I am the last one,' I explained. 'And thank God they will not be Maharajas,' I added.

Again the old man looked blankly at me for a few seconds, but there was still no sign of any understanding in his eyes. I might have been speaking a language he did not understand. Did those who were in charge of treasure always have to be so dumb?—I asked myself—their minds incapable of going off outside the groove of dog-like devotion to their jobs? I wondered if he took bhang or some other kind of dope.

'Let us be thankful that neither Dada-maharaj nor I were called upon to go in there for an emergency,' I said, 'He went only twice, and so am I, going only twice …'

He shook his head. 'Dada-maharaj went in only once,' he said.

'Only once, when he was the Yuwaraj. He never came after he became the Maharaja. We requested him to come every year when he used to camp at Bulwara. He always made an excuse.'

'I want to go in now,' I told him.

At last his eyes lit up. 'I hope the Bedar king is going to treat this visit as an emergency,' he said softly.

I laughed, as much with relief at the measure of his response as with my own thoughts. 'A sort of emergency,' I said. 'Yes, something like that.'

'I shall go and make the arrangements, the lamps and everything.' He turned to go.

I stopped him. I had waited for him to ask me what was going to happen to his clan, almost shut away from the outside world for nearly two hundred years. But since he did not appear to think of it, I told him what I had in mind.

'I shall make provision for all of you. Put some of the older ones on pensions and try to give the others some land. You need not be afraid of the future.'

He gave me a level stare. 'We have never worried about that, Bedar King,' he said. 'We knew that the Bedar would not forsake us. There is an oath that binds us to him. We never had any fear that the Bedar king would leave us in the wind.'

It was a pathetic kind of loyalty. I had half a mind to tell the old man to go and help himself to some of the gold, but I knew it would have shocked him to the core.

I did not stay in the room with the oil-flame lamps for long. I had not even curiosity left. I had taken with me the two duelling pistols, oiled and cleaned and looking almost ready for use. I put them back in the faded velvet case which had been their resting place since the days of Louis XIII. They fitted snugly, butt to muzzle, back into the dents they had made for themselves. Even during the minute or so I was there, I was beginning to be conscious of the smell of dead roses emanating from the garments in the boxes. Moved by some impulse I cannot explain, I sat down briefly on the golden throne of prince Murad. And then I got up and walked out, aware of a good deed done, of debt paid off , that whatever my father and I had removed from the place of curses had been given back.

I had made up my mind to leave Begwad for a few months as soon as the inauguration of the new administration was over. I was mentally braced for what was coming. Indeed, I had a feeling that all things considered, I had performed my tasks without discredit. But I wanted my wife and children to be away from Begwad at the time of the inauguration ceremonies. I wanted to be alone on my last day as the ruler of Begwad, and I was a little annoyed when I found that my wife was reluctant to go away.

'I want to be here,' Kamala told me with unaccustomed firmness. 'I am the Maharani; I too want to see it through.'

'It is all over already,' I said. 'There is nothing more to see through. It is … it is like waiting for the train to pull out after the good-byes have been said.'

'We will just send the children away with Miss Groves,' she said. 'I want to remain here. I am your wife. It is my duty to remain by your side. It is also my right.'

'I want to be alone for this, Kamala,' I said, 'and don't say "I want to be here" again.'

'It feels so horrible … quite shameful. Like running away. Leaving you alone to face things, in your adversity.'

Her voice broke down. She was leaning forward, with her teeth pressing her lower lip, her eyes bright with moisture, and the way the light fell on her face, she looked breathtakingly lovely. I caught her face in my hands and kissed her gently on the nose, and then I gathered her into my arms and held her close to me.

I went on holding her, conscious of a sudden lifting away of tension, pressing my face into the softness of her chest and grateful for its comfort and warmth.

'The door is open and the butler will be bringing in tea at any minute,' Kamala reminded me.

I did not release her. 'You must train the servants not to bring tea at inconvenient moments,' I mumbled.

She ran her fingers through my hair. 'There haven't been many inconvenient moments lately,' she pointed out.

I released her then. 'Why do you want to be here?' I asked.

'Because I want to be near you. Besides …'

'Besides what?'

'It's just that I don't want you to face it alone. You might do something a little rash, something which someone close to you, someone who loves you, might be able to prevent.'

'Do you think I am going to break down?'

'I know you won't.'

'Then what?'

'Darling, don't be angry, but I feel so frightened.'

'Frightened!' I felt like laughing. 'What is there to be frightened of, now? They cannot take away any more than they have.'

No, they could do no more damage. It had come and gone, like a tremor in the earth; now there was only the debris. The debris and those who were near and dear to you, those who wanted to stand by you.

'Please don't be bitter. They can take away much more. We still have so much.'

'I am not being bitter,' I protested. 'I am completely relaxed.'

'Relaxed!' Kamala shook her head. 'No, you are not relaxed. You are tense, knotted up. You mumble in your sleep and gnash your teeth and say things. I have lain awake for hours, terrified, not knowing whether to wake you …'

'You should have. What have I been mumbling?'

'It is all rather indistinct. Sometimes it is like some verse. Something like "the vengeance of sheep can be a terrible thing". But most of the time you keep repeating "This I have sworn, this I swear".'

'Oh.'

'Abhay, what is it that you have sworn? What are you going to do? Sometimes you act so much like your father that it makes me feel frightened. Darling, you are not alone. There are your children, there is me. We are not outsiders …'

'I can't think what I could have been dreaming about,' I told her. 'But please listen to me. I want you to go. Not because you are an outsider, but just because you are so near to me. I want you to go away for my own sake, because I love you.'

The words had slipped out of my mouth as though at a confessional, and Kamala stared at me for a few seconds. Then I saw her wipe her eyes with the end of her sari. 'You have never told me that before,' she said. 'I have always hoped that you would, some day.'

'Always is so long,' I said. 'Always is ever so long.'

Kamala looked at me anxiously. 'Darling, what are you talking about?'

I laughed. 'Sometimes it comes after many years … it cannot be there in the madness of youth … and then one day it hits you …'

'What are you saying?' Kamala said again.

'I am telling you that I love you,' I told her, and I felt wholly sincere as I said it.

'It is nice to be loved. It seems silly to talk of love after two children … but it feels, it feels wonderful. Please give me your handkerchief.'

I gave her my handkerchief. 'Once this is over, we will go on a honeymoon,' I said. 'We'll go to strange, exotic places, romantic places …'

'What is it that you are afraid of, Abhay?' she asked. 'What do you think is going to happen?'

Somehow I did not resent her curiosity. Suddenly I wanted to tell her, share my burden with her.

'I really don't know, I said. 'It is just a vague feeling. Something to do with the Bhils. I don't think they quite trust me. And if they start an agitation or anything like that, they will come in for a lot of punishment. They are our charge, the Bhils. I don't want them to be hurt more than can be helped.'

'But you have done your best. You can have nothing to blame yourself about.'

'It is so difficult to see one's way clearly through all this. For one thing, they will be finished as a separate clan, as a distinct ethnological sub-heading: the Bhils of Bulwara. They are all grouped together now, because they live in the valley. It will not be possible for the Government to resettle them all together…' We went on talking, as man and wife, about our problems. I was grateful to find someone I could confide in, to whom I could pour out the doubts that had been haunting me.

In the end, I was able to persuade her to go away with the children. Three days before the durbar, I drove my family to the station. There was a lump in my throat as the train moved away, carrying my son and my daughter waving wildly, and my wife poised, smiling and dignified and tearless—a Maharani conscious of the need for keeping up appearances.

As I stood looking at the departing train, I had a feeling that the play was coming to an end, and I was aware of the dramatic neatness of the ending. I was eager for the last three days to pass, for the end to be clean and swift.

It was the day before the final durbar. I was sitting on the balcony of my father's bedroom, sorting out the papers in his desk which I had arranged in neat piles on the glass-topped coffee table before me, when I heard the crunching of car wheels on the gravel drive leading to the main porch. Very few cars were permitted to use the main gate or the central porch of the palace, and I remember thinking that one of the other rulers who had come for the durbar had come to pay me a call.

A few minutes later I heard the sound of footsteps on the carpet behind me. I was reading one of my own letters, sent to my father from college, describing a cricket match and explaining why I had not done better in the Sanskrit paper, I was still a part of that moment, more than ten years in the past. I looked round in annoyance and stared at the woman who stood in the doorway wearing a white sari. It took me a second or two to realize that she was my mother. For a moment I wondered why she was wearing a widow's white and had come out without the red dot on her forehead which was compulsory for all Hindu wives, and then my mind was back in the present.

It was more than six years since I had seen my mother, but was not surprised that she looked as strikingly lovely as ever. Middle age had only added a sort of chiselled perfection to her features.

Whose fault was it that we had not seen each other for all those years? Hers or mine? Or was it no fault of either of us?

She came and sat down on the wicker chair on the other side of the coffee table, and looked at me with a touch of anxiety, just as she had whenever I came home from school or college.

'Don't say "How thin you have become!" Maji.' I said.

She gave me a quick smile. There were wrinkles round her eyes that had not been there before. 'But you are looking thin, Abhay. You look as though you haven't been sleeping well.'

'You look as though you always did,' I told her.

Mother smiled again. 'Tell me. Abhay, is this thing getting you down too much?'

'I expect it is, rather. But it is all going to be over tomorrow. And I sleep very well, Mother, like a log.'

'You must get away from all this. Go away for a long time.'

'I am going, Maji. We are all going to Calcutta. Then I want to go to Mussorie. Perhaps a trip to Europe later in the year.'

It was extraordinary how we had slipped into a groove of conversation as though we had been seeing each other every day. Or was there something brittle, something artificial in the things we had been sayings, as though we were subconsciously trying to cover up our real feelings behind the banalities of small talk?

'I have missed you, Abbay. You are the only person connected with all this ... with my past, that I have really missed,' Mother said. 'That I will go on missing.'

Her words made a small smear of guilt on my conscience, for on my part I had not missed her at all. 'I hope you have come to live here, Maji,' I said. I had a feeling that the ice was breaking up, that we were no longer being protected by the screen of small talk.

She shook her head slowly, taking a long time to answer. Then she said, 'No, Abhay, quite the opposite, in fact. I have come to say good-bye.'

'Where are you going, Maji?'

'I am going to Karachi; to Pakistan.'

'With that ... with Abdulla Jan?'

She winced, her face paled, her eyes hardened. 'As you wanted to say, with *that* man.'

'But you cannot go there, Maji. It is foreign territory now. They are killing thousands of Hindus every day. It is here that you belong. With us.'

'No, I don't belong here. I belong there, on the other side of the border.'

Something in her expression made me ask:

'Have you ... you haven't married him, have you?'

She looked straight into my eyes, almost defiantly. 'We were married last week.'

'You are nothing but a bitch, a shameless woman of the streets! You cheap whore!' I cried out, stung by I know not what tortured emotions. And I realized the horror of my words only when I saw the shock and the anger in her face. I hung my head in shame and disgust. 'I am sorry Mother,' I said. That was all there was to say.

'I may be a bitch, but I am no longer a shameless woman of the streets. I was one, all these years when I lived with a man in sin. But remember I had been abandoned by my husband—I was a discarded woman.' Her eyes were hard, her voice dry, her words like the pricks of a scalpel.

'I am sorry, Maji,' I said again. 'Please forgive me.' My own private life was a morass of guilt. Who was I to talk of sin, of abstract standard of morals? I who had never been faithful to Kamala and carried no taint of sin within me, what right had I to feel outraged at my mother's degradation?

But my mother did not want to forgive me easily. It was her right to punish me for the pain I had caused her. Her face, which had no make-up, was dead white, and had the hardness of glass.

'A bitch but not a whore any more … now that I am married.'

'I'm sorry, Mother.'

'And yet it was you who gave me the courage to run away from misery to happiness … to a man I loved. It was then that I felt that you were at least partly mine—not wholly his.'

'I hope you are happy, Maji. I hope you have found what you were seeking.'

'Who can say what anyone is seeking? And yet I can say I am happy—happy because I have found what I never had, a place of honour in a man's house. I am the wife, the lady of the house, a share in the joys and sorrows of the husband. Here I was nothing. I was never even told when they operated on your nose—as though I had nothing to do with you.'

'It was I who wanted no one to be told, Maji,' I said. 'I wanted to spare you the anxiety.'

'And do you know this is the first time that I have entered this room, his room, when all those other women, one after the other, even my maid-servants were admitted. They came and sat here, sat where you are sitting … shared his bed. I never came. I was only the wife, the Maharani, confined to the end of the palace.'

'Please, Mother,' I implored. 'Please.' She was hurting me and I knew she would go on hurting me, but I deserved it all.

'I am no longer something to be hidden like sin, hidden behind bamboo curtains as though I had some kind of deformity. It was—it was like being an animal, a leper kept in segregation, until I went away, preferring to be a woman of the street, as you have said, to being a Maharani in darkness … never knowing what it was to be a complete woman.'

'Have you changed your religion too?' I asked. 'Become a Muslim?'

'Yes.'

'Oh, my God!' I said. 'Oh, my God!'

'Why don't you say it? Why don't you say what is in your mind?' she taunted me.

'I have nothing to say, Mother. Nothing.'

I had nothing to say. All I could think of was her ardent, almost passionate devotion to her gods, her veneration for the seven satis in the family, of the time when I entered her prayer room and she had tears in her eyes. And then I found myself thinking of my father's religion, flamboyant, loud, almost defiant. I was glad he was not alive to be subjected to this final mortification—the Bedar Maharani marrying her lover and changing her religion.

'And I can assure you that I did not become a Mohammedan because he wanted me to, but because I wanted to belong to my husband's religion, belong completely to him … hold nothing back that I had to give.'

There was a soft buzzing in my head, and somewhere at the back a nerve pounded as though it were going to burst. Why was I being given this extra punishment? Was this my reward for venerating the father-image I had created in my mind out of a man who was a good rifle shooter and who made a fetish of manliness, teaching me never to break down under punishment, never to squeal, the man who quoted from the scriptures to justify his waywardness in thought or in action? This was his retribution, not mine—the punishment was rightly his.

'I came because I wanted to see you before I went away. But perhaps it was inevitable that you should cause me this additional pain, just at the moment of parting. When an illusion that one had nursed all one's life is shattered it cannot help hurting. To think that for all those years, it was you that kept me here, for whose sake I was willing to go on enduring, whom I went on loving even when you disowned me the moment I did what I should have done … you, the embodiment of purity abandoning something which had been polluted, you who could bring yourself to call your mother a whore!'

'It wasn't me, Mother, you know it wasn't,' I cried out. 'It was something that possessed me … it was …'

She gave a hard, bitter laugh. 'You asked whether I had found what I was seeking. What I was seeking was just what you accused me of—what a woman's body and mind burn for.'

'Oh, please, please, Mother.'

'It was you who mattered. You who caused me the pain when you disowned me … when you stopped writing and I used to lie awake for news of you, haunted by forebodings. You who kept me tied to this place; not him. And when he died, I'm not ashamed to say that I could not even bring myself to feel sorry—I who cannot prevent myself from crying when one of my canaries gets hurt. That is what you and he have done to me.'

'He is dead now, Mother,' I said in sudden exasperation. 'Do you mind not saying anything about him?'

She stared at me in anger, almost as though I had said something rude. 'Oh, I should have known better,' she said. 'You were always his boy; his in spite of everything I did for you. I am sorry I was carried away. You will always be what you are, and I will always love you, my son, my only son.'

I said nothing, I hung my head.

'I think I had better go now,' my mother said, and her voice was normal again. 'There is no point in lingering here. Goodbye, and God bless you!'

No, there was no point in her lingering in the room, my father's room which had been denied to her all the time she had lived in the palace. I found myself wishing she would go.

She stood up and walked away, as she had always walked, with the grace of a court dancer leaving the stage after bowing to the applause, walked away as though unaware that she was taking with her a part of myself.

In the archway, she stopped. 'I almost forgot,' she said. 'I have settled my affairs, here … the house and the land and things. They are yours. I want you to take them. The papers are with Harikishore …'

'I have no use for your estates, Maji,' I said. 'I have enough of my own.'

'Who knows, some day you might have need of them the way things seem to be going with you.'

'And how will you live, Mother?'

'I will live as a wife should live, on what her husband gives her,' she said proudly, almost defiantly, and then she added: 'I am going as I came, taking nothing from here; a woman, not a Maharani.'

And then she was gone.

I wanted to shout to her to stop, to get up and run after her, try and comfort her and comfort myself, assuage the wounds of my mind as I had done in the past. But I did nothing of the kind. I sat gazing at the spot where she had stood, under the marble arch with the lotus design, knowing that I should never see my mother again.

31

'Julay-Julay!'

Early in the morning on the day of the durbar, I had a moment of sheer panic when I was told that it looked as though the Bhils of Bulwara were likely to clash with Charudutt's police.

I had not expected the Bhils to come, and my first thought was one of annoyance, that they should have created this complication for me on my very last day as ruler. But it was only a fleeting thought. In a moment, its place was taken by a wave of gratefulness that they should have come to attend my very last durbar.

I had just finished dressing. I was standing in front of the looking-glass while the bearer was putting on my medals, thinking how unfamiliar I looked to myself in my Major's uniform, when Sumer Chand, my A.D.C., came and told me that Charudutt was waiting to see me. 'He says it is extremely urgent, Your Highness,' Sumer Chand said.

I felt no particular animosity towards Charudutt, but was not very much inclined to see him either. 'Tell him I can't see him,' I told Sumer Chand.

'It is something about the Bhils, Your Highness. He says he might have to open fire on them.'

'Oh, the bloody swine!' I said. 'Oh, my God!' But even after that I hesitated a little before sending for Charudutt.

As I went into the verandah, he rose to his feet and gave me a stiff salute. I asked him to sit down.

'What is it?' I asked.

'It is the Bulwara Bhils, Your Highness. They have come carrying their spears.'

I almost felt like laughing. 'But what's wrong with that? They always carry them. That was how they came to my father's durbars. You should know that. They would feel undressed without their spears.'

'But my orders are not to let them come armed. It is a precaution against any breach of the peace.'

'Whose orders?'

'The Political Officer's.'

'Well, it's his problem then, not mine.'

'But there are several thousand of them … and more trooping in. I have had to halt them on the polo ground. They are clamouring to be allowed to go on to the durbar. They say they will force their way.'

'And I suppose if that happens you just open fire and shoot down as many of the poor devils as you can.'

'Those are my orders. But naturally, we shall give all possible warning … do as little damage as possible, shoot only below the knees.'

'Oh, below the knees.'

'Only as a last resort, Your Highness.'

'Then why come to me? What do you think I can do?'

'You can go and talk to them, Your Highness. Explain to them they cannot come into the town armed. They will listen to you.'

'Did the P.O. send you?'

'Yes, sir.'

'All right,' I said. 'I will come and talk to them. But only on one condition. I don't want any of your men hanging around. I want them all withdrawn before I go. And I want you to tell the P.O. that I am not doing it for his sake or for yours. It is just that I don't want you to go shooting them down.'

'But how will they be controlled, then?'

'They don't need to be controlled, they are not cattle. They are gentlemen. I'll send word that I'm coming to talk to them.'

He hesitated for a second or two. 'Just as you say, Your Highness,' he said. He was being very formal, very correct. He rose to his feet and put on his cap. He saluted stiffly and turned on his heels, just as though he were on a parade ground. It was quite a performance.

For a moment I wondered whether to change from my uniform into something more familiar to the Bhils, but decided against it. After breakfast, I drove to the polo ground.

The ground was a seething mass of bronze bodies, all wearing little coloured twists of rope as turbans, and standing or squatting in separate groups according to their villages. The spear-heads glinted in the morning sun. As I stopped the car and walked towards them, they rose to their feet and began to yell, and some of them hurled their spears high into the air and caught them again.

I raised my hand for quiet. 'Julay-julay!' I greeted them.

'Julay-julay!' they yelled. 'Julay-julay!'

'When I visited you last week,' I said to them, 'I came away sad, not knowing whether you had accepted me as one of yourselves—for you and I are one people. Now, I know that you have. Because I know that you would not have come all this way just to be present at the ceremony of my handing over my powers, unless you had accepted me as your own. And I am no longer sad. Some of you must have had to walk as much as fifty miles. Why have you come?'

'To be with you.'

'To help you, if you need our help.'

'You are our man—our King.'

'We shall fight for you—die for you.'

'This is no time to talk of fighting,' I warned them. 'Or of dying. But you certainly can help me. And I want your help … need it. I know you will not deny me that help …'

'We will deny you nothing!'

'Not even our lives!'

'Then the only way you can help me is by leaving your spears here, each village in its own group. I shall arrange to put my own guard here so that your spears are not touched by outsiders. You go and attend the durbar. On your way back to Bulwara, you can collect your spears.'

'But why cannot we take our spears with us as always?' one of them asked.

'We are not going to kill anyone,' another said.

'The new government does not understand such things. They are city people, not jungle dwellers such as you or I. They do not understand our customs.'

'We don't want a sarkar of strangers! We don't want any other rule but the Bedar's.'

Things were not going as I had planned. I wanted to cut them short before they did something rash.

'Stop cackling like women!' I yelled. 'Dammit, I can almost hear the bangles!'

Some of them gave way to laughter but most of them looked guiltily at one another. In a few seconds, they were silent.

'I know exactly what you are going to do,' I said. 'You are going to leave your spears here because I am telling you to do so. I may not be your ruler any longer, but remember that there are ties that bind us together that nothing can sever, for we are the same people—brothers! Julay-julay, brothers!'

'Julay-julay!' they yelled. 'Julay-julay! Julay-julay! …'

And that, as far as I was concerned, was my farewell to the Bhils as their ruler: Julay-julay, which meant both greetings and good-bye and covered all the range of human contacts, the correct punctuation mark for the end of a relationship the origins of which were lost in the mists of legend.

I walked away from them quickly. I did not trust myself to look back.

They were docile as lambs throughout the ceremony, listening intently to speeches they could barely understand, serenely unaware that they were the targets of warnings contained in two of them. In his opening address, speaking in English, the Political Officer made a veiled reference to them, saying that while the new government was going to promote the interests of all classes, it would tolerate no threats or any kind of demonstration from anyone who had enjoyed special privileges in earlier regimes.

Kanakchand was much more venomous and much more explicit. Looking directly at me, he warned us:

'… if there are any people who still think in terms of past loyalties, I warn them that we shall deal with them severely.' And he brought down his fist on the table with a thump. 'The new regime is the regime of peace and progress, but it is determined to brook no threat to its well-being. Those who are not with us will be shown no mercy … we shall be ruthless with those who oppose us, who incite others, or who subvert the loyalty of the people … ruthless!' He banged the table again.

Some of the people clapped, the uncomprehending Bhils among them, and Kanakchand talked on. I was only half listening to the speech. Already I felt separated from the present. Whatever was happening had nothing to do with me. The play was already over, and this was nothing but a gathering of all the actors for a final curtain call. I and the other thirteen rulers who were present belonged to the dead, like ghosts hovering over the scenes of their pasts.

I could not keep my eyes from straying to the faces of the others, all sitting on the same kind of ornately carved chairs that had been brought over from our administrative building, all looking dazed and numb as though in a state of shock. I felt sorry for them even though I had little in common with many of them. They were trying to take it bravely and not succeeding. They were gripping the armrests of their chairs hard and staring fixedly ahead, but I could see that their minds were far away. They were only waiting for the show to be over, as though for release.

Their faces haunt me still. Next to me was the Maharaja of Tilkatta whom I had always called 'uncle'. Gnarled and bearded, he had always looked like a lithograph of the days of Queen Victoria when Indian princes were said to be like the trees in autumn, the epitome of flamboyance. Now he was looking like a shadow of himself, wizened and wrinkled in his plain white clothes; his face, which had always reminded me of weathered teak, was now the colour of a snake's belly. His head shook slightly all the while as though with some kind of internal tremor. His eyes were red as coral and his pupils like dull marbles. I felt suddenly guilty and shifted my gaze. I realized that he had dosed himself heavily with bhang, hashish or some other dope to brace himself for the ordeal.

The only other man in uniform was Snappy Baindur, the Maharaja of Ninnore, who had broken my nose at school, sitting at the other end from me. He was dressed as a squadron leader, and wore a row and a half of medal ribbons. Snappy must have been trying to catch my eye, for when I looked at him, he gave me a broad wink. Then he held up both his thumbs, telling me not to let it get me down.

And suddenly I wondered if I too was looking as though I had taken it as hard as some of the others.

32

Evidence of Misconduct

'... cannot but view with concern You Highness's close association with the group of ex-rulers known to favour an agitation against the constitutional settlement arrived at ...'

Personally I could see nothing wrong in the idea of some the ex-rulers getting together and forming a union to put forward their grievances jointly, if that was what the Rulers' Union was doing. But the fact remains that I did not join the Union and did not attend any of its meetings as a non-member. By nature I do not think I am the agitating type, being more inclined to take the fences as they come, and the only reason I can think why anyone should have connected my name with the Union may be that I had my friends among its more active members.

For nearly a whole year after the merger of our states, I was almost constantly in the company of one or other fellow-ex-ruler, as though we had gravitated closer in our decline. There is no denying that we rather tended to talk in circles in those days, about what we had lost and what we could have done to prevent it. But even if, at times, our thoughts were bitter and our language far from refined, I cannot recall any of us even vaguely suggesting that we should set up some kind of people's agitation in our erstwhile states.

For instance there were at least half a dozen ex-rulers who were members of the Union present at the Maharaja of Tilkatta's pig-sticking meet. The Tilkatta meet was an annual fixture, rather like our own Tatwal duck-shoot, and I went merely out of politeness, because my father had always made a point of going. Actually I had very little in common with either the host or the other guests. They were in a different group, both as regards age and temperament, and were inclined to harp too much on their misfortunes. All the same, I ended up by inviting all of them to our own duck-shoot at Tatwal later in the year. I now realize that to anyone with a suspicious mind, this gathering of the same group of ex-rulers in out of the way jungle lodges must in itself have given the impression that we were up to some kind of mischief.

> '… *and whereas Your Highness has been known to have been in close touch with individuals suspected of helping some of the ex-rulers to transport their valuables abroad* …'

That was Snappy Baindur's tiger shoot, to which he had invited Punch and Minnie.

Kamala was away in Akheti, to be with her mother who was recovering from a heart attack. I had gone to Calcutta for the tennis tournaments. Snappy too had come from Ninnore. We were sitting in adjoining chairs, watching the semi-final of the doubles matches when Snappy asked me to his tiger shoot. The players were changing sides.

'Some friends of yours are coming,' Snappy said. 'Major Farren and his wife.'

'Punch and Minnie?' I asked.

'Punch and Minnie,' Snappy said. 'Very attractive woman, Minnie.'

The name came from nowhere and fell like a stone on water, setting up its own ripples in my mind. It was three years since I had seen Minnie, and yet the mere mention of her name could still cause a flutter of anticipation, a quick spasm of pain and longing.

'He is a bit pompous, but she's fun,' Snappy said. 'And my God, she's all there.'

'I didn't know you knew them,' I said.

'They came to Ninnore about two years ago; I think with a letter of introduction from your father. Now he has written saying he wants to shoot a tiger. I'm also hoping to do a little business with him. Do come, it will make things easier all round.'

I wanted to ask what sort of business Punch was engaged in now, but before I could do so, they had resumed the game.

Punch and Minnie came to the shoot in a chauffeur-driven Buick, laden with matching cow-hide and crocodile-leather luggage with gold fittings and their monograms worked into the leather. Punch had grown rather fat, but his swagger, his snorts, his boisterous laughter, were all there. If possible, they were a shade diluted and mellowed by time to go with his new personality, with the cigars and the dark pin-striped suit and the rotundity, the air of assurance and success, even of opulence.

Minnie was wearing a sky-blue dress that could have been made only in Paris, with hat and shoes to match. She looked positively dazzling, even if it was the ensemble that struck one first. She looked different, for somewhere in the process of developing into a professional beauty, she had lost that air of helplessness, the wide-eyed look of uncertainty and the earthy sensuousness which she had always exuded. Now she looked perfectly poised, enamelled and slightly predatory, like a successful film star, an orchid under glass, exquisite, without blemish. I could not visualize her riding along the Mall at Simla on a shaggy tatt any more.

There was a moment of disappointment, a sudden shrinking back from this new, slightly synthetic stranger that was Minnie, and then, with the release of some emotional valve, I found myself in the grip of a bitter-sweet anticipation, the joy and the pain of reunion I had experienced whenever I saw her after a separation. And there was too, in spite of myself, a sharp stab of jealousy at the way her eyes lit up when she was saying hullo to Snappy.

Could I still be in love with her? Was this what they meant when they said that a man was capable of love but once, or was is merely some capricious twist of nostalgia, what they called a conditioned reflex?

Somehow I got the impression that Punch was not very pleased to see me. 'Gosh!—didn't expect to be seeing you here,' he said to me. 'You never said anything about Abhay coming, Snappy?'

'I wasn't sure of getting him,' Snappy explained.

'It is always nice to see Abhay,' Minnie said, and she gave me a private smile all to myself. 'Thank God there is someone to hold my hand while Punch goes shooting tigers.'

'But of course it's great to be seeing you, Scrapper, good old Scrapper,' Punch said. He beamed expansively at me and gave me a thump on the back.

It was a long drive to Snappy's tiger shooting camp deep in the Sattawan range, a small, straw-roofed bungalow that looked quite lost in the vast forest. We had dinner on the wide, open verandah in the light of a hissing pressure lamp and to the sound of the night-time din of the jungle.

We were all tired after the drive and retired early. I was just about to get into bed when I heard a knock on the door, and there was Punch walking on tiptoe and carrying a glass in each hand. He gave me a conspiratorial wink.

'I was just about to have my nightcap when I said to myself how nice it would be to go and have a chat with Scrapper over a drink,' he explained, and handed me a glass.

'Why, thanks, Punch,' I said. 'It's really most thoughtful of you. I was just about to turn in, but it's always a pleasure to have a drink with you.'

'Oh, come off it, Scrapper,' Punch said with a disarming smile. He sat down on the wing chair and drew it close to mine. 'You know jolly well I want to have a business chat with you. There will be hardly any time for it tomorrow when we start chasing the tigers.'

I had an idea it was coming, and I felt sorry for Punch because I was determined to have nothing to do with it. He was the picture of prosperity, sleek as an advertisement, dressed in pure silk pyjamas and Morocco slippers and a shiny, wine-coloured dressing gown with a monogram, but he looked too eager and slightly nervous. He also looked flabbier and more wilted than in the afternoon.

'A business chat, Punch?' I said.

He had heard rumours, Punch said, from one or two of the Maharajas whose names he did not want to mention and for whom he had been doing a good deal of business, that I might have rather large quantities of stuff that I might like to have sent away.

'Sent away, Punch?'

'Taken out, y'know,' he explained, and jerked his thumb towards the window. 'Out!'

'What sort of stuff?' I asked.

'Good old Scrapper,' Punch said, and nudged me in the ribs. 'Got a reconditioned Dakota as good as new. Range—well—from here, fifteen hundred miles easy. Oh, easy.' He took a leather cigar case from his pocket and held it out to me, and when I declined, he took a cigar and lit it.

'You mean jewels, Punch?'

'Any old stuff. We can handle four thousand pounds at a time—oh, easy.'

He looked like an oversized baby playing a game with a cigar, and I felt that the game was wearing him down. He did not have Minnie's hardness, I found myself thinking; she would have handled this much more efficiently.

Where was Minnie? Was she working on Snappy? If she was, I was sure that she was doing it with her customary efficiency. And again I felt a prick of jealousy towards Snappy.

'I really cannot think of anything I want to send out, Punch,' I said.

'Dammit, they're all talking in whispers about your family treasure, and you come and tell me there's nothing—you, my wartime pal.'

He is too easily hurt, I thought, and shows it too. It was like boxing. There were a few who could go on pretending that they had not been hurt. He was like a bulldog who had been fed on pap and gone soft.

'I didn't say I have nothing. I said that I don't want anything sent out.'

He looked suspiciously at me. 'Tell me, has Snappy been talking to you?'

'Oh, no, Punch; Snappy hasn't said a word.'

'Nor you to Snappy, I hope.'

'Oh, no.'

'Then don't tell me you have been doing business with someone else—Watson, or someone. You have to be jolly careful who you deal with, old boy. You don't know what happened to Kirwatti's stuff—the old man is nearly out of his mind. And here am I, your old pal, offering to help you out, just for old times' sake …'

'It really is most considerate of you, Punch. But there is nothing I want sent out.'

Punch snorted and waved his cigar. 'Oh, come off it, Scrapper,' he said a little impatiently. 'Everyone knows you people have stuff that you can't possibly have absorbed here—the market won't bear it. Even little pieces get talked about, and then the Government is on your tails like a shot.'

'I'm sorry I cannot help, Punch,' I told him.

'Help! Dammit, I thought I was trying to help you—just for old times' sake. Well, don't say I didn't offer. I am just on my way. The Middle East first and then the States. Amazing the amount of stuff the Arabs can handle—Egypt too. Salim Ali, who buys for both Ibn Saud and Farouk, absorbed the whole of Tilkatta's stuff. Shakes you …'

'Not … not the state jewels?'

He gave one of his snorts, and I was glad to see that he looked quite composed once again. 'What you don't know won't hurt you, chum. And we really would appreciate it, Minnie and I, if you did not, well, offer any advice to Snappy. Ruin the whole trip for us. We're about to fix a biggish deal here, and let's hope it doesn't go sour on us.'

'Why, of course, I won't say anything to Snappy, Punch. What Snappy does is his own business.'

'Good, oh! That's the way to look at it. Well, sorry we couldn't do a little business together. Minnie'll be most disappointed. Thanks for the drink.'

'It was your drink, Punch,' I reminded him.

The next day was disappointing. We took two beats for tiger and both were blanks. When we returned to the bungalow, we were all pretty tired.

'No tea, thank you,' Punch announced. 'I want a drink. Cool and tall and full of whisky.' He looked quite worn out and his face had become all red with the sun.

'It is always like this on the first day,' I said. 'I'm sure you will shoot something really worthwhile tomorrow.'

'Actually, if you weren't feeling so tired,' Snappy said, 'I was going to suggest that we should go and sit up over a kill after dinner, just you and I, Punch.'

'Oh, no!' Punch groaned. 'Not on your life; not tonight.'

'It was only a thought,' Snappy said. 'Let's see if you feel like it, after a drink and a bath.'

'Why don't you go, Punch?' Minnie said.

'You too!' Punch said and made a face at her.

'It's rather fun, sitting up for a tiger at night,' Snappy said. 'We usually sit only until midnight … and remember you only have two more days.'

'I'm sure you'll enjoy it, Punch,' Minnie said.

I felt sorry for Punch, for he looked nice and comfortable slumped in his canvas chair, sipping his whisky, and his eyelids drooped. 'Oh, but you're bound to get a tiger in the next two days,' I said. 'No need to sit up for one at night.'

'Thanks, pal,' Punch said.

But he must have felt really refreshed by his drink and his bath, for when he came out into the verandah, he had again changed into khaki and announced that he would go and sit up for the tiger.

We had early dinner, and then Punch and Snappy got into the jeep, bristling with rifles and searchlights, while Minnie and I stood in the verandah wishing them luck and waving them off.

We watched the headlights snaking along the winding road, and when they disappeared Minnie moved closer to me and held my hand. The perfume she wore was all around us. I had the odd feeling of being a part of a scene and also of watching it from a distance. I kept wondering to myself how Minnie was going to handle her role.

We stood side by side, not saying anything for a long time, just listening to the hum of the jungle below, to the hiss of the Petromax behind us and to the sharp explosive sounds made by the beetles as they banged into the lantern. And we watched the millions of fireflies flickering in the trees around us, all together as though controlled by a switch. We still had not said anything when the servants cleared the table and bade us good night. At last we were alone.

In the harsh, white glare of the Petromax, Minnie's face looked incredibly beautiful and severe, like a flawless porcelain mask. She had changed into a low-necked green dress and was wearing the pearls I had given her.

'Well?' Minnie said.

'Well what?' I asked.

Minnie chuckled to herself and put her hands on my shoulders. 'Here we are,' she said.

I looked into her eyes and thought of the girl I had taken out to dinner. They both had the same expression, the eager, anxious look. 'Minnie, you look wonderful,' I said.

'Aren't you glad to see me?'

'Of course I am,' I said.

'Tell me the truth. Do you ever think of me?'

'Of course,' I said. 'I'm always thinking of you.' Minnie gave a queer little shrug. She turned and walked up to the pressure lamp hanging by a length of wire suspended from a rafter. She turned off the pressure. There was a loud hiss of escaping air. In a moment we were in total darkness, just a part of the jungle night.

'Where are you?' Minnie said.

'Here, Minnie.'

'I can't see you. Please light a match.'

I lit a match and she came and stood close to me before it went out. In the darkness, she put her hands on my shoulders again and drew me to her. 'Kiss me,' she whispered.

I leaned forward and kissed her. She took my head in her hands and I felt her lips hot and hungry on mine. 'Oh, darling,' she whispered. 'Oh, darling!'

It was wonderful to be in the darkness and in each other's arms, and yet I was conscious of a part of myself watching us.

'Wait,' Minnie said. 'Wait, darling,' and she wriggled out of my arms. I heard the sound of a zipper opening and the rustle of silk dropping on the ground. Then she was in my arms again, her cold, hard, naked body pressing into mine.

'Oh, darling, I have missed you,' Minnie whispered.

'Minnie?' I asked. 'Is this ... is this something to do with business?'

I could feel her body stiffen in my arms. 'Business?' she asked.

'Something to do with what Punch was discussing with me last night?'

I could feel her go rigid. She pushed herself away, and then I felt the sting of her fingers on my cheek as she slapped me. 'You swine!' she hissed. 'You bloody, lowdown swine!' And she lashed out at me again. But this time I was able to ward off her blow. I caught her in my arms and pulled her to me with all my strength. For a moment, only for a moment, she was limp in my arms, as though she would have dropped on the floor if I had let her go, and then she was thrashing wildly to get free. 'Let me go! Let me go! Oh, let me go!'

I let her go, and as she fumbled in the dark for her clothes, I lit a match and held it for her. I thought the hard, porcelain look on her face had gone. She looked flushed and warm and more desirable than ever, and then I found that she had burst into sobs.

I held another match for her while she pulled her dress over her head, and another while she walked away, groping along the whitewashed wall of the verandah, holding her head down because she was still crying.

> '... *and whereas Your Highness is known to have attempted to have items of State jewellery included in the inventory of private assets* ...'

It would have been really surprising if there had been complete accord between the princes themselves and those who were empowered to decide what was their personal property and what was not. We were all required to put up the inventories of our personal assets to our respective scrutiny boards. By and large, our relationship with the local authorities was not such that they would have accepted our inventories without question.

In the past, hardly any of the princes had bothered to keep any sharp distinction between what was their own and what belonged to their states, and some of the lists of private property submitted to the boards included items which by no stretch of imagination could have been regarded as private—one prince even wanted the state aerodrome to be included in his private property. One or two princes in our own union were known to have put up inflated lists and there were rumours of an understanding between them and one of the members of the board that the demands would go through.

It was Lala Harikishore who brought up such a proposal to me. 'Why doesn't Your Highness include the Karbala dairy farm as a private asset?' he asked.

'But it was started for the city—to augment the milk supply,' I said. 'They will never agree to anything so blatant ...'

He gave me a sly smile. 'I have been assured that it can be done,' he said.

'Assured? By whom?'

'By Lala Chandar Prashad.'

Lala Chandar Prashad was one of the members of the commission appointed to scrutinize our lists.

'Well, well; why is he being so kind?'

'Not kind, Your Highness. He wants to be kept covered …'

'Covered?'

'As they say in business. Ten per cent.'

'No, no,' I said. 'I don't want the farm. It can go to the state.'

'But they will only ruin it, Your Highness. All those Jafrabad buffaloes, the Saiwals … the valuable Danish separators, the plant.'

'We shall have to be resigned to seeing many of our things ruined, Lalaji,' I said.

'Well, His Highness of Kirwatti is getting his state dairy farm included in his property, all the grazing lands too, and the Raja of Konada is getting his saw mill …'

'All for ten per cent, what do you call it … cover.'

'That's right, Your Highness.'

'No, no, we don't want to give anyone any coverage.'

'In that case His Highness might find that the scrutiny might be, well, perhaps harsh …'

'I don't care,' I said. 'I don't want to kow-tow to them any more than I have to.'

Perhaps it was not a wise decision. I have often wondered if that was the reason why they disallowed my mother's jewellery. Even the customary bridal ornaments that my grandfather had had made for my mother at the time of her wedding were excluded from my list of personal property.

… and finally, whereas on 7th January, 1949 …'

It must have been building up somewhere within me for a long time, and it came to the surface too suddenly for me to be able to suppress it, like a fifth column of the subconscious suddenly breaking out into the open. It is even possible that it was merely an explosion brought on by just the exact combination of circumstances, a number of separate rages and frustrations buried deep in my mind finding release when they came upon a familiar set of props.

And perhaps the date too had something to do with it. It happened to be the anniversary of my father's death.

I now realize that the way things were going, it was a serious lapse on my part to have sent money to the Bhils of Bulwara. I can only say that I had meant well. The poor wretches were still clinging to their lands, but they had not been allowed to cultivate them because they were to be taken over before the crops could be harvested. As a result, the Bhils had no crops and nothing to live on. On learning their plight, I had sent them ten thousand rupees to tide them over until they were paid the compensation for their lands.

For nearly a year, there had been almost constant trouble in the Bulwara valley. No alternative holdings were being offered to the Bhils, and the authorities were unwilling to pay compensation until they had actually surrendered their lands. The Bhils had become increasingly truculent, declaring they would not move until they were given alternative sites.

I don't know how the Government could have solved the problem. It was certainly not going to be easy to find cultivable land to resettle twenty thousand farmers, and of course, it was quite impossible to find it in one lot.

I could see the difficulties but I could not see any solution. On the very day I returned from Snappy Baindur's tiger shoot, three of the Bulwara leaders came to see me.

'We have decided to resist any efforts to shift us by force,' one of them told me.

'But that would be suicidal,' I warned them. 'If they have to remove you by force, they can do it … make no mistake.'

'Then what should we do, Maharaj?' he asked. 'What is there for us to do? We are being thrown out of our houses and holdings. We were not permitted to sow our crops. We have nothing to eat. If it had not been for the money you sent us, we would have starved. They cannot ask us to quit and then give us no other land to cultivate.'

'Now listen,' I said. 'It is not obligatory for the Sarkar to give you alternative land. But under the law they must give you fair compensation. If you are reasonable, they might try and resettle you on other land. But in that case they will deduct the price of this land from your compensation. If you create trouble, they will show you no mercy.'

'But why don't they pay us?' the youngest of the three said. 'Then we will go. We do not even know how much they are going to give us.'

'In the people's raj, it always takes time for such things.'

'The compensation officers have been openly asking for money, that's what they want, money …'

'The patwaries, kanungos, tahsildars, all want money,' another said, and they all laughed.

'They say that if we pay them fifty rupees per guntha, they will recommend that we should get a hundred rupees more for each guntha, but that if we don't pay them anything, they will take years to decide.'

'That's the answer then,' I said. 'Pay them fifty and get double that in compensation. They won't make difficulties then.'

They again laughed and shook their heads. 'Where are we to get the money, Maharaj? Your officers were quite satisfied with fowls and eggs whenever they came touring, and once a year some honey and bananas or a bottle of rum. These new officials want cash, even before they do anything.'

'You will just have to learn to live with that now,' I said. 'These are the—well, these things cannot be avoided in the people's sarkar.'

'Please tell us what we are to do, Maharaj, we have come to fall at your feet.'

'You are our ma-baap, Maharaj, please tell us what we are to do,' the other two echoed.

I was no longer their mother and father, but I was ready to give them what help I could.

'I think that some of you should go and see the Chief Minister himself and explain things to him. I am sure he will intervene. If you promise to quit immediately you receive compensation, I am sure he will have it paid without delay.'

'But we have offered that, Maharaj. They don't trust us.'

'But you haven't been to see the Chief Minister. You and half a dozen others go and see him. I'm sure he will agree—and remember not to take your spears with you.'

They all shook their heads doubtfully. 'And what will we tell our people in the meantime, giver of food? They are harassed by the police every day … now we have to supply eggs and fowls to hundreds of policemen camped in our villages when we ourselves live on one roti a day. The people are resolved to do something. Who is to make them understand? They are angry, they want to fight. Every day, they talk of fighting the police.'

'Oh my God!' I said. I had had no idea that the situation had deteriorated so much.

'They listen to us no longer, they laugh at us when we tell them to be patient …'

'Accuse us of wearing bangles,' the younger man said.

'Look, on second thoughts, the best thing for you would be to vacate your lands without delay. That will give them no cause to suspect you. Then you should make an appeal to the sarkar to settle your compensation and also to try to give you other holdings.'

They looked at each other and shook their heads like bullocks warding off flies. 'They will not listen to us, Maharaj. Our people are no longer in a mood to leave their lands quietly and then be at the mercy of the sarkar. They will shout us down if we give such advice.'

'There is only one thing. They will listen to you,' another said.

'You come and tell them to go, and they will go,' the third one said. 'You come and pacify them. Otherwise they will not go. There will be trouble.'

'Of course I will come and talk to them,' I offered. 'I shall come whenever you want me to. Look, the day after tomorrow is Dada-Maharaj's death anniversary. I will come then. You go back and send word to all the villages that I'm coming. We must settle this without trouble. I will come to Bulwara. You get them all gathered in front of the camp. I'll be there by noon.'

Next morning, after I had returned from my before-breakfast ride, I was told that Charudutt was waiting to see me. It seemed that he had come to serve some sort of order on me. There was something in Charudutt's face, a suggestion of triumph, that gave me a twinge of alarm.

He came in, gave his parade-ground salute, and handed me a sealed envelope. 'I have been directed to bring back a receipt,' he said.

I told the A.D.C. to sign the receipt and give to him. The order was on Government paper and it was signed by the Chief Secretary to the Government. It read:

> 'Whereas the Government of Padmakoshal has reason to believe that Your Highness has been instigating the tribal population of the Bulwara district to resist the efforts of the Government to evacuate the valley for the purpose of the Bulwara hydro-electric dam, and that you are actively supporting their agitation by distributing large sums of money … And whereas any visit by Your Highness to the Bulwara District at this juncture would, in the opinion of the Chief Secretary to the Government of Padmakoshal, be likely to incite the people to acts of violence, the Chief Secretary hereby directs that until further notice, Your Highness will not leave the city limits of Begwad without the permission in writing of the said Chief Secretary …'

I like to think that I did not give away my feelings by any change of expression to Charudutt, who was still waiting, hat in hand.

'That will be all, Superintendent,' I told him. 'You have my permission to leave.'

I sent word to the Bhils that I could not come, and worried myself sick all day about what would happen to them now. Perhaps if Kamala had been with me, we could have talked it over and I might have been less agitated about the whole thing. As it was, I had to take a sleeping tablet that night.

The next morning, as I was dressing, I was once again fairly composed. I had my tea on the balcony, listening to the music of the sehnais coming from the drum-gate. I glanced quickly through the newspaper and I only vaguely remember seeing an item tucked away in one of the middle pages about some ceremony they were going to have that morning under the chairmanship of the Education Minister, Shri K-C. Gaur.

I was careful not to transgress the Chief Secretary's order, and confined my ride to the city limits. And that was the only reason why, on my way back, I passed the school where they were having the ceremony.

The scene was something I had seen before, many years earlier. The props were all in their places: there were streamers of bunting, rows of cars parked in the drive, arches made of bamboos and hoardings of welcome, the grounds had been sprayed with water to keep the dust down, the drive was swept clean, there was even the faint trace of khas in the air—everything was the same. I halted at the main entrance under a hoarding which, in letters a foot high made of gold paper pasted on red calico, proclaimed:

Welcome To Our Beloved Minister

I dismounted, handed the reins to one of the policemen at the entrance, and walked in.

I stood right at the back, behind the rows of chairs and the people who were standing. Over the backs of the elite of Begwad and the schoolboys in their best clothes all leaning forward, I could see like a stage setting, the platform where the high-backed chair brought over from our administration building had been placed behind a table draped with green and white cloth. The garlands were all heaped on a tray and the brass flower vase was just as I remembered it. Kanakchand had just begun his speech.

'We are giving the people a new deal, just as we promised,' he told them. 'The people have come into their own—the people; you,

I, all of us. We are the masters. Where are the masters of yesterday; I ask you, where are they?' He held his hands wide to give extra meaning to his question.

He was wearing a black and white achkan and snow-white churidars, and because of the slight puffiness that his face had acquired, his lips now looked permanently retracted.

'Look at the great changes we have brought about, brought about in so short a time. Here was this high school which throughout its existence was never a proper high school, but merely pretending to be one … going by a false name. Today we are making it a real high school—a full-fledged high school. My people, we give you this gift, so that no longer will our children have to go without the benefits of higher education.'

He paused for the applause to die, and held up his hands in a gesture of blessing.

'Ashokraj High School! How false! False in name, false in deed, false in everything. It may have belonged to Ashokraj, it certainly was not high.'

He paused again, knowing there would be laughter and more applause. He waited for it to die down and again held up his hands.

'We have no compunction about changing a name associated with the old order, a name rooted in falsity. I give you the new name: "The New National High School". It is both national and high. Instead of a false coin, I put before you this shining new coin: "The New National High School".'

Again there was applause. I found myself clapping my hands with the others. His audience was wholly with him.

'And consider the change, my comrades. Consider the great change. Can you believe it that in this same place, almost fifteen years ago now, I had the experience of being flogged. Yes, horsewhipped—beaten until I fainted. Such things were possible in those days. I ask you, can it be possible today—in the people's raj, in our raj, yours and mine? Answer me, can such a thing be possible?'

'No-o-o-o!' they answered him. 'No-o-o-o!'

'And I was punished for no fault. My only crime was that I was a poor boy trying to win a scholarship. But time has had its revenge, my friends. The man who wielded the whip is no more. All that he stood for is gone. Today the will of the people prevails. The day of beating up little boys for their zeal to learn has ended …'

'But the fault was yours too,' I yelled. 'You had cheated to win the scholarship.'

The words had slipped out without my realizing it; and yet, once I had spoken them, they made me taste a new kind of power, for they had achieved the dead silence that swept like a cold wave upon the audience.

Over the dimness that separated us, Kanakchand glowered in my direction in angry defiance, but there was also a quivering, frightened look on his face. He still cannot take it, I said to myself. He was one of those who would always squeal, one of those unfortunates who had not learned to take their punishment without showing it.

'Whoever said that must be a relic of the old order,' he thundered. 'Nursing a twisted, stunted mind and groping in the darkness of the old days. I challenge him to come here. I defy him. Let him come here on the platform instead of making a cowardly remark from the back.'

He waited, panting, his arms akimbo, still peering in my direction. Then he went on again:

'What has happened to the man who flogged me? His power is gone, his money is gone, he himself is gone. I, whom he whipped, have the honour to be one of your Ministers. It is they who are finished; it was we who finished them. It was the sacred oath of the Praja-mandal, those of us who worked and suffered for the advent of the people's raj … we were determined to wipe them out. This we had sworn—this we have fulfilled.'

I felt a black rage sweep over me, hitting me almost with a physical force, and I was conscious of nothing except the snarling, insolent face on the platform. I only vaguely remember pushing through the throng of applauding men and children and rushing up the steps, clutching the riding crop in my hand. I saw him close, staring at me in utter disbelief, insolent no longer but cowering, shrinking, frightened; the face of a schoolboy in the grip of terror. I raised the crop high. I brought it down.

'This I have sworn,' I was muttering to myself. 'This have I fulfilled.'

Suddenly I was at peace with myself. I turned and walked up to the red velvet chair behind the table and sat down. I remember sitting quite calmly, not conscious that I had done anything out of the way. The people were rushing towards the exits and one or two children screamed. The police had come running from all directions. About half a dozen of them made a ring around Kanakchand; others were crouching all around me as though trying to capture a dangerous criminal. I saw Charudutt coming up the steps, his face grim, his eyes narrowed with hatred. While he was still a few feet away, he halted.

I laughed. I threw the crop on the table and it fell in a neat coil beside the tray of garlands.

I was sitting in the room with the tiger rug, leaning against the bolster. The butler had just handed me a fresh drink. The six-thirty news was on:

'… In the Bulwara riots, the violence of the mob compelled the police to open fire twice, but there were only minor casualties …

'This is the Regional Broadcasting Service, giving you the news.

'The Maharaja of Begwad, His Highness Abhayraj Bedar the third, has communicated to the Government his decision to abdicate his title and renounce his privileges as an ex-Ruling Prince, preferring this course to submitting to a commission of inquiry into his conduct and in particular to his part in the violent agitation carried out by the tribesmen of the Bulwara valley.

'And that is the end of the news.'

Somewhere a switch turned. A woman's voice came on in place of the man's. 'Commentary after the news follows in just thirty seconds from now,' she announced.

There was a blare of music for the next half minute and then the commentary came on. I leaned forward, not wishing to miss a word, but it took me some time to realize that there was to be no mention of the Bhils or myself in the commentary. A dry male voice with an unresponsive tongue was giving out the details for the plans for a further rise in the production of newsprint.

Epilogue

1st November 1958

'The President will make the journey from Begwad by helicopter, arriving at Bulwara ten minutes before the ceremony.

'The Bulwara hydro-electric dam, situated in one of the most picturesque parts of the country, is the third largest dam in India. The valley now under water was once the haunt of the dreaded Pindaries. The foundation stone was laid seven years ago by the Chief Minister of the then Union of Padmakoshal states. The road on which even a jeep could go only with difficulty then is today a magnificent four-lane highway.

'The width of the river itself at the dam site was less than a thousand feet, but the great concrete wall is 4,329 feet long. The reservoir forms a lake 117 square miles in area and has a capacity of twenty-five thousand million cubic feet of water. The height of the dam from the bottom of the valley is 287 feet.

'The fort of Patalpat which, less than two hundred years ago was the stronghold of the Pindaries, is today more than two hundred feet under the water ...'

(Extract from an official press release)

About the Author

Manohar Malgonkar (1913-2010) was an eminent post-Independence writer whom R.K. Narayan once referred to as his 'favourite Indian novelist in English'. He was hailed as 'one of India's most exuberant storytellers' in an article published by *The New York Times* in 1965. Born near Belgaum, Malgonkar was the grandson of the prime minister of a former princely state of Dewas. He served in the army during World War II, was a big-game hunter, a farmer, a mine owner and an adventurer. Later, he started working as a journalist and thereafter took to book writing. His works are as diverse as his personal life and have a blend of history, romance and military life. Some of his major works include *A Bend in the Ganges*, *The Devil's Wind: Nana Saheb's Story* and *The Sea Hawk: Life and Battles of Kanhoji Angrey*.

Also available from HarperCollins *Publishers* India

'This captivating real-life fiction is a must-read ... It's a tribute to one of our unsung heroes.'

—Girish Kuber, author and editor, *Loksatta*

'A classic of our times ... ageless, tragic, relevant and a reminder of the lessons history holds for us.'

—Urvashi Butalia, author and historian

'Imaginative and inventive, yet never losing sight of authenticity ... this rediscovered classic gleams like one of Nana Saheb's own lost gems.'

—Avik Chanda, author

30 Years *of*

HarperCollins *Publishers* India

At HarperCollins, we believe in telling the best stories and finding the widest possible readership for our books in every format possible. We started publishing 30 years ago; a great deal has changed since then, but what has remained constant is the passion with which our authors write their books, the love with which readers receive them, and the sheer joy and excitement that we as publishers feel in being a part of the publishing process.

Over the years, we've had the pleasure of publishing some of the finest writing from the subcontinent and around the world, and some of the biggest bestsellers in India's publishing history. Our books and authors have won a phenomenal range of awards, and we ourselves have been named Publisher of the Year the greatest number of times. But nothing has meant more to us than the fact that millions of people have read the books we published, and somewhere, a book of ours might have made a difference.

As we step into our fourth decade, we go back to that one word – a word which has been a driving force for us all these years.

Read.